I0819945

THE PAPYRUS TRILOGY

Zoran Živković

The Papyrus Trilogy

FG-RS0008L-5
ISBN: 978-4-908793-01-1

Cover: Youchan Ito, Togoru Art Works

Neoclassic Fleurons font
used with permission of Paulo W–Intellecta Design

Cadmus Press

cadmusmedia.org

THE
PAPYRUS TRILOGY

The Last Book
The Grand Manuscript
The Compendium of the Dead

Zoran Živković

Cadmus Press
2016

Contents

The Last Book

Translated from the Serbian
by
Alice Copple-Tošić

Nothing about the death seemed violent, so there was no reason for an investigation. But the owner of the Papyrus Bookstore panicked. No one had yet lost their life in her store. She called the police as well as an ambulance.

I got there at the same time as the ambulance. While the doctor went about his work, I stood to one side and looked around the bookstore. I hadn't been there before. You could tell by the details that the place had character. The potted plants were well cared for, the decorations on the mantelpiece above the small fireplace were nicely arranged and there was no sign of the dust that inevitably goes along with books.

"There's nothing for you here, Inspector Lukić," said the doctor, taking off his plastic gloves. "It was a natural death. Heart failure most likely. We'll know more after the autopsy. Whatever it was, it probably happened in his sleep. All you can do is envy him." He chuckled softly. "He'll never even know he died."

"What was the time of death?"

"Sometime between five and six. The old man had been sitting here dead for at least two hours and no one even noticed. It's a heartless world we live in."

"So it seems," I said and moved aside to let the orderlies pass with a stretcher carrying the body under a green sheet.

The doctor nodded. "I'll see you next time, Inspector, when the circumstances are more exciting."

Once we were alone in the bookstore, I approached the owner. She was a willowy woman with long red hair and a freckled face. There was a youthful air about her, but she was probably close to thirty-five. She was dressed in a dark blue tweed suit with a matching blouse of a lighter shade. Narrow reading glasses hung from a ribbon around her neck. Standing in front of the cash register counter, she didn't know what to do with her hands, which is often the case with people who can't hide their anxiety.

I held out my hand to take her mind off the dilemma if only for a moment.

"Inspector Dejan Lukić. Good evening."

"I've had better evenings. Vera Gavrilović, owner of the Papyrus." She paused and then added almost reluctantly, "Miss."

"Would you like to sit down?" I asked.

"No, thank you. I'm fine like this."

"Have you ever seen a dead person before?"

She looked at me for a few moments in silence, then shook her head briefly.

"It's always a shock the first time. Particularly if the deceased is not a stranger. Did you know him?"

"I don't remember seeing him before. But lots of people come here. I can't remember them all."

"If it's any consolation, it doesn't get any easier even when you're used to seeing the dead."

"I don't suppose I'll have to get used to it."

"I think that's a safe bet. A bookstore is the last place one would expect to find a dead body. This is the first case I've heard of."

"Let's hope so."

"Would you mind telling me what happened?"

Miss Gavrilović sighed deeply before she began.

"Just like I do every night, a little bit before eight I announced that the store was about to close. Some people headed for the cash register with the books they wanted to buy and the rest went out the door. It wasn't until the last customer left that I realized I wasn't alone."

She turned to the right towards an armchair upholstered in worn-out dark-green plush. Three more like it were placed in the other corners of the bookstore.

"The old man's head was bowed over the book in his lap. He seemed to be reading, but I had a notion he was asleep. There's nothing unusual about that. Some people come here in winter, mostly to get warm. They take a book, settle into an armchair and stay there until closing time. Most of them actually do read, but some, particularly the elderly, soon nod off. I don't mind as long as they don't snore."

She shrugged her shoulders as though exonerating herself.

"I went up to the armchair and told him that we were closing, but he didn't move. I said it again in a louder voice, then put my hand on his shoulder to shake him a little. His body just tilted to the side. . . ."

I nodded my head. "Disagreeable, I know. But the worst is over."

"Is it?"

I looked at her questioningly. "What do you mean?"

"If the word gets out, our customers might start to give us a wide berth. Death isn't the best recommendation for a bookstore."

"There's no reason for this to get out. It was a natural death, not a crime. It could have happened to the poor old man anywhere. It happens almost every day. No one will take any notice." I smiled, then repeated the words I'd heard not long before. "It's a heartless world we live in."

The bookstore owner sighed once again.

I took a look around.

"You have a nice bookstore. I would have preferred not to come on business."

"I'm afraid we don't have many books that would interest a police inspector. The books we sell are mostly serious literature."

"Then you sell what interests this police inspector."

"Really?"

"My degree is in literature."

"And you went to work for the police?"

"I went to work where there was a job. Being well-versed in literature wasn't a handicap. On the contrary, it's often helped me."

"Detective novels? But they aren't really serious literature."

"Would you call *Crime and Punishment* or *The Name of the Rose* light literature?"

"No, of course not. But I wouldn't categorize them with detective stories either."

"Nevertheless, they can be read like one."

"I suppose so. Let's not go into the complex issues of literature right now, it's not the right time. I'll be more than happy to exchange thoughts with you on such topics if you come another time. Unofficially."

"With pleasure." My eyes swept over the tall shelves filled with books once again. "Goodbye, Miss Gavrilović."

"Goodbye, Inspector."

2

INSPECTOR JOVAN PETRONIJEVIĆ, MY colleague, raised his eyes from the newspaper when I entered the office.

"Dr. Dimitrijević called a little while ago. About the autopsy he performed. He asked for you to call him back. It's about this, isn't it?"

He handed me the tabloid he regularly read. I took it and looked at the bottom of the page where he was pointing. The brief news item was entitled "Death in a Bookstore." So a snooping journalist had found the incident newsworthy, probably because of where it happened. Miss Gavrilović would not be pleased, even though it would all be forgotten the next morning.

"That's right."

"Finally a case tailor-made for you, eh?" he said with a note of derision.

"Literature and bookstores are not exactly the same thing. That should be clear even to a guy who rarely opens a book." I gave him back his newspaper. "Anyway, there isn't any case. The old man died a natural death. I went there for nothing."

"That's not what I'd say, judging by Dr. Dimitrijević's voice."

I looked at him, mystified, but he plunged back into the newspaper without a word.

I called the autopsy department. A shrill female voice told me to hold the line. A good three minutes passed before Dr. Dimitrijević answered.

"Hello, Inspector. Sorry to keep you waiting. Things don't seem to be as simple as they looked to me last night."

"How so?"

"The old man didn't die of heart failure. By the way, his name was Predrag Todorović. He was a retired piano teacher. There was no one to inform about his death. He lived alone, if you don't count three cats. His wife passed away several years ago. They didn't have any children."

"Then what was the cause of his death?"

The receiver went silent for a few moments.

"Nothing."

Now it was my turn to fall silent.

"Come again?"

The doctor cleared his throat before continuing.

"You see, there's no medical reason for Mr. Todorović to be dead. He didn't have a heart attack, a stroke or any of the usual causes of sudden death. In addition, he was surprisingly fit for his age. Much younger people would have envied the condition he was in."

"But he did die?" I hesitated briefly. "Didn't he?"

"Yes, indeed. He is very dead. If he wasn't when we took him away, I doubt he would have survived the autopsy."

I frowned. His cynical sense of humor wasn't to my liking. But in his line of work it probably couldn't be avoided.

"So how do you explain it?"

"There's no simple explanation."

"Is there a complicated one? People don't just die for no reason. Something must have caused it."

"There might be a complicated explanation if I were to let my imagination run wild. But it would be so far-fetched that I hesitate even to mention it."

"Please don't hesitate. Flights of fancy make the world go round."

He chuckled. "I thought it was money."

"Money, too, of course. So, let's hear it."

"Certain artificial substances exist that can cause death without leaving any trace. When they take effect, a person simply stops living. They are snuffed out, so to speak, just like Mr. Todorović. Seemingly for no reason. I've never come across them in my work, of course, but I've read about them in the literature."

"Artificial?"

"Yes. It takes a very well-equipped laboratory to synthesize them. There's no way to make them at home. Thank heavens."

"But why are they synthesized? Who might be in need of them?"

"Well, you'll have to ask that of the National Security Agency. I'm just an ordinary medical examiner."

There was another bout of silence.

"The National Security Agency resorted to lethal substances in order to do away with a retired piano teacher with three cats who dropped by a bookstore to get warm?"

"I told you the explanation would be far-fetched."

"Will you cite that as the cause of death in the death certificate?"

"Of course not."

"So what will you put?"

"What I know for sure. That the cause of death is unknown."

"And that will be enough?"

"Yes, it will. Unless. . . ."

"Unless?"

"Unless there's another case of a death with no cause in the near future."

3

IT WAS ABOUT A quarter to eight when I entered the Papyrus. Even though it was almost closing time, there were still a dozen customers in the bookstore. Most of them were standing by the bookshelves, pondering the titles on the spines or leafing through books. Three of the armchairs were occupied. I examined the people sitting in them. No one looked asleep. Miss Gavrilović was working at the cash register where two customers were waiting to be served.

I approached the closest bookshelf and took out a book at random, then went to the free armchair, unbuttoned my coat and sat down. The springs had given out long ago so I sank down very deep. My knees were at the height of my navel. It wasn't until I'd settled in that I realized it was the armchair in which Mr. Todorović had died the night before. Without a cause.

I opened the book in the middle, but kept my eyes over the top. The line in front of the cash register had doubled in the meantime. I tried to judge which of those in the armchairs had come to the bookstore because of the books and which had come to get warm. The woman with salt-and-pepper hair in a gray coat and matching beret must have been quite shortsighted.

She was holding the slim volume right up to her eyes, hiding her face. The gentleman in the plaid jacket holding an unlit pipe was flipping through the pages of a book full of illustrations. The young man with a long, bright-red scarf and conspicuous earring in his left ear was concentrating on the page in front of him.

A little before eight, when Miss Gavilović announced in a slightly raised voice that they were about to close, the gentleman with the pipe and the young man got up right away. The young man headed for the cash register, while the older gentleman, not without effort, put the unwieldy book back on the top shelf of the nearest bookshelf. Then he took his coat from the coat rack at the entrance and promptly left.

The lady with salt-and-pepper hair didn't lower her book until the line at the cash register had disappeared. She placed it in the large handbag on her lap and headed for the door, walking slowly as though unwilling to exchange the warmth and light of the bookstore for the dark and windy November streets.

I'd failed dismally once again. She had looked the least suspicious to me. I'd been certain that the young man had been there for ulterior motives, and yet he was the only one to buy a book. That's what happens when you let prejudice get the better of you. I personally would never wear an earring, but a good police inspector must not be misled by personal preferences.

When the bell above the door stopped ringing after the old woman had left, I turned towards the bookstore owner. She smiled and headed towards me. I stood up and shook her outstretched hand.

"Good evening, Inspector."

"Good evening, Miss Gavrilović. I hope that the customer who just left paid for the book she took with her."

"She didn't get past you? Of course not. A successful inspector must have an excellent eye."

"Should I have intervened?"

"I thought your job was to take care of more serious crimes than petty theft."

"During breaks between serious crimes, petty theft is a good way to stay in shape."

"You would have been wrong to intervene. There was no theft involved. She bought that collection of love poems long ago, and with the book came the right to read it here. She visits us regularly on Thursday afternoons. She always sits in the same armchair. If it happens to be taken, she stands next to it with stubborn patience until it's free."

"The Papyrus seems to attract real characters."

"She's among the more moderate. We have considerably more eccentric customers. Do you know what we call them? Off the record, of course."

"What?"

She smiled again, this time with a twinge of discomfort.

"Patients."

"I suppose they deserve the name."

"You be the judge. There's another customer, and whenever he drops by, which is at least once a week, he always buys the same book. As many copies as we have on hand. This has been going on for more than a year. We've sold him almost 150 copies."

"Maybe he's the author."

She laughed resoundingly.

"That hadn't crossed my mind. But why would a writer deprive his readers of the chance to buy his book?"

"Oh, I can think of at least two reasons. Perhaps he isn't satisfied with what he wrote. Or, on the contrary, he's overly satisfied and feels that no one else is worthy enough to read his work."

"That would be the highest form of egotism."

"Few writers can boast of their modesty."

"I have yet to meet one. And I know quite a few."

"Why don't you simply ask the customer if he's buying his own book?"

"Because life is not always simple. Discretion comes first at the Papyrus. We don't go into our customers' motives, although from time to time I'm just dying to find out what they are. For example, I'd love to peek inside the head of the woman who spends hours in front of the same bookshelf rearranging the books on it. She tries to do it inconspicuously, waiting for moments when she thinks I'm not looking her way."

"Rearranges?"

"Yes. We arrange books by title. At first I thought that for some reason she preferred books to be arranged by author. But that wasn't it. For a while I tried to find some pattern in the way she arranged them, without success. Either I'm not astute enough or there isn't any pattern."

"Why don't you ask her not to rearrange the books?"

"Because then we'd lose a good customer. After venting her urge to rearrange the books, she always buys several of them. Most often expensive editions. And that's more than enough compensation for the disorder she leaves behind her."

"Perhaps I might take a look at her disorder."

She eyed me with reproach. "To show that you're cleverer than I am?"

That put me on the spot. "Of course not. I just thought. . . ."

"Well, all right," she said, cutting off my stammering. "I'll call you the next time she comes. Then we'll see just how clever you are. You might be disappointed in your detective skills, but at least you won't be the only one looking for hidden meaning in this bookstore."

"Is that so?"

"There's an old math professor among the patients.

He also visits us regularly, but nothing he does is hidden. He politely asked for permission to carry out some sort of research. Once he tried to explain what it was all about, but mathematics has never been my strong suit. Even a hypotenuse is beyond me."

"I like numbers."

"And you studied literature."

"They aren't as unrelated as you might think."

"The professor would certainly agree with you. His notebook is full of numbers and symbols. He takes books off the shelves according to some key, leafs through them until he finds the right spot, then takes out his pocket calculator and crunches the numbers. After writing down the result, he goes to the next book. For hours on end. It's a real obsession."

"Does he buy any of the books in the end?"

"No. But it doesn't really matter. I'm indulgent towards him because he's so nice. It's like he's the Papyrus mascot. Customers stare at him because he looks like Einstein: small, disheveled gray hair, bushy mustache. And he's charmingly absentminded. Sometimes his shoelaces are untied, or his coat is buttoned the wrong way. Once he even came in slippers. In the snow."

"Mascots are always useful."

"Indeed. But you can't weigh everything by its use. At first glance one might say we get the most use out of one patient who is the exact opposite of a thief. But he gives us the most headaches."

"The opposite of a thief?"

"That's right. He doesn't steal books, he brings them in. Even though we keep our eye on him, he always manages to sneak at least one of his own books onto the shelf."

"Why does he do that?"

"Who knows? At first we thought that he wanted to get rid of some worthless books and he thought this was better than throwing them away. But some of the books he left us were truly valuable editions. He was furious when we tried to give them back, claiming they weren't his. We couldn't keep them, of course, because we hadn't bought them legally. Whenever he leaves, we spend huge amounts of time looking for what he's left behind."

I glanced around the empty bookstore.

"Appearances can really be deceptive. This place looked harmless to me when I came here yesterday for the first time."

"The Papyrus isn't exceptional. Every bookstore has its patients. But regardless of their eccentricity, they're basically harmless. There was no need for you to come on business again."

"Why do you think I'm here on business?"

"Because someone like you doesn't go into a bookstore right before closing time unless it's official. Unless you came for that book, which I doubt."

She indicated the book I was holding.

With a contrite look, I went up to the shelf and put the book back in its place.

"I wanted to see if there was any bad fallout from the report about last night's incident that was printed in a tabloid."

"Oh, none at all. Contrary to my expectations, we had considerably more visitors than usual. The world we live in is not only heartless, it's also depraved. Death seems to be the best publicity after all. A cynic might want things to continue that way."

I glanced at my wristwatch.

"It's almost eight thirty. Excuse me for keeping you so long. One more thing. Do you remember noticing anything unusual about the man who died here last night?"

"Unusual?"

"Did someone go up to him, did he talk to anyone?"

She gave it some thought.

"No, not that I remember. But I told you that I

didn't pay any attention to him. Something might have gone unnoticed. Why do you ask? Is there anything suspicious about his death?"

"No, no. Nothing suspicious. Everything's clear. This is only a routine inspection."

She looked at me probingly for a few moments, but didn't say anything.

"Good night, Miss Gavrilović. The next time I come I promise it will definitely not be on business."

"I'd like that. I enjoy talking to you. Although I did most of the talking. You certainly know how to get a person to open up."

"What kind of police inspector would I be if I didn't?"

"Good night, Police Inspector."

4

I HAD BOTH HANDS on the wheel, slowly making my way through the morning rush hour, when my cell phone rang. It rang five times before I managed to take it out and answer.

"Dejan, it's Jovan. Miss Vera Gavrilović just called from the Papyrus Bookstore. She wants you to call her back right away. It seems they've had more trouble over there. She left her cell phone number. Have you got it already?"

"Where would I get it?"

"Just asking. You might've jotted it down."

"There wasn't any reason. I thought the case was over."

"Even if it was, and it clearly isn't, I certainly would've asked for the phone number of a lady with a voice like that."

"You would've been wasting your time. A guy who's proud of the fact that he doesn't read could never impress a lady with a voice like that."

"Since when has being well-read got anything to do with it?"

"Since always. It's just that you never took any notice. Give me the number."

I hung up after he gave it to me, then pulled over to a free spot by the curb and stopped the car. I don't like to talk on the phone while I'm driving.

She answered after the first ring.

"Hello."

"Miss Gavrilović? Inspector Dejan Lukić speaking."

"Thank you for calling so quickly."

"What happened?"

"I'm afraid we'll have to see each other on business again. There's been another death in the Papyrus."

Since I was slow to answer, she asked, "Are you there?"

"Yes. Sorry. Tell me more about it."

"I don't know very much. About ten minutes ago my colleague who works the morning shift called me. She was terribly upset. All she managed to say was that someone else had died, and then she had to hang up because the ambulance had just arrived."

"I'll be there in ten minutes. How about you?"

"I'm already in the car. I should be there about the same time unless I'm held up in traffic."

I took the rotating light out of the glove box and put it on the roof of the car. Freezing rain completely soaked my coat sleeve. I turned on the light but not the siren. The sound gets on my nerves.

In spite of my head start, I reached the Papyrus after Miss Gavrilović. She was just getting out of her car which was parked next to the ambulance. She raised the collar of her coat, ran the short distance to the store entrance and waited for me there.

"As if this awful weather wasn't enough," she said dejectedly.

I held the door open for her, then followed her in. Orderlies had just picked up the stretcher. I went up to the young doctor and showed her my badge. I hadn't met her before. She was blond, short and plump, with too much makeup for my taste.

"Inspector Lukić," I said. "What have you found?"

"You didn't have to come, Inspector. It was an ordinary heart attack. It's the third one this morning. Today is one of those days that are fatal for people with heart disease. We'll have our hands full."

"Are you sure?"

Her eyes flashed. "Do you have any reason to doubt my diagnosis?"

"Of course not. Excuse me."

"In any case, you'll get the official report from the autopsy, so you'll see for yourself."

"Give my regards to Dr. Dimitrijević."

She looked at me briefly without saying anything, then nodded and headed after the orderlies.

I went up to the cash register counter where Miss Gavrilović was standing with a woman who could have been younger than her, but looked older. Probably because everything about her was vintage, from her hairstyle to her clothes and bearing. She had short, straight black hair, thin lips and oversized glasses. She wore a plain dark business suit and low-heeled shoes. Unlike the doctor, she didn't seem to use any makeup at all. That extreme didn't appeal to me either.

"Inspector Lukić," said Miss Gavrilović, "please let me introduce Miss Olga Bogdanović. The two of us are co-owners of the Papyrus."

"Nice to meet you," said Miss Bogdanović, with the flicker of a smile that barely disturbed the seriousness of her face. Her handshake was limp. "Vera has told me about you. She admires your affinity for literature. But you've fallen short as a policeman. You assured her that there would be no more deaths in our bookstore."

"I miscalculated. The Papyrus doesn't seem to be a typical bookstore."

"It certainly isn't. It wouldn't be good, though, if corpses made it atypical."

"Corpses can be useful too. One might say they pick up business."

"Do all police inspectors have a morbid sense of humor?"

"Not all of them. Just those with an affinity for literature."

"Olga, please," interrupted Miss Gavrilović. "Inspector Lukić isn't to blame for what happened. He's trying to help us."

"I hope this is the end of your troubles," I said. "Please tell me what happened."

She pushed her glasses up her nose with her middle finger.

"The woman was the first customer after I opened at ten. It's never very crowded here in the morning, particularly not in rain like this."

"Had you seen her before?"

"I think so, but not often."

"Did anyone come in after her?"

"No, not until the ambulance arrived. Please keep your questions for the end, after I've told you what I have to say. Your interruptions distract me."

"Of course. Sorry."

"She browsed through the bookshelves for a while, then chose a book and sat down there."

She indicated the armchair to the right of the cash register counter.

"That's where the man died the night before last," said Miss Gavrilović.

"That's right. Had she known that, I'm sure she would have chosen another armchair."

"Maybe she wasn't superstitious," I mumbled.

"Excuse me?" said Miss Bogdanović. She didn't have to frown to look like she was frowning.

"Nothing. Please continue."

"She was immersed in reading, and I was busy with

work at the cash register. We have the most bookkeeping to do on Friday. Some ten minutes might have passed before I looked in her direction again. I could tell right away that she was dead."

"Do you have experience in judging whether someone is dead?"

"No experience is needed when you see a head thrown back, mouth open and eyes staring fixedly at the ceiling. It was a dreadful sight. It sent shivers all through me."

"You didn't hear any sound?"

"Should I have?"

"A heart attack is usually accompanied by a death rattle, and it isn't silent."

"Maybe the poor thing didn't die of a heart attack."

"The doctor thinks she did."

"But you have your doubts."

"Should an ordinary police inspector doubt the findings of an expert?"

Miss Gavrilović once again prevented any sparks from flying between us.

"I forgot to ask you yesterday, Inspector. Has it been confirmed that the old man died of heart failure?"

"Todorović. Predrag Todorović. He was a retired piano teacher."

"That's sort of what he looked like."

"I haven't received the medical examiner's report." It was only a partial lie. Strictly speaking, that conversation over the phone was unofficial, and I hadn't received anything in writing yet. "They are proverbially slow when a crime's not involved. You have to understand, they have their hands full."

"I could never be a medical examiner." The frown on Miss Bogdanović's face turned into an expression of disgust.

"And I would love to spend my time with books. That's what I studied, after all. But someone has to do the dirty work. It seems that even the world of books has its share."

Miss Gavrilović went to the chair that had already scored two deaths.

"I wonder if we should remove it. The customers have started to avoid it, and after this second death no one will sit in it any more."

"How did they find out that Mr. Todorović died there?" I asked, joining her.

"Oh, I must have mentioned it to someone. I don't remember. And rumors spread so fast. Yesterday that armchair was glaringly empty during my whole shift. How was it in yours, Olga?"

Miss Bogdanović stayed next to the cash register counter. "I suppose it was the same. I didn't pay any attention."

I looked at Miss Gavrilović. "It wasn't quite glaringly empty."

"It wasn't?"

"No. Don't you remember, I spent about fifteen minutes in it."

"Oh, yes. But I didn't count you. You're not a customer. You were here on business."

"That fine distinction would have been little help to me if there's something about the armchair that causes heart attacks."

Silence reigned.

Miss Bogdanović was the first to break it. "That's ridiculous. How could an ordinary armchair cause heart attacks?"

"I don't know. It's the only thing, however, that connects two sudden deaths."

"So why didn't you have a heart attack?"

"Maybe the armchair spared me because of my affinity for literature."

The sound Miss Bogdanović let out was like a cat spitting.

"Your behavior is quite out of place!" she said stiffly. Her tight lips formed a thin line. "The unfortunate souls who died there deserve respect, not ridicule."

She turned and headed briskly towards the door behind the cash register counter that evidently led to a back room.

"Don't hold it against her," said Miss Gavrilović when we were alone. "All this is too much for Olga. She'd never seen anyone dead before either."

"It's my fault. I went too far. This weather seems to be having a bad effect on me too."

"No one likes it. Joking aside, what do you think we should do with the armchair?"

"Nothing. The best thing is to leave it where it is."

"Someone might sit in it."

"You said that the customers avoid it."

"But what if someone sat in it anyway?"

"Then take careful note of what happens. And call me at once. You have my cell phone number."

Miss Gavrilović opened her mouth to say something else, but the bells above the entrance prevented her. A young man and a girl entered the bookstore. She looked towards the door to the back room, but it remained closed.

"It's time I left," I said, saving her from an awkward situation. And saving myself too. Had we continued our conversation, I would soon have had to face questions that I was unprepared to answer. "I've got my hands full too. I'll wait for you to call me."

I smiled at her and left the Papyrus.

5

I STARTED WHEN THE telephone rang.

I was in my office. Inspector Petronijević had gone out early in the afternoon, saying he would not be back. Dusk had descended long ago. No light was on except my desk lamp, illuminating an open book.

"Hello?"

"Good evening, Inspector Lukić. Dr. Dimitrijević speaking. I didn't expect to find you still in your office."

"What time is it?"

"Twenty past six."

"That late? I got caught up in a case and didn't notice the time flying by."

I put the marker ribbon between the pages and closed the book.

"Before I get down to brass tacks, I'd like to ask you something. I hope you don't mind. It's a personal matter."

"Go ahead."

"Are you married?"

I laughed.

"If I were, I doubt I'd still be at work. Why do you ask?"

"I lost the bet."

"Bet?"

"For some reason I was convinced you were married. My misconception will cost me a large bar of hazelnut chocolate."

"Who's going to get it?"

"My colleague, Sonja Vidić. You met her this morning."

"The blonde?"

"This one clearly doesn't fit the stereotype. She reached the infallible conclusion that you're not married."

"Based on what? We barely exchanged two words."

"Perhaps there are signs that only women see. They certainly escaped me."

"I assume it was her idea to bet on a hazelnut chocolate bar."

"Yes, it was. How do you know?"

"I've got an eye for signs too. Especially when they're conspicuous."

"In any case, she proved more skillful at judging men than in diagnostics."

"The heart attack?"

"Yes."

"She snapped at me when I asked if she was sure."

"Considering the circumstances, you shouldn't hold it against her. She asked me to send you her apologies."

"I'll accept it if half the chocolate goes along with it. Tell her that I'm actually doing her a favor."

Dr. Dimitrijević chuckled. "I think I'll leave that part out."

"The cause of death is again unknown?"

"I'm afraid so. Miss Ljubica Mitić wasn't exactly in the pink of health like Mr. Todorović. But her ailments only made her life miserable, they didn't threaten it. She had rheumatism and asthma."

"What did you find out about her?"

"There are some similarities with the first case. She was also involved in the arts. She was a painter. Before and after she retired. She also loved cats, but in moderation. She had one of everything. One cat, one husband, one daughter who started a family of her own long ago."

"She doesn't look like someone who'd be of interest to the National Security Agency either."

"No, she doesn't."

"What will you write in the death certificate this time?"

"Nothing for now. I'll leave the cause of death blank. I think I'll drop by the Papyrus to sniff around a little. There might be something in the bookstore that's unhealthy for pensioners with an artistic streak."

"I haven't ever heard of anything so selectively harmful."

"Me either."

My cell phone rang.

"Just a moment." I put the receiver on the desk and reached for the inside pocket of my jacket.

"Hello?"

"Inspector Lukić?" Miss Gavrilović's voice was at least one octave higher than usual.

"What happened?"

"Can you come right away?"

"Did someone sit in the armchair?"

"Someone else has died."

"Don't touch a thing. I'm on my way."

I thrust the cell phone back in my pocket and picked up the receiver.

"Here's a reason for you to go to the Papyrus straight away. We have a third corpse."

6

As soon as I entered the bookstore, I glanced at the ominous armchair. A middle-aged woman in a cute little hat was sitting there, a book in her lap. She was bewildered and frightened, but certainly not dead.

I looked around the Papyrus. Never before had I seen it this full. There must have been twenty customers, also looking quite alive. The commotion they made suddenly quieted down and all eyes turned towards me. Then they started to move, making a pathway from the door to a distant bookshelf on the left. Before they had freed the way completely, I caught sight of a body lying at the foot of the shelf with books scattered all around.

As I walked through the two rows of people, it struck me that I should be worried. Even though I was convinced that I didn't look at all like a police inspector, none of them had had any trouble recognizing me as one. I clearly have the wrong impression about myself. I would also have sworn that absolutely nothing about me indicated I wasn't married, and yet that lady doctor had needed just one look to pin the label on me.

Miss Gavrilović was standing closest to the body. She appeared more composed than I expected.

"No one has touched anything," she said softly when I reached her. "And I also asked the customers to wait until the police arrived. I hope I did the right thing."

I smiled at her. "You did superbly. If you decide to give up the bookstore after all this I'll find you a job with the police."

She smiled back, but immediately turned serious again.

Even before I crouched down next to the body, I recognized the young man. A large book partially covered his face, hiding the earring, but the bright red scarf was there, like a wide streak of blood. I stuck my hand under the scarf and felt his jugular vein. There was no pulse.

I examined the scattered books, then looked up at the shelf. The upper rows had been partially emptied. I stood up, took off my coat and covered the body with it. Silence filled the room.

"We'll have to rehabilitate the armchair," I said to Miss Gavrilović. "What happened?"

"I don't exactly know," she said in a small voice. "My eyes were riveted on the woman sitting in the armchair. Those were your instructions, right?"

I nodded.

"I heard some sort of commotion, and then the books started to fall. At first I thought the shelf had collapsed. Although that's impossible, of course. It wasn't until I went over there that I saw the young man on the floor."

"He was here last night too."

"That's right. He was a regular customer. A student of veterinary medicine. He was extremely fond of poetry." Her voice turned into a moan. "This is dreadful. . . ."

I put my hand on her shoulder. I knew I had to say something, but nothing suitable came to mind. In my confusion, I did something completely unnecessary. I took out my badge and raised it in the air, as if no one knew that the police had arrived.

"Inspector Lukić. Thank you for your patience and for waiting. Was anyone nearby when the young man fell?"

Everyone looked at each other in surprised silence for a few moments. Then a girl cleared her throat. She was small, with very short dark hair and a snub nose, wearing loud, flashy clothes. She was chewing gum.

"I was standing next to him." She pointed to the place where the young man's legs were sticking out from under my coat. "There."

"Did you see what happened?"

"He suddenly began to wave his arms like he was having an attack or something. He started knocking books off the shelf, and then collapsed."

"Out of the blue?"

"That's what it looked like."

"What was he doing before that?"

"He was leafing through a book."

"He didn't talk to anyone? No one went up to him?"

She shook her head. "I don't think so."

The bells above the door rang sharply and Dr. Dimitrijević entered the bookstore accompanied by two orderlies. One was carrying a folded stretcher.

"Everyone please leave the bookstore," I said in a loud voice. "We have to carry out an investigation." I looked at the dark-haired girl. "Thank you."

"Is he dead?" she asked softly, her voice uncertain.

"Yes, unfortunately."

Her eyes glistened. It seemed like she wanted to say something else but couldn't find the words. She took out her chewing gum, held it between her fingers, then turned and joined the bulk of murmuring customers heading towards the exit. Only two went towards the cash register to pay Miss Gavrilović for the books they had chosen.

Dr. Dimitrijević handed me my coat.

"This is yours, I assume."

I nodded, took the coat and placed it on a nearby armchair. Standing there, my eyes skimmed over the bookstore that looked much bigger now that it was empty.

Miss Gavrilović soon joined me. After seeing out the last customer, she had turned over the sign on the door, so it now said "Open" on the inside. She looked at me fixedly without speaking. Although she clearly had questions, she probably thought it would be inappropriate to talk while the doctor was crouching next to the deceased young man.

He got up a few minutes later and signaled to the orderlies, who started to unfold the stretcher. Then he came up to us.

"If this were the first case, I'd swear it was heart failure."

"At his age?" I asked.

"You can't imagine how many young people have heart disease."

"But you doubt that it was his heart?" said Miss Gavrilović.

Dr. Dimitrijević looked at me.

"At first it seemed that the previous two died of heart failure," I said to Miss Gavrilović. "But they didn't."

"So what did they die of?"

A few moments passed before I answered. "The cause hasn't been established yet."

"Looks like this will be another one," said the doctor. "Perhaps there's something strangely unhealthy in your bookstore, madam."

"Miss," I corrected him. "Miss Gavrilović. Excuse me, I forgot to introduce you."

The doctor took off his plastic gloves and held out his hand. "Dr. Dimitrijević. Nice to meet you."

"Strangely unhealthy, Doctor?"

"Three deaths in three days can scarcely result from pure chance. And deaths whose cause we are unable to determine."

"But. . . ." she said, then stopped. "But what could there be that's . . . unhealthy . . . in a bookstore?"

"To be honest, I haven't a clue. I would like to take a closer look at the Papyrus. With your approval, of course."

"Certainly. When would you like to do it?"

"Right away, if it suits you. You would be closing soon anyway, wouldn't you?" He indicated the black bag he'd placed on the floor. "I have all the equipment with me."

"How long will you need?"

He looked at his watch. "It's seven-fifteen now. I wouldn't stay longer than eight-thirty. Would it bother you if I was alone while I work?"

"Of course not. I'll come back at eight-thirty to lock up the store."

"Does that include me?" I asked.

"Yes, please. If you don't mind, perhaps you could come back at eight-thirty too?"

"My pleasure," I said.

The doctor turned towards the orderlies who had placed the young man's body on the stretcher and covered it with a green sheet. He nodded curtly. This had already become a routine in the Papyrus. They lifted the stretcher and headed towards the door.

"Excuse me for a moment," said Miss Gavrilović and headed towards the back room.

I picked up my coat from the armchair and put it on.

"What are you looking for?" I asked the doctor in a low voice.

He looked at me for a long moment, then shrugged his shoulders. Miss Gavrilović came out dressed in a dark coat. She had an umbrella over her arm.

"I'll see you at eight-thirty, doctor," she said, then looked at me quizzically.

We headed for the door at the same time. I opened it for her and followed her out.

We stood in front of the Papyrus briefly in silence. A small overhang protected us from the unremitting downpour. Then we both spoke at the same time with the same words.

"Would you. . . ."

We both fell silent with embarrassment.

"Excuse me," said Miss Gavrilović, the first to break the silence.

"I interrupted you."

"No, I interrupted you."

"I wanted to ask whether you might need company until eight-thirty."

She smiled broadly. "Yes, thank you. Would you care for some tea? Or is that a distasteful invitation for a police inspector?"

"Contrary to popular belief, police inspectors adore tea. Particularly if they are partial to literature."

"I know an excellent teashop close by."

She opened the umbrella and offered it to me. As it was small, we had to walk very close together to stay out of the rain.

7

THE TEASHOP HAD ONLY four small tables. A young couple was sitting at one. Their heads were close together as they chatted and they took no notice of the new customers. It was warm inside, the light was subdued and a multitude of fragrances swirled about the air, colliding intoxicatingly, mingling and complementing each other.

We chose a corner table. It had a small lamp with a dark-red shade and a dish with several sections containing condiments for tea. We put our coats on the coat rack nearby and sat down.

A short, oldish man with thin graying hair, slanted eyes and a rheumatic walk came up to the table.

His narrow pants and Mandarin jacket buttoned all the way up were the same color as the lampshade. He bowed and smiled at Miss Gavrilović.

"Good evening. Welcome. A bit early today?" I had never heard such a foreign accent. The words were drawn out and each one seemed to be followed by an exclamation point.

"Good evening," replied Miss Gavrilović, returning his smile. "We closed early."

The old man bowed again.

"Not many customer when rain? Empty here too. Tea is best for cold weather. Tea and book. But people not know what is good." He sighed. "Like usual for you? And what would gentleman like? The same, yes? When two, should drink same tea, old saying."

He looked at me and I looked at Miss Gavrilović. It seemed to me that she blushed, but it might have been just the dark-red glow from the lamp.

"I recommend fig tea," she said. "Unless, of course, you fancy something else. Almost every fancy can be met here."

"Should we question the saying? Besides, I've never tried fig tea before."

The old man bowed once more and left.

"I drop in often after work. I discovered the teashop by accident. It opened recently. I didn't care much for tea before, but now I'm addicted."

"I enjoy a good cup of tea. Linden tea. Sometimes I think I should try another kind, but the force of habit wins out. That's how it is with men who live alone."

She looked at me without speaking for a few moments.

"You're not married, are you?" she asked at last, lowering her voice a little.

"I've already been labeled once today. Does it really show that much?"

She nodded with a smile.

"What makes it so obvious?"

She indicated my right hand.

"You're not wearing a wedding band."

I wanted to slap my forehead. So much for the quick-witted detective.

"That doesn't mean a thing," I said, trying to get out of the awkward situation. "Maybe I only wear it when I'm with my wife."

"You don't need to resort to such cheap tricks. A wedding band wouldn't stand in the way. On the contrary. Some women consider it a challenge."

"So then I should wear one?"

She laughed.

"Then you wouldn't have to explain why you're not married."

"I don't have to this way either."

"That's right, you don't. But you might volunteer the information."

"Isn't it obvious?"

She looked at me askance, then shook her head.

"Police inspectors don't make the best husbands. Their marriages don't last long as a rule."

"Not even when they have a degree in literature?"

"Particularly not then. There's something unnatural about that combination. It repels both women who, in spite of everything, have no preconceptions about police inspectors, and those who aren't alienated by well-read men." I stopped briefly. "Would you, for example, marry someone like that?"

The old man's return spared her from having to answer the question.

"Tea made of figs," he said, placing a porcelain teapot and two cups before us. "Very good for conversation. People happy when drink it."

He poured the steaming green liquid into our cups. The fragrance of figs overpowered the mixture of aromas surrounding us.

Then came the inevitable bow. "Now you enjoy," he said, retreating with a smile.

"May I?" asked Miss Gavrilović, indicating the sectioned dish.

"If you please."

She took the covers off three sections. Using the tiny spoons in them she scooped up a bit of orange powder from the first, something that looked like brown sugar from the second, and shreds of a dried black plant from the third. When she stirred all of that into my tea, the green turned yellowish-brown. I must have puckered my brow, because she gave a little laugh.

"It took a lot of experimenting with various condiments to discover this combination. Don't be fooled by appearances. I'm sure you'll like it."

I raised the cup, but her hand placed gently on my arm stopped it from reaching my lips.

"You have to be patient and let it cool off. Tea should never be drunk when it's scalding."

I put the cup down and she withdrew her hand

"So what is your explanation?"

"My explanation?"

"For the 'Miss'."

"Oh, that." She looked at her cup as she stirred it with a spoon. "The bookstore, of course. It doesn't leave much time for other things."

"How unusual. I thought that only happened when you worked for the police."

"It all looked different to me when Olga and I opened the Papyrus seven years ago."

"What went wrong?"

"I had a starry-eyed approach to running a bookstore. I thought of it as something artistic, and it's primarily a commercial undertaking. Sometimes it seems that we aren't much different from a grocery store, at least with regard to the paperwork."

"I envy you that grocery store."

She glanced at me warmly, then turned her eyes back to the whirlpool in her cup.

"We wanted the Papyrus to become sort of a literary salon. That's what the armchairs are for. We had eight in the beginning. But instead of a select clientele we got our patients."

"Have you ever thought of doing something else?"

"No, I haven't. In spite of all the drawbacks, I love working in the bookstore. It gets under your skin."

"Enough to make you sacrifice your private life?"

Her eyes lost their warmth.

"I could ask you the same thing. What is it that ties you to police work when it deprives you of a private life?"

"Like you said, it gets under your skin."

We sank into silence. The young couple at the other table got up and headed for the door. After they left, the only sound in the teashop was the spoon ringing in her cup.

She soon stopped stirring it.

"I think it's cooled off enough. Go ahead and try it."

I took a cautious sip of the brown liquid.

"It's like what I drank before wasn't tea."

She lit up again.

"That's nice."

I took a big sip, then another. If I'd been alone, I would have emptied the cup. As it was, I set it on the table reluctantly.

"You know," I said, "it's not all that bad with your patients. At least you're getting some excitement."

"Indeed. Too much, I'm afraid. Particularly now with this onslaught of deaths in the Papyrus." She stopped and her face turned serious. "Do you think we'll have to close?"

"Why?"

She hesitated a bit. "Well . . . if they continue."

"They won't continue. You have greatly surpassed the average number of deaths in a bookstore."

"But if the doctor finds something. . . ."

"What is there to find?"

"I don't know. But he's looking for something, isn't he?"

I glanced at my watch. "We'll know soon whether he found what he's looking for."

"Maybe we shouldn't have left him alone in the bookstore."

I laughed. "Don't worry, he's not in any danger. Medical examiners don't die, not even in detective novels. And since we're on the subject, I'd like to ask you something."

"Yes?"

"Do you have any reason to stay in the Papyrus after Dr. Dimitrijević leaves?"

"I'll stay at least another half hour. I mentioned the paperwork, and I have to take care of those scattered books. Why do you ask?"

"Would you mind if I keep you company? I'd like to try to find a book."

"I would enjoy your company very much. Being alone in the bookstore has lost its charm. I'd be glad to help you. All the books are in the computer. What book are you looking for?"

I sighed. "I don't know."

She studied me, puzzled.

"You don't know the title?"

"No."

"Or the author's name?"

"Not even that."

"Then how do you think you'll find it?"

"I'd recognize it if I saw it."

"Then the computer won't be of much help."

"That's what I thought."

"Do you know anything at all about the book you're looking for?"

"It's a detective novel, I assume."

"We don't have many of them, unless they're serious literature. We already talked about that."

"I don't know whether this is serious or light literature."

"Have you read it before?"

"I'd say I have."

"You'd say?"

I raised my cup and finished the tea.

"All of this must seem puzzling to you."

"Why not try to explain it a bit?"

"I'll try, but I'm not certain that it will be much clearer to you. It's not even clear to me. Everything started the first time we spoke. When you called the police after the first death in the Papyrus. Do you remember?"

"How could I forget it?" she replied with a smile.

"As I was listening to you, I had the strangest impression. It was like I knew what you were going to say the moment before you said it."

"*Déjà vu*?"

I raised my eyebrows and shook my head.

"It's more like *déjà lu*."

"I've never heard of anything like that."

"Neither have I. But that's certainly what it seemed like. As though you were speaking sentences from a book that I'd read."

"But how could I? I don't read detective novels."

"I don't read them much either, but what I said at the time seemed to come from the same book."

She sipped a little tea. Her cup was still more than half-full.

"Maybe you shouldn't attach too much importance to one strange impression. I experience *déjà vu* from time to time, but I let it pass. What else is there to do?"

"It's not just an impression."

"It's not?"

"No. Everything that's happened since our first conversation has looked to me like *déjà lu*. Even here in the teashop."

She stared into my eyes.

"Now I'll turn out to be a character from some dime-store novel," she said, smiling again.

"Does this resemble a dime-store novel?"

Her expression showed that she wasn't certain how to answer. In the end she sidestepped the issue.

"All that's left is for you to search the bookstore. I hope you find that mysterious book. I'd like to read it, regardless of whether it's serious or light literature."

She raised her cup again and finished her tea.

"We have to go," she said, putting it down, then turned towards the old man. Although he was absorbed in something behind the counter, he somehow caught her look and trotted over to our table. I took out my wallet as he came up, but he shook his head.

"Mister not pay because first time here. So come again. I hope tea made of figs pleasant. Enjoy talking?"

"Very much," said Miss Gavrilović, glancing at me briefly. "Fig tea is a real inspiration to interesting conversation."

The old man bowed twice, smiling broadly.

"I happy. You me see again soon."

When we drew together again under her umbrella, she took my arm. This seemed to give us more room.

8

As I SHOOK OUT the umbrella in front of the entrance, Miss Gavrilović went inside the Papyrus. I followed after her, and the bells rang out again when I closed the door.

She turned and looked at me in bewilderment. It took a moment before I realized why. There was no one in the bookstore.

Then a rustling noise was heard in the back room. I

signaled Miss Gavrilović to stay by the entrance, then headed in that direction. I was halfway there when the door behind the counter opened and Dr. Dimitrijević appeared.

"Ah, you're back. Right on time. I just finished."

He started to take off the plastic gloves. A gauze mask was hanging under his chin.

"I didn't know that the back room would interest you too," said Miss Gavrilović.

"It's part of the bookstore."

"But customers aren't allowed back there."

"Someone goes back there, don't they?"

"No one but me and my colleague who is co-owner of the Papyrus. Does this make us suspects?"

"Suspects of what?"

"Why, of what's happened. Three deaths."

"How could you be suspects? These aren't murders but natural deaths."

"What from?"

Dr. Dimitrijević went up to one of the armchairs. He took off the mask and put it and the plastic gloves into the bag he'd placed there.

"I don't know yet. I might find out something after I examine the samples."

"Samples?"

"Yes. I took samples of various materials in the bookstore."

"Like what?"

"Paper, for example. That's what there is in here the most, which is understandable, so it might be the primary source of trouble."

"How could paper cause such serious trouble as death?"

"Some people are allergic to paper."

"But they would stay away from a bookstore."

"Not necessarily. Perhaps they had no idea that danger was lurking. An allergy can develop to just one type of paper. All others types are completely harmless, while that one is literally fatal."

"I had no idea. That makes bookselling a high-risk job."

"Rest assured, paper allergies are extremely rare."

An ironic smile appeared on Miss Gavrilović's face.

"Would you call an average of one case a day rare?"

"Oh, paper doesn't have to be behind all three deaths. Other things cause dangerous allergies too. Dust, for example."

"Dust? But there isn't any dust here. We take great pains to keep the bookstore clean."

"I agree completely. Your orderliness would be the envy of some pharmacies. But regardless of how much you try to remove the dust, it always comes out the winner. Particularly where there are lots of books."

"So what should we do?"

"You shouldn't do anything. If that's the reason someone died here, then they're probably the only person in the whole city liable to die from bookstore dust. That's even rarer than being allergic to paper. The same can be said for ashes."

Miss Gavrilović and I turned our heads towards the fireplace at the same time.

"Ashes?"

"Yes. The literature cites cases of serious allergies to ashes. But it's the least probable. That happened when some dangerous matter was burned, and you, as far as I can tell, use ordinary beech wood."

"Maybe we should install some other kind of heating."

Dr. Dimitrijević shook his head.

"Certainly not. You have to understand that there is no full protection as far as allergies are concerned. Even if you were to turn the bookstore into a hermetically sealed and sterilized chamber, that would still be no guarantee. And then who would come to buy books?"

"No one," replied Miss Gavrilović softly.

Dr. Dimitrijević smiled.

"That's enough talk about the samples I took. I've only frightened you unnecessarily. There's no reason to worry. You've just had a stroke of bad luck with three people dying in the Papyrus within a short interval and from uncommon causes. But this has certainly come to an end. I hope it won't discourage people from visiting the bookstore."

"It hasn't so far," said Miss Gavrilović. "Quite the contrary. The first case was like a lure. We'll see what happens after the two today. I dread to think of what the tabloids might do. . . ."

"Don't worry," said Dr. Dimitrijević, waving his hand dismissively. "Whatever they write won't hurt you. Tabloid readers don't go into bookstores like this and your customers don't read the tabloids."

Miss Gavrilović let out a sigh. "Let's hope so."

"All right, I have to go now. I'll talk to you soon, Inspector. Would you mind giving me your cell phone number?"

"Of course."

He took out his phone and wrote the number into the address book.

"Thank you. Goodbye, Miss Gavrilović. I don't know whether you'll take this as a compliment, but the Papyrus is one of the nicest places I've worked."

"Thank you for the compliment," she replied with a fleeting smile.

He headed for the door, took his coat from the coat rack, put it on and left. After the bells died down behind him, there was a protracted silence.

"Inspector Lukić. . . ." said Miss Gavrilović at last, but I interrupted her.

"Dejan."

She gazed straight into my eyes for a long while. There wasn't any dark-red light to hide her blush.

"Dejan."

"Yes, Vera?"

It seemed like she wanted to say something else, but changed her mind at the last moment.

"If there's anything I can do to help you. . . ."

"Thank you, but I don't see how you can since not even I know what I'm looking for. How about if I help you clear up these books?"

I indicated the scattered volumes on the floor.

"No, no, it will only take a second. You go ahead and start your search."

She went into the back room to leave her coat and I hooked mine on the coat rack. Then I went up to the closest bookshelf. I turned around when I heard her come out. Our eyes met briefly. We both smiled.

I'd been overly optimistic when I said I'd recognize the book if I saw it. I hadn't the slightest idea what it looked like. It might end up right in front of my nose without my being aware of it. There was an ever greater probability, however, that it was all in my mind. There actually was no book.

Indeed, giving it some serious thought, as befits a police inspector, how could a book describe everything that was actually happening to me? It couldn't, of course. This was reality, not literature. How could I allow my formal education to stand in the way of my work?

On the other hand, the impression of *déjà lu* was truly powerful. I'd never experienced anything like it before. Worst of all was the realization that I'd fallen into a trap with no way out. Just before I said something I knew the very words that would inexorably follow, like an actor who has learned his role by heart. I'd tried to alter the inevitable several times and say something else, but it hadn't worked.

My eyes slid slowly over the book spines. From time to time I took out a volume and leafed through it briefly. It took Vera about ten minutes to put the shelf in order. Then she went to the cash register and concentrated on her paperwork. It was completely silent in the bookstore, nothing like the agitated place I'd entered some two hours before.

"Having any luck?"

I put the book I was holding back on the shelf and turned around. She looked at me over the top of her reading glasses that were halfway down her nose.

"None at all. Have you finished?"

She took off her glasses which hung on a ribbon around her neck and put them in a drawer under the cash register.

"Not quite, but I'll finish the rest tomorrow. Today's excitement has exhausted me."

I went up to the counter.

"Me too. It takes fresh eyes to look for something you know nothing about. I'll continue tomorrow, with your permission."

She smiled.

"Of course. But there might not be any more need for the search."

"Why?"

She came out from behind the counter and stood in front of me.

"I must confess I'm quite impressed. You should have been a writer. You have a wonderful imagination."

I shook my head. "I don't understand."

"You know, Dejan, I've been hit on a number of ways, but no one's been as inventive as you."

I stared at her with blinking eyes.

Her smile broadened. She stroked my cheek.

"That idea about *déjà lu* was really clever. And the inevitability of what happens next."

"That's not it. . . ." I started to say, but she interrupted me.

"You didn't have to go to such pains. But I'm flattered in any case. So, what inevitably happens next?"

I sighed.

"Now there is an inevitable parting until tomorrow. Any other sequence of events would be characteristic of dime-store novels, and the book I'm looking for doesn't seem to be that."

I stroked her cheek too.

"Although right now I'm really sorry it isn't."

9

I WAS GREETED IN the office by my colleague Petronijević's broad smile.

"Congratulations," he said. "No less than the front page."

He showed me the tabloid in front of him.

I picked up the newspaper. A photo of the Papyrus window display covered almost the entire lower half of the front page. Above it was the large headline "Lethal Bookstore," with three exclamation points at the end. The note at the bottom of the picture indicated the story was on page nine. I turned the pages hurriedly until I found it.

My attention was first drawn to another large photograph. A skull and crossbones had been placed over the shelves full of books. The brief story was put together in typical tabloid fashion.

From the outside, Papyrus Bookstore looks harmless. But don't be fooled by appearances! Don't go inside if you care for your life! It's one of the most dangerous places in town! Three innocent book lovers have lost their lives in that bookstore in the past three days! The cause of their deaths is still unknown. Reliable police sources have told us they expect new victims.

I felt like snarling. I could just imagine how Vera would feel if she got hold of the newspaper.

"Disgusting!" I said. "That bit with the skull and crossbones could only be the work of a pathological book-hater."

"Nothing they wrote is incorrect."

"The part about expecting new victims is remarkably incorrect."

"Well, aren't they expected?"

"Why would they be expected?"

"The boss wouldn't call you in to talk if it was all over."

"When did he call me?"

"At nine-thirty. He said to go see him right away."

"Wonderful. It's high time we talked about the reliable police sources mentioned by the tabloids all the time."

"I doubt he'll be very interested."

He took the newspaper out of my hands and stuck his nose back into it.

I left my office and headed down the corridor, then knocked on the last door on the right. The brass plate said "Chief Inspector."

"Come in!" droned a voice.

I opened the door. Chief Inspector Đorđević was sitting behind a large desk dominated by two symmetrically placed bonsais. Behind it was an enormous aquarium full of green reflections.

"Ah, Inspector Lukić, take a seat."

He indicated the left of two armchairs facing the desk. I sat down, wondering why he never offered me the one on the right.

"What's going on in that bookstore? The Papyrus, isn't it?"

"Yes, the Papyrus."

"Nice name for a bookstore. Where do you get so many dead bodies in a place like that? Three, right?"

"Yes, three."

"What does the medical examiner say?"

"I haven't received his official report. Unofficially, the cause of death is still unknown."

"Unknown?"

"It isn't something commonplace. Dr. Dimitrijević is currently checking out some less common possibilities. Violent allergic reactions, for example."

"Allergic reactions—to what?"

"As far as I understand, there are several candidates. Paper, dust, ashes, for example."

He got up from his leather armchair, took out his handkerchief, bent over the right bonsai and wiped the miniature treetop.

"Dust is really unbearable. I cleaned the tree this morning and you can already draw a line with your finger." He turned towards the aquarium. "Maybe I should protect it with something. I didn't know such things could be lethal."

"It seems that they can. In very special cases."

He shook out his handkerchief and put it back in his pocket.

"Isn't three very special cases too much in only a few days? How many, exactly?"

"In three days."

"Did anything similar ever happen in the Papyrus before?"

"No, nor in any other bookstore to my knowledge."

"Is it possible they're not a coincidence?"

A few moments of silence passed before I answered the question.

"What are you getting at?"

"Oh, you know already, we live in violent times."

"Are you saying that someone might be behind this?"

"Maybe you shouldn't exclude that possibility. The world is full of psychopaths and there's no short supply of terrorists either."

"I would expect terrorists to choose a larger target than a small bookstore."

"You never know. If they're using some sort of biological weapon, it makes no difference where they start. The least conspicuous starting point the better, actually. Psychopaths don't aim high, anyway."

"What do you propose we do?"

"We can't do much until we get the medical examiner's findings. Then we'll see. We might even have to ask for help."

"From the National Security Agency?"

"Yes. They are the only ones properly equipped to fight against terrorism."

"I'd say that won't really be necessary. If my intuition serves me right, this is something less dramatic than terrorism."

"I've always respected intuition in our work, but be on your guard just in case. Maybe you could drop by the Papyrus from time to time in the days ahead."

"That's what I intended to do."

"Wonderful. You're a bookworm anyway, so you won't stand out there."

I smiled.

"I'll take that as a compliment."

"Compliment or not, I couldn't send Inspector Petronijević to a bookstore, could I? Just one look and they'd know he was the police."

"But he'd go unnoticed in a tabloid."

Now he was the one to smile.

"To each his specialty. They all have their importance."

"Of course."

"All right, that's about it."

I got up and headed for the door.

"Report back to me immediately if something new turns up," he said as I opened it.

"OK, Chief."

Just as I started down the corridor, my cell phone rang. The number of the Papyrus flickered on the small screen.

"Hello?"

"Inspector Lukić?"

"Speaking, Miss Bogdanović."

"I hope I'm not disturbing you." Her voice was aloof.

"Not at all."

"Would you mind coming to our bookstore?"

I stopped walking.

"It's not. . . ." I began after a brief hesitation.

"I'm afraid I have to disappoint you. No one else has died. But we're having other problems."

"I'll be there right away."

10

I FOUND TWO CUSTOMERS in the Papyrus. There was a tall girl wearing a colorful woolen cap, a leather jacket that barely reached her hips and jeans tucked into high boots. She was standing next to a shelf to the left of the entrance, leafing through a large book. Her mouth opened and closed without a sound as she sang along to the music coming through small earphones.

A middle-aged balding man was sitting in one of the armchairs. He'd placed his coat on his lap with his scarf over it and his hat on top. An umbrella was leaning against the side of the armchair. He would have been much more comfortable if he'd left it all by the coat rack. And if he'd had glasses with the proper prescription, instead of holding his book with arms stretched out to his knees.

I went up to Miss Bogdanović, who was standing at the cash register behind the counter. Too bad she didn't use just a little makeup to hide her pallor. She didn't hold out her hand, for which I was grateful. I don't like shaking hands with a dead fish.

She looked at her watch.

"Shouldn't police inspectors be faster?"

"We're fast when there's a reason to be." I looked around the bookstore. "I don't see anything here that should have made me rush with a wailing siren."

"That's because you're not looking carefully. Shouldn't a detective have an excellent flair for observation? Particularly if he's not unfamiliar with books."

This time I looked around the premises more carefully. Everything looked the same as when I'd left the night before. I was just about to tell Miss Bogdanović that I wasn't there to play cat and mouse with her, when she nodded impatiently towards the nearest shelf. I went up and studied it for a while. Then I went back to the counter.

"The books aren't arranged by title."

"Congratulations," she said ironically.

"Thank you. Only I don't understand why that's a job for the police."

"Because someone switched them during the night. And as we know, the bookstore is closed at night."

"When did you notice that they were rearranged?"

"Just before I called you. A customer was looking for a book. I went up to the shelf to get it, but it wasn't where it should have been. I quickly discovered that many others weren't either."

"Just on that shelf or on all of them?"

"Just on that one."

"How long were you in the bookstore before you discovered it?"

"About an hour and a half. On Saturday we're open from nine until three."

"You spent an hour and a half here and everything seemed fine, and you expected me to notice at first glance that it wasn't?"

She repeated a movement that I'd caught the last time: she pushed her large glasses up the bridge of her nose. This was a way to gain time.

"I'm not a detective."

"But you're here every day. Does it take an excellent flair for observation to notice such a conspicuous change?"

"I didn't take notice." Her voice became more strident. "I had more important things to do than look at the books. Vera didn't finish her work last night, so it was left for me to do. It seems she wasn't in a mood to work."

She looked at me in reproach.

"Did you talk to her?"

"She called me before she closed the bookstore. She told me everything that happened. If I understood correctly, the new death in the Papyrus didn't stop you from enjoying a cup of tea."

"Fig tea is an excellent pick-me-up regardless of the occasion. Especially after a death. I heartily recommend it. It has the best effect, though, when it's tea for two."

Her lips formed a thin line.

"And what do you intend to do about it?"

"About what?"

"About the break-in at the Papyrus, of course."

"Break-in?"

"Don't you understand that someone broke in here during the night and rearranged the books?"

"I understand that someone changed the order of the books, but not that someone broke into the bookstore. When you opened the door this morning, did you notice anything unusual about the lock?"

She gave it some thought.

"No, I didn't. But that doesn't mean a thing. Thieves are surely smart enough to pick more complicated locks than ours and leave no trace."

"Oh, yes, professionals are highly skilled at that. But why do you think this has anything to do with thieves? Was anything stolen?"

She looked like she wanted to say several things at the same time, but couldn't decide which one to say first. Her eyes flashed behind the glasses.

"Nothing was stolen!" she said, almost shouting.

The man in the armchair raised his eyes from his book.

"Don't take me literally," she continued in a lower voice after the man's gaze had returned to his knees. "I wasn't thinking of a thief but a burglar."

"You suspect that a professional broke into the bookstore during the night just to rearrange the books?"

"Well, what other explanation is there?"

"There's a rule in police investigations, you see, that rarely fails. Occam's razor. The simplest explanation is the most likely."

"I don't understand what you're trying to say."

"Why do you assume that someone broke into the bookstore when someone could have entered quite legally?"

"What do you mean, legally? There are only two keys, mine and. . . ."

She stopped, mouth open. When she spoke again, her voice was still low, but it trembled with anger.

"What nonsense! You don't suspect that we did this, do you?"

"I don't suspect anyone. I'm just checking the most likely possibilities. All right, you didn't come here last night and rearrange the books. Then all we have to do is check with Ve . . . Miss Gavrilović."

Another reproachful glance inevitably followed.

"But why would she create such chaos?"

I shrugged my shoulders.

"We don't know that she did. Did you call her to tell her what happened?"

"Yes, I did, but no one answered. When she doesn't work on Saturday she sleeps in."

"Would you please try again?"

She hesitated a bit before going into the back room. When she returned, she seemed puzzled.

"This is unusual. There's still no answer. She's never slept until almost noon before. I called her on her cell phone too, but she can't be reached."

"Maybe she decided to go away for the weekend. You shouldn't hold it against her. The past few days have been quite turbulent."

"But it's not at all like Vera to go off without letting me know."

"We all grow up some day."

The only thing that stopped her from exploding was the girl who came up to us just at that moment. She handed Miss Bogdanović the book she'd been leafing through and a credit card. She didn't stop mouthing the words as the sale was rung up, then headed for the door, her steps following the inaudible rhythm.

"Miss Gavrilović told me about your. . . ." I stopped, ". . . .patients. One of them is a woman with this very inclination, right?"

I indicated the shelf.

"I don't like it when Vera calls our customers that. It isn't fair."

"What would you call them?"

"We're all eccentric in one way or another. You are certainly no exception."

"I don't rearrange books on shelves."

"But there must be something else you do. I wonder if the eccentric tendencies of a police inspector are as harmless as that."

We regarded each other for a few moments as though through gun sights.

"Do you know," I said, breaking the tense silence, "whether that woman. . . ."

"Mrs. Dragana Stojanović," she said interrupting me. "Curator of the Museum of Modern Art."

"So, was Mrs. Stojanović in the bookstore last night?"

"No, she wasn't."

"Are you sure?"

"Vera would have told me if she had been."

"Maybe it didn't seem important compared to other events. Or she didn't notice. There was quite a crowd here."

"But she would have noticed that the books were rearranged when she came back from the teashop. There wasn't any crowd then. Actually, just the two of you were left in the end, right?"

"That's right. But as you said, Miss Gavrilović was not in a mood to work, and that's when one doesn't take the greatest care."

Invisible gun sights rose between us again. She spoke first this time.

"The best thing would be to check that with Vera when we finally contact her. I'm confident she wasn't completely . . . careless."

I took out my cell phone.

"Will you give me your permission to take a few pictures of the shelf?"

"How could I refuse to give a police inspector my permission? Wouldn't that be against the law?"

"That wouldn't be against anything. Except your conscience, perhaps."

"Oh, do I have you on my conscience? Go ahead. I only hope your pictures don't appear in a tabloid."

Now I was unable to keep my voice down. Luckily, the man in the armchair had kindly decided that our temperamental conversation no longer concerned him.

"It's clear to me that police inspectors aren't your favorite type. But if you think that I have anything to do with what was published today, you're terribly mistaken. I find it no less disgusting than you."

It looked like she was trying to think of a retort, but in the end all she did was lower her eyes to some papers on the counter.

I went up to the shelf and took several close-up pictures so I could get a good look at the titles on the spines. The flash was not enough to raise the eyes of the only customer in the store from the book on his knees.

When I headed back to the counter, the bells above the door rang out.

"Your patie . . . eccentrics are interesting," I said to Miss Bogdanović. "I'd like to meet them sometime."

She nodded briefly towards the door.

"Here's your chance."

I turned around and looked at—Albert Einstein.

11

THE RESEMBLANCE WAS UNCANNY. As the mathematics professor walked briskly towards the counter, I had the overwhelming impression that the great physicist in person was coming towards me. He had the same short stature, the same gray hair sticking out on all sides under his hat, the same mustache that covered his upper lip. His bow tie was crooked and the collar of his coat was raised on just one side.

He took off his hat and bowed first to Miss Bogdanović and then to me.

"Hello, my dear miss. Hello to you too, sir."

"Hello, Professor," said Miss Bogdanović, as I returned the bow.

"I came as soon as I heard what happened," he said, putting his hat back on. "Three deaths already. Dreadful, dreadful."

"There's nothing to be done. People don't choose where they die. It could happen anywhere. Our luck's been rather tough the past few days."

"Hah, luck!" shouted the professor, forcing the man in the armchair to raise his head briefly again. "Luck has nothing to do with it! It's all much more . . . serious!"

"Really?" said Miss Bogdanović in the voice of a mother whose child has just said something very imaginative.

"To be sure!" said the professor, disregarding her tone. "And I, of course, am to blame for it all. I wasn't fast enough." He shook his head several times. "Inexcusable, inexcusable."

"I advise you to be careful, dear Professor. It isn't wise to accuse yourself in the presence of the police." She turned towards me. "This is Inspector Lukić."

I held out my hand.

"Dejan Lukić."

He bent back a little, looked me over, then accepted my hand.

"Ah, I see. Indeed, indeed. Atanasije Nedeljković. Retired professor of mathematics. I'm afraid the police have nothing to do here."

"It looks that way to me too," I said. "Our business is with violent deaths, not natural ones."

He looked at me with pity.

"Natural, do you say? Well, now, you're in for a surprise."

"You don't think it's that?"

"I certainly do not."

"Why?"

"Because everything clearly points to something else."

He stuck his hand into the left pocket of his coat and then into the right. Then he checked the inside pocket and finally found what he was looking for in the back pocket of his pants. The notebook had greasy spots on its brown cardboard cover. He tapped it with his free hand.

"It's all written here. All of my research."

"Research?" I asked.

"Yes. Here, see for yourself."

He handed me the notebook with a proud look on his face.

I slowly turned the pages filled with tiny numbers and symbols. Unlike the professor's general air of distraction, everything was neat, just as befits a mathematician.

I gave him back his notebook.

"Unfortunately, I have trouble finding my way in mathematics. My field is literature."

"Mr. Lukić is a new type of police inspector," interjected Miss Bogdanović with an amused smile. "He's a real paragon of erudition."

Professor Nedeljković looked me over again.

"Indeed, indeed. As a matter of fact, this is about literature."

He put the notebook in the inside pocket of his coat.

"About literature?" I repeated.

"Correct. Those are all the traces I found. In countless works of literature. Covered up, hidden, disguised traces. Invisible to the ordinary eye. Believe me when I say it was not at all easy to find them. I've invested decades in it. An entire life, one might say."

"What traces?" I asked after a moment's hesitation.

Before he had a chance to answer, the man in the armchair came up to us.

"Excuse me for disturbing you," he said to Miss Bogdanović. "Would you be kind enough to reserve this book for me? I'll come and pick it up on Monday."

He handed her a book with a business card tucked into it.

"Certainly, sir," replied Miss Bogdanović, placing the book under the counter. "See you on Monday, then."

"Goodbye."

"What traces?" I asked again, after the ringing of the bells above the door had subsided.

The professor didn't reply at once. He looked around the empty bookstore as though fearing that someone might hear him.

"Traces of the last book," he said at last in a soft voice.

"The last book?" said Miss Bogdanović. "You never mentioned it to me before, Professor."

"I didn't, because it was a secret. But now the secret is out." His arm gestured broadly, taking in the premises. "The last book is somewhere in here."

"In what sense is it the last?"

A few moments passed again before he answered.

"After it, there are no more."

"But if there aren't any more books, we'll be without a job. Would you like us to close the Papyrus? Where would you go to do your research?"

"Not only the Papyrus is in danger. Everything is in danger. The whole world."

"Really? Why, that's dreadful, Professor. Is there any hope for us?"

"There might be, if I find the last book soon."

"Then you must start looking right away. We can't let the world go to ruin, can we?"

"What does the last book look like?" I asked after the professor had already headed towards the closest shelf. I endured Miss Bogdanović's reproving look.

He stopped, turned around and shook his head.

"I don't know. No one does. That's the biggest problem. It's different every time. You don't recognize it until it's too late."

"Why do you think it's in the bookstore?"

"Aren't three deaths enough proof? It's here, there's no doubt about it. I had a feeling it would turn up here the first time I set foot in the Papyrus. That's why I kept coming back. But I wasn't fast enough to stop it. Sad, sad."

I wanted to ask something else, but Miss Bogdanović headed me off.

"Let's not detain the professor. He has an important task before him. He has to save the world. Please go on, Professor."

Professor Nedeljković started searching through his

pockets again until he found his notebook. He leafed through it briefly, then began to draw his finger down one of the pages, following his notes. Then he bent down and took a book out of the lowest shelf. Before he opened it, he turned his head briefly towards us, then positioned himself so that we couldn't see what he was doing.

"You clearly have no experience with eccentrics," said Miss Bogdanović in a low voice. "You should never be surprised at what they come out with. Or ask them superfluous questions. The best thing is to humor them, regardless of what they say. And don't strike up a conversation with them."

"Thank you for the advice."

"You should be even more grateful for my interrupting you. If I hadn't, he would have bent your ear with his crazy ideas. And I doubt that police inspectors have time to spare."

"Eccentrics aren't the only ones who act irresponsibly towards police inspectors' time. Normal people give us headaches too. They often call us for unwarranted reasons."

She cast me a furious glance.

"It didn't look unwarranted to me."

"In any case, everything's all right now. At least according to the Papyrus' standards where things can be much more exciting."

Her lips seemed to vanish from her face.

"Do you always have to be insufferable?"

"Not always, only on my way out. Goodbye, Miss Bogdanović. Please say hello to Miss Gavrilović when you get in touch with her."

When I turned and headed towards the door, something resembling a hiss came after me.

"That's the very first thing I'm going to do."

12

The only source of light in the office was a large monitor. It was still daylight when I sat down at the computer. I didn't notice when it got dark. At one point I raised my head because my neck had a crick in it and was surprised to see that the windows were filled with darkness.

I hadn't expected the work to take that long, but it ended up being rather tedious. The photographs I'd taken showed almost three hundred books in nine rows. First I noted down all the titles. Even though I'd taken a close-up, it wasn't always easy to read what was written on the spines, even after zooming in very close.

Once I had completed the preliminary work, I started to mark in red the titles that were not in alphabetical order. Then I copied them one by one into a new window. I stared at the short list for a long time, trying to make some sense out of it.

The first thing I wondered was why these particular books had been rearranged and not others. Their literary value was hardly any criterion. Along with several very important works were some quite mediocre novels. I would have to ask Vera—or better yet Miss Bogdanović—how they had found their way into a bookstore that prided itself on its impeccable literary taste.

Then it crossed my mind that the choice actually had nothing to do with the titles. The books might have been singled out according to some other characteristic. Their format, for example, or binding or the color of the cover. For some reason the idea about color seemed particularly attractive.

I minimized the window with the list of book titles marked in red and re-examined the photograph of the bookshelf. But soon I realized it had no pattern either. It had large and small books, both hardback and paperback, and the colors were a hodgepodge.

I maximized the list of rearranged titles again and stared at it. I don't know how long I stayed like that. As time passed and fatigue slowly got the better of me, I started to accept the idea that all of this effort was in vain. Vera was right. Whoever had rearranged the books, Mrs. Stojanović or someone else, had most likely done it without aim or purpose. There was no meaning hidden there.

Feeling depressed, not so much for the failure as for having wasted my time, I reached for the mouse to close all the windows and turn off the computer, but my hand stopped in mid-air. Although the volume of my cell phone was turned down, its ringing in the dead silence made me start.

"Hello?"

"I wanted to thank you for the greeting. It was nice to hear."

"Vera," I almost shouted. "How are you?"

She laughed.

"Fine. Were you expecting otherwise?"

"No, of course not. Except that Miss Bogdanović was upset when she couldn't get hold of you on the phone."

"That's Olga for you. Sometimes she's overly protective."

"Like an older sister?"

"She's two years younger than I am. That's why her protective attitude seems so out of place."

"I'd say you're not alone in receiving such treatment from her."

"Did the two of you cross swords again?"

"Oh, nothing special. I'm used to it by now. I know how to handle her sarcasm."

"I'm sure you give as good as you take. Even so, there was no reason for her to trouble you."

"It's always better when it turns out that there was no reason for the police to come. In any case, if I hadn't gone to the Papyrus today, I would have missed the chance to meet Professor Nedeljković."

"Ah, our Einstein. Olga told me that she got you out of an unpleasant situation. Sometimes he's a real bore."

"I found him interesting. Too bad Miss Bogdanović took away our chance to talk."

"You can always make up for it. I'll call you the next time he appears on my shift, then you can talk to your hearts' desire."

"Since we're on the subject of your patients . . . or should I call them eccentrics?"

"Only when Olga is around."

"Did Mrs. Stojanović drop by last night?"

"I already told Olga. I don't think she did, but I'm not completely sure. It was really crowded."

"You didn't see anyone else fooling with the books?"

"No, I didn't. My attention was focused primarily on the cash register and that armchair, and then on what happened."

"Someone did rearrange the books, though. Miss Bogdanović thinks that it was done during the night."

"That's in her nature. She always thinks the worst."

"You locked the door last night, didn't you?"

"Of course. And no one came in after you left, worried about the endangered honor of serious literature."

I cleared my throat at this jibe, which made Vera laugh again.

"I hear that you took a picture of the shelf. So, have you proven to be more astute than me? What did you find out?"

I sighed.

"Nothing. I spent the whole afternoon searching, but haven't been able to find any sense. It's really exhausted me."

"Then would fig tea do you some good?"

"Very much so. Am I to understand this as another invitation to the teashop?"

"It's nice there, but I know a place that's even nicer. And I picked up all the condiments they have in the teashop." She hesitated briefly. "Of course, if this fits into your scenario of *déjà lu*."

"It fits in perfectly. Since it's a serious work of literature, the writer would refrain from going into the details of drinking more fig tea. He would know that an intimation is much more eloquent than an exhaustive description. Tell me."

"What?" she asked, bewildered.

"The address where this new fig tea awaits me."

"Oh, that. Of course."

Since I didn't have any paper and pen on the desk, I wrote Vera's address under the list of red titles on the screen.

"I'll be right there."

"I'll be waiting."

I put my cell phone back in my pocket. There was no need to take a notebook from the drawer and write down her address because I'd memorized it. In any case, it would stay in the file. I reached for the mouse to save it, but my hand stopped in mid-air again.

It's happened to me before. I'm struggling to find a solution, but nothing seems to work. And then something briefly interrupts me. When I go back to the problem, the solution appears right away, as though I'm looking at the whole thing from a completely new perspective.

I couldn't believe I'd spent hours there, when it was so obvious it stuck out like a sore thumb. But sometimes simple things are the hardest to see. Now it seemed that the first letter of each book on the list had suddenly become very large and was flickering.

Very clearly written in a vertical along the left edge of the screen was: LASTBOOKHERE.

With feverish movements I saved the file and then opened the window with the photograph containing the last in the sequence of books not in alphabetical order. I felt like shouting "Eureka!" when my suspicions turned out to be right. After the second book whose title began with an "E" was a small space that I'd overlooked before. A space that had previously been filled by a book.

13

The corridor extending in front of me seemed endless. It steadily decreased in perspective, but no final point could be seen. Although I'd been walking for a long time, I didn't seem to be making any progress.

The walls, floor and ceiling were lined in worn-out dark-green plush. It looked like I was in some gigantic, infinitely long jewelry box. The lighting was muted, with no visible source, as though the plush itself was shining.

Doors appeared at irregular intervals on the right-hand side. They seemed to be fused to the wall. If it weren't for their round doorknobs I wouldn't have noticed them. I tried to open several of them but they were locked so I stopped trying. I would have passed by this one too if I hadn't heard knocking on the other side.

I stopped and stared in confusion at the rectangle with its barely discernible edges. Then I looked up and down the corridor.

"Come in," I finally said, almost in a whisper, then repeated it in a louder voice. "Come in!"

The door opened towards me slowly. I had to move back a little to get out of the way. When it had swung to ninety degrees, I finally saw who had opened it.

The woman in a gray coat and beret with salt-and-pepper hair was smiling ear to ear. Somehow I knew that the thin volume she was holding was a collection of love poems.

She gestured broadly towards the room behind the door.

I wavered a moment before stepping inside. I wasn't particularly happy in the never-changing corridor, but for some reason I didn't feel like going inside. Yet how could I refuse her kind invitation?

I crossed the threshold with slow steps and the woman quickly closed the door behind me. I was in a small room furnished with nothing but an ordinary wooden table and two stools. On the left-hand wall was a washstand with an oval mirror above it. The woman went there straight away, placed her book on the small shelf under the mirror, turned on the faucet and started to splash her face.

Two men stood up as soon as I entered. A chessboard without any pieces was in the middle of the table between them. It was illuminated by a bare bulb hanging on a wire from the high ceiling. The man holding an unlit pipe was wearing a plaid jacket, while the one with slanted eyes was in narrow pants and a Mandarin jacket buttoned all the way up. The former nodded curtly and the latter bowed deeply several times.

While the woman continued to wash her face, making a larger and larger puddle on the bare floor, the two men came up and took me by the arm, one on either side. I wouldn't let them commandeer me at first, but I finally warmed to their smiles and repeated bows.

We crossed the room, rounded the table and headed for the wall behind it. It was not until we got up very close to it that I noticed the round doorknob. We stood still for a few moments in front of the door that I couldn't make out until, just like before, there came a knock from the other side.

This time the door opened inwards. As it swung open I had a widening view of shelves full of books. I felt two hands gently nudge my back. Less unwilling than a moment before, I walked into the new room.

If someone had opened the door, they stayed behind it. All the walls were covered with books, from floor to ceiling. The furniture here was even sparser. To the left, next to the middle of the wall, was a solitary armchair covered with the same plush as the corridor. A stooped, gray-haired man was sitting in it.

As soon as I entered he stood up, turned towards the bookshelf and started to draw his finger over the head-high row of books. His search soon came to an end. He took out a book, then returned to the armchair.

When his hand moved towards the cover to open it, I opened my mouth to shout, "Don't do it!" but no sound came out. I wanted to dash over and wrench the last book from his hands, but my body had stopped obeying me. I stood rooted to the spot by the open door and watched helplessly.

The old man opened the book and leafed through it briefly. The moment he stopped on a page and became engrossed in reading, he started to erode. His body began to fall apart and crumble as though composed of countless globules. Starting with his feet, the globules fell off and evaporated before they reached the floor.

The man was shrinking rapidly before my very eyes. After his legs came his trunk. When his shoulders had disintegrated, the erosion suddenly stopped. The sight of a head and two arms not connected to it, with hands still holding the book, was more appalling than the preceding erosion. I wanted to cry out, but still did not have control of my voice.

A cry finally tore out of me when there was nothing on the armchair but the book. The shackles seemed to drop off my body that same instant. I flew out of the library, but what awaited me in the first room only intensified the nightmare that had found me.

Instead of the men from before, two chess pieces were sitting at the table. The white king was wrapped in a plaid jacket and the black king was wearing a dark-red Mandarin jacket. The pieces bowed to me, the white one curtly and the black one deeply.

A giggle came from the washstand. I raised my eyes when the woman turned around. But I didn't see her face. Where it should have been was a flat surface of skin with water dripping off it, as though she'd washed off her face by frenzied scrubbing.

I let out another cry and then rushed to the door. Icy fingers of fear gripped my chest when I couldn't open it. As the giggle behind my back grew louder, I pulled frantically at the doorknob. Suddenly it dawned on me what I had to do.

A knock would most likely have been enough, but the terror I felt made me pummel the door with my fists. It opened instantly. I jumped out as if I had springs on my feet and ran screaming down the corridor, not daring to look at what was happening behind me.

14

My ears were still filled with the scream from my dream, when I sat straight up in bed, eyes wide open. I realized the same instant that something was wrong, but several feverish moments passed before I figured out what it was. I had to shake my head to dispel the dream that was still pulling at the edges of my consciousness. I wasn't in my own bedroom.

I jerked when a hand touched my shoulder.

"You were having a dream," said Vera softly

I turned and stared at her, but the outline of her raised head was all I could discern in the darkness. Luckily, she couldn't see me any better, otherwise the expression on my face would have frightened her for sure. I slowly sank back onto the pillow.

She caressed my cheek.

"Was it terrible?"

"I can't remember the last time I had a bad dream."

"Maybe my bedroom doesn't agree with you."

I stroked her hair.

"It's much nicer than mine."

"We'll have to double check that. Shall I turn on the light?"

"How could an inspector be afraid of the dark?"

"I've never liked inspectors who aren't afraid of anything."

"I didn't say I'm not afraid of anything."

"All right, what are you afraid of, mister fearless inspector?"

"The dark."

She giggled and patted my stomach lightly. Then she snuggled up to me. I put my right arm around her.

"I have bad dreams sometimes too. Do you know what's the worst about it?"

"What?"

"When you wake up and there's no one else in the room."

I turned my head and kissed her on the temple.

"Now there is. You can have all the bad dreams you want."

This time she tickled my stomach.

"What were you dreaming?"

"Something ridiculous. You know what nightmares are like."

"Mine always seem to have some meaning. The only thing is I can never quite grasp it."

"I thought that only happened in literature."

She laughed again.

"Didn't you say this resembles something you already read?"

I lowered my hand a little and tickled her around the waist. She squealed and twisted, throwing her leg over mine.

"That's right. I read that the main female character is

very ticklish. Should we check this out in other places too?"

She shook her head briskly where it lay on my shoulder.

"No need, no need."

In the silence and darkness that surrounded us, the fragrance of Vera's skin struck me more than anything else. Soft and musky, intoxicating. I kissed the top of her head.

"I don't know if what I dreamed has any meaning, but it got me thinking. Do you remember the first death in the Papyrus?"

"How could I forget it? Mr. Todorović."

"That's right. Do you remember by any chance which book he was reading when he died?"

She didn't answer immediately. Finally, I felt her shake her head again on my shoulder.

"I'm afraid not. I was too distressed."

"Of course. Do you know what happened to it after the orderlies took away the old man's body?"

"I probably put it back on the shelf. What else could I have done with it?"

"Yes, that seems the most natural. But you don't remember?"

She shifted her head from my shoulder to the pillow.

"No, I'm sorry. Why is the book Mr. Todorović died with important?"

"It's probably not. I just wanted to check something. And what about the second case?"

"Do you mean which book was the woman reading?"

"Yes, Mrs. Mitić."

"Olga would be the one to know. Although I doubt she took any notice under the circumstances. She panics more easily than I do."

"You didn't put it back on the shelf?"

"I don't think I did. Actually, I'm certain I didn't."

"The hardest will be to establish which book the unfortunate young man was reading. The book he was holding was mixed in with those he knocked to the floor."

"Why try to find out, anyway? Do you suspect something?"

"No, no. It just crossed my mind that there might be a thread that links the three deaths."

"A book?"

"Yes. The same last book."

Vera withdrew her leg and moved a little away from me.

"But why does it matter? Even if they did read the same last book, those people died natural deaths." She hesitated an instant. "Didn't they?"

"Of course they did. There's no book connected to any of them dying."

"Then why not consider the whole thing closed? Why look for threads to link three unfortunate cases?"

"I'm not. It never would have crossed my mind if it weren't for the bad dream."

Neither of us spoke for a few moments. Then Vera snuggled up to me again.

"Well then, we'll have to make sure all your future dreams are good ones."

15

I COULDN'T GET BACK to sleep for a long time, while Vera was soon slumbering. Had I been alone, I would have tossed and turned, but I had to lie there quietly so I didn't wake her. It was almost daybreak when her even breathing and warm body finally put me to sleep.

I was wakened by a kiss on the forehead. I must have looked at her in such surprise that she laughed.

"It's only me."

I rubbed my eyes.

"Good morning."

"Morning is way along."

"What time is it?"

"Ten past eleven."

I was wide awake the same moment.

"That late?"

"So what? It's Sunday. Can't police inspectors sleep in at least on Sunday?"

"Life is rarely kind to police inspectors."

"Here's our chance to make up a little for that injustice."

She picked up a tray from the night table by my pillow, waited for me to sit up, put it in my lap, then sat on the edge of the bed. When she took the lid off the teapot for a moment and glanced inside, the smell of the hot beverage mixed with that of fresh zwieback. She put the lid back in place, filled my cup and started to add the condiments.

"Then I haven't been misled," I said.

"Misled?"

"This really was an invitation to tea. I was beginning to think that was just a pretext."

She looked at me with narrowed eyes, then raised her hand and started to sprinkle some greenish powder on my head that should have gone in the tea.

I grabbed her wrist, pulled it over the tray and kissed it. Everything was done with a soft touch so I wouldn't spill what was in my lap.

"It's been a very long time since anyone brought me breakfast in bed."

When she smiled, all the freckles on her face seemed to smile with her.

"It's been a very long time since anyone in my life has deserved to have me bring him breakfast in bed."

My hands reached for the tray to put it back on the night table. Breakfast could wait a little. But then came the last sound I wanted to hear.

We stared at each other. A look of defeat crossed her face and mine filled with regret. She finally got up, went to the chair where I'd hastily thrown my jacket the night before, took my cell phone out of the inside pocket and handed it to me.

"Hello," I said sharply.

"Dr. Dimitrijević. I'm sorry to disturb your Sunday morning. We have to meet."

"What happened?" I asked in a milder tone.

"There's been another death without a cause."

"What? Where?"

Vera sat down on the edge of the bed again.

"Not in the bookstore. You'd better come to the Institute."

"I'm on my way."

I put down the cell phone, ended the call with a press of my thumb and sighed.

"I should have turned it off."

"Are police inspectors allowed to be out of touch?"

"Those who are always in touch end up without a private life."

"Those who want a private life don't become police inspectors. They do something else, like literature."

"But if literature were my job, would I have caught the eye of a pretty bookstore owner?"

"The fact that you caught the eye of a pretty bookstore owner has nothing to do with your job."

"So what does?"

"I don't have time to explain. You're in a hurry, aren't you?"

She put out her hands to take the tray, but I wouldn't let her.

"Not so much that I have to go without fig tea." I smiled. "Sometimes you have to make do with the consolation prize."

"The first prize isn't going anywhere. It will be waiting for you to come back. Preferably with your phone turned off. . . ."

16

THE INSTITUTE OF FORENSIC Medicine looked forbidding inside and out. Although a bright color would have been unseemly for the two-story building's façade, there was no reason for the sickening mouse-gray color that looked mournful even when the weather was nice, and yet more so on a rainy autumn day. As soon as you stepped inside you were struck by the penetrating smell of chemicals that stayed with you long after you had left, refusing to let the idea of unnatural death leave your mind.

This place was never crowded and today it was quite empty. The doorman barely raised his eyes from the television when I showed him my badge. He waved me through, then turned his attention back to the soccer match.

I went along numerous corridors and up the stairs that led to Dr. Dimitrijević's office, which must have been the farthest from the entrance. Even though I walked normally, my steps echoed on the tiled floor as though I was marching. The same white tiles covered the walls, and everything else was also painted white: the ceiling, doors, handrails in the stairwells, and the windows that looked onto the inner courtyard. It was only in this place, and then again on a Sunday when it was empty, that the source of Dr. Dimitrijević's cynical sense of humor became clear.

I knocked on the door with a brass plate bearing his name.

"Come in!"

He got up from his desk where he'd been working as soon as I entered. White was the dominant color in his office too. The metal cabinet on the right was the only thing that clashed. A multitude of colorful plush animal figures, mostly rabbits and bears, was visible through the glass doors. Rumor had it that each of them denoted one of the doctor's autopsies and that he would stop that job when there was no more room in the cabinet.

"Ah, you're here already," he said in a tone that did not indicate whether it meant praise or reproach. "Let's go to cold storage. My colleague Dr. Vidić is there."

"Cold storage" was a room with large drawers along one whole wall where the Institute's charges were kept. In the middle was the autopsy table and next to it was a small table on casters full of instruments that were not intended to make anyone feel better. Dr. Sonja Vidić was sitting at the computer in a corner. Her makeup was garish even for a Sunday morning. Next to the monitor was a large bar of chocolate.

She stood up when we headed towards her.

"Hello," I said.

She replied with a nod and an awkward little smile as she hurried to lick the chocolate off her teeth.

"Dr. Vidić discovered the new case," said Dr. Dimitrijević.

"And it's all to your credit," she finally said. Her tongue had not done the best of jobs.

"Me?"

"You planted a seed of doubt in my mind. Here again at first glance I would have sworn it was heart failure. But the autopsy didn't reveal a thing. There was no reason for the woman to die."

"Where did she die?"

"At home. She was a widow and lived alone. Her husband died long ago in a traffic accident and she never remarried. The cleaning lady, who comes on Sunday, reported the death. First she rang the bell and when no one answered she opened the door with her own key. She found her on the living room floor. She'd been dead around thirty-six hours."

"So she died on Friday evening?"

"Yes. Some time between eight and midnight. It's hard to determine it more closely."

I thought this over briefly.

"Could I have a look at her?"

"Certainly."

She opened one of the drawers and a wave of cold air escaped. Then she lifted the sheet off the head. The woman was in her mid-fifties and had long dark hair. Death always uglifies the face, but I could still see that she'd taken care of her looks.

I nodded and Dr. Vidić closed the drawer.

"Do you know her?" she asked.

"No."

"Things are getting more complicated, it seems," said Dr. Dimitrijević. "We aren't restricted to the bookstore any more."

"I hope it's not an epidemic," added Dr. Vidić.

"Of what?" I asked.

She shrugged her shoulders. "Dying for no reason."

I nodded towards the closed drawer. "What did you find out about her?"

Dr. Vidić went over to the computer table and picked up a notebook. She turned several pages.

"She was a curator at the Museum of Modern Art. . . ."

"Dragana Stojanović?"

She raised her eyes from the notebook.

"You've heard of her?"

"Yes. Yesterday, for the first time."

They both looked at me in bewilderment.

"We don't have an epidemic. We're still restricted to the bookstore. Mrs. Stojanović may have been in it on Friday evening."

"When the young man died?" asked Dr. Dimitrijević.

Dr. Vidić leafed through her notebook again.

"Lazar Žigić, veterinary student."

"Yes. Tell me, was there a book near Mrs. Stojanović's body?"

Dr. Vidić thought for a moment.

"I don't think so, but I can't be sure."

"Did the cleaning lady clean the living room before you arrived?"

"It's not likely. She was too upset."

"Did she stay in the apartment or leave with you?"

"We all left. I locked the door with her key."

"Would you mind giving me the key? I'd like to go there and look around a bit."

"Of course."

She went to the computer desk again, picked up a medium-sized white envelope and shook a key out of it onto her palm. Then she wrote something in the notebook, tore out the sheet and handed it to me along with the key.

"That's the address."

I smiled at her. "Thank you."

"Why do you want to know if there was a book near her?" asked Dr. Dimitrijević.

"Because, in the absence of simple solutions, we might have to resort to complicated ones."

"What are you getting at?"

"You mentioned certain artificial substances that can kill without leaving any trace."

"Yes, I did. But I also told you that it's impossible to get hold of them. Unless you're implying that the National Security Agency is mixed up in this."

"For the moment let's leave aside the question of how to get hold of the substances and who is mixed up in this. Right now I'm more interested in how they can be used."

"That depends on the substance. If it's a liquid, it would be enough to sprinkle a few drops where they could come in contact with skin. If it's a powder, you simply shake a bit where you expect something will be touched."

"In both cases couldn't that be a book?"

"Yes, it could."

"Do you mean to say," interjected Dr. Vidić, "that this might be the work of someone imitating *The Name of the Rose*?"

I smiled at her again. "I didn't know you were interested in literature."

"Did you think I was only interested in autopsies?"

"Of course not. . . ."

"If that's true," said Dr. Dimitrijević, coming to my rescue, "then we are in serious trouble. Although I still don't see how anyone could get hold of the substances. Maybe I should make a few inquiries of friends who have contacts with the Agency."

"That would be very useful. But be discreet. We don't want to alarm them needlessly. I might be on a wild goose chase."

"Of course."

"All right, I'm off to look at Mrs. Stojanović's apartment."

Dr. Vidić went up to a cupboard next to the computer table and took out a pair of plastic gloves.

"Take these. Wild goose chase or not, they won't do you any harm."

17

NEVER BEFORE HAD I seen so many paintings in one room. The living room walls were covered floor to ceiling with frames of various sizes that fitted together like parts of a mosaic without leaving any empty space. It was hard to concentrate on just one picture because those around it necessarily entered my field of vision.

This variegated puzzle was interrupted in just one place between two tall windows by a narrow bookcase, filled with books. They were primarily on art history, but there were also works of literature. All without exception were deluxe editions. Nothing low-priced would have suited the expensive gallery surrounding it.

I stared at the high column of books. At first it seemed they were not in any special order. But that would have been highly uncharacteristic of Mrs. Stojanović. And then I realized that an order did exist, just not the one I'd expected. The works were arranged not by title but by author.

I got out my cell phone and took a few pictures. My intention was to check them out later on the computer, but impatience got the better of me. After all, I wasn't in any big hurry. I approached the bookcase and ran my eyes over the spines on the top row.

I reached the lower half of the bookcase without finding any deviation from the alphabetical sequence of authors' names. I briefly considered giving up, but then continued. In the second-to-last row I felt the bitter taste of disillusion. As though someone had broken a promise they'd made to me.

But it turned out they'd kept the promise after all. The order was finally disrupted in the bottom row. I felt like shouting "Eureka!" If anything ties me to the job of police inspector, it is moments like this when stubborn persistence pays off. When some seemingly nonsensical search is not devoid of meaning.

I sat on the floor so I could see better. The last five books should not have been there. The authors' names belonged to rows much higher up on the shelf. I quickly put their first letters together—and the wind went out of my sails. What I got did not form anything coherent.

I then made an acronym of the titles, but this didn't lead anywhere either. I stared at the five books in frustration for a few moments, then took out a pencil and notebook and wrote down the names of the writers and the book titles. This was an easier way to study them than written vertically on the spines.

Before I was able to tackle the riddle of the list in my notebook, the telephone on a corner table started to ring. I raised my eyes, uncertain what to do. The phone rang twice more while I got up from the floor. As I walked towards it, the answering machine came on.

The recorded female voice stated an inadvertent lie. She would not, unfortunately, be able to return the call. A beep sounded and then a male voice was heard that made me stop in mid-step.

"I have wonderful news, Mrs. Stojanović," said Albert Einstein's double. "It's here! This time there's no doubt about it! You'll see it tonight! At the usual place, at nine. Everyone will be there. They're all so excited. Just imagine! The last book! Finally! We'll be waiting for you!" He stopped briefly, then quickly added, "Don't try anything by yourself. You know how dangerous it is."

After he hung up, there was another beep, then complete silence. I stood there in the middle of the living room, one foot forward. The voice and what it said were surprising, but this was not why I was standing there stock-still. One of the words he'd spoken had stood out from the others, as though written in italics. But in spite of this obvious fact, I hadn't recognized it right away.

When it finally dawned on me, I raised the notebook quickly and circled five letters. Nothing. Then another five. And the meaning finally surfaced. There was an acronym, not of the first letters but of the last. It would have slipped right past me if Professor Nedeljković hadn't used that adjective, even though I should have guessed it. The books were the last ones on the shelf, too.

First I tried with the titles, without success. The message was in the last letters of the authors' names.

A very brief message.

I MUST.

I snapped out of my torpor, turned around, went back to the bookcase and knelt down. I reached out towards the bottom row, but pulled back my hand before it touched the books. I took the plastic gloves Dr. Vidić had given me out of my coat pocket and put them on.

I wanted to take the first of the five books, but when I grasped it, I realized it was not standing up straight. I checked the second-to-last row and the two above it. All the books were tightly packed. The last row had looked like that too, but it was just an illusion. A book had been removed from there, but it was impossible to identify the place because the other books were arranged so as to look as though every space were filled.

I stood up and looked around the living room. There weren't any books outside the bookcase. I thought of looking in the other rooms, but just then my cell phone rang in my pocket.

"Hello?"

"Dr. Dimitrijević speaking. Would you mind dropping by again? Commissioner Milenković from the National Security Agency is here."

18

The doorman at the Institute of Forensic Medicine was now the epitome of diligence. The presence of two agents in the foyer undoubtedly had some bearing on this. The television behind him was turned off and he was needlessly standing. He scrutinized my badge as though he hadn't seen it an hour ago. He finally nodded his head. I passed by the agents and headed for Dr. Dimitrijević's office.

He greeted me with the same double-entendre as before.

"Ah, you're here already."

"As fast as I could," I replied.

He indicated the free chair of the two facing his desk.

"Please sit down. This is Commissioner Milenković."

We shook hands before I sat down. Commissioner Milenković was a short, balding, stocky man in his fifties. Had I met him somewhere else, I never would have thought that he worked for the National Security Agency. He looked more like a barber or dentist. But what kind of secret police would have its members easily recognizable?

"The Agency's pathologists are in cold storage right now. They're going over our autopsy findings."

"Don't they trust your expertise?"

"We do," replied Commissioner Milenković. "It's just that we're better equipped."

"Does this mean you're taking over the case?"

"No. Go ahead and continue with your investigation. We'll work together."

"I didn't think this would interest you."

"We're interested in everything that is a threat to national security."

"Do you think we're dealing with something that serious?"

"Maybe not. But we're paid to be paranoid. Not a single possibility should be ruled out."

"Terrorism?"

"Among other things. Please tell me what you've found."

"Almost nothing. Over a short period of time, we have three deaths in the Papyrus Bookstore and one outside it. What they have in common is the absence of a cause of death. Dr. Dimitrijević probably explained the medical side of the case to you."

"I explained that we didn't find anything," said the doctor. "We'll soon see if our colleagues from the Agency have better luck. As the Commissioner said, they're better equipped."

"Is there something about the Papyrus that singles it out from other bookstores?" asked Commissioner Milenković.

I shrugged my shoulders. "Perhaps the fact that they care about serious literature. But that's hardly important in this matter."

"You never know. You studied literature, didn't you?"

I looked at him for a few moments before answering. "You're well-informed."

"That's my job. Do the events in the Papyrus look like some work of literature to you?"

I glanced at Dr. Dimitrijević who lowered his eyes.

"If you mean *The Name of the Rose*, there are certain similarities."

"Would you mind giving me a summary of the book?"

"You didn't read it?"

"I don't get around to reading much."

"Too bad. You'd be even better informed."

"I'll try to read *The Name of the Rose*. In the meantime, I'd appreciate your summary."

"A series of murders takes place in a medieval monastery. It turns out that they are caused by a book whose pages are coated with poison. The victims lick their finger to turn the pages and that's how they're poisoned."

"Clever. Is there a book here that links the four murders?"

"The three who died in the bookstore were reading a book right before they died but, as far as we know, not the woman who died in her apartment."

"She was a regular at the bookstore too, wasn't she?"

"Yes."

"Did the other three read the same book?"

"We don't know. No one paid any attention to that."

"Too bad."

"Maybe it didn't make any difference what they were

reading. It didn't have to be just one book like in *The Name of the Rose.*"

"That's right," nodded Commissioner Milenković after giving it some thought. "It could have been several books."

"One book or more," said Dr. Dimitrijević, "if this is an imitation of *The Name of the Rose*, then we're up against a serious adversary. Someone has access to a poison that's extremely hard to detect, if at all. Do you think, Commissioner, that terrorists might have got hold of such a weapon?"

"It's unlikely, but not completely impossible. Finding out which substance was used is of utmost importance. That will lead us to its source and then we'll follow that trail."

"If anything was actually used," I said in a low voice.

Commissioned Milenković looked at me askance.

"What do you mean?"

"Maybe this has nothing to do with *The Name of the Rose.*"

"Do you have some other theory as to how four people could die apparently without cause?"

I shook my head.

"No, I don't."

"All right. Then we'll concentrate on the only theory we have at this moment."

A cell phone rang, but the tone was different from mine. Commissioner Milenković reached for his pocket.

"Yes?"

He listened for a while without talking, his eyes half closed. Then he put the phone back in his pocket.

"They want to see me in the autopsy room."

"Shall I go along too?" asked Dr. Dimitrijević.

"No, no. Please wait for me here."

I turned towards the doctor after the commissioner had left. He didn't wait for my question.

"I didn't call them, if that's what you think. I didn't even get a chance to call my friends who have contacts with the Agency."

"Then what happened?"

He opened his arms.

"I haven't a clue. They've got their people everywhere." He stopped, then chuckled. "Unless they read it in the tabloids."

I nodded my head.

"That's more than likely."

"Was there anything interesting in Mrs. Stojanović's apartment?"

"Someone will be happy she died. Her heirs will inherit an enormous art collection."

"Were there any books?"

"A bookshelf full."

"Did any one catch your eye?"

"There wasn't time. Just as I started to look, you called me to come back here."

I put my hand in my pocket to give him back the keys to Mrs. Stojanović's apartment, but I took out my cell phone instead since it had suddenly started to ring.

"Hello?"

"Inspector Lukić," said Commissioner Milenković, "we need to take a look at the Papyrus Bookstore. Would you mind calling Miss Gavrilović to open up for us?"

"Certainly," I replied after a moment's hesitation. "I'll get right back to you."

As I waited for Vera to answer, a host of questions swarmed through my head. How did they know the name of one of the owners of the Papyrus? Why did he want me to call specifically her and not Miss Bogdanović? And why did he assume that I knew Vera's private phone number?

"Hi Vera, it's Dejan. Would you mind going to the Papyrus right away? My colleagues want to take a look at the bookstore. They think it would be best to do it on a Sunday when there aren't any customers."

"Did something happen?" asked Vera, her voice subdued.

"I'll tell you all about it. I'll be there too."

The receiver was silent for a few moments.

"All right. I'll be at the Papyrus in about fifteen minutes."

I pushed the button to call the last number to call me.

"Miss Gavrilović will be at the Papyrus in about fifteen minutes."

"Wonderful. Thank you." I thought he would end the call, but then he spoke again. "Just one more thing, Inspector. Have you heard of the last book?"

"The last what?" I asked, desperately hoping my voice wouldn't give me away.

"It doesn't matter," replied the commissioner a moment later. "We'll talk about it some other time. You'll be coming to the Papyrus too, won't you?"

"To be sure."

19

In addition to Commissioner Milenković, seven more members of the National Security Agency left the Institute of Forensic Medicine—three women and four men. They got into two cars that looked more used than new, of different makes and colors, and not exactly clean. My car followed them not far behind, joining this inconspicuous column.

When we got there, Vera was already in the bookstore. She was standing at the counter. I rushed to be the first to enter. I went up to her, smiled and caressed her left hand.

"Everything's all right."

My words didn't ease her worried look.

Commissioner Milenković headed toward us while the others fanned out, examining the bookshelves. One of the two agents from the Institute's foyer was stationed by the entrance.

"Hello," said the commissioner with a smile. "Miss Gavrilović, I assume?"

She nodded and shook his outstretched hand.

"Commissioner Milenković," I said, introducing him. "National Security Agency."

Vera's eyes narrowed.

"The secret police have never visited us before."

"There was no reason before," replied the commissioner.

"And now there is?"

"People rarely die in bookstores. The Papyrus seems to be an exception. Four deaths in three days is more than a good reason."

Vera eyed the commissioner and then me in bewilderment.

"Three, not four," she corrected him in a half-questioning tone.

The commissioner turned his head towards me.

"You haven't told her yet?"

"I didn't have the chance."

"What didn't you tell me?"

"Mrs. Dragana Stojanović," I began slowly. "The curator . . . your old customer . . . do you remember?"

"Yes?"

"She died. In her apartment. Last Friday."

"Oh."

She covered her mouth with her hand.

"Without a cause," I added. "Isn't that right, commissioner?"

He looked at me briefly, but did not reply.

"As you can see," he said to Vera, "there are very convincing reasons to examine the Papyrus. With your permission, of course."

"Of course," I replied. "Miss Gavrilović won't insist on a search warrant."

The commissioner smiled again.

"Thank you. We'll be through in no time. Would you mind staying somewhere in the vicinity? I might have to ask you some questions."

Vera nodded her head.

"Wonderful. I recommend the Mandarin Teashop. It's close by. You must have heard of it. They have an excellent selection of tea. They say the fig tea is particularly good. I'm sure that Inspector Lukić would be happy to keep you company. I'll join you as soon as we're finished."

20

We headed down the street. She handed me her umbrella but did not take my arm. Not even our shoulders touched.

As I searched for the right words, Vera beat me to it. Her voice was cold and tense.

"What does all this mean, Dejan?"

I put the umbrella in my left hand and put my right arm around her shoulders. I thought she might put up some resistance, but she didn't.

"I'll tell you everything I know. But I don't know much."

She stopped and looked at me piercingly. We stayed like that for a few moments.

"How does he know about the teashop?" she asked after we continued walking. "And particularly about fig tea?"

I shook my head.

"I have no idea. All I can do is guess. He said it to upset you. It's an old secret police trick. A way of showing that they know a lot about you."

"Let me hear your guess."

"I'll just upset you even more."

"It doesn't matter."

"Someone told them about our visit to the Mandarin Teashop."

"The owner?" she said in disbelief.

"No one's excluded. But I doubt it."

"Then who else?"

"There was a young couple there."

She turned her head towards me and looked at me in confusion.

"I don't remember."

"You paid no attention. You were preoccupied with other things."

Her voice took on a tinge of reproach. "I thought you were too."

"I was, of course. But that didn't dull my powers of observation. Even when an inspector falls in love, he's still an inspector in one part of his brain."

When she clung to me, it felt like she was shaking.

"But why on earth would the secret police shadow us?"

"They've clearly been interested in the Papyrus for some time already."

"Do you mean since the dying started?"

"Probably even earlier."

"But what could possibly interest the National Security Agency in an ordinary bookstore?"

"Perhaps it isn't altogether ordinary."

She stopped again briefly.

"What do you mean by not ordinary? You're frightening me, Dejan."

I held her more tightly in my arms.

"The dying isn't ordinary."

"Didn't you say that they were natural? You confused me a little while ago when you said—without a cause. What did that mean?"

We had just reached the teashop. As she made for

the entrance, I held her back. She looked at me questioningly.

"Let's walk a little more. It's rather romantic like this in the rain."

She opened her mouth to say something, but waited until we'd moved further away.

"Why didn't we go inside?" she finally asked in a needlessly low voice. "I'm cold."

"Because we might not have been able to speak freely."

"Would they spy on us again?"

"Not necessarily. They might not have done it the first time either."

"Well, then, how could they. . . .?"

"We mentioned the teashop and fig tea in a telephone conversation."

We walked a bit in silence.

"Do you mean they're eavesdropping?"

"That's the normal procedure."

"And they say we don't live in a police state."

"In a police state where even the police are tapped."

"But how could they eavesdrop in the teashop? We wouldn't be talking over the phone."

"They might have planted a bug. That's another thing they often do."

She shook her head.

"I don't believe it. But we'll have to go to the Mandarin Teashop even so. The commissioner said he'd meet us there."

"We'll go a little later. We don't have to right away."

We continued in silence for a while. The sound of a passing car periodically joined the even drumming of the rain and our splashing footsteps. Before us stretched an empty street.

"Well?"

"What?"

"What does it mean—without a cause?"

"It means that there was no medical reason for any one of the four deaths. At least as far as Dr. Dimitrijević was able to ascertain."

"I don't understand."

"I don't understand either. Maybe Commissioner Milenković's team will be able to figure it out. They are better equipped than ordinary pathologists."

She thought for a minute before asking her next question.

"Do they suspect something?"

"The Agency never makes its suspicions public. But from a short conversation with the commissioner I got the impression that they think it might be terrorism."

She stopped and moved away. The right half of her body was in the rain.

"Terrorism?"

I pulled her back under the umbrella.

"That's the Agency's primary job, taking care of national security. They're examining the possibility that a terrorist group is using a new biological weapon here."

I could tell by the restless darting of her eyes that she was pondering which of a multitude of questions to ask first.

"How do they use it?" she said at last.

"Through books, for example. They poison a book with an invisible and extremely lethal substance. Anyone who comes in contact with it dies. And it leaves no trace."

She stopped again and shook her head. I made a semicircle and turned us back in the direction from which we'd come.

"Let's go to the teashop. That's enough romanticism in the cold."

"That's why you asked me which book they had read before they died," she said after a few steps.

"Yes."

"But why the Papyrus?"

I shrugged my shoulders.

"Maybe by accident, maybe not."

"If it's not by accident, what is there in our bookshop that would attract terrorists?"

"For example, the fact that you don't have video surveillance like the big bookstores."

"I've been trying for some time to convince Olga that we should install it. But she's against it. She's not at all partial to technical innovations."

"Cameras would seem out of place to me too in the Papyrus."

"But they would ward off terrorists."

"If they're at all behind it."

She looked at me askance.

"You're confusing me, Dejan."

"I'm confused too. I'm groping in the dark."

"Who else but terrorists could be killing our customers?"

"A serial killer who is no less informed than terrorists about new biological weapons."

A good minute passed before she spoke again. In the meantime, the rain increased and the wind picked up.

"Why would a serial killer pick the Papyrus? Because we don't have surveillance cameras?"

"The reasons might be more complex and not merely of a practical nature."

"For example?"

"It might all be connected to literature."

"How could murders be connected to literature?"

"I don't know. It's just a feeling. Although, of course, there is still no proof that anyone was killed."

"Let's hear what Commissioner Milenković has to say."

"I'm afraid we won't hear anything from him."

"But he'll have to tell us something. Particularly if terrorists are involved."

"If terrorists are involved, they'll close your bookstore for a while. Without an explanation."

"That would ruin our business."

"They would ruin a lot more than the Papyrus to remove a threat to national security."

She sighed deeply.

"And if they conclude it's not terrorists?"

"Then they'll hand the case over to us. Serial killers are beneath the dignity of the secret police."

We reached the teashop. I pushed down the handle but didn't open the door right away.

"While we're waiting for the commissioner, let's keep the conversation to small talk. About tea, for example. OK?"

She looked at me at length and then nodded.

21

I HAD NEVER MADE so much small talk in my life. When Commissioner Milenković finally appeared, it was almost four-thirty.

In the meantime, I learned in great detail about the medicinal and general beneficial effects of Eastern teas. Vera began the conversation, but even though she was a real expert compared to me, her knowledge was nothing compared to the owner's. Since there were no other customers in the teashop, he joined us after a while and stayed at our table until the commissioner arrived.

It was a pleasure to listen to the owner not only because of the interesting things he said, but also his manner of speaking. His faulty syntax was full of comical word combinations and several times I was unable to stop myself from laughing. He didn't take it badly and laughed along with me, although I didn't understand what he found so funny.

He went to great pains to explain to us the beneficial effects of lotus tea. We looked at each other, baffled, at the expressions "locked down," "hard inside," "not want be born." It wasn't until he pointed to the restroom door and circled his finger several times around his watch that Vera caught on.

"It's for constipation," she said, blushing.

He gave an even more picturesque explanation of when to use something that was listed in the menu as butterfly powder tea. He struggled for a time to find the right words, but since we didn't understand, he put on a pantomime act. First his hands described the form of a vase in the middle of the table, then he pretended to put a flower inside it. Rendered by his raised finger, the flower stayed upright for some time, and then slowly began to droop, as though fading. When the elixir of butterfly power was poured into the vase, the flower suddenly rose upright again.

We both understood at the same time, so no one had to say what this tea cured. The old man beamed when he read on our faces that he'd been able to explain it without a word.

This time we didn't drink fig tea. When I ordered it, the teashop owner recommended something else.

"Algae tea good for head."

Vera frowned. "I don't have a headache." She turned toward me. "At least not in the literal sense."

"This not for head ache. This for head work."

I wasn't sure what he meant by that until I tried the algae tea. Only two sips were needed to make me feel fresh, as if after a restful sleep. It seemed as though my thoughts of a moment before had been shrouded in a veil that had now vanished, making my perception clearer. My head really did work better.

The drink had a favorable effect on Vera too. I don't know about her thoughts, but she started to relax. She finished her cup before me and struck up a cheerful conversation about tea with the old man. She didn't seem at all like the owner of a bookstore that was being searched by the secret police that very moment.

When Commissioner Milenković finally entered the

teashop, Vera greeted him with a reproving, not frightened expression.

"Are you closing the Papyrus, Commissioner?" she asked defiantly as he took a seat at our table.

Instead of answering, he turned to the old man who had got up as soon as the teashop door opened and was now standing next to the table, smiling.

"Beetroot tea, please."

The owner bowed without speaking and went off to prepare it.

"I thought you preferred fig tea."

"Red beet is excellent if your triglycerides are high." He indicated my cup that still held a bit of tea. "You two had something else too."

"This one is recommended for a long wait," continued Vera in the same tone.

He looked at her briefly in silence.

"There are a lot of books in the Papyrus, Miss Gavrilović."

"Which quite befits a bookstore. So, are you closing it?"

He shook his head.

"We have no reason to do that."

"You didn't find anything?"

"Nothing that would require such a drastic measure."

"So it's not about terrorists?"

Commissioner Milenković threw a glance at me.

"Someone has needlessly frightened you."

"But what about the sudden deaths?"

"They happen."

"As often as this? And without any cause?"

"There is always a cause of death. It just has to be found. We're working on it."

Vera picked up her cup. It was not until she brought it to her lips that she realized it was empty. She placed it back on the saucer.

"Will there be any more?"

"Who can predict the future?"

"What if there are?"

"Then we'll meet again."

The old man came to the table carrying a tray with a small teapot and a cup. He placed them in front of Commissioner Milenković and poured out the tea.

"Mister wait a bit, not drink hot. Hot not good for blood."

"I know. Thank you."

He took the spoon and stirred the tea in silence, waiting for the teashop owner to move away.

"Would you like to try some beetroot tea?" he asked Vera, indicating the teapot.

"No thank you. My triglycerides are fine."

"Lucky you. Do you mind if I ask you something? People with eccentric behavior drop by the Papyrus from time to time, don't they?"

"Eccentric behavior?"

"Yes. There's all kinds. One interests me in particular. Instead of buying books, he leaves his own. Do you know who I'm thinking of?"

Vera didn't answer right away. She watched the spoon making circles in the commissioner's cup for a few moments.

Her voice was subdued when she answered. "I do."

"Can you tell me something about him? What's his name? What does he do for a living? Where can we find him?"

"I avoid any familiarity with the customers. Particularly with eccentrics."

"This doesn't seem to be a hard and fast rule. You knew the name of the last person who died and where she worked. Mrs. Stojanović, museum curator. She had eccentric proclivities too. She arranged books on the shelves as she saw fit. Isn't that so, Inspector Lukić?"

We looked each other straight in the eye, until Vera spoke again.

"Mrs. Stojanović was an exception. Customers with eccentric behaviors are not in the habit of introducing themselves. Quite the opposite. In any case, the man who brings his own books didn't. I don't know anything about him."

"I'd like to ask you to call me if he appears again. Here's my number."

He took out a pen and notebook from his inside pocket, wrote down a number, then tore out the page and handed it to Vera.

"Should we be wary of him? Is he dangerous?"

"He won't be if you call me as soon as you see him."

"I'll call you."

The commissioner stopped stirring his tea, then grimaced and took a big sip.

"It tastes awful, but it's very healthy." He put down his cup. "Does the last book mean anything to you?"

Vera looked at me before she returned with a question.

"What last book?"

The commissioner turned his head towards me briefly too.

"Everyone's surprised when they hear about it."

"About what?" asked Vera. "I don't understand you."

"Please keep your ears open if anyone mentions the last book. It might be important."

"Do you want me to give you a call?"

"I'd be very grateful."

"Have I been promoted to secret police informer?"

"You can't expect the police to help you if you don't cooperate with them. Isn't that right, Inspector Lukić."

"You told me that we'd work together too. But shouldn't cooperation, by definition, be two-way?"

"You of all people should know that you can't say everything in this job."

"Not everything, but maybe something might be said. That way we'd work together better."

The commissioner finished his cup with another frown.

"The best way to work together is if you don't hide anything from me." He stood up. "Excuse me. I have to leave. Here's the key to the bookstore, Miss Gavrilović."

He took it out of his coat pocket and put it on the table along with some change for the tea. He was already at the door when he turned around and came back. This time he reached for his pants pocket, took out a bill and put it on the table next to the key.

"I almost forgot. This is for the book. I took the liberty of helping myself. I hope you don't mind."

"Which book?" asked Vera, perplexed.

"*The Name of the Rose*. I was told it's a must-read."

22

We didn't stay there long after the commissioner left. Being limited to small talk had made Vera restless.

When we got up to leave, the old man gave each of us a little bag with ideograms written on them.

"Algae tea," he said with a bow. "Maybe head need work when not in teashop."

This time I paid, but the amount was so small that I wondered how he could keep his business going with such low prices and so few customers. He must have had more customers in the evening or on nicer days.

There was a real downpour when we left. We reached the bookstore almost at a run, holding the umbrella in front of us, more like a shield than over our heads. Vera promptly took out the key, but I grabbed her hand before she had a chance to put it in the lock.

"You must be hungry."

She looked at me quizzically and then nodded.

"I am. All I had was breakfast."

"I didn't even have that. Let's go get a bite to eat."

"I just wanted to take a look."

"You can come back to the bookstore later." She hesitated, so I added, "We'll be freer to talk at a restaurant."

It took her a few moments to understand. She went up to the display window, pressed her nose against it and shielded the sides of her face with her hands.

"I can't see anything," she said, stepping back.

"You'll see better when the lights are turned on. But not what they left behind them. They're professionals. Let's go."

We took my car. She opened her mouth to say something as soon as we got in, but I put my finger to my lips to silence her. She gave me a sideways glance, then turned forward and stared out the windshield where the wipers were swishing furiously. I laid my hand briefly over her folded hands in her lap and smiled at her when she looked at me, but this didn't ease her worried expression.

I chose a restaurant where I'd never been before in a neighborhood full of small restaurants and cafes. Inside, we were assaulted by the smell of spicy food and beer. One of the four tables was occupied and being served by an extremely fat waitress with fuzz on her upper lip. I didn't like the music they were playing, but fortunately it was low.

After we'd ordered, we put our heads together over the table and started talking almost in a whisper. This was unnecessary, since no one was paying any attention to us, but paranoia had taken its toll.

"This is dreadful," said Vera. "My life is completely disrupted."

"It's best just to ignore it. Act normal, like before."

"How can I when I know I'm under constant surveillance?"

"You're not the one under surveillance. The Agency is interested in other people."

"Of course I'm under surveillance when they can hear every word I say in the bookstore." She screwed up her eyes when something else occurred to her. "Maybe they can see me too? They installed cameras too, not just microphones, didn't they?"

I sighed.

"Probably. But look on the bright side. Now you won't have to quibble with Olga about putting in surveillance cameras."

Her voice rose slightly. "You may think this is funny, but you're a victim of the Agency too. You can't even talk in your own car."

"I'd be a victim if I didn't know they were listening. The commissioner let me in on it."

"Why on earth would one police department tap another? Aren't you all part of the same team?"

My fingers slipped through my hair.

"Of course we are. But departments exist so they can work independently. That's how the police are organized. It goes without saying that we work with each other, but as you've seen, such cooperation is understood in different ways. Sometimes it goes smoothly and sometimes it's done by other means. Like wiretapping, for example. I agree that it all must look complicated to people from the outside."

"Very complicated. But let's put aside internal police relations for the moment. What does it mean that they won't close the Papyrus?"

"It means that they probably didn't find any trace of terrorist activity."

We were interrupted by the waitress who brought our soup and hoped we would enjoy our food. She had an incongruously high-pitched voice for such a big woman.

Hunger got the better of our curiosity. We ate our soup in silence, more rapidly than good manners allowed. Vera didn't speak again until we were well into our main course.

"What traces were they looking for?"

I shrugged my shoulders between two bites.

"I don't know. Certainly something to do with books. I'm sure they checked them all."

"All? Do you know how many books we have?"

"A lot, I know. But I also know how efficient they are. In any case, they were there a long time."

"If they didn't find anything, why did they put us under surveillance? You told me that anything less than terrorism was beneath their dignity."

"Maybe it isn't less."

"But the commissioner said. . . ."

"The commissioner said very little. He's very skilled at saying almost nothing. He didn't say it wasn't about terrorism. If they didn't find anything and they're still interested in the Papyrus, terrorism is still part of the game."

She chewed pensively for some time.

"Wouldn't it have been better for them to close the Papyrus?"

"Why?"

"The fact that they found no evidence doesn't mean anything. If terrorists are using this new biological weapon, as you said, then maybe it can't be detected. It's quite possible that poisoned books are still on our shelves."

I shook my head.

"No, it isn't. If there were any, someone from Commissioner Milenković's team would have been hurt. Don't forget, they checked every one. If they weren't safe, they wouldn't let you stay open."

She drank half a glass of mineral water.

"But if all the books are safe, then what did those people die of? As the commissioner said, there must be a cause of death."

"Of course there must. It could still be a book."

Her fork stopped halfway to her mouth.

"How could that be if none of them is poisoned?"

"Because the one that's poisoned isn't in the bookstore any more."

"Do you think someone bought it in the meantime?"

"Or stole it. Which amounts to the same thing. Regardless of how they got hold of it, they had to die too. If the book is at all to blame, it seems to be very lethal."

She stopped chewing.

"Mrs. Stojanović. . . ."

I nodded.

"That means that the book is in her apartment."

"If it is, I didn't recognize it. I was there around noon, after they removed the body. All the books were on a shelf in the living room. None of them seemed suspicious."

She placed her knife and fork on her plate and wiped her mouth with her napkin.

"Did you tell Commissioner Milenković about it? He could send his people to find it."

"There was no need to tell him," I replied, laying down my own cutlery. "He knows about Mrs. Stojanović's death and has probably sent a team to her apartment. In any case, if the book is there, it can't hurt anyone any more. Danger is lying in wait elsewhere."

The waitress came up and cleared our plates.

"Would you care for coffee?" she squeaked.

I looked at my watch, then at Vera and shook my head.

"No thank you. May I have the check, please?"

"Where?" asked Vera after the waitress left.

"Whoever poisoned the book—terrorists, a serial killer or someone else—will see that it's no longer on the shelves. Then what will they do?"

Vera didn't have time to reply because the waitress came up just then and put a plate with the check in front of me. I looked at the amount, took out a bill and nodded to indicate I didn't need any change. In return I received a smile that made her fuzz quiver.

"He'll poison another book in the bookstore," said Vera softly when we were alone again.

"Not likely. He has to assume that the bookstore is under surveillance. Even if neither you nor Olga notices him, he won't slip past those monitoring the Papyrus surveillance cameras."

"So then what?"

"There's no need to expose himself to danger and poison a book in the bookstore. He'll bring a new poisoned book."

"They'll see him when he puts it on the shelf."

"Not necessarily. He could do it without being seen. Didn't you tell me that one of your patients always manages to sneak one in even though you keep a sharp eye on him? By the way, you really don't know who he is?"

Vera looked at me in surprise.

"I really don't know. I wouldn't venture to lie to the commissioner. And why would I anyway?"

"I was hoping that you were on my side."

"Of course I'm on your side. But I didn't suppose that meant I should lie to the police."

"I'm the police too."

She sighed.

"Just so I don't end up a victim of your complicated relations, it would be a good idea for you to tell me what to do. That will make it easier to be on your side."

"If that patient appears again, please tell me first."

"But the commissioner. . . ."

"Tell the commissioner too. A little later. That way you won't be breaking any rules."

She looked at me for a few moments in silence, then nodded.

"Although, that really won't be necessary," I continued.

"How's that?" she asked me, puzzled.

"All your telephones are certainly bugged. Mine

too. But we'll turn the tables on them. Not even the Agency is omnipotent. Tomorrow I'll buy two new cell phones. We'll use them only in special circumstances. For everything else we'll talk normally over our old telephones."

She shook her head.

"How can I talk normally when I know they're listening?"

"It's not so hard when you know that they know that you know they're listening."

She raised her hands, palms turned towards me, and waved them.

"I won't even try to understand that."

"You don't have to. All you have to do is act normally, just like no one's listening."

We looked at each other briefly in silence. Then she got up and so did I.

"What's that last book the commissioner mentioned?" she asked as I helped her put on her coat.

"We don't have time for that right now. But I'll tell you everything I know if you invite me for tea again tonight. Fig tea, not algae, of course."

She smiled and caressed my cheek.

"Of course."

23

I DROVE VERA TO the bookstore. During the ride we talked about the weather. Her bearing was artificial, like an inexperienced actress. It wouldn't be easy for her to overcome her anxiety and accept the fact that they were listening.

After she unlocked the door, she turned and waved to me. I replied with a flash of the high beams and drove off.

The floor where I had my office seemed eerily empty late on Sunday afternoon. The duty inspectors were on the ground floor. I didn't turn on the light when I went in. Although it was dark, enough light filtered in from the outside for me to recognize the contours of the furniture. I hung my coat on the coat rack, sat at the desk and turned on the computer.

First I had to check something. I typed in the password, then found the file I'd been working on the night before. About twenty-four hours should have passed since I'd last opened it. But as I'd suspected, this was not the case. Someone had opened the file with the list of red book titles and Vera's address at eleven minutes past midnight. Someone with no obstacles to getting around passwords. Someone who could get in anywhere. I didn't have to see for myself that the same had happened to the files with the pictures of the Papyrus shelves, and probably all my other files.

I turned off the computer and stayed there for some time, drumming my fingers on the desktop. I was seething with anger, but not so much for their breaking into my protected space. I'd worked long enough in the police to know that a password is only a semblance of protection. What filled me with anger was that I wouldn't be able to do what I'd come to do without being watched. They would monitor everything I did with the computer just as though they were standing behind my back.

If another monitor wasn't silhouetted behind mine, the idea might not have occurred to me so quickly. I rushed over to my colleague Petronijević's desk and turned on his computer. I'd thought my conscience would prick me harder, but I hardly felt it at all. The rules of the game that had been forced upon me left no room for the luxury of conscience. In any case, I wouldn't jeopardize anyone's privacy. I wasn't at all interested. I would only use the computer to gain access to the police data base.

Yes, but unlike those I was trying to outsmart, I

wasn't all-powerful. For me there were obstacles. I stared dully at the flickering cursor in the box where I was supposed to type the password.

I wracked my brain feverishly and it dawned on me some twenty seconds later. The solution seemed almost pathetically simple, but that was probably why it worked. As my right index finger flew across the keyboard, asterisks appeared one after the other. I pressed enter and—let out a shout. But of course!

People are predictable in any case and police inspectors are no exception. Quite the contrary. What else would Petronijević choose for a password but the name of his favorite tabloid!

As I opened the data base, I was briefly filled with paranoid fear. What if my computer wasn't the only one they were monitoring? But I had to take the risk. If I wanted to do things the safe way, I would have to go to some other place outside the building and there was no time for that. After all, even if they monitored what I was doing, they'd have a hard time understanding my intentions.

I typed in "Atanasije Nedeljković." His last name was rather common, but not his first, which allowed me to hope that there wouldn't be too many candidates. And indeed, the list contained only three items. I took out my notebook, wrote down the addresses and phone numbers, then turned off the computer.

I didn't go back to my own chair, however. It would be safer to use Petronijević's telephone. There at least there was no problem with my conscience.

When I dialed the first number, an elderly woman asked me warily why I wanted Mr. Nedeljković. I said that he had won a mixer in a lottery organized by the telephone company for its long-time subscribers. She replied that if the company really cared about its subscribers, they should know that he was no longer among the living. Specifically, Mr. Nedeljković had died four-and-a-half years ago. I expressed my condolences and she said thank you, then asked in a milder tone if his heirs could receive the mixer. I promised to look into it and call back the next day.

A child answered the second number. No, Papa wasn't at home. No, Mama wasn't either. They were on a trip. Yes, Papa's name is Atanasije. All right, call back again. 'Bye.

I didn't have to call the third number to know whose it was, but I wanted to make sure he was still at home.

"Hello?" said Albert Einstein.

I hung up the phone, grabbed my coat, rushed out of the office and ran down the corridor. Luckily, of all three addresses Einstein's was the closest.

24

I PARKED THE CAR a little bit before Professor Nedeljković's building. I chose the opposite side of the street because I had a better view of the entrance. There were no passers-by and almost no traffic either in the rainy autumn evening. Before me stretched two rows of intermittent lights and chestnut trees with bare branches like hands reaching for something in the darkness.

The rain was a nuisance. I couldn't leave the windshield wipers on all the time, and the wall of water that poured over the windshield blurred and distorted my view. Someone might even leave the building without my being aware of it. All I could do was turn on the windshield wipers briefly from time to time. Then the world would come into focus, but not for long.

I would have been more at ease if the heater was on too. The short ride hadn't been long enough for the car to warm up, so the temperature inside was soon about the same as it was outside. I raised my collar and tightened my coat around me, as though this would make me warmer.

I hoped that by suddenly hanging up I hadn't upset the professor and forced him to leave before I got there. I also counted on him having no reason to use a side exit from the building. Then I would lose any chance of being at the mysterious gathering in a little over an hour.

The minutes dragged by slowly because nothing happened. This kind of senseless time wasting had always been the hardest part of my job as an inspector, even though I knew it was necessary and unavoidable. If only I could have passed the time reading, but that was clearly unthinkable. There wasn't any light in the car, but even more important, if I delved into a book my attention would be taken away from the reason for my being there.

When new headlights shone in my rear view mirror, the dim blue numbers on the digital clock above the speedometer indicated that in three minutes it would be eight-thirty. It was the fourth car to appear since I'd parked on this poorly lit street, but unlike the previous three, this one didn't just pass by. It was moving slowly and the motor was barely audible. I sank deeper into the seat.

The car stopped as soon as it passed by mine. Without the windshield wipers it was hard to see whether anyone else was in it but the driver. I thought there was a passenger, but wasn't sure. The car stayed there about a minute and a half. No one got out of it and no one came up to get in. It left as slowly as it had come and finally turned right onto a boulevard.

There could be a simple explanation behind this. It might have been a young couple, for example, stopping briefly on a side street to exchange caresses. But the car could have belonged to the Agency just as well. How had they got there? They'd seen what I'd looked for in Petronijević's computer. They weren't sure right away what I was after, but they'd finally figured it out. They have a lot of bright people working for them.

But maybe they hadn't tracked me down through my colleague's computer. A much simpler way to follow my movements suddenly occurred to me. If they'd bugged my car, there was no reason not to add a GPS device. That way they would know where I was at any given moment. If this had crossed my mind earlier, I could have found another car, but now it was too late.

Not more than a minute after the street was empty again, the front door to Professor Nedeljković's building opened. I rushed to turn on the windshield wipers. The rubber whisked over the windshield twice, removing the watery curtain for just a moment. But it was enough to recognize the stooped figure with his hat pulled down, gray hair poking out from under it.

The professor got into a small car parked near the entrance. He had trouble starting it and the sound of a coughing motor could be heard above the drumming rain. I thought it was going to die, when the mechanical death rattle turned into a not quite even rumble.

He maneuvered briefly out of the parking place and took off. I waited for the car to move away and then headed after it. I didn't turn on my headlights until the professor had disappeared into the boulevard. The light traffic made it easy to tail him, but more conspicuous too. So I kept at a greater distance, always leaving at least one car between us.

The fact that Einstein probably hadn't the faintest idea that he was being followed worked in my favor. Unlike me. I looked in my rear-view mirror frequently to check whether someone might be shadowing the shadower, but didn't notice anything suspicious. There was no trace of the car that had stopped for a moment on the professor's street. This, of course, didn't mean that my movements weren't being followed, just that it was by means of GPS.

When we left the boulevard after a long drive, I couldn't tail him any more without being seen. We proceeded along a broad, well-lit street towards the fashionable part of town, full of luxury family homes behind tall fences. Since I couldn't count on a car to cushion us, I had to give the professor a one-hundred-meter advantage.

At one point when we entered the winding little streets that led to the villas, I turned off my headlights. The street lighting here was spare, but I could still see well enough. Ahead and behind. No one came after me.

The car I was following started to disappear from sight, turning in an unknown direction at the end of short streets before I reached them. I opened the window a little so that the sound of the motor could tell me which way to continue. Although the rain was lighter, it still splashed in through the narrow opening at the top.

At the beginning of a street lined on both sides with dense hedges at least two-and-a-half meters tall, just when I concluded that I should turn left at the next intersection, the rumbling motor stopped. Except for the falling rain, everything around me suddenly went silent.

I parked the car, closed the door quietly and hurried to the intersection. I peered around the corner just as the professor slipped through a gate in the fence some seventy meters ahead. His car should have been in the vicinity, but the street was empty. I didn't have time to tackle that mystery right then. I turned left and headed along the narrow sidewalk full of puddles, keeping my head bowed because of the rain.

The fence next to me was tall and made of metal, with menacing spikes at the top. When I reached the gate, I didn't see any sign on it, not even a house number or a bell. There was just a small head-high rectangle. I hesitated a moment, but really had no choice unless I wanted to stay outside in the rain.

I knocked on the gate.

The rectangle pulled back the same instant and a dark void appeared in the opening. Confused, I stared at it for a moment until I understood what was expected.

The password!

But how could I know the password? Icy tentacles of panic started to run up my spine. I was already resigned to the fact that all I could do was turn and run for my car, when I heard myself say three words.

"The last book."

The rectangle closed. Nothing happened for a long moment. And then the gate began to open.

25

THE GATE OPENED JUST enough for me to pass through and then closed right behind me. I was surrounded by darkness. I could see only two rows of small lights like runway markers along the path to a villa in the middle of a garden. It was some fifty feet away, totally darkened, with just the upper part visible in the reflection from the urban night sky.

Two hands came out of the gloom to my right, holding something. I had to strain my eyes to recognize the long robe. I hesitated slightly before turning my back to the invisible checkroom attendant. I stiffened when he kept his hand on my shoulder after I had put on the robe, but the squeeze only lasted while he raised the hood. My head disappeared completely inside it, narrowing my field of vision to the space directly in front of me.

Once he had let go of my shoulder, I headed down the path. The soles of my shoes made a scrunching sound on the wet gravel. As I advanced, I had the increasingly uneasy feeling that my movements were being watched by penetrating eyes—not only from behind but from all around. My steps quickened involuntarily.

The path did not end at the porch in front of the entrance as I'd expected. There were steps that led downwards. At the bottom was the outline of an arched opening, a muted glow emanating from its depths. I started down cautiously, feeling the edge of the steps with my foot.

The opening was the beginning of a corridor that descended under the villa at a gentle slope. The hood prevented me from seeing it all at once. I could have raised it a little, but hesitated. I still had the feeling that they were watching me, and curiosity could have given me away.

Some twenty paces later I stopped at the end of the corridor. The hood was still lowered, but my field of vision was considerably broader. Three steps separated me from the large, round room I'd reached, so I was looking at it from above. This was not the only entrance. Three more corridors were placed at ninety degree intervals.

The lighting was subdued. The four lamps placed between the entrances had screens in front of them so they couldn't be seen. While I was still in the corridor an unknown smell reached my nose, rather like thyme, but with aromatic enhancements. Now I detected its source. Small vessels with something smoldering inside were hanging from black chains just under the lamps.

The circular room was filled with people in robes. There must have been at least fifty of them. Most of the robes were brown like mine. This uniformity was disrupted by four bright red mantles around the edge of the underground amphitheater's empty center.

I would have preferred staying where I was because I could take in everything with one glance, but this wasn't an option. I had to join the others as soon as possible to avoid arousing suspicion.

I descended the three steps and moved a little to the left, staying behind the others, my back against a marble wall. Not a single hood turned towards me. The heads inside them were bowed and their hands crossed on their chests. I took this position too.

It was only when I got this close that I could hear murmuring, like a prayer or mantra. It was barely audible so I couldn't make out the words. The footsteps of the last three to arrive from the other corridors were heard above this subdued background and then everything was quiet for several minutes. I assumed it was almost nine, but if I were to look at my watch I would have disturbed the stillness that held sway.

The lighting suddenly began to dim and we were soon in total darkness. The murmuring stopped. Everything sank into silence. Then a spotlight flashed from the highest point of the domed ceiling. The beam was directed at the only unoccupied part of the amphitheater that was guarded by the red robes.

I raised my head like the others so I could see better. A good half-minute passed before anything started to happen. At first it seemed that some kind of elevation was rising in front of me beyond the multitude of hoods. It gleamed in the glow of the spotlight.

Not until the figure was shoulder-high did I realize it was a white robe. It continued to rise until it was waist-high above us. Its back was turned to me and its hood was up, so there was no way I could see the face.

When it stopped rising, white sleeves separated from the trunk and stretched out to the side. They described two arcs and crossed above the head, stayed in that position briefly, then slowly descended.

"Brothers and sisters," echoed a deep male voice. "You realize how careful we must be. There have already been mistaken announcements of the last book's arrival. And you all know what comes next. This is why I did not speak up after the first death. It could have been the work of someone who had lost faith and patience. It would not have been the first time that murder was used in the simple-minded belief that it would make the prophecy come true more quickly. I was also silent after the next two deaths, although almost every doubt was dispelled that the long-awaited moment had finally arrived. I had to be absolutely certain. The final proof was given to me not by one of the uninitiated, but by one of us. Sister Dragana was blinded by the selfish desire to appropriate the right that belongs to the Grand Master alone. She had the audacity to reach for the last book—and was inexorably punished on the spot like an ordinary infidel."

A wave seemed to course through the brown robes in front of me.

"Do not mourn her. She got what she deserved. But let us put her aside, for her death is as unimportant as the others. Let us turn to the happiness that lies ahead. May your faces light up with joy. May your souls be filled with rapture. May you be seized with infinite pride that fate has granted you what it withheld from the members of our order in past times."

He paused briefly for dramatic effect. When he spoke again, his voice was like thunder.

"Are you ready humbly to receive the redeemer who is coming to save our world from ruination?"

"We are!" replied the multitude in unison.

"Are you ready humbly to bow down before our one and only master and ruler?"

"We are!" echoed even more stridently from all sides.

"Are you ready to face the ultimate truth?"

"We are!" Everything seemed to tremble from the force of the exclamation.

There was another pause and then his arms began to rise again. This time his hands were not empty. When the two arcs met, there was a blue book above the white hood.

Staring at it, I was a little late in joining the others. They were already on their knees when I started to bend down. Luckily there was no one behind me to notice this discrepancy.

The silence that reigned seemed to have something of the thunderous acclamation of a moment before. The Grand Master let it draw out a bit and when he finally spoke, his voice was threatening.

"But are you really ready? As I delve into your thoughts, what do I find hidden in some of them? Doubt! What if this isn't really the last book? Your distrust hurts me deeply, but I will forgive you on this great day. Will you believe me if you see it with your own eyes?"

The only answer was silence.

"All right," continued the Grand Master after waiting a few moments. "If that is the only way to dispel your doubts, then you will see the last book in action. There is another reason for this as well. Tonight we are not alone."

The robes around me started to rustle.

"Someone has joined us uninvited, naively hoping to pass unnoticed. Now the intruder will pay for his stupidity. But there is no reason to grieve because of this. We are actually bestowing on him a great honor as the first to be judged by the last book openly and not in secret."

There was no time to act. Kneeling with my head bowed, I didn't even hear the red guards approach me. Firm hands grabbed me and lifted me up. The resistance I tried to offer was easily overcome. As they carried me, I saw all the brown robes rise to their feet.

When we reached the central space, the Grand Master had already descended from the square dais he'd been standing on. Apparently it had risen from the floor because nothing had been there when I arrived. They took off my robe, laid me on top of it and held my hands and feet over the side.

"Ah, it's our inspector," said the man in white. Even

though he was standing next to me, his face was still hidden. "How appropriate. It's high time we sent a clear message to the police that they are powerless against us."

He raised the blue book again, waiting for the brown robes to crowd around the dais. It was at an angle so I was unable to read the title on the cover. He held it briefly over his head and then started to lower it, opening it at the same time. All I could figure out was that he intended to put it in front of my face.

But he didn't lower it all the way. The pounding of rapid footsteps could be heard in the corridor I'd taken. Several people were approaching at a run. The Grand Master shouted a word I didn't understand. The spotlight shining down on me from above, forcing me to squint, went out the same instant.

I couldn't tell what was happening in the darkness surrounding us. I heard a commotion and some sounds I didn't recognize. They were still holding my limbs. Then I felt the dais start to descend. When the upper part was flush with the floor, the hands released me. I stayed there without moving, not knowing what to do in the dark.

The beams of at least five flashlights cut through the gloom when the footsteps reached the end of the corridor. They searched around the amphitheater until one of them found me. Then they all came straight at me because no one else was there. I had no idea how and where so many people could have disappeared in no more than twenty seconds.

I covered my eyes with one hand and started to get up as they approached. They lowered the beams slightly so as not to blind me. I still couldn't see who was holding the flashlights, but it made no difference. I knew who they must be.

"Everything would be much simpler, Inspector Lukić," came Commissioner Milenković's voice from the darkness, "if you wouldn't play hide and seek with me."

"Why do you think I'm playing hide and seek with you?"

A beam of light hit my face again. I frowned and turned my head a little to the side.

"What are you doing here in the dark?"

"It was light until you turned up."

"That's not an answer to my question."

"You wouldn't be in this place unless you already knew the answer."

The beam slid below my chin.

"Where are they?"

I shrugged my shoulders. "That's what I'd like to know."

"How many of them were there?"

"About fifty."

"They can't be far away. We have to act fast. We'll talk another time. You'll have to excuse us now. We'll continue on our own. Escort the inspector."

One beam turned back towards the corridor.

"This way," said a male voice.

I had just climbed the three steps, following the beam, when the commissioner's voice sounded once again.

"Did you see it?"

"What?" I asked without turning around.

"The last book, of course."

"I saw a book. I don't know if it was the last."

"You don't give up on the hide and seek, do you."

"Is there any better game to play in the dark?"

I waited for him to make a comeback, but there was only the sound of movement behind me.

"Let's go," said the man who was lighting my way.

The lights along the path were turned off but the gate in the metal fence was open, letting in the illumination from the street lamp, so the flashlight was not needed.

Nevertheless, the agent stayed at the top of the stairs, guiding his beam in front of me, until I went out.

Two other agents were waiting out front. They didn't say anything to me. We just glanced at each other and then I headed for my car through the rain that had picked up again.

26

"It's stone-cold," said Vera, sipping the tea. "Shall I make some fresh?"

We were lying in the gloom of her bedroom. The picture window across from the bed looked like an animated arabesque. The torrential rain produced shifting patterns on the glass that were illuminated from the other side by the reddish glow of the city.

"Isn't it a bit late for tea? It must be midnight already."

"How could I disappoint your expectations?" she asked, placing the cup on the night table. "You came here for tea, didn't you?"

"I did, but that's not what I got."

"You little liar! It was steaming when you got here."

"Maybe so, but I wasn't allowed to drink it."

"It didn't seem to be of utmost importance to you."

"And I thought you'd be dying of curiosity to hear what I had to say. But that was clearly the last thing on your mind."

"How could I know that you had something to tell me? You didn't act at all like someone who wanted to talk."

"Really? So how did I act?"

"You know perfectly well. In any case, what difference does it make? You can tell me now. Unlike the tea, your story hasn't turned cold, has it?"

"No, it hasn't. But maybe it should be avoided before sleeping. It might cause insomnia, like tea."

"Is it that bad? But you're the one who has nightmares, not me. So, let's hear it."

I didn't reply at once. I listened to the monotonous drumming of the rain for a while, interspersed with the distant noise of nighttime traffic.

"I saw the last book. It has a blue cover."

A moment of silence ensued. Vera cuddled up to me and pulled the cover up to her chin.

"Where did you see it?"

"Under a villa where its followers meet."

"The last book has followers?"

"Yes. You know one of them. I reached the villa by following Professor Nedeljković."

"Einstein? I had no idea he could be mixed up in something sinister. He gave the impression of a harmless patient."

"I think it will turn out that other Papyrus patients aren't harmless either. Even though I didn't see any of their faces, because they were covered by hoods, I'd be willing to bet that several of your bookstore customers were at the meeting of the secret order."

"What kind of secret order?"

I sighed.

"From what I was able to gather, it's one of those waiting for the end of the world."

"What does a book have to do with the end of the world?"

"Its advent denotes the beginning of the end."

"I don't understand."

"I don't understand much either. Now that the book is here, something terrible is supposed to happen. Probably only the members of the order are to be spared from the pestilence. But not even all of them. Mrs. Stojanović allegedly paid with her life for deciding to act independently."

"She was part of that group too?"

"She was. My intuition tells me that the Grand Master

of the order is someone you know. It's too bad you weren't there with me. You might have recognized his voice."

"You didn't invite me to go with you."

"How could I expose you to danger? As it was, I only got out by the skin of my teeth."

"Really?" Her voice became softer.

"If Commissioner Mileković hadn't appeared in the nick of time, the book would have carried out my sentence."

"What sentence?"

"I didn't have a chance to find out. The Grand Master opened it above my head and started lowering it toward my face when the Agency burst in. As you can see, sometimes they come in handy."

"That's all he did? Lower the book toward your face? He didn't force you to touch it, turn the pages?"

"No."

"So how could it harm you if you weren't in physical contact with it?"

I shrugged my shoulders.

"I don't know. He held it and opened it without any protection. With his bare hands. He did maintain, though, that only the Great Master could safely handle the book. Allegedly it had no impact on him."

Vera shook her head on the pillow next to me.

"You don't believe such nonsense, do you? How could he alone be immune to the poison that was fatal to everyone else?"

"Of course I don't believe it."

"Then how can you explain the fact that the book didn't harm him?"

I stared for a while at the undulating curtain of rain on the other side of the window before I answered.

"I can see only one explanation. The book is not the least bit poisonous."

27

I WAS RUNNING LIKE mad down the plush-lined corridor, although I didn't know why. No one was chasing me. All I had was the feeling that I'd experienced something unpleasant back behind me, but I couldn't remember what it was.

I slowed down and started to walk at a normal pace. There was no reason to rush because I couldn't get anywhere. The corridor extending before me was endless. I didn't have to turn around to verify that it had no end in the other direction either.

When my heavy breathing calmed down, I could hear music coming from somewhere up ahead. It was barely audible. I was filled with anxiety. Was I rushing to a concert? If I was, then I was late.

I picked up my pace again. But the music didn't get louder, not even after I'd covered a considerable distance. It was still soft, as though retreating before me.

I came across doors periodically on both sides of the corridor, but without any inscription. How would I recognize the one that would take me to the concert? All I could think of was to press my ear against them.

I quickly abandoned the first door I pressed my ear against. Although subdued, the lion's roar covered me with goose bumps. I stepped back from the second one as soon as I recognized the sound of a blazing fire. I didn't stay long at the third door either. What if it didn't hold fast and the waterfall thundering inside crashed into the corridor with all its force?

I approached the fourth door warily. It opened before my ear even touched it. I started, ready for more nastiness, but all I saw was an elderly woman with a violin who obviously suffered from rheumatism. She opened her mouth to say something to me, but an asthma attack got in the way. Struggling to catch her breath, she signaled with the bow to enter. I hesitated a moment, then accepted her invitation.

There was a small stage at the far right of the room, its curtains open. Two easels were in the middle, their canvases covered with the same plush that lined the corridor. There was only one armchair in front of the stage.

Coughing all the while, the violinist joined two other musicians behind the armchair. The young man with a double bass had a bright red scarf around his neck, and the middle-aged woman with long black hair and a well-groomed look was holding an oboe.

They waited for the elderly woman to catch her breath, and then all three heads in unison motioned towards the armchair. I hesitated briefly once more before I took the only seat.

As soon as I sat down, the lights began to dim. We were in darkness for a minute and then a spotlight flashed behind my back and illuminated the two easels. Music sounded at the same time.

Nothing happened for a few moments. I watched the scene before me without moving, surrounded by the slow tones of a sonata. I thought I'd heard it somewhere before, but played by other instruments.

As though pulled by invisible fingers, the covers suddenly began to fall down. Soon they were lying on the floor underneath the easels, and two profiles appeared on the canvases. The woman on the left looked pale and the woman on the right seemed extremely pink. When I looked more closely, I realized what it was. The one on the left had no makeup and the one on the right was overly made up.

The sonata's tempo quickened. As though reciprocating this acceleration, the paintings came to life. With harmonious movements, the two women reached for something beneath the lower edge of the canvas. When their hands returned to the framework of the canvases, both were holding the same blue book.

The two heads started to move. When they were facing completely forward, their eyes seemed to be looking straight at me. Their lips curved into a smile.

I suddenly understood what was about to happen. My body strained, wanting to jump up from the armchair and prevent it, but try as I might, I was unable to move. I couldn't even open my mouth to shout them a warning.

The music quickened even more. Now it was a whirlwind of tones announcing the high point of the show. The eyes on the paintings turned away from me and focused on the books. I screamed in my head not to do it, but not a whisper left my mouth.

The change began as soon as they opened the books. It was more conspicuous on the left-hand painting. That which is pale fades more easily. When the pale woman had completely disappeared from the painting, still smiling, the pink one became pale. But she too soon faded into nothingness. The blue books stayed in the middle of the paintings a few moments longer, as though refusing to accept the fact that no hands were holding them, and then fell below the frames, down to where they had been a moment before.

The music stopped, but silence did not reign. At least not for me. Ringing filled my ears as I watched in disbelief. The plush covers rose from the floor and covered the canvases where two empty female profiles now glistened in their centers.

When the covers were back in place, the spotlight went out. Once again we were briefly in the dark, and then the ceiling lights came on. The very same moment I felt that I could move again.

I jumped out of the armchair and turned around angrily, wanting to tell the musicians what I thought about their concert, but I was struck dumb. The instruments were still there, but not those who had played them. In their stead were three new musicians.

A flaming form was holding the violin, a lion was raised on its hind legs behind the double bass, and the oboe was protruding from the top of a waterfall. All three were frozen, but I realized at once that this would not last very long. At any moment the fire would blaze, the lion would roar and the waterfall would thunder.

I scrambled for the door and pulled it frantically towards me, feeling the clutches of panic tearing at me, and then finally understood that it opened outwards. I burst out of the room and sped down the corridor.

28

It was five-seventeen when my eyes popped open. Luckily, this time I didn't sit bolt upright in bed so I didn't wake Vera. Her peaceful sleep was uninterrupted.

At first I stared straight ahead in disquiet, my eyes filled with the images from the dream, and then slowly relaxed in the silence and gloom of the early morning. I tried to go back to sleep, even though I was afraid I'd be in the plush-lined corridor again, but couldn't.

Since I was wide awake, there was nothing to do but think. First about the dream that was still powerfully with me, and then about the previous dream and everything that had happened since the case started on Wednesday evening.

But my thoughts were jumbled. Seemingly at random, fragments of unimportant conversations and disconnected little things came back to me. None of it made any sense. Or at least I couldn't make it out.

The window started to pale at six-thirty. That's when the feeling of *déjà lu* appeared again out of the blue. Actually, it had never left me. It just subsided periodically so that I wasn't as aware of it. Now for some reason it was heightened.

I was certain that I'd come across a description of

just such a daybreak in some book. The main character was lying in bed awake. The only sound he heard was the even breathing of the woman sleeping next to him. He was staring at the rain pouring down a window, trying to solve a mystery, but the answer eluded him.

The mystery would be solved if I could remember what happened next in the book, but even though I knew I'd read it to the end, subsequent events were beyond my reach. A veil like a curtain of rain seemed to cover them, allowing me to catch a glimpse of what was behind it, but not letting me see clearly. Too bad I didn't have windshield wipers. One swipe would have clarified everything.

Vera woke up at twenty to eight. She seemed ill at ease to see I wasn't sleeping.

"Don't look at me," she said sleepily. "I'm not pretty in the morning."

I cuddled up and kissed her.

"Of course you are. I'm the one who's going to look wretched all day for lack of sleep."

She looked at me tenderly.

"When did you wake up?"

"Around five-thirty."

"Another nightmare?"

I nodded my head.

"This is getting worrisome. It seems that making love to me doesn't agree with you."

I laughed.

"What does making love have to do with bad dreams?"

"You always have them afterwards."

"That 'always' is only two times."

"There weren't any exceptions."

"All the same, we'll have to increase the sample. If nightmares still haunt me after, let's say, the twentieth time, we'll see what we can do."

"What can we do? We'll stop. How can we let you lose your beauty sleep?"

"We certainly won't stop. Furthermore, the best thing would be to work on increasing the sample immediately."

She kissed me, but moved away.

"Morning isn't when I'm at my best for that. In any case, it wouldn't count towards increasing the sample now. Unless you fall asleep afterwards."

"I'd love to sleep a bit longer, but I have to go to work."

"Me too. This week I've got the morning shift."

"But if I were to be invited again for tea tonight. . . ."

"Fig tea. . . ."

"Fig tea, of course. Although the one for 'head work' would be useful too."

"Doesn't your head work well?"

"Clearly not well enough. The riddles around me are only increasing."

"You can have it right away for breakfast. If you give me a bit of time, I'll bring it to you here again."

I shook my head.

"You'll spoil me. I'd rather help you get it ready."

She kissed me again and then we both got up.

Some forty minutes later we were finishing breakfast in Vera's kitchen. The algae tea had refreshed me in no time. It must have had strong stimulating ingredients. Some of them might even be on the list of substances my colleagues from the narcotics department were interested in, but it made no difference. I would have agreed to something even more illegal if I had known it would clear my foggy head.

"So, how does the book kill if it isn't poisoned?"

Vera had asked that the night before, but I hadn't answered, just shrugged my shoulders. She didn't insist, but the question hovered between us.

"I don't even have a theory," I said, lowering my cup. "But I suspect it all hinges on that question."

"Do you think it will reappear?"

"It has to. It would make no sense for it to disappear right now."

"At least we know what it looks like now."

"The cover might change. Just because we know it's blue."

"A book can't change its cover just like that."

"A lot of things that can't be done have already happened here."

"So what should I do?"

I stared at the empty cup in front of me for some time.

"I don't know anything better to tell you than to try not to open any books. The last book is only dangerous when it's open."

"But how can I not open any books? I run a bookstore."

"It won't be easy. You'll have to be resourceful. If you think it's impossible, you always have a choice."

"What choice?"

"To close the Papyrus for a while."

Vera shook her head vigorously.

"I can't close the Papyrus."

"I know. Anyway, I doubt that it would resolve anything. Someone had a reason to connect your bookstore to the last book. They would wait for you to reopen the Papyrus and then continue where they left off."

Vera lowered her eyes.

"That's not very encouraging."

I stretched my hand across the table and placed it over hers.

"Everything will be all right."

"How do you know that?" she asked softly.

"Intuition," I replied, my voice also low. "It's never let me down."

"I'd like to rely on something more tangible."

"The only more tangible thing I can give you right now is a new cell phone that isn't bugged. We'll drop by the first store we see and buy two of them. If you notice anything unusual, don't do anything. Call me immediately. Send me an SMS message if you don't want anyone to hear what you have to say to me."

29

"THIS THING OF YOURS is causing quite a stir," said my colleague Petronijević with an affected grin, slightly raising the tabloid spread out in front of him.

"Really?" I replied grumpily.

"Bodies are starting to appear outside the bookstore and now some secret orders are involved."

"They managed to write something about that too? How did they find out so fast? Let me see."

He turned the newspaper towards me. The upper half of the page had a large picture of the iron fence with spikes at the top and the outline of the villa's roof against the night sky. Across the picture in slanting letters was the swaggering headline "Sect kills with book!"

"Never underestimate investigative journalism."

"Or well-informed sources."

"There are no better-informed sources than those working on the case."

"Or those tailing them."

"You're the one who hacked into my computer, not me into yours."

"I just needed to use it. I didn't go into your files. By the way, I couldn't have gotten in if you'd been a little smarter when you chose your password."

"I changed it. It won't be so easy any more."

"Think so? In any case, the computer incident doesn't justify your tailing me last night."

He turned the newspaper back towards himself and stared at it.

"You can always file a report if you have proof," he said without raising his head.

"Why would I do that? Well-informed sources don't bother me. But I'm not the only party working on this case. I'm afraid the other one might run out of understanding for investigative journalism."

He didn't answer and pretended to read. I took off my coat, hung it up and went into the corridor.

As I walked towards the chief inspector's office, I felt the effect of the tea was fading. I wanted another cup, but wouldn't be able to satisfy this addiction because I'd left the bag with the ideograms at Vera's.

I knocked, waited for the chief inspector to answer, then entered. He was standing next to the aquarium, gazing down on it.

"Ah, it's you. Perfect timing. I was just about to call you. Please sit down."

As usual, he indicated the left armchair.

"They just called from the Agency," he continued once I had sat down.

"I assume they have some complaints."

"How would you know that?"

"I haven't heard of them ever calling to praise someone."

The chief inspector smiled bitterly.

"That's right. Their complaint is that you're not cooperating enough."

"I could make the same complaint about them."

"Their answer would be that they don't have to cooperate. You know what they think they are. Demigods."

"If the demigods are unhappy with my cooperation, why don't they take over the case from us?"

"That's what I asked them."

"And what was their answer?"

"Nothing specific. They just said that for the time being it was best to continue with a two-pronged approach."

"Maybe the problem would be resolved if you assigned the case to someone else."

"I proposed that to them too, but they nixed it. They insist that you stay. Beats me why."

"Maybe they think I know something they don't."

The chief inspector sat at the large desk between the two bonsais.

"Do you?"

"I don't know what they know, so I can't say. That's the main drawback when you work with them. You never know where you stand."

"All right, so what exactly do you know? How far have you got?"

I sighed.

"I don't have anything for sure. The simplest assumption is that someone from the secret order of the last book is behind the mysterious murders in the Papyrus."

"The Agency thinks they're the main suspects too."

"I thought the Agency wasn't interested in secret orders."

"Maybe they think this is linked to something bigger."

"The ways of the demigods are mysterious. Did they say whether they caught anyone last night?"

"As far as I understand—they didn't. They were left empty-handed. I'd say they hold that against you too."

"The results would've been better if we'd been better coordinated. Just a few more moments and I might have found the solution."

"Really?"

"I was very close to the last book."

"What is that book, anyway? Why do they call it the last?"

"They believe that its advent heralds the end of the world. Secret societies and sects usually hinge on that."

"I've heard various stories about the end of the world, but none revolved around a book."

"Even if it doesn't portend the end of the world, this book is not wrongly named. It was the last one for those who opened it."

"How's that?"

"First I thought it was poisoned, modeled after *The Name of the Rose*, but that doesn't seem to be it."

"So what could it be?"

I shrugged my shoulders.

"I don't know. And neither does the Agency. I think that's what interests them most in this case. If it was just about some secret order, regardless of how twisted their beliefs, they'd be happy to leave it to us. But the weapon that was used here might end up in far more malicious hands."

"Who used the weapon? Who's behind the whole thing?"

"As far as I understood last night, there were previous attempts to speed up the prophecy of the last book's advent. I don't know how lethal they were, but the member of the order who is pulling the strings now is very adroit."

"To be sure, arranging deaths whose cause even the Agency can't figure out."

I smiled.

"Although, when you think about it, this weapon is not exactly for mass destruction, and that's what really interests the Agency."

"How's that?"

"In order for the last book to work, it has to be opened. And how many people in our day and age open books?"

"Hey. People do read."

"What is the last book that you read?"

The chief inspector thought it over, then shook his head.

"You caught me by surprise, but I'll remember."

"Did you read *The Name of the Rose*?"

"Not yet, but it's on my night table."

"You're safe while it's that way."

He looked at me suspiciously for a few moments.

"We're not going to recommend that people stop reading, are we? We've got to solve this case as soon as possible. Devote all your time to it. You can count on any help you need."

I got up from the left armchair.

"Thank you."

On leaving the chief inspector's office, I caught sight of Petronijević coming towards me, a silly smile on his face.

"You have a visitor," he said with a wink.

I stared at him briefly as he walked down the corridor, then hurried to my office.

I didn't recognize her at once. How could I when I'd never seen her with any makeup?

30

"Miss Bogdanović," I said, perplexed, "what a surprise."

She was sitting on one of the two chairs next to a small round table across from our desks. Although she certainly hadn't overdone it like Dr. Vidić, what little she'd used seemed conspicuous on her face that was unaccustomed to makeup.

"I hope a pleasant one," she said, extending her hand.

I expected a limp handshake, but was wrong. She shook my hand firmly and held it somewhat longer than an ordinary handshake required. After she had released it, I sat down in my chair.

"Pleasant, to be sure. Any inspector would be happy to receive the visit of an attractive lady."

Makeup was not the only new thing about her. I wasn't an expert on women's coiffures, but she certainly didn't have hair like this when I'd seen her before. Instead of being straight, it now had gentle curls, was somewhat lighter and seemed more luxuriant. She was no longer wearing her huge glasses—she had probably replaced them with contact lenses—and her thin lips now seemed fuller.

She'd also changed clothes. She was still wearing a suit, but the dark business suit had been replaced by a light-blue fluttery one with a matching blouse, its top buttons undone, better suited to bright spring surroundings than the grayness of yet another rainy fall day. Finally, the high heels lifted her up and made her slender.

She smiled.

"Attractive lady? I never expected to receive a compliment from you."

"Why not? You certainly deserve it. You look very nice today."

"Thank you. I didn't think you'd notice."

"How could I not notice?"

"Do men in love notice other women?"

"Even men in love notice women who make an effort to be noticed."

"Vera might not like to hear that."

"There's no reason for her not to like it. In any case, I'm sure that the change in you won't slip by her either."

"Maybe it will."

"She'd have to be blind not to see it."

"She is blind."

I stared at Miss Bogdanović, then shook my head.

"I don't understand."

"Color blind. Vera is colorblind."

"Ah, I see."

"For her, all the colors on me will just be shades of gray. You didn't know about her deficiency?"

"No, I didn't."

"Vera isn't as perfect as she seems."

"I doubt that she'd like to hear you revealing her defects."

It seemed that new sparks between us were inevitable, but when she spoke again her tone was conciliatory.

"I'm not here about Vera. I came to tell you something."

I waited a few moments for her to continue, but all she did was scrutinize me.

"What?" I asked, to break the unpleasant silence.

"My dream."

Now I was the one to stare at her without speaking.

"Do you believe in dreams?"

"In what way?"

"In that they reveal something important to us."

I shrugged my shoulders.

"My dreams are usually muddled."

"Everyone's dreams are like that. But something is often hiding under the apparent confusion."

"Even if that's true, I can't figure them out."

"I usually can. This last one, however, has me completely bewildered. You have to hear it. You're involved."

"Me?"

"I dreamed about you last night."

"Really?" I asked, not knowing what else to say.

"Yes. But I feel uncomfortable talking about it."

"Why?"

She lowered her eyes.

"I was painting you in my dream."

"What's so awkward about that?"

"In the nude."

My eyes turned downward too.

"Nude?" I repeated, as though hearing the word for the first time.

"On a large canvas, life-size."

Only the rain beating on the windows was heard for a while.

"So how did I turn out?" I tried to make my voice sound playful.

"You turned out great. A perfect likeness."

"Was I posing for you?"

She shook her head rapidly.

"No, you weren't."

"Then how do you know it was a perfect likeness if you didn't see me without any clothes on?"

She glanced at me briefly, perplexed, and then lowered her eyes again.

"I don't know, of course . . . I suppose . . . But that's not important. There was no problem with the body. The trouble began when I started with the head."

"Is the head important in a nude?"

She raised her eyes.

"Of course it's important. A nude without a head is just plain . . . obscene."

"So what was wrong with my head?"

"The fact that it didn't want to stay yours."

"What do you mean—didn't want?"

"I painted your face, but it changed after I drew the last stroke."

"Did I become someone else?"

"No. That was the catch."

"I don't get it."

"Neither do I. It was still you, but it wasn't."

"How is it possible to be and not be me, even in a dream?"

"You looked like yourself, but you weren't you. It was like the face of your twin brother appeared on the painting."

"I don't have a twin brother."

"Then your double. Someone who looked an awful lot like you, and yet there was something different."

"What was it?"

She shrugged her shoulders.

"I can't really say. It was something elusive. At first I wasn't quite sure, but as soon as you started to snicker, I knew it wasn't you."

"I was snickering in the painting?"

"Yes. Or rather, not you but the other one. The painting came to life, the lips curved and there was this awful giggle. The dreadful sound made my flesh creep. I wanted to scream but I couldn't. I woke up terrified."

We spent another few moments listening to the rain.

"I'm sorry that my nude upset you so much."

Her eyes flashed.

"It wasn't your nude that upset me, it was that demonic laugh! Do you always have to be so derisive? I came here hoping you'd help me, not to be mocked."

"Excuse me, Miss Bogdanović. I didn't choose the proper words. I certainly did not intend to mock you. How may I help you?"

She continued to stare at me until the flashing diminished.

"I don't know," she said at last. "That dream certainly means something, but it escapes me. I thought you might be able to interpret it because you're part of it."

"I was never good at interpreting dreams. Besides, as you yourself said, it was my double who upset you, not me."

"Who do you think it could be?"

I shook my head.

"No idea. I have yet to meet any double."

"That doesn't mean you don't have one."

"That's true," I agreed.

"Beware of him, if you ever meet."

"I will. Thanks for the warning."

It seemed that Miss Bogdanović wanted to tell me something else, but then changed her mind and stood up. My colleague Petronijević appeared at the door the same moment.

"I hope I'm not disturbing you," he said with a showy smile.

"You're not. We just finished our conversation. Let me see you out, Miss Bogdanović."

As we waited for the elevator, something crossed my mind. I quickly took out my pen and notebook and wrote down a number. I tore off the sheet and handed it to her.

"I have a new cell phone number. If it isn't urgent, it's better to send me an SMS."

She opened her mouth to ask for an explanation just as the elevator arrived.

31

Soon after I got back to my office, an SMS message came on my new cell phone. At first I thought that Miss Bogdanović had remembered something else from her dream or was simply trying the new contact with me, but it was from Vera.

"Come if you can."

I grabbed my coat and rushed out, followed by Petronijević's puzzled and curious look. I didn't have the patience to wait for the elevator and ran down the four flights of stairs to the underground garage.

As soon as I got the car out onto the street, I reached for my old cell phone and called the bookstore.

"Hello, Papyrus Bookstore," said Vera. Her voice did not seem particularly troubled.

"Is everything all right?" I asked.

"I don't know," she replied softly.

"You don't know?"

"I've never seen so many people in the bookstore on a Monday morning."

"I'm on my way."

I put on the rotating light and hit the gas pedal. Luckily, the morning rush hour had already passed, so I arrived in less than ten minutes.

I opened the door to the Papyrus and looked inside in amazement. With the exception of Vera behind the counter, there wasn't a living soul inside.

"Where are they?" I asked as I went up to her.

"They left. All of them. Just after I finished talking to you."

"How many of them were there?"

"More than thirty, I'd say. They started to come a little over half an hour ago. One by one or in pairs. There were at least fifteen of them when I realized that something was wrong. I should have called you right away, but I didn't think fast enough."

I smiled at her.

"You thought just right."

"Too many telephones," she said almost in a whisper.

I nodded.

"What did they do?"

"They were moving around all over the place. It was unusually lively for a bookstore. Like a cocktail party. I didn't know where to look."

"Did they take books out of the shelves?"

"I think so. But I'm not sure. My view was mostly blocked."

"Did they say anything to you?"

"Two of them asked me for some unusual books. I'd never heard of them. They asked me to check the data base but I didn't find anything."

"Did you recognize anyone?"

"I think that three or four of them have been here before. I don't know anything about them."

"Were any of the patients here?"

She shook her head. "None of the extreme cases."

I looked around the empty bookstore and sighed.

"They returned the last book."

Vera stared at me without speaking for a few moments.

"Where is it?" she whispered at last.

I made a sweeping gesture with my arm.

"Out there somewhere."

"How do you know?"

"It was all an act. Blocking your view, asking you to look for nonexistent books. But you weren't the only one they wanted to deceive. Two or three actors would have been enough for you. The whole ensemble was here to deceive other, considerably more vigilant eyes."

"Do you mean. . . .?"

I took out the old cell phone and hit the buttons rapidly with my thumb. The phone rang in my ear nine times before someone finally answered.

"I'm listening."

I raised my eyes to the upper corners of the bookstore.

"Which way should I look?"

"Whichever way you want."

"Where did they put it?"

"I don't know."

"So, we're still playing hide-and-go-seek? Then don't complain about my lack of cooperation."

"Don't you think I'd be there already if I knew where it was? We're poring over the footage, but haven't found anything yet. They're extremely clever."

"Did you follow them when they left?"

"They were clever there too. We lost them."

"All of them? There were more than thirty."

"There were more than fifty in that villa and they disappeared without a trace in twenty seconds."

"Why didn't you catch them while they were in the bookstore?"

"Because I wanted them to leave the book. Right now it's more important than they are."

"You could have got your hands on both them and the book."

"Maybe. But maybe not. Don't underestimate them. They certainly had contingency plans if we'd burst in while they were there. We're dealing with a very serious opponent."

"So what now? The book is here and we don't know where. Why don't you come here with your whole team and look for it?"

"It's more convenient to search for it here. We're comparing the footage of the shelves before they arrived with how they look now. On the other hand, you could look for it since you're there already. You're the only one to have seen it, by the way. You know what it looks like."

"I know what it looked like last night. But it might not be the same any more. The blue cover might be gone, for example. If they're really that clever, they could have taken care of that. They probably did."

"It's not inconceivable, but you should still try. We have to do everything we can so an innocent customer doesn't find it first."

"Wouldn't the best protection for the customers be to close the bookstore for a while and take out all the books?"

I smiled at Vera contritely as she glared at me in alarmed reproach.

"Nothing would come of it. When the Papyrus reopened they'd bring the last book again. Why would there be only one copy? We're actually lucky that they only care about this bookstore for some reason. We'd be in an awful fix if they spread to the others."

I was silent for a moment.

"All right, I'll look for it."

"Very good. It seems our cooperation is improving."

I looked at the upper corners of the Papyrus again, then shook my head. I switched off the phone, put it back in my pocket and turned towards Vera.

"I hope you don't mind if I stay here and keep you company."

The dejection on her freckled face of a moment before turned into a radiant smile.

32

I HUNG UP MY coat and started a slow inspection of the shelves. Vera was at the counter, doing something on the computer next to the cash register. When our eyes met periodically, we smiled at each other. I knew that she wanted to talk to me, but held back because other ears would hear our every word. After a while, probably because she didn't like the silence surrounding her, she turned on some soft background music.

It soon became apparent that my chances of finding anything were very small. If a new book had been put on the shelves, Commissioner Milenković's people would have found it by comparing the footage of before and after the order members' visit. Since the adherents of the last book knew that they would be carefully watched, they wouldn't be foolish enough to bring a book that hadn't been there before, and particularly not one that I could recognize.

They'd probably been prudent and put the last book in the cover of another book that they'd seen there previously. They'd removed the harmless book and slipped the dangerous one into its place. It could now be any one of the thousand books in the bookstore. Well, maybe not just any one. I could ignore the volumes whose format didn't fit the last book's. The problem, however, was that the vast majority of the books in the Papyrus were in the customary format of prose editions.

The only way to find the last book would be to make a systematic check. Every volume of this common format would have to be examined, but one person couldn't do the job. The Agency would have to do it, precisely because they were better protected than I was. The last book might not be poisoned, but it was lethal nonetheless. Regardless of how it worked, my chances of coming to harm if I found it, defenseless as I was, were much greater than if the commissioner's well-equipped team discovered it.

Although I realized my efforts were in vain, I kept on examining the shelves, for several reasons. I had nothing else to do. I could have taken a book, sat in an armchair and read, but I wasn't at all in the mood. In addition, if I stopped, I would be forced into a discussion with Commissioner Milenković, and that didn't appeal to me either. I also doubted that Vera would approve of my giving up.

Finally, I stayed by the shelves because the impression of *déjà lu* had appeared once again. As my eyes slid over the book spines, it seemed to grow stronger, while it weakened whenever I looked in another direction. The book I was trying to remember seemed to be here, somewhere in front of me, affecting me, but insidiously, eluding me like words on the tip of the tongue that you simply cannot remember.

I had just stood up after examining the lower part of a shelf, when a sudden thought made me stop in mid-step towards the next. I put two things together that had previously been separated. Did the haunting impression of *déjà lu* have anything to do with the last book?

I jumped when Vera touched my shoulder. Lost in thought, I hadn't heard her approach.

She smiled.

"You seemed to have wandered off somewhere."

I returned her smile.

"I was lost in thought."

"Would you like some tea? Or maybe you aren't supposed to interrupt what you're doing?"

She raised her eyes to the ceiling.

"Of course I can. I'd love some tea."

"I'll order it from the teashop. Which one would you like?"

"I'd love to have some fig tea, but I think it's a bit

early for that. Then maybe algae. It can be drunk anytime."

Vera sent me a short, meaningful look, then went to the back room to telephone.

Ten minutes later an Oriental boy in a dark-red Mandarin jacket and narrow pants who couldn't have been more than twelve entered the bookshop. He closed his umbrella skillfully with one hand, came up to the counter with almost balletic steps and set down a tray with a teapot and two cups. He poured our tea without putting the umbrella away.

I took out a bill but the boy shook his head.

"Papa says pay later when come to teashop."

It was not until I heard the voice that I realized she was a girl. She bowed, then gracefully glided out of the Papyrus, seeming almost to float.

I looked at Vera in disbelief when we were alone.

"Papa?"

"I was amazed to hear that too."

"Maybe it's not so strange."

"What do you mean?"

"With an unlimited supply of butterfly powder tea available. . . ."

"She's very sweet, isn't she," said Vera, interrupting me. "Did you think she was a boy at first too?"

I nodded my head.

"It's remarkable how deceptive appearances can be," she said.

"Yes, remarkable. I come across that constantly in my work."

Vera looked like she wanted to comment on that, but changed her mind, probably because of those who were listening. She drank a little tea, then changed the subject again.

"It's not crowded today."

"If you don't count what happened this morning."

"Yes, if you exclude that. I wonder whether it's just

because it's Monday. Normally there are fewer customers in the first shift, especially when it's raining. Or have we finally gotten a bad reputation and people are staying away?"

"I'm sure it's because of the rainy Monday. You'd have to be really addicted to books to go to a bookstore at this time and in this weather."

"But there's not a single customer."

"Look on the bright side. The fewer the customers, the less the chances of the last book harming anyone."

"But without customers we might as well close the bookstore."

"There's no reason to close it. This certainly won't last much longer. We'll soon solve the case of the last book. And then it can become a great advertisement for you."

Vera smiled bitterly.

"That's not the kind of advertising I want."

We drank our tea in silence for a while. My mental vigor quickly returned. I knew it would last an even shorter time, but this didn't spoil my good mood.

"What shall we do about Olga?" asked Vera after placing her empty cup on the tray.

"About Miss Bogdanović?"

"Should we warn her that the last book is back here again?"

I shook my head.

"She's better off not knowing. It would only needlessly upset her."

"But if something happens on her shift. . . ."

"Nothing will happen. I doubt you'll have many customers in the afternoon either. Besides, you enjoy special protection." I raised my eyes. "Isn't that right, Commissioner Milenković?"

Of course there was no answer from the ceiling. After I finished my tea, I went back to examining the shelves. The feeling of *déjà lu* was now suppressed, so I could concentrate on the titles without feeling encumbered. I was on duty here but soon, probably because of the tea, I felt off duty. I stopped looking for the last book, telling myself that the effort was in vain. Instead, I did something more enjoyable and innocuous. I selected the books that I would buy and read when things calmed down.

Preoccupied with this, I lost track of the time. I thought it was just a little after one, and it was already two-twenty when Miss Bogdanović appeared. She was back to her old self: straight hair, dark suit, flat shoes. Her face was without a trace of makeup. Her morning radiance had completely disappeared.

She seemed ill at ease to see me in the bookstore. When Vera went into the back room for her coat, she spoke to me in a low voice.

"Did you tell her that I visited you?"

"Why would I do that?" I asked, my voice equally soft. "Your visit was official."

She eyed me piercingly for a long moment.

"Official, of course."

Vera appeared at the door with her coat and umbrella.

"I hope you have more luck," she said to Miss Bogdanović. "No one's come in all day."

"No one?"

She hesitated a moment. "With the exception of the two of us, no one's set foot in the bookstore."

"Maybe the customers will start to come now, when I'm alone. Booklovers don't like the police keeping tabs on them."

"Olga, please. . . ."

"I'm just joking. Inspector Lukić doesn't mind, does he?"

"How could I?" I asked, putting on my coat. "I don't like the police to watch me either. But maybe that's because I'm a booklover myself."

"Oh, yes, how could I have forgotten?"

"Let's go," said Vera quickly, keeping the first sparks from igniting.

We had already opened the door when she turned around and smiled.

"See you later."

The thin lips turned up a little too.

"See you."

Rain drummed heavily on the umbrella as soon as we stepped out from under the small overhang.

"Do you have any suggestion?" asked Vera, taking my arm.

"I'd really like another cup of tea."

"For 'head work'?"

"It wouldn't be worth it. My head won't work until I get a bit of sleep."

"I don't know any tea to put you to sleep."

"I hear that the one made of figs can be used for that too."

33

I RAN FOR A long time before I became aware of the change. Nothing disturbed the uniformity of the plush-lined walls around me. The doors had disappeared. I stopped in bewilderment. The corridor stretched out endlessly in front of me. Why would I continue in that direction if I couldn't get anywhere? I should go back the other way.

I turned around and looked in the other direction that was also never-ending. That same moment I realized why I was running. I was fleeing something. Nothing was actually chasing me, but I knew that some danger was lying in wait for me there. I didn't dare go in that direction. I had to continue in the other one. Maybe the doors would appear again. Infinity is very long.

But it turned out to be quite short. When I turned

around again, I was no longer facing a corridor with no end in sight. The end was right in front of me. The corridor stopped at a wall with a door in it. It was different from all the others I'd seen before. It wasn't part of the plush background that could only be detected by a slit along the edge. The door before me was made of solid brown wood with an ornate brass handle.

There was also a head-high bronze plaque. I had to move back a little to read what it said: "Last Book." How strange for something like that to be written on a door. I placed my ear against the plaque and listened, but couldn't hear anything. I waited a bit, then knocked. No one answered.

A few moments passed before I turned the handle and cautiously pulled the door. I expected someone finally to say something on the other side, but only silence came from within. When I'd opened it far enough, I poked my head inside.

I was prepared for any kind of oddity, but not an ordinary study. The walls were almost completely lined with bookshelves. In the middle of the room was a low, round, glass-topped table between three armchairs. Three brick-colored flowers poked out of a flowerpot upon it. The two corners that I could see had tall, narrow loudspeakers.

There was a large desk facing the door. The only light in the room came from a desk lamp next to a monitor, its beam illuminating the keyboard and mouse on a yellow pad. A dark red, opaque curtain was drawn across the tall window behind the desk.

I lingered in front of the door, reluctant to enter. There was no one inside, but I'd be trespassing just the same. Why would I go into someone else's study? Suddenly it seemed that the sight before me was not completely foreign. As though I'd already seen it somewhere, but that was probably because all the rooms where writers work resemble each other.

In any case, it seemed to be much pleasanter inside than in the gloomy corridor where I was standing. I stepped in and closed the door behind me, thinking that I'd come up with an excuse if the owner appeared. In any case, I wouldn't do anything objectionable. I would just look around a little. I love books.

I couldn't see all the titles in the poor lighting, but among those that I read there wasn't a single one that I wouldn't want to have in my own library. If the owner showed up, I could offer to buy all his books. Without checking any further. I was convinced that I would like all the works, even those I couldn't see.

After I had made a round of the shelves on all four walls, I stopped briefly in the middle of the room, contemplating my next move. I could read one of the books, but thought it was better to leave them alone. The owner probably wouldn't like it. I wouldn't like for some stranger to nose around my library either.

I sat down in one of the armchairs and stayed there until my patience ran out. I hadn't come this far down the endless corridor just to sit there idly. I got up and went to the only place in the room I hadn't been. I pulled back the chair on its rollers and sat at the desk.

I kept my hands in my lap. Here I had even less right to touch anything than on the shelves. But I didn't have to touch anything. As though reacting to my presence, the monitor came to life the moment I looked at its dark surface. A white background replaced the black, and then text started to appear in the upper part. All by itself.

I heard the sound of typing on the keyboard, but my hands were still in my lap. My eyes dropped to the lettered keys in front of me. Invisible fingers seemed to be playing on them as they went up and down. I raised my eyes to the monitor again. The passage had just reached its end. I drew closer and began to read.

I heard the sound of typing on the keyboard, but my hands were still in my lap. My eyes dropped to the lettered keys in front of me. Invisible fingers seemed to be playing on them as they went up and down. I raised my eyes to the monitor again. The passage had just reached its end. I drew closer and began to read.

I didn't wait for the writing to continue. I jumped up from the chair, knocking it over as I did so, and rushed to the door. But the wall where it had been was now completely lined with books. I turned around in fear, thinking I was on the wrong side, that the door was on another wall. But bookshelves surrounded me completely. There was no way out of this room. I was deafened by the ear-splitting scream that came out of my mouth.

34

Hearing my scream, Vera ran into the bedroom. Her terrified expression told me better than any mirror what I looked like. I was sitting up in bed, staring straight ahead, my eyes as big as saucers. She hesitated momentarily at the door before drawing near, then sat down next to me and laid her hand on my cheek.

"Again?"

I looked at her for several seconds as though not recognizing her, before nodding.

"This is becoming serious. We can't risk making love any more."

I put my head on her shoulder and she began to stroke my hair.

"We will make love. There won't be any more nightmares."

She moved away. I raised my head.

"How do you know?"

"I just do. It's over."

"What's over?"

I didn't reply at once. I was at a loss for words.

"Everything. . . ." I said at last, conscious of how insufficient and bewildering this was.

"Everything?" she repeated.

I drew my fingers through my hair and stared out the window. Rain was pouring against the backdrop of the night.

"It's still raining," I said, changing the subject. I wasn't ready just yet to go into an explanation.

She gazed at me quizzically, then graciously accepted the change.

"Tomorrow the weather will finally clear up. I heard it on the news."

"It's about time. Speaking of time, what time is it?"

"It's almost nine."

"Nine? You shouldn't have let me sleep that long."

"I would have woken you if I'd known for sure you'd have a nightmare. But I was hoping. . . ."

I thought of telling her it was a good thing she hadn't woken me, but that would have brought us back to a topic I now wanted to avoid.

"This was actually a daymare."

She smiled.

"Yes, day. There was another reason to wake you, but I didn't. Your new cell phone rang. I took both of them out of the bedroom."

"The new one?" I said in amazement.

"Yes, the new one. Then you got an SMS message on it."

"But how could that be? You're the only one who knows the new number."

She shrugged her shoulders.

"Maybe the Agency. . . ." I said, and then remembered. "Miss Bogdanović!"

I almost jumped from the bed.

"Olga?"

"Yes. I gave her the new number. If anything happened in the bookstore, she was to call me first."

"You didn't tell me. Had I known, I would have woken you."

"I forgot to tell you. That was wrong of me, but it didn't seem important."

"It's probably nothing serious, otherwise she would have called me when she couldn't find you."

"Let's hope so. Where are the telephones?"

"In the kitchen."

We rushed there together. I picked up the new phone. The missed call had been at 8:07 p.m.

"Is this her number?" I asked Vera, showing her the little display.

She nodded.

The SMS was from the same number. It had been sent six minutes later. I started to read it.

"I called you but no one answered. You told me to call if anything happened. This might be important. When you were here on Saturday, a customer reserved a book. Do you remember? I put it under the counter. He was supposed to come and pick it up today, but he didn't. When I went to put it back on the shelf, I saw that it was a different book. The title was the one professor Nedeljković mentioned: The Last Book. *Call me."*

I slapped my forehead with the palm of my hand.

"But of course! What an idiot I am. . . ."

"What happened?" asked Vera, her voice subdued.

I handed her the phone. I waited on tenterhooks for her to finish reading.

"Dejan. . . ." she began.

"Quick! Call her!"

Her hand shook as she dialed the number. Just when I thought that no one would answer, the call went through.

"Maja? Where's Olga?"

Her face began to pale as she listened without a word. She found a chair and sat down.

"I'm on my way," she said before hanging up.

She raised her eyes towards me. They went glassy and welled with tears.

"Olga. . . ." she sobbed. "She's dead."

I bent down and put my arms around her. She got up from the chair and we clung to each other. I could feel the sobs shaking her body.

"What happened?" I asked softly after she'd regained some composure.

"Maja is her sister. They live together. Or rather, they lived. . . ."

She started to cry again. I waited for her to calm down, stroking her hair.

"Olga brought the book home. She collapsed as soon as she opened it. An ambulance came right away, but she was already dead. They've just taken her to the Institute of Forensic Medicine. . . ."

"What about the book?"

I repeated the question because she just stared at me blankly, as though not understanding.

"They took the book too," she said at last. "I have to go see Maja."

I kissed her on the forehead.

"I'm going to the Institute. I'll call you as soon as I learn anything."

35

I DASHED PAST THE doorman at the entrance to the Institute. He was the same one as on the day before, watching television again. He shouted something but I didn't turn around and he didn't come after me.

My footsteps rang through the dark corridors and stairs of the building as I hurried to Dr. Dimitrijević's office. I didn't turn on any lights, relying on the weak streetlight that came in through the large windows to help me find my way. I knocked briskly when I reached his door. Silence was all I got in return. I pushed down on the handle, to no avail.

I stood there indecisively for a few moments, then headed for cold storage. The door was locked there too. I banged my fists in frustration on the white metal, but noise was the only result.

I thought of going back to the doorman, but then it dawned on me that I could phone Dr. Dimitrijević. I reached into my pocket, took out my cell phone—and realized it was impossible. I was holding the new telephone. The old one was on Vera's kitchen table. In the commotion before leaving I'd left it there, and the doctor's number was in it.

If Vera had still been at home I could have called her, but she wasn't. We'd left together. I was already on my way to the ground floor when it occurred to me that my old telephone's memory was not the only memory I could use. I had one too. I'd always been able to remember numbers. After strenuous effort, a number finally surfaced from the depths of my memory. I wasn't sure it was right, but what was there to lose? I would simply hang up if it was wrong. I quickly dialed the number.

I sighed heavily when I heard Dr. Dimitrijević's voice after only two rings.

"Hello?"

"Inspector Lukić."

"Inspector! I've been trying to get hold of you for some time, but no one answered your cell phone."

"The phone you called isn't with me."

"I have to see you right away. Where are you?"

"In your Institute."

"You're already here? Then you know?"

"I know. I looked for you in your office and then in cold storage, but both places were locked."

"Are you by cold storage right now?"

"Yes."

"I'll come and get you."

As I waited for him, I realized how convenient it was that I'd forgotten the old phone. If I'd used it, other ears would have heard us.

Rapid footsteps soon came from one end of the corridor. I headed in that direction to meet Dr. Dimitrijević.

"I thought you'd be here," I said when we met, jerking my thumb back towards cold storage.

"There's no need for an urgent autopsy. We know we won't find any cause for Miss Bogdanović's death. Let's go."

We returned in the direction I'd come from.

"Where are we going?"

"To the chamber."

"The chamber?"

"It's a hermetically sealed chamber for examining highly infectious, poisonous and radioactive samples."

I stopped in my tracks. Dr. Dimitrijević took two more steps, then stopped as well and looked at me questioningly.

"The book. . . ." I said in half a voice.

He nodded.

"Someone wants to examine it?"

"Yes. Dr. Vidić. She just went in."

"She can't do that!" I shouted and jumped at Dr. Dimitrijević, pulling him by the sleeve. "Take me there immediately!"

He looked perplexed, wanting to ask something, but held back. He led the way as we rushed down the stairs to the first floor, traversed a long corridor and finally reached a metal door that didn't have an ordinary lock. The doctor took a card out of the breast pocket of his white coat and swiped it through an opening on the door jamb. Four little red lights flickered and then turned green. He had to use both hands to pull the handle and open the door.

I darted in before him. The center of the white room

contained a cylindrical chamber some two meters in diameter that stretched from floor to ceiling. There was a small head-high window on the rounded door that I reached in two steps, then looked inside.

If I hadn't known it was Dr. Vidić, I wouldn't have recognized her. She was wearing a yellow plastic suit like a diver's that covered her completely, with a helmet on her head. Behind her rose a shelf full of chrome instruments, bottles and glass vessels. She was sitting at a little table in the middle of the chamber. A blue book was on it. Unopened.

I banged on the little window frantically. The helmet turned towards me. An extravagantly made-up face looked at me through the visor. She smiled.

"Don't open it!" I screamed.

She tapped the helmet at ear level, then shook her head.

"I can't hear you." Her voice came out of a speaker somewhere behind me.

Dr. Dimitrijević laid his hand on my shoulder.

He indicated one of the buttons next to the card slot on a small control panel by the door.

I pressed it unnecessarily hard.

"Don't open it!" I shouted again.

The smile on the brightly colored lips broadened.

"Don't be afraid, Inspector. I'm safe here. Nothing will happen to me."

"You don't understand! It's not a normal book. It will kill you if you open it!"

"Of course it won't kill me, regardless of how abnormal it is. Now we're going to discover its secret."

She turned her head back to the table. Her hand reached out to open the book, but stopped in mid-air. She looked at me again, still smiling.

"I dreamed about you last night, Inspector. You really frightened me. You had two faces. I have to tell you my dream when I come out."

I pushed the button again vehemently.

"No!"

My scream still seemed to resonate in the white room while I watched, face pressed against the window, powerless to do anything, as she opened the cover. At first nothing happened. She looked like a strangely dressed reader engrossed in an ordinary book. And then her head collapsed on the table, covering the blue volume.

36

As I TURNED IN alarm towards Dr. Dimitrijević to ask him to open the chamber, someone started banging fiercely on the other door. The doctor and I glanced at each other and he rushed towards the entrance to the white room.

Commissioner Milenković burst in. Before the doctor closed the door behind him, I caught sight of two men in raincoats in front of it.

"Where is it?" asked the commissioner, wasting no time.

I might have tried to pull something if I had had a chance, but Dr. Vidić was more important now. I clung to the faint hope that we might be able to help her, although I knew it was too late. I pointed to the chamber.

"In there. Doctor, open it! Now!"

He had already put the card in the slot, but hadn't swiped it. He stayed riveted to the window a few moments, then removed his card and stepped back from the door.

He shook his head.

"I can't take the risk. . . ."

The commissioner went up to the chamber and looked inside.

"What happened?" he asked, turning around.

"She went inside to examine the book," replied the

doctor, his voice now hesitant. "Something happened. I don't understand. She was thoroughly protected."

"Open it, for God's sake!" I shouted. "We can't leave her like that."

The doctor shook his head again.

"I can't take the risk. We might all get hurt. This is something . . . dangerous."

"No one will get hurt!" I said, still screaming. "The book is harmless until it's opened. You brought it here and nothing happened to you."

The doctor moved a little further from the chamber. I looked at Commissioner Milenković. We stood there stock-still in a silence of just two or three seconds that seemed infinitely longer.

"Give me the card," said the commissioner intransigently, putting out his hand.

The doctor hesitated a moment before handing it over.

The commissioner stood there briefly holding the card as though uncertain whether to use it himself or give it to me. Then he turned and swiped the card through the slot. Four little green lights went on, like in the corridor. No effort was needed to pull the door open. It opened by itself. The commissioner moved to avoid it.

It was too cramped inside for both of us to enter. Had there been an opportunity, I would have tried to get in first, but the commissioner was closer. He stopped for a second at the entrance and then went inside. I drew closer in order to see better and to help him carry out Dr. Vidić.

First he placed three middle fingers on her jugular vein. The thin plastic of her suit made him keep them there longer than usual. Finally he turned his head towards me and shook it.

Behind me came Dr. Dimitrijević's sobbing sigh. His cynical sense of humor which helped him get through daily encounters with death was insufficient protection for him now.

The commissioner stood behind the chair, grabbed Dr. Vidić under the arms and started to pull her upright. The yellow helmet hung limply. He set her back against the chair. I thought he would lift her up all the way, but he took out his hands and looked at the table. Then he turned towards the doctor and me and repeated the question he'd asked when he first entered.

"Where is it?"

I didn't understand what he meant at first.

"The book," he added impatiently, reading the incomprehension on my face.

I leaned a bit to the right to get a better look at the table that was partially obscured. There was nothing on it. I shrugged my shoulders.

The commissioner first looked at Dr. Vidić's lap, then bent down and checked under and around the table. He got up and stood there a while. When he came out, he took another good look at the small space inside the chamber, then closed the door.

"Are you sure it was inside?"

The question was directed at both of us. Dr. Dimitrijević was the first to answer.

"Absolutely. She took it in with her."

The commissioner turned towards me.

"I watched her open it," I said. "I tried to stop her, but she wouldn't listen. She collapsed on the table over the book."

The commissioner was silent for some time, staring at me hard.

"Why?" he asked at last.

"Why what?"

"Why did you try to stop her from opening the book?"

"Because all those who opened it died."

"But it makes no sense," interjected the doctor.

"Closed or open, the book couldn't have harmed Sonja. She was wearing armor that was impenetrable to any kind of germ or poison. Even radiation. She was in a hermetic cocoon."

"The cocoon was not completely impenetrable," I said in a somewhat subdued voice.

The doctor looked at me circumspectly.

"What do you mean?"

I didn't reply at once. I looked at Commissioner Milenković.

"The visor."

"The visor?" repeated the doctor. "What could pierce glass as thick as your finger?"

"What Dr. Vidić saw."

The doctor shook his head.

"I don't understand you."

"What did the doctor see when she opened the book?"

"Some text, I suppose. What else?"

"That's right, the text of the book."

He glanced at me without speaking.

"And?"

The silence that surrounded us was broken by the commissioner. His voice was also low.

"Reading the last book killed her?"

"Like the others," I replied. "The book isn't poisoned. No one's imitating *The Name of the Rose*. It's more complex. Whatever's written in the last book kills."

"That's . . . that's. . . ." said Dr. Dimitrijević trying to find the right word, "out-and-out voodoo."

"Do you have any explanation that's a bit less voodoo?" asked the commissioner.

"No, I don't, but I'm convinced there must be a natural explanation. . . ."

"This might not be unnatural," I replied. "It's just that we'll have to expand the definition of a natural explanation."

"I didn't expect two serious policemen to act so unreasonably. . . ."

"It's hard to hold onto reason when a book disappears from a closed chamber right before your eyes."

I thought the doctor would reply, but all he did was shake his head.

"How did you reach that conclusion?" asked the commissioner.

"In my dreams," I said, telling the truth after hesitating briefly. "It happens to me often. I have awesome dreams."

"Lucky you. I don't remember mine." He paused. "What could be written in the last book that is so lethal?"

I shrugged my shoulders.

"I haven't a clue," I lied.

37

Commissioner Milenković left right away, while I stayed in the room until the orderlies came to pick up Dr. Vidić's body. When they took it to cold storage, Dr. Dimitrijević seemed to collapse. He didn't even try to hide his tears. I realized he must have felt something more than mere sorrow for a lost colleague.

"I won't be able to do the autopsy," he said in a broken voice. "I'll have to ask someone else. . . ."

"Why is one necessary? You know you won't find anything."

"Protocol. It wasn't a natural death. Miss Bogdanović will have to have one too."

"Why was Dr. Vidić the one who examined the book?"

"She insisted on doing it. She always was ambitious. I was wrong to let her. It should have been me in the chamber."

"Would you have acted otherwise if you'd been there in her stead?"

He looked at me for a few moments in silence.

"Would I have listened to you and not opened the book? No, I wouldn't. But it would have been better for me to die than her. She was so young. . . ."

"She would still be alive if she'd listened to me."

"She was convinced that she was thoroughly protected. How could she have known? Even though I witnessed the whole thing, I still can't accept what happened. It was so . . . unscientific. What kind of dreadful book is that? And how could it disappear?"

I shook my head.

"I don't know. But I'll give everything I've got to find out." I paused. "If it's at all possible," I added in a lower voice.

He wiped the tears from the corners of his eyes.

"What if it appears again somewhere?"

"Now at least we know for sure that it's harmless until it's opened."

"Some of us know, but not the others. It could turn up in the Papyrus again or in some other bookstore and lie in wait for an unsuspecting victim."

"It won't turn up."

He eyed me suspiciously.

"How do you know?"

"Intuition."

"That's not very scientific either."

"I'm afraid I can't offer anything more scientific right now. I've got to go."

I patted him on the shoulder, then we shook hands. I wanted to say something else to him as we parted, but nothing consoling came to mind. I didn't even say good night because it didn't seem fitting. The night before him would be anything but good.

The doorman was on his feet. His eyes followed me as I passed by, but he didn't say anything. I was halfway to my parked car when I realized something was amiss. I looked around in confusion and then it hit me. There was no steady drumming of the rain; the rain had stopped. I raised my eyes. The streetlights weren't very bright here so I could gaze at the clear night sky where several little points were flickering. I smiled. I hadn't seen the stars in weeks.

I sat in my car but didn't leave right away. My eyes swept over the almost empty parking lot, then I took out my cell phone and called Vera.

"It's me," I said when she answered. "Where are you?"

"I'm still with Maja." Her voice sounded depressed. "How about you?"

"I just left the Institute of Forensic Medicine." I paused. "I don't have good news."

Vera was silent for a moment.

"I wasn't expecting any. What happened?"

"The book took another victim."

There was another period of silence.

"Who?"

"Dr. Vidić. Do you remember her?"

"What happened?"

"She opened the book even though I warned her not to do it."

"That awful book!" Vera's voice grew stronger. "Did you finally get hold of it?"

"No, I didn't. It disappeared."

There was another pause in the conversation.

"How could it disappear?"

"I'll tell you when we see each other. Will you be at Maja's much longer?"

"I might spend the night here. She needs me tonight."

"Certainly. So I'll call you tomorrow."

"I'll go to the Papyrus in the morning. I have to put up a sign saying the bookstore won't be open for a while."

"Vera. . . ."

"Please, let's not talk about it now," she said, interrupting me. "We'll talk tomorrow. 'Bye."

She hung up before I had a chance to say goodbye. That hurt me for a moment, but I didn't hold it against her. How could I? I knew how she was feeling. And she certainly held me responsible for everything that had happened. Rightly so. If I hadn't been sleeping, her friend would still be alive.

I started the car and headed home. I hadn't been there for days. Luckily, I didn't have any pets that needed care. The three brick-colored flowers in the flowerpot on the coffee table in my study were all that needed my attention. I would water them as soon as I got there. Hopefully they hadn't wilted.

38

I WAS STUCK IN the morning rush hour on my way to work when my cell phone rang. It sounded seven times before I finally managed to pull over to the curb and answer it.

"Vera," I said, without waiting to hear her voice. Her new number was on the display and it couldn't have been anyone else.

"Dejan! I almost gave up."

"I'm in the car. I couldn't answer any faster. Where are you?"

"In front of the teashop."

"What are you doing there?" I asked, perplexed.

"You told me to call you if I saw the patient who leaves his own books."

"Yes?"

"He turned up. He wanted to enter the Papyrus but I kept the door locked. I showed him the announcement that the bookstore was closed. Then he raised a book."

She fell silent.

"Vera?"

Her voice was trembling. "I finally saw it."

"Everything's all right. Then what happened?"

"He went off. I didn't know what to do. I put on my coat and went out to call you so that no one else would hear me. He didn't get very far. He just stood there like he was waiting for me."

"And?" I said after another bout of silence.

"I took out the telephone, but he started moving again. I hesitated a little and then headed after him. I was just about to call you when he reached the teashop. He turned towards me, then entered. I got here to the entrance and then called you. What should I do? Should I go in too?"

"No!" I said, almost shouting. "Wait for me in the street. I'll be there as fast as I can."

I was just about to hang up when Vera's voice came from the receiver.

"What about the commissioner?"

"What about him?"

"Should I call him too? He asked me to, remember?"

"Call him," I said after a moment's hesitation. "But not right away. Wait a bit. Do you have the other cell phone with you?"

"No, but I have your other phone. I picked it up this morning when I dropped by my apartment."

"Great. Call him from it."

I put the telephone back in my pocket, hastened to put the rotating light on the roof, turned on the siren and with screeching wheels got back into the traffic. Behind me came the angry honking of the car I almost hit.

I reached the teashop in thirteen minutes, although it seemed a lot longer. I barely escaped two more accidents.

Vera was standing in front of the entrance looking anxious. I kissed her, but she barely returned it.

"All of them are inside," she said softly.

"All of them?" I repeated.

"I didn't have time to call the commissioner. Just as I was dialing his number, he came running this way with six or seven men. He just nodded his head before rushing into the teashop."

I wanted to slap my forehead.

"He knows my new number because I called Dr. Dimitrijević from it last night and he must be intercepting his calls too. I should have connected things."

"That's not all. . . ."

I looked at her in confusion.

"What else?"

"Others went inside right after."

"What others?"

"Those who were in the bookstore yesterday morning. Not all of them, maybe about fifteen. I recognized some of them. Einstein was one. He smiled at me. . . ."

I stared dully at Vera.

"I underestimated the order. One more slip-up."

"What now?" she asked.

"I'm going into the teashop too. I have no choice." I smiled. "I couldn't miss the denouement, could I?"

"What about me?"

"What about you?"

"You don't expect me to stand here in the street, do you? I want to go along."

I shook my head.

"No. It might be dangerous."

"No, it won't."

"How do you know?"

"Intuition."

"Vera. . . ." I started, but she interrupted me.

"You were wrong not to take me to that villa. Do you want to make another mistake?"

I had no time to think of how to stop her and she

was standing closer to the teashop door. She turned, opened it and went in. All I could do was rush in after her.

39

It took a few moments for our eyes, accustomed to the sunny but cold day, to adjust to the reddish gloom of the teashop. We stopped next to the entrance. Before I was able to see properly, a familiar voice came from somewhere in front of me.

"Welcome."

The old man was standing behind the counter, smiling. Two other figures in blazers were next to him. One I had already met—the twelve-year-old girl I had thought was a boy. But which one of the identical twins who bowed, also smiling, was she?

The mystery only deepened when their father introduced them.

"Son and daughter."

He didn't indicate who was who.

Vera briefly returned the bow and then I did too.

"Please," said the old man, coming out from behind the counter and indicating a table. He could have chosen any of them. There were no customers in the teashop.

"We didn't come for tea," I said.

"Tea very useful now. Already prepared."

I shook my head.

"We don't have time. Where are they?"

Ignoring my question, he turned towards the twins and signaled with a nod. One of them took a tray from behind the counter with two cups on it and brought it to the table the old man had chosen, then pulled the chairs out a little for us.

Vera beat me to it again. Before I was able to object, she went up to the table and sat down. I hesitated briefly, unhappy that she had taken the initiative, then joined her.

The other child took the cups off the tray and placed them in front of us, then joined their father and brother or sister who were standing next to the table. They looked at us, still smiling.

Vera was faster once again. She brought the cup to her lips and drank a little tea. Her face lit up but she didn't say anything.

As I raised my cup warily, I noted that the tea wasn't steaming. Indeed, it was lukewarm. But that was not the only surprise. I'd been certain that he would serve us algae tea, but this one had an unfamiliar taste. It was a little bitter, something like cornelian cherry and yet different.

I glanced at Vera questioningly—and realized that something was wrong. Her eyes were fixed on me, but as though not seeing me. She still seemed serene, but also numb, stiffly holding the cup in midair between her mouth and the saucer on the table.

"Vera?"

She didn't move.

I put down the cup and almost jumped out of my chair.

"What's going on? What did you give her?"

"Miss Vera all good," replied the old man calmly. "Wait for you come back. Now you must alone."

I stared at him for a few moments.

"Where?"

"There."

He pointed to the left. I turned, but all I saw was a dark-red curtain covering part of the wall between two tables. The twins went up to it and pulled it open, like theater curtains. Behind it was a door. One of the twins reached for the handle and opened it, and the other gestured broadly, inviting me to enter.

Before I left, I glanced at Vera once more. She looked

like the living statue of a young woman happily drinking tea with an invisible friend.

I turned around when I reached the door. Nothing had changed. The old man was still standing next to the table by Vera, as though on guard. The smile never left his face.

I thought that the twins would just let me go in and then close the door behind me, but they entered first. I hesitated just a second and then followed them.

I couldn't tell where we were. It was dark. What little light there was came from the teashop. But even that disappeared when a child's hand closed the door behind us.

The total darkness lasted only a moment. The light went on seemingly by itself, but its source wasn't visible. It seemed to come from all around, as though the walls, floor and ceiling covered with worn dark-green plush were radiant.

Before us was a short corridor. There was a door in the middle on either side. They were also dark-green and barely visible. A third door at the opposite end of the corridor disrupted the uniformity of the plush. It was made of heavy wood.

The twins skipped ahead of me, their movements supple and light. I thought that they could have hung in midair if they'd wanted. They stopped in the middle and stood on either side of the left-hand door. They didn't say anything, but I understood they expected me to join them.

As I headed towards them, the feeling of *déjà lu* suddenly flooded through me. It was stronger than ever before. I was still staring at a windshield blurred by rain, but now I seemed to see through it a little bit, to set eyes finally on what was hidden on the other side.

As I stood in front of the door, the windshield wipers went on for an instant. Even before one of the twins opened it, I knew what I would see behind.

Eight people filled all the places at a long table that stretched out from the door. Commissioner Milenković was sitting at the other end, at the head. The Agency's men were numb just like Vera, each holding a half-raised cup of tea.

I nodded and the other twin closed the door. I turned towards the door on the opposite side. The first child reached for the handle, but I waved my hand dismissively. There was no need to open it. The windshield wipers were powerfully at work. The plush and wood behind it became completely transparent.

The table here was twice as long. Only one of the sixteen figures was not wearing a brown robe with the hood raised. Dressed in white, the Grand Master was sitting at the same place as the commissioner. The order members resembled monks toasting something in a monastery refectory.

I looked at the brother and sister. I didn't have to say a thing. They skipped back to the entrance where they awaited me.

I turned and headed resolutely for the wooden door at the end of the corridor. At the end of the last book. *Déjà lu* stopped being an elusive chimera. Before me was the shining clarity of a sunny day. I no longer needed any windshield wipers.

I knocked lightly.

"Come in!" replied a very familiar voice.

40

THERE WAS NO REASON to remain in the study at the end of the corridor for very long. I knew everything before I went in, so no superfluous explanation was needed. The conversation was light and cordial, as befits people who know each other well. Even better than identical twins. It was actually the kind of conversation a man has with himself when he's in an amiable mood.

Returning to the corridor, I was in darkness once again and then the walls, floor and ceiling started to shine. The brother and sister were waiting for me at the other end, bowing and smiling. I answered their smile and headed towards them.

I stopped briefly in the middle of the corridor. I didn't have to turn left and right and look through the locked doors. No one was sitting at the long tables. There weren't even any tables. Or rooms where the tables had been. The two plush-covered doors were false. They didn't lead anywhere.

The door from the teashop to the corridor was also an illusion. I went through it after one of the twins opened it and the other drew the dark-red curtain. Nothing but a wall was left behind me, the one that had always been there.

I found Vera in the same position in which I'd left her, stock-still, holding her teacup chest-high. Her eyes were centered on the empty seat across from her, as though looking at someone there. Only the old man had left. She was alone in the teashop.

I approached and pulled back the chair. She came to life the instant I sat down and lowered her cup to the saucer.

"I've never tasted tea like this before," she said as though continuing a briefly interrupted conversation. "What do you think it's made of?"

"Cornelian cherry?" I replied.

She shook her head.

"The taste is similar, but I think it's something else." She looked around. "Where's the old man? I'll ask him."

I nodded towards the door behind the counter that led to a back room.

"He went in there."

A shadow suddenly crossed Vera's face.

"Where are the others? Commissioner Milenković

and his men? And the members of that order? At least twenty-five of them went in."

"They're not here any more. It's all over for them."

She examined me circumspectly.

"What do you mean, over?"

"The commissioner will soon close the case as unsolved. That happens periodically in police work. There are no new crimes and the old ones go unexplained. As for the secret order, they'll conclude it was another false manifestation of the last book and keep waiting for the real one."

"But the last book is here. I saw that patient carrying it half an hour ago. What happened to him?"

"Nothing. He played out his role and brought us all together in the teashop."

"Why?"

"For the denouement. The last book will be here just a little while longer. Until we finish this conversation."

"I don't understand you, Dejan," she said after a moment's silence.

"I know. But that's not the main problem. Even when you do understand, you'll have a hard time accepting it."

I could tell by her eyes that a multitude of questions crowded her head. One finally prevailed over the others.

"What does this conversation have to do with the last book?"

"It's part of it. Part of the last chapter, the fortieth."

Her eyes narrowed.

"What. . . .?"

"The last book is the story of everything that happened since I first entered the Papyrus last Wednesday to this denouement right now."

"But that's impossible. . . ." She paused. "How do you know? Did you read it?"

"If I had, I would have died like the others who

opened it. They perished because they started to read it."

"You can't die from reading a book. . . ." she said after a slight hesitation.

"You can, unfortunately. In a very special case. When realities cross."

"Realities cross?"

I sighed.

"This will be the hardest to explain. When you write prose, there is your reality as the writer and the reality of the book. They are strictly separated. Think of them by analogy to a world made of matter and antimatter. You know that from physics? They mustn't come into contact because they would annihilate each other. When two realities cross, annihilation appears in the form of the death of the person who comes into contact with the artifact from the other world. Not physical contact. No one would have come to harm if they'd just held the last book without opening it. But as soon as they started to read it, to read about themselves, the two realities became hopelessly intertwined and they were—annihilated. No trace was left of this annihilation, so the cause of death could not be established."

Vera just shook her head for a while in silence.

"That's preposterous. . . ." she said softly.

"Preposterous, yes," I agreed. "But the only plausible explanation."

She mechanically raised her cup to take a sip of tea, but put it back on the saucer before it reached her mouth.

"If what you say is true, if the book is lethal to anyone who tries to read it, then shouldn't that apply to you too?"

"It does."

"Then how do you know what's written in the last book?"

My answer was not immediate. We looked into each other's eyes across the table.

"I didn't have to read it," I said at last. "I wrote it."

"You?"

"Yes, me. But not this Dejan who's sitting across from you right now."

"Oh? Is there another one?"

"There is. The author of the last book. From another reality. But that's not his name."

"What's his name?"

"It's similar. He based the book's main character on himself. We are more than identical twins. We are the same."

"Is he an inspector too?"

"No, just a writer. But I'm a writer too."

"I didn't know that."

"Neither did I. Not until I got home last night and went into my study. By the way, our studies are identical. Even the same flowers in a pot on the table. You'll see when you finally come to my place."

"How do you know what the other writer's study is like?"

"I was in it."

"You were in . . . his reality?"

"Yes, just a moment ago. While you were sitting here."

She shook her head.

"No you weren't. You were right in front of me the whole time."

"It just looked that way to you. But that's not important now. I turned on the computer in my study last night and found a file with thirty-nine chapters of the last book."

"Then why didn't you know before that you were writing those chapters?"

"I wasn't allowed to know. That would have caused chaos in the last book. I had to be part of the story.

Only some sort of presentiment was possible. Do you remember when I mentioned the feeling of *déjà lu*?"

"Yes."

"It wasn't about some book I'd read long ago and forgotten, but about this one that I had written—that we actually both wrote. At the same time."

"But why did you have to write it too?"

"Because that was the only way, as a writer, that I could read the last book safely. Otherwise this denouement would not be possible. And what kind of detective story would it be without a resolution to the plot?"

This time she took a sip of tea. I thought briefly of stopping her so she wouldn't go numb again, but then realized that wouldn't happen. I didn't need to leave my reality any more.

She gestured vaguely around herself after putting down her cup.

"So our reality is only . . . some writer's . . . fiction?"

"No. It's as real as his. Only his has impacted ours for the last seven days, which is the duration of the last book. That impact will stop in just a few minutes."

"Why did it have to be that kind of impact?" she asked in a subdued voice, after giving it some thought.

"What kind?"

"Why did he decide to write a detective story? Couldn't he have chosen something serious?"

"Actually, he did. He doesn't think detective stories are nothing but light reading."

"Maybe they aren't, but at least there wouldn't have been so many deaths. Six real people, including Olga, lost their lives just because he wanted to show that a detective story can be serious literature. That's cold-hearted and unforgivable."

"People die in serious literature too. Sometimes many more."

"That's little consolation."

"You're right. That's why he wants to make amends while we're still in the last book."

"Amends?"

"Yes. It won't bring back the dead, of course, but it will make your life more pleasant. And it will remove any doubts. Everything I just told you still seems utterly unbelievable, doesn't it?"

She nodded her head.

"Utterly."

"But you would believe your own eyes, wouldn't you?"

She eyed me questioningly.

I stood up and held out my hand.

"Come here."

I led her to the teashop exit.

"Close your eyes," I said when we reached the door. "Don't open them until I say so."

She looked at me in confusion for a few moments before she closed her eyes.

I took her out into the street. The brilliance of the clear day forced me to squint after the semi-darkness of the teashop.

"Now open them."

She opened them, but quickly closed them again. And then cautiously, as though for the first time, she raised her eyelids halfway. She stayed like that a long time, eyes narrowed, until they adjusted. Finally she opened them wide.

All the freckles on her face slowly curved into a smile.

"Colors. . . ."

The Grand Manuscript

Translated from the Serbian
by
Alice Copple-Tošić

I PARKED THE CAR in the only free spot in the small parking area outside the building at 12 Oak Street. The name had surely been chosen by someone with a sense of humor. There were three trees on the short street: two lindens and a chestnut. When I got out of the car, my head was filled with the fragrance of a nearby flowering linden whose crown was bathed in the glow of the streetlights. A warm wind rustled its broad leaves.

I made for the entrance to a five-story building with a flat roof. Since it was not even nine-thirty, most of the windows were lit up. Lamplight was interspersed with the grayish, flickering radiance of television screens. Little eddies of dust and scraps whirled about the asphalt.

As I approached the entrance, a light went on in the foyer behind the glass door and a short, plump woman appeared. Since the light came from behind her, I was unable to get a good look at her face.

"Inspector . . . ?" she asked, opening the door a crack.

"Inspector Dejan Lukić," I replied. "Good evening."

The door opened wide and the woman moved aside to let me in. Now I could see her better. Although she had a youthful appearance, she was certainly over forty. Her short red hair was cut in a bob reaching just below her prominent double chin. Large thin-framed glasses and full bright-red lips filled her round face. She was wearing what seemed like a colorful poncho over her beige blouse. Her dark skirt reached below mid-calf, and her plain black shoes had low heels, although one would have expected them to be high. A large leather briefcase hung from her left shoulder.

"Good evening," she said after closing the door behind me quickly. She held out her hand. "Miss Ljubica Aksentijević. Literary agent."

I did not expect such a firm handshake from a woman of her size.

"So we are colleagues," I said with a grin.

She raised her eyebrows. "Colleagues?"

"Agents."

"Oh, that. I never liked that title. It sounds too. . . ."—she pondered briefly as though looking for the right word—". . . .inaccurate. There's nothing police-like in my work. Quite the contrary."

"Nevertheless, our paths have crossed." She seemed to hesitate about replying to this and then let it drop.

"Excuse me for not waiting for you outside. The wind shatters my nerves."

I nodded. "It does that to lots of people. Even when they are indoors. On windy days people act more strangely than usual."

"It has no effect on you?"

"Not much."

"That makes me feel a bit better. If the wind bothered you like it does me, I'd feel bad if it turned out that I've summoned you in this weather for no good reason."

"Don't you worry about that. It's always best for everyone when it turns out that the police have been summoned for no good reason."

The corners of her mouth lifted briefly. "I hope that's the case here too. Although. . . ."

If she had intended to finish the sentence, she was interrupted when the light in the entrance suddenly went out. Had I not moved, or had I looked for the switch on the left-hand wall, nothing would have resulted. But I reflexively turned to the right—and the collision was inevitable.

First her "Oh!" was heard in the dark as her head collided with my shoulder and then my "Excuse me," accompanied by a brief groan as her heel smashed the toes of my left foot (had she been wearing high heels, she would have made a hole in the casual shoe), followed by her "Sorry." Finally, the light came back on.

We stood there for several moments in silence, filled with unease, avoiding each other's eyes. She rubbed her right temple with the tips of her short fingers and I barely held back from inspecting my trampled foot.

"Let's go," she proposed at last. Without waiting for my agreement, she circumvented me and headed for the elevator at the far end of the foyer. To left and right were other glass doors leading to apartments on the ground floor.

Thanks to mirrors on three walls and the ceiling, the elevator looked considerably more spacious than it actually was. When she raised a finger to press the button for the fifth floor, I was disconcerted to see the same movement multiplied all around me. For a moment I couldn't tell which was the real person among all the likenesses. I wasn't even sure which one of me was real.

The confusion must have shown on my face because she smiled.

"It's even more unpleasant when you ride alone. I avoid this elevator when I'm not with someone else. I prefer the stairs, even though I'm in no shape to climb them. I'm all out of breath after seventy-two steps. But that's how it is with smokers. You don't smoke?"

"No."

"Of course. A police inspector has to be in excellent shape."

"Most of my colleagues smoke. Some are even chain-smokers."

"Then how do they handle stairs?"

"They use elevators whenever possible. Not even psychedelic ones put them off."

She opened her mouth to reply, but there was no time. The elevator stopped smoothly and the door opened at my back almost without a sound. I hesitated a moment and then stepped out backwards. Had I tried to turn around in the cramped quarters, we might easily have collided again.

She came out after me and gestured toward her right. "This way."

Before following, I glanced the other way. The elevator was in the middle of the corridor. Two doors faced each other at the far end. The opposite side was the same. The floor was covered with thick dark-red carpeting and each wall had four red drawings on a white background at regular intervals; at a fleeting glance they did not seem to show anything specific.

Miss Aksentijević stopped at the left-hand door. There was a peephole between two plaques. The upper one was small and plastic and bore the number 19, and the lower one was large and made of metal and had nothing written on it because there was no need. The shape of the plaque was sufficiently articulate. Would anyone but a writer have chosen the trademark of a stylized goose quill dipped in an ink pot?

It took a while for Miss Aksentijević to dig a set of keys out of her briefcase. It consisted of at least fifteen keys of various shapes and sizes. And then a full minute passed before she found the one she was looking for.

"Here it is," she said contritely, handing it to me. The set jingled under the key. "See for yourself."

I slid the key into the lock. It entered about halfway. I pushed harder but it would go no further. I tried to turn it left and right, also with no result. I took it out and inspected it. It seemed all right to me.

"Are you sure it's the right one?" I asked.

"Absolutely. I always remember where I keep each key. It's seventh from the end."

I looked at the key ring that held the set together.

"From which end?"

"From the left," replied Miss Aksentijević self-confidently.

I turned the ring over in my hand. What had been on the left was now on the right. I waited for her to say something, but she remained silent.

"Would you mind if I tried a few more keys?"

"Go ahead, but I'm certain. . . ."

She didn't finish her sentence because we were plunged into darkness a second time. It was darker than in the entrance hall. Down below a quantity of light from the street poured in through the glass door. Even though the window at this end of the corridor was large, it looked onto an unlighted area and was not much use.

Both of us might have reached for the nearby switch on the wall, but after the embarrassment we'd experienced five floors below, we stood stock-still, each waiting for the other to turn on the light. One of us would have done it eventually had something not snapped at our backs. Then a deep, menacing growl filled the corridor.

2

I TURNED AROUND AT once. I felt Miss Aksentijević brush against me, squeezing as far as she could into the narrow space between my back and the door. She mumbled something unintelligible and grabbed my left bicep.

It was not complete blackness in front of me. The lights were not on in the neighbor's apartment, but a weak glow came through the open door and outlined the vertical rectangle. It did not seem artificial which meant it probably came from a window somewhere in the background. The center of the dimly illuminated door frame was filled by the outline of a tall, thin figure standing on the threshold. The growling came from near its legs.

"I would advise you to keep still," rasped a male voice. "Even the slightest movement will trigger Adam and he is a dangerous dog."

Miss Aksentijević's grip tightened even further. She repeated something in a low voice but I still could not understand.

"There is no reason for Adam to attack us," I said, trying to appear unruffled. "Our intentions are not at all dishonest."

"Except that you're trying to enter a stranger's apartment."

"It's not a stranger's. . . ." objected Miss Aksentijević, but I interrupted her.

"There's a good reason for it."

"No doubt. That's what all burglars think."

"How dare you. . . ." came a raised voice behind my back. This time the sentence was left unfinished because the growling increased.

I placed my hand over hers on my arm.

"We can easily prove to you that we're not burglars."

"Soon you'll get a chance to prove it to the police."

He raised his half-clenched right hand to his head.

"You don't have to call the police," I said. "The police are already here. I am an inspector."

The cellphone remained a little longer by his ear. Then he lowered his hand, and we fell into a brief silence.

"Show me some identification. But don't make any sudden movement. Whatever you try, you won't be faster than Adam. Even in the dark."

"Why don't you turn on the light? It will make it easier for all of us."

"Easier for you, sure. Adam and I don't mind it like this. So?"

I disengaged my hand from Miss Aksentijević's fingers, reached into my jacket pocket and took out my badge. I extended it forward slowly. I was certain that the growling would rise again, but the dog remained silent.

"Shall we turn on the light anyway?" I proposed once more, when he had taken the badge. "You'll see better."

A quarter of a minute passed before he replied. "You can see with your fingers too and you don't need light to do it, Inspector Lukić."

The dark outline moved slightly to the left, the switch sounded and the lights went on in the corridor. Miss Aksentijević quickly let go of my arm and put her hand over her mouth, but a sigh of relief slipped out nonetheless.

The tall man with the large German shepherd in front of him seemed even more elongated by his long black smoking jacket. His wide-collared shirt and the scarf around his neck were also black. Had he been dressed more cheerfully, I would not have thought he was over forty-five, but in this get-up he seemed ten years older. His thick salt-and-pepper hair was pulled back in a ponytail. His face was thin with regular features and a high forehead.

The most remarkable thing about him was his eyes. The jade-green color seemed to shine from within. Never before had I seen such eyes in a man. But in spite of their brilliance, his eyes were empty, unfocused, looking somewhere off to the side of us.

"Sorry," said the man, raising the badge in the direction of my voice. "I had no way of knowing that you were an inspector."

"Of course you didn't," I replied, taking the badge. "Its not easy to recognize a police inspector even when . . . it's not dark."

I stopped myself at the last moment from saying—". . . .even when you can see." I had no experience of talking with the blind.

"Is something wrong with Miss Jakovljević?"

"We hope everything is all right."

"If it were, would you be here so late with her agent?"

"How do you know. . . .?" said Miss Aksentijević without finishing the question. She was no longer standing behind my back, but was still next to the door, her eyes mostly fixed on the dog.

"I don't forget a voice. I heard you when you came before."

"Do you eavesdrop on your neighbors?"

"I don't have to eavesdrop. I have acute hearing and those who can see usually talk needlessly loud."

I got the better of Miss Aksentijević, who had already opened her mouth to say something. "Voices do not reveal professions. How did you know she was an agent?"

"Voices reveal more than you imagine, Inspector. If you know how to listen, of course. But I didn't reach this conclusion from her voice. I found out from Miss Jakovljević. She mentioned you."

"Really?" Miss Aksentijević's voice was a mixture of surprise and displeasure.

"If you recognized the voice of Miss Jakovljević's agent, why did you think it was a break-in?" I asked.

"I had my reasons."

"What reasons?" asked Miss Aksentijević sharply.

The jade eyes turned toward her. Not past her but straight in her face as though he could see her. And even more—see through her. The man, however, did not reply. Tense silence surrounded us.

"Forget about that now," I said, breaking it finally. "When did you last. . . ."—even though I did not say "see," the pause gave me away—". . . .hear Miss Jakovljević?"

His head turned toward me and his eyes turned blind again. "The day before yesterday. She dropped by to see me on Wednesday evening. We had a little chat. I didn't hear her after that."

"Do you mean, she didn't drop by anymore?"

"Not only that. The door to her apartment hasn't opened since then."

"That's what I told you. . . ." interjected Miss Aksentijević. She was no longer bristling, as though suddenly changing her opinion of the blind neighbor's acute hearing.

"You might have missed it. It could have happened when you were asleep."

"I did not miss it. I sleep very lightly. Miss Jakovljević is still inside."

"Oh, please do something." Miss Aksentijević's voice had regained the hysterical tone it had had when she called the police a little over half an hour ago. I had had to take great pains to calm her down.

"Thank you for your help, Mister. . . ."

"Teodosijević. Branislav Teodosijević."

He held out his hand, but before I had a chance to shake it, we were plunged into darkness again. I stood there bewildered, uncertain what to do. He could not know that the lights had gone out, and if I tried to turn them on, the dog might attack me. He had been good-natured enough while there was light, but my ears were still ringing from his growling in the dark.

Just as I concluded that the best thing would be to propose that Mr. Teodosijević push the light button by his door again, he did it without any prompting. As though replying to my puzzled look, which he could not see, he said tersely:

"Three minutes and forty seconds."

I thought of asking him whether the blind had an acute sense of time too, but did not have the chance because he had extended his hand again. The tiny hand of Miss Aksentijević gave a stronger handshake than that of Mr. Teodosijević, although his was almost twice the size.

"Inspector Dejan Lukić. Nice to meet you. Please forgive us for disturbing you."

"Nice to make your acquaintance, even under such circumstances, Inspector Lukić. I'm sorry if Adam frightened you."

"He didn't," I lied. "It's the same with policemen as it is with doctors. People usually meet them when there's something wrong. I hope this will turn out to be harmless."

He seemed to search briefly for the proper reply and then said, "If I can be of any assistance. . . ."

"Thank you, but there's no need." I paused briefly, then added, "For now."

"Then I'll be seeing you."

He turned, let the dog go in before him and then returned inside. Once the door had closed with a click, my eyes were drawn to the brass plaque under the peephole. It was also without an inscription: in the form of a painter's palette.

3

Miss Aksentijević shook her head and sighed, then turned toward Miss Jakovljević's door.

"Please hurry," she said and, still upset, motioned with her chin to the keys in my hand. "Something must have happened to Jelena . . . Miss Jakovljević."

Before I started examining the keys, I thought of a way to prevent the problem that awaited us in about two minutes.

"When the lights go off again, please turn them back on."

A smile briefly softened the anxious expression on her face. She nodded.

Of the sixteen keys, five fit the type of lock. I tried them one after the other. Three would not go in at all and only two got in halfway through the hole.

Even though I knew it wouldn't work, I tried to turn them.

"None of them is the right one," I said.

She took the set of keys briskly from my hand and selected the last key I had tried.

"Of course it is," she said angrily. "This is the key to Jelena's apartment."

"Maybe it is. But it does not open the lock."

"It clearly does not open the lock. Because it is locked from the inside and the key is in the lock. It doesn't take a highly insightful inspector to draw that conclusion."

Now I was the one to sigh.

"Highly insightful inspectors avoid drawing rash conclusions."

"Rash? This couldn't be more obvious."

"In my line of work you quickly learn that what is obvious does not always have to be right."

Impatience joined the anger on her face.

"Instead of having this pointless discussion, you should break into the apartment as soon as possible. That's why I called you, after all."

"Then you should have called a burglar. Although he would have had a hard time saving you from Adam. The police don't break into apartments without a strong reason. We only do so once we establish that it really is necessary."

"Isn't it here?"

"Not necessarily. Let's assume that you are right and it is locked from the inside. That still does not mean that something is wrong with Miss Jakovljević. She simply might not want to open the door."

She looked at me in disbelief. But before she had time to answer, we were surrounded by darkness. From the thud that was heard I would say she hit the switch with her fist.

"Hogwash!" she almost shouted. "Of course

she would open the door for me. Why in the world wouldn't she?"

"Maybe she's writing and does not want to be disturbed. Writers are often like that."

"How do you know what writers are like?" She did not even try to hide the disparagement in her voice. "I'm certain you don't meet them very often in your line of work."

"We meet all kinds of people. But there are other ways to get to know writers. By studying literature, for example."

She eyed me suspiciously.

"You studied literature?"

"You would be surprised to learn all the things police inspectors have studied. I know of one, for example, who studied paleolinguistics. The science of the languages of the oldest human communities."

"I know about paleolinguistics," she said, offended. "But what's the use of literature in police work?"

"To help an inspector properly handle a case like this, you might say."

She stared at me for a few moments. Her eyes showed that she was hunting feverishly for a comeback.

"Well, Inspector," she said at last, "here is proof that you are not handling it very well."

She reached inside her purse again, rummaged around a bit and then took out a cellphone. She pressed several buttons nervously with her thumb. She did not bring it to her ear but held it in her hand.

"Listen," she said tersely and put her ear to the door. I did the same. A moment later, from inside the apartment there came the sound of a soft chirp that repeated itself at regular intervals. She did not hang up until the eighth ring, as though wanting to be completely sure I had heard. Then she returned her phone to her purse and looked at me in triumph.

"Would a writer who doesn't want to be disturbed

leave their cellphone on? And the landline is also on, I checked."

"Probably not," I agreed. "But this opens up a new possibility."

"What new possibility?"

"A writer who did not want to be disturbed would not have a telephone with them."

She wrinkled her brow. "I don't understand you."

"Miss Jakovljević left her cell at home because she did not need it wherever she withdrew to write in peace."

"But she didn't go anywhere. She's in the apartment. You heard Mr. Teodosijević."

I lowered my voice almost to a whisper. "I got the impression that you don't trust him."

She glanced briefly at the neighboring door. If she had thought of replying to this, the lights going off again prevented her. This time the sound of the switch was barely heard.

"In any case, the door is locked from the inside," she said, also softly.

"What if it isn't?" I replied in a normal voice.

She looked at me briefly once again, without a word. "It is. Didn't you just establish that yourself? The key won't go into the lock."

"That might be because it's the wrong one."

"It always worked before. How can it not work now?"

"The lock has been changed."

She started to shake her head. Her mouth was half-open, as though she wanted to say something, but some time passed before she finally spoke.

"Who changed the lock?"

"The only one who has a right to: the owner of the apartment. I assume that is Miss Jakovljević."

Another pause ensued.

"Why would she change it?"

"Because she doesn't want anyone to enter her apartment when she's not there."

"But that's ridiculous. I'm her agent."

"Writers might have secrets even from their agents."

"They didn't teach you much about the relationship between writers and agents in your literature studies."

"I don't recall they ever mentioned agents."

She bit her lower lip. The bunch of keys jingled in her hand. I thought she would explode for sure, but she kept her temper in check.

"Does that mean you won't do anything?" Her voice was trembling.

"I'll do the first thing that a police inspector has to do before he does anything else. I will try to establish the facts. Are we unable to unlock the door because it is locked from the inside or because the lock has been changed? And to establish that, I will need the help of a burglar."

"Burglar?"

"Former. Inspector Tanasije Vesić was a virtuoso burglar before he became a policeman."

"Do the police employ burglars, even former ones?"

"Only if they've never been apprehended and sentenced. The police did everything they could to pin something on him. He drove them crazy with his exploits, but all their efforts were in vain."

"Even so, he was a thief and there's certainly no room for thieves in the police force."

"He never stole anything."

She looked at me, puzzled.

"What kind of burglar doesn't steal? So why did he break into places?"

"He couldn't resist the challenge. He chose only the most difficult and famous locks. Not a single one remained unpicked. He wasn't at all interested in what was behind the door. He would just move something inside as proof that he had opened it. That was his trademark."

"Oddball. But what's the good of having him join the police?"

"Enormous benefit. It's always better to use a gentler procedure than brute force. Like here, for example." I nodded my head toward the door in front of us. "In particular because he'll know in a moment whether the key is in the lock. And if it is, there will be no need to break down the door. Which is quite unpleasant, by the way. He will open it quite elegantly."

"So have him come at once."

"Not all policemen are on call around the clock, Miss Aksentijević. I don't think Inspector Vesić is on duty tonight. I'll have to check."

"But this is urgent. Something might have happened to Jelena!"

"I don't want to seem callous, but if something truly has happened to her, I'm afraid we are way too late to be of any assistance. You should have called us a lot earlier. Please excuse me for a moment."

I removed my cellphone from the inside pocket of my jacket and moved down the corridor.

"But how could I. . . ." Miss Aksentijević started to say behind my back. She was interrupted by the darkness once again. I took another two steps, stopped and waited for her to turn the lights back on. But this did not happen. I thought with a sigh that I would have to search for the switch on the wall, then remembered that this was not necessary. I pushed one of the buttons on the phone at random. The screen lit up and I looked for Vesić's number on my contact list.

Less than a minute later I headed back towards Miss Aksentijević. My eyes were already adjusted to the darkness so I was able to see her plump outline against the weakly lighted window at the end of the corridor.

"I'd say we've had enough of playing hide-and-seek," I said, making peace.

About ten seconds passed before the lights finally went back on. As I walked toward her, reproving eyes shot daggers at me, but she did not speak.

"We're in luck. Inspector Vesić will be here in about forty minutes."

"Forty minutes?"

"He lives way over on the other side of town. Even if he used his flashing light, he would only get here at most six or seven minutes earlier."

"What'll we do here for so long?"

"We don't have to stay here. In the end we would alarm the entire building by constantly turning on the lights, and I'm sure you wouldn't like us to remain in darkness all that time."

"Would you like it?"

"I'm used to waiting in even worse conditions than darkness, when it can't be helped. But that's not the case here."

"So, where shall we go? It's not much better down in the foyer where I was waiting for you to arrive and it's really windy outside."

"On my way here I noticed a café-bar not far away, just around the corner. We could wait for Inspector Vesić there." I paused, then added: "We can go by car, if you like, although it's quite close."

She turned indecisively towards the door to Miss Jakovljević's apartment and then to the one across from it.

"Let's walk," she said at last. "My nerves are shattered enough already, so the wind can't do me much more harm."

A smile flickered at the corners of her mouth.

This time I got into the elevator first and turned to face her. As the doors began to close, I noticed something that I had missed on the ride up. I had probably been confused by the three mirrors around me and the one on the ceiling, so that standing with my back to the doors, I had not seen in the reflection that they were lined with mirrors too. I quickly lowered my eyes to the floor. Covered with the same red carpeting that lined the corridor, it was an island of reality surrounded by infinite illusion. I left the elevator slightly dizzy.

The wind dispelled it as soon as we exited the building. Miss Aksentijević bowed her head and drew the poncho around her. Whirlwinds played about our feet. After passing through the conical glow of the streetlight next to the linden, I looked briefly at the building. Seven steps later I stopped and looked at it again.

I did not reply to Miss Aksentijević's questioning expression, but continued toward the café-bar. There was no need to upset her, particularly since I was not even certain myself. Perhaps I had not paid close enough attention, but I would have said that, on my way there, the row of four windows on the upper left-hand corner had not been lit. Now a weak glow emanated from the last window but one.

4

Not until we were already quite close did I realize that it was not a café-bar but a teashop. It was located slightly below street level. A wrought iron fence extended in front of two arched windows. Three tall steps led down to the entrance where a metal sign in the shape of a teapot hung above the door.

Herbal fragrances and semidarkness welcomed us inside. Banquettes covered in dark-brown leather lined three walls. Eight little round tables on spindle legs were placed in front of them, each with two round chairs. Subdued lighting came from behind screens along the cornices. Only the fourth wall with the bar facing the entrance was better lit.

The dozen customers were sitting mostly on the banquettes. I could only make out their shapes in the darkness. The melody of a stringed instrument competed with the din of voices. If the steam from the tea cups had been more abundant, I might have thought I'd stepped into an old-fashioned opium den.

Only two tables were free. I gestured toward the one in the far right-hand corner next to the window and Miss Aksentijević nodded, so we headed in that direction. She took off her poncho, settled on the banquette and placed it next to her, while I sat on the right-hand chair.

A large woman broke off her conversation with the man behind the bar and came briskly toward us. She had short, thick hair that resembled a yellow brush. Her brown dress, the same shade as the leather banquettes, was sleeveless, emphasizing her muscular arms. There was an older look about her, although she was probably still in her thirties. If she'd played sports in her younger days, most likely it had been the shot put or hammer throw.

When she reached our table, I noted a brass pin on her lapel in the same shape as the sign above the entrance.

"May I help you?" she said in an aptly deep voice. Her lips turned up briefly in the hint of a smile.

"Tea, please," said Miss Aksentijević.

The woman narrowed her eyes.

"Do you ever go to bookstores?" Her voice was effortlessly reproving.

Miss Aksentijević eyed her suspiciously.

"Sometimes," she replied warily.

"What would happen if you went into one and said, 'A book, please'?"

"This is not a bookstore," said Miss Aksentijević after another brief hesitation.

"No, it isn't. But it isn't an ordinary teashop either. You can't order just any old tea here."

"Then what should I order? You don't have a menu."

She gestured toward the little table that was empty except for a green ceramic teapot figurine. Dried flowers in a variety of colors sprouted out of the holes in the lid.

"We don't have one because it's not necessary. We concoct teas tailor-made to each customer."

"How do you determine the fit?"

"The customers usually help. They tell us what ails them."

"Then this is a doctor's office, not a teashop."

"Many of our teas are indeed medicinal."

"Well, there's nothing ailing me."

"Everyone's got something ailing them, even if they're not aware of it."

Miss Aksentijević's eyes began to flash.

"The wind bothers her," I interjected. "Do you have any tea that might help?"

As she answered me, the teashop proprietor kept her eyes on Miss Aksentijević.

"We have tea for every ailment."

"Wonderful," I said. "Then perhaps you could find something fit for me."

"What's ailing you?"

"Illusions."

The shot putter's head finally turned toward me. She looked at me in silence for a few moments.

"I'll see what I can do for you," she said at last.

She turned and headed back to the bar. Even though she was wearing soft-soled shoes, her steps echoed above all the other noises.

"I don't like teashops," said Miss Aksentijević dejectedly after the proprietor had left the table.

"We'll certainly be more comfortable here than waiting in the corridor. Besides, we won't be here for long." I paused and smiled. "And tea against the wind might do some good."

She looked at me dubiously.

"How can a police inspector be so gullible?"

"Don't underestimate tea. I've tried some that work wonders."

"They get rid of illusions?" she asked mockingly.

"That too."

"What are these illusions that are troubling you?"

"Police work is full of illusions, ambiguities. It's not all that easy to figure them out. What happened tonight is no exception."

"Is that so?" Her voice turned serious.

"Yes. I have several dilemmas. Perhaps you could help me get rid of one even without the tea."

"Which one?"

"When was the last time you saw or heard Miss Jakovljević?"

"The day before yesterday. We spoke on the phone Wednesday evening. I already told you that during our first conversation. Don't you remember?"

"How could I have forgotten? Barely an hour has passed since then. But people are usually upset when they phone the police, particularly if they don't know the person they're talking to, and so something important slips their mind. You didn't say whether you called her or she called you."

"I called her. Why is that important?"

"I'm trying to establish something. On her cell or home phone?"

"Home phone. She was at home, if that's what you want to find out."

"That doesn't necessarily mean that she was. She could have set it up so any call to her home phone when she wasn't there was transferred to her cellphone."

"But her cell is at home. You heard it."

"She might not have only one. The transfer can be heard by a change in the ring tone. Did you notice that by any chance?"

"No, I didn't," she said without a second thought. "You're barking up the wrong tree. Jelena certainly answered the phone from her apartment. That's the only place she could have been."

I looked at her inquiringly. "Doesn't she ever go out?"

"Rarely when she's writing. And when she's under a deadline, like now, she doesn't budge."

"Sounds almost like a hermit."

"Not almost—absolutely. It's only students of literature who imagine that writers lead a leisurely and exciting life. In reality, it's lonely and full of hard work."

"But not even hermits can do without the outside world. They have to get hold of food, for example. How does Miss Jakovljević get food supplies if she doesn't go out?"

"I brought her fresh food every other day."

"Literature studies deplorably underestimate the invaluable contribution of literary agents."

Miss Aksentijević pressed her lips together, but before she could say anything, heavy steps echoed once again. The teashop proprietor was carrying an oval tray with two steaming bell-shaped cups. She came up to us and set first the dark-green one in front of Miss Aksentijević and then the white one in front of me. The tea in my cup was reddish and in hers it was blue.

"I hope it has an effect," she said to me. "It isn't easy to deal with illusions."

"You're telling me."

She smiled as she turned to Miss Aksentijević.

"You certainly won't be bothered by wind anymore."

She turned at once and headed towards the bar so Miss Aksentijević was again unable to bluster in reply. All she did was push the cup angrily away from her, spilling some into the saucer.

"Won't you even try it?" I asked.

"You're to blame for everything," she said almost in a growl. "First you brought me to this awful place and then you even mentioned the wind to that . . . that . . . woman. See what it's come to."

"The only thing you complained about was the wind. If I were better acquainted with literary agents, I would know what else troubles you."

"Whatever it is that troubles us, tea certainly can't get rid of it."

"To be sure. That was just a promotional wisecrack. Try the tea, you might like it."

"How could I like something that is such a revolting blue? And in a green cup?"

"Would you rather have red tea in a white cup?" I asked, pushing my cup toward her.

She shook her head. "No, thanks. The life of a literary agent isn't easy, but at least we aren't troubled by illusions."

"Yes, illusions would certainly get in the way of grocery shopping. While we're on the subject, when was the last time you took them to Miss Jakovljević?"

She looked at me darkly for several moments before she replied.

"Wednesday about noon. I brought them today too at the same time. I buzzed the intercom but she didn't answer. At first I thought she was still sleeping. That would not be unusual. She stays in bed later when she has spent the night before working. I toyed with the idea of going up to her apartment and leaving the food, but I would have wakened her up that way."

"Didn't the buzzing of the intercom wake her?"

"She turns it off before she goes to bed. The telephones too."

"The telephones are not turned off."

"The intercom might not be either. I couldn't establish that by myself. If I had, I would have called you earlier."

"What did you do when she didn't answer the intercom?"

"I went home to put the food in the refrigerator. I called her by phone around two."

"The house number?"

"First the house number, then the cell."

"Did you think she'd gone out somewhere?"

"What else could I think?"

"Even though she was up against a deadline?"

Miss Aksentijević sighed deeply.

"We all have our breaking points. Jelena has had no trouble coping with deadlines until now, she's a real professional. But she's only made of flesh and blood."

"How do you think she would react if she reached that point?"

She shrugged her shoulders. "I don't know. At first I assumed she'd gone out for a walk. That would do the least harm. If she were to recharge her batteries like that, it would be easier to spend another night working."

"Wouldn't she have told you she was going out? Or at least answered your call?"

"Maybe she didn't feel like having to explain me. She knew that I would scold her."

"You would have scolded her?"

"That's my job. Do you know what some writers call agents? Especially the lazy writers."

"What?"

"Slave drivers."

I smiled. "I can imagine you with a whip in your hand."

"If only I could use that whip to drive lazy policemen," she replied, smiling in return.

"When did you suspect that she hadn't gone for a walk?"

"After seven. It was already getting dark. If she really had gone for a walk, it was high time she returned. The sooner she started writing the better. But she still didn't answer either phone. I consoled myself for a while, thinking that she was engrossed in her work and that was why, but I finally realized that she couldn't be ignoring all my calls. Why would she keep the phones on if she didn't want to answer them? And so, just before nine, I went to Jelena's apartment again. You know the rest."

I got to thinking.

"You didn't call her yesterday?"

"There was no reason. I didn't want to disturb her."

I indicated the white cup that was just barely steaming.

"Are you sure you won't?"

She shook her head.

I drew the saucer to me, raised the cup and took a tentative sip. The tea had a bitter and sour taste but I was unable to recognize a single ingredient. I found it pleasant. In two sips I drank almost half the cup.

Miss Aksentijević raised her left arm and looked at her watch.

"Just a bit longer," I said. "When is that deadline that's giving Miss Jakovljević such a headache?"

"Monday. My headache is worse than hers."

"Why is that?"

"It seems you really know very little about literary agents."

"You are the first one I've ever met."

"If the manuscript of the novel is not ready by Monday, I will be the one to face the publisher, not Jelena. That's an agent's primary duty, not buying groceries."

"Do you expect problems with the publisher?"

"Problems? I'll be crucified, that's what will happen to me. He'll ask to break the contract."

"Is that so terrible?"

She looked at me like a teacher would a backward pupil.

"Is it terrible? Not at all. We'll only have to return the large advance and then pay even larger damages."

"Both of you? Isn't the contract only in the writer's name?"

"It is. But there is also a contract between the writer and their agent. I get fifteen percent of the author's earnings, but I have to pay that same amount in case of non-fulfillment of the contract."

"That's rather unpleasant."

"I had to be ready to make concessions to become Jelena's agent. She's a very lucrative author. There aren't many like that, so my colleagues fought for her tooth and nail."

"Fifteen percent is still less than eighty-five percent," I noted with a grin.

"Little consolation. Do you have the slightest idea how much that fifteen percent advance and damages amount to?"

I shook my head. "No, I don't. I thought there wasn't much money in literature. At least that's the impression you get from lit classes."

She sighed once more, then waved her hand dismissively.

"Forget literature classes. That's not the real world. Jelena can certainly afford it, but I simply don't have that much money. I might even end up in prison."

"There's another similarity in our jobs," I said with a smile.

She looked at me, puzzled. A moment later, when she realized what I was referring to, she opened her mouth to retort, but I was faster.

"Can't the deadline be extended?"

She stared at me crossly a few moments before answering.

"We've already extended it twice. He won't agree to a third extension."

"Why did you let such a dangerous contract be signed when you knew that Miss Jakovljević is unreliable when it comes to deadlines?"

"She's not unreliable," said Miss Aksentijević, almost shouting. Two or three customers turned their heads towards us briefly from neighboring banquettes. Once the heads had turned the other way, she continued in a voice that was softer than necessary. "She never was before. Until this book. She would finish the books on time. Even considerably before the deadline."

"Why is the new book an exception?"

She shrugged her shoulders. "I don't know. From the very beginning everything about it has been somehow . . . unusual."

"Unusual?"

"Yes. To begin with, Jelena would always give me the manuscript to read while she was still writing it. She wouldn't let anyone else read it. This time, however, she won't let me either. Without any explanation. The only thing I know about the book is its title." She stopped briefly, as though thinking twice, then added: "*Find Me*."

"Interesting title."

"Have you read anything by Jelena? Or are you like all those who study literature and have a high-handed prejudice against detective novels?"

"The first thing you learn when studying literature is to get rid of all your prejudices, particularly the high-handed ones, and then that there is only one essential division in fiction: good and bad. Many great works could be classified in the detective genre. That by no means stands in the way of their being great."

"But you haven't read any of Jelena's books?"

"There are a lot of books I haven't read. Luckily, it's easy to atone for such a sin. I will certainly read one of Miss Jakovljević's books."

"What a surprise it would be if you liked it."

"Why a surprise?"

"Because Jelena has recently started to lose faith in what she writes, even though it has made her famous. And rich. It's as though she's had enough of detective novels."

There was no time to reply to this because my cellphone started ringing in the inside pocket of my jacket. I took it out, told my colleague Vesić that we were on our way, then stood up.

Miss Aksentijević started to rummage through her

briefcase, looking for her wallet, but I gently took hold of her arm.

"Allow me. You might be facing bankruptcy, and every cent will be dear."

She hesitated briefly over what to say to this, then nodded her head with a grin.

"Thank you."

She put on her poncho and I quickly finished my tea. Then I went up to the bar, put a bill in front of the teashop proprietor and motioned her with my hand to keep the change. The response to this was also a smile. As before, it did not seem to suit the stern face.

"Might I ask you something?" I said.

"Inspector, isn't it?" she replied tersely.

"Is it that obvious?"

"No. You look more like someone whose field is literature."

"How did you guess?"

"By the way you drink tea."

"I had no idea you could tell someone's profession from that."

"And not only their profession, if you have a practiced eye."

"Would you recognize a writer too?"

"Artists are the easiest to recognize. They are my most frequent customers." Her gaze swept over the people in the semidarkness. "There you have three musicians, two painters, a sculptor and a writer."

I took a look at the banquettes along the walls, but was not even certain who was holding a teacup just then.

"Amazing," I said.

She bowed briefly. "Which writer are you interested in?"

"Miss Jelena Jakovljević. Does she ever come here?"

"Has something happened to her?" she asked in return.

"Everything's all right. I'm interested in her as a reader, not as a policeman. I love her detective novels."

"Really? Which one is your favorite?"

Her piercing glance seemed to plunge into my blinking eyes. The seconds drew out, hopelessly slow, which is what happens when you get caught in a lie.

When I finally answered: "*Find Me*"—I had the impression that someone else had said it.

Now it was her turn to blink. Then she nodded her head towards the entrance to the teashop.

"Your girlfriend's losing patience," she said in a low voice. "Come back another time when you don't have company."

5

As we drew near to the building, I took a good look at the façade. Fewer of the windows were now alight. All four on the upper left-hand corner were dark. There was no fear that Miss Aksentijević would follow my eyes as her head was bowed and seemed to protrude from a teepee.

Inspector Vesić was waiting for us in front of the entrance. Miss Aksentijević looked at him in predictable disbelief. Nothing about him reflected the conventional idea of a police inspector. And if there is a notion about the appearance of famous retired burglars, he would have had trouble fitting that too.

He looked like a polished businessman: graying hair, rather small stature, stout, with ruddy cheeks, round wire-framed glasses, a thin mustache above his upper lip, dressed in an elegant black suit with a dark-red bow tie and a hat. He was carrying an oversized briefcase with as many as three security locks.

He took off his hat and bowed as we approached.

"My respects, madam. Good evening, esteemed colleague."

"Miss," I said, correcting him. "Miss Ljubica Aksentijević, literary agent."

"Nice to meet you," she said. The smile softened her puzzled expression.

He took her extended hand but not to shake it. He bent over, brought it to his lips and kissed it lightly.

"Literary agent? How very nice to make your acquaintance. I might be in need of your services."

"Do you write?"

"Now and then. Lyric poetry."

"Lyric poetry?" Miss Aksentijević made no attempt to hide her disappointment. "I'm afraid there's absolutely no demand on the market for any kind of poetry right now. But if you had something along the lines of . . . a memoir. . . ."

Silence fell momentarily. Inspector Vesić threw me a quizzical look and I looked at Miss Aksentijević, also quizzically.

"The life of a police inspector," she hastened to add, rescuing us all from the awkward situation, "must be full of excitement. Detective stories are quite widely read. Both fictitious and real."

"Unfortunately, there's nothing exciting about my work. It's almost the same as a locksmith's. Nothing like a detective story." He paused a moment and then gestured toward me. "But if you're interested in really sensational detective stories that are also true, you have Inspector Lukić here."

"Is that so?" said Miss Aksentijević, turning toward me inquisitively.

"Yes," continued Inspector Vesić, "some of his cases outdo any and all fiction."

I gave him the same look he had just given me.

"My colleague is just joking," I said. "Look, this case is among the most exciting I've covered. And you tell me—who else would want to read about it?"

There was no reply. Her eyes went back and forth

from Inspector Vesić to me. Then she stuck her hand in her briefcase and took out some business cards. She handed one to each of us.

"Don't hesitate to call me if you decide to write something of your memoirs. I would be delighted to represent you as your literary agent."

"Perhaps this is not the most suitable moment for a business conversation," I said, taking the card and putting it in my pocket. "You're in a hurry, if I'm not mistaken."

"Of course," replied Miss Aksentijević with a ring of discomfort and then reached into her briefcase again for the set of keys.

As we entered the foyer, Miss Aksentijević and I hesitated. Inspector Vesić hesitated too and looked at us in bewilderment.

"After you," I said at last, nodding toward the button.

She smiled, then pushed it. We continued towards the elevator, leaving Inspector Vesić without an explanation.

All three of us watched in silence as the red numbers slowly changed on the small display above the door while the elevator descended. The fact that it came from the fifth floor did not have to mean anything special. No doubt somebody lived in the two apartments at the other end of the corridor.

It was not until the doors opened that I realized we had a problem. Had Inspector Vesić been slimmer we could all have fitted in, but as things stood it would be very tight. Who ever thought of putting such a cramped elevator in a five-story building? Particularly since there was plenty of room.

Miss Aksentijević was the first to enter. She stood with her back against the mirror on the far wall of the elevator. When Inspector Vesić went in after her and did not turn around toward the doors, she looked at me anxiously over his shoulder, realizing what would happen if I tried to enter too.

"I'll take the stairs," I said, sparing her grief.

She replied with a fleeting smile and Inspector Vesić, who was misled by the mirrors, turned around to see what was the matter. He had no chance to ask anything because the doors started to close that very moment. Miss Aksentijević clearly had not hesitated to push the button for the fifth floor.

A wide stairwell wound around the elevator with a brass handrail extending along either side. With my very first step I began counting the stairs. I had tried for a long time to get rid of this habit. I would switch my thoughts to something else, try to mix up the numbers, but nothing worked. Part of my consciousness always continued to count undisturbed. I finally gave up when it turned out that there was a benefit to this shortcoming. In my line of work it's sometimes useful to know the exact number of stairs.

Just as I was headed for the fourth floor, the lights went out. The stairwell had no windows so I was plunged into pitch blackness. I swore under my breath. Widening the elevator would certainly be too expensive now, but it wouldn't cost a thing to adjust the lighting timer to a longer interval. Three minutes and forty seconds were insufficient under ordinary circumstances, let alone in an emergency.

I could have continued since I knew there were six more steps to the landing, but I had no reason to rush. Miss Aksentijević would be pushing the button any moment. She was probably aware of my predicament. I felt for the handrail on the left and drew close to it. The seconds continued to draw out, however, and I was still stranded in the dark.

I had already decided to continue when I was suddenly filled with foreboding. Nothing external caused it. Nothing disturbed the impenetrable darkness, nor did any sound reach my ears. Nevertheless, I had the distinct impression that I was no longer alone on that short stretch of stairwell. Someone seemed to be rushing down the handrail on the other side.

I was uneasy, wanting to do something, but nothing suitable came to mind. At first I thought of stretching out my arms, but I might have lost my balance that way. And I didn't exactly feel like reaching for someone I knew nothing about. Would it be better to speak? While I was figuring out what to say, the lights came back on.

There was no one to be seen. I hesitated just a moment and then rushed down the stairs, reaching the ground floor in no time at all. But it was empty. I thought of going out in front of the building, but dropped the idea. If someone had opened the door, I would have heard it in the total silence. I looked around the foyer, wondering where else someone could have gone. The two glass doors leading to the apartments were closed. If they had been opened I wouldn't have missed that either.

And then something crossed my mind. What if I'd had the wrong impression and someone was going up, not down? It's easy to lose your orientation in the dark. I rushed toward the fifth floor, two steps at a time. I was already quite a ways up when I realized I should have taken the elevator. What if the lights went off again? No, there would be enough time, barely a minute and a half had passed since they had come back on.

Miss Aksentijević and Inspector Vesić were standing in front of the door to Miss Jakovljević's apartment. They stared at me in bewilderment when I burst into the corridor next to the elevator. I glanced briefly the other way and then headed toward them. But I stopped after the second step and turned my head toward the stairwell, peering in that direction a few moments.

Something had finally thrown the counter in me out of kilter. What I had been seeking for so long was clearly a combination of excitement, haste and taking the steps two at a time. I had counted seventy-five and not seventy-two, the number of steps Miss Aksentijević had mentioned. I would have achieved that number too if I had continued my initial climb. From the first floor to the third there were four times nine stairs. There had to be the same number from the third to the fifth floor. Where had I miscounted, adding three nonexistent stairs? I shook my head and then continued down the corridor.

"Was someone chasing you?" asked Miss Aksentijević as I reached them.

"Ghosts," I replied with a smile.

"It took you a long time to climb up for someone being chased by ghosts. I could have got here faster myself, even without the ghosts."

"I would have got here faster if you hadn't hesitated to turn on the lights."

She wrinkled her brow. "I didn't hesitate at all. I pushed the button as soon as the lights went off. Isn't that right, Inspector?"

Inspector Vesić nodded. "That's right. Don't be taken in by the tricks of inspectors who don't stay in shape."

I gave him a hard look and then waved my hand dismissively.

"All right, forget it. Let's get down to business."

Inspector Vesić took off his hat and handed it to me. Then he interlaced his fingers, turned his hands palms outward and straightened his arms. His knuckles cracked. He shook out his hands and thrust his left hand into the inside pocket of his jacket. He pulled out two little round steel rods about fifteen centimeters long and as thin as knitting needles.

Those picks were the only tools he used. He never opened his briefcase, although he always carried it with him when he was on duty. He refused to reveal the contents, causing imaginative stories to be spun. All that was known for sure was its considerable weight. Should conjectures reach his ears, he would merely smile. His reply was that he would open his briefcase when he had to. There had been two or three attempts to open it without his knowledge, but no one had managed to get anywhere with even one of the locks.

Now he placed it on the floor next to him, lifted his pant legs a little and knelt down by the door. He twirled the little picks briefly between his fingers before inserting them into the upper and lower parts of the lock. Just as he started to move them ever so slightly, we were plunged into darkness.

I heard Miss Aksentijević rush over to the switch. It didn't take her long to feel for it on the wall. She was already quite experienced. When the lights came back on, the little picks were no longer in the lock.

"It's locked from the inside," said Inspector Vesić. "The key is in the lock."

"What did I tell you?" said Miss Aksentijević triumphantly, almost in a shout.

"Can you remove it?" I asked, disregarding her interruption.

"I can try," he replied. His calculations were always qualified. He never made promises and always kept them.

He reversed the picks and inserted them into the lock once more. Before getting down to work he closed his eyes. To a casual observer he might have appeared quite motionless. This petrified scene seemed to slow down the passage of time. I glanced at Miss Aksentijević. The little twitches around her mouth indicated her barely contained impatience.

When the lights finally went out again, the sound I heard made me think she had jumped as she headed for the switch. But before she had a chance to push it, Inspector Vesić's sharp voice stopped her.

"Leave them off!"

We remained in the dark. I wondered how he had known, without looking, when the lights had gone off. He must have been able to tell through his lowered eyelids. I had no answer to my other question: why did he prefer to work in the dark?

Now with our sense of sight excluded, time passed even more slowly. All that disturbed the silence was the periodic rustle at my back caused by Miss Aksentijević's fidgeting.

When the key fell to the parquet floor on the other side of the door, a sound that we would otherwise have barely heard, it seemed almost like an explosion. I started and Miss Aksentijević let out a choked "Ah!"

"Shall I unlock it or will you use the key?" asked Inspector Vesić in an even tone.

"We'll use the key," I replied. "Lights, please."

They were back on before I had finished my sentence. Miss Aksentijević started rummaging through her briefcase at the same moment. It was some time before she pulled out the set of keys. She tried to avoid me as she headed for the door, but was stopped by my outstretched hand.

"Allow me."

She stared angrily into my eyes for several moments but did not object. She opened her hand and let me take the keys. Inspector Vesić, who was already on his feet, moved a little away from the door. I handed him back his hat, then approached and started to search by memory for the five keys that fitted that type of lock.

When not even the third one turned out to be right, I was sorry I hadn't accepted his offer to unlock it with the picks. It would certainly have been faster. And then, finally, the fourth key made a full rotation along with a click.

6

I PLACED THE KEYS in the outside pocket of my jacket and then took latex gloves from the inside pocket and put them on. As I started to open the door, Miss Aksentijević drew close to me.

"Please wait here," I said to her, keeping the door closed.

"But I have to go in," she said adamantly. "Jelena. . . ."

"If something is wrong with Miss Jakovljević, you might not want to be inside."

She covered her mouth with her hand. "You think. . . ."

"There is no need for conjecture. I'll find out what has happened soon enough."

"Even so, I want to see. . . ." There was a ring of hysteria in her voice.

I looked at Inspector Vesić. He stepped forward and placed himself between the door and Miss Aksentijević, forcing her to take a step backward.

"Listen to the inspector," he said to her calmly. "Just be patient a little longer."

It seemed she would keep insisting, but nevertheless refrained.

I went inside quickly and closed the door behind me. I was in semidarkness. Faint streetlight filled a window that was four or five meters away. Little could be made out in that weak light. It seemed there was a short hallway in front of me that led to other rooms. There was the outline of a door in the middle on the right. It was ajar.

First I groped around the right-hand wall and felt a wooden surface under my fingers. It was ribbed, not smooth. Narrow vertical spaces separated sections that were about an inch wide. I didn't have to reach up to the hooks at the top to recognize a coat rack. I had one like it at home. Nothing was hanging on it.

I turned to the other side and felt for the switch, then had to squint when the entrance was illuminated by a strong light.

The window that had now turned into a dark oblong was flanked by the multicolored spines of books on shelves, and below it was a round glass table with metal legs and four metal chairs. To my left, next to the entrance, was another door, probably to the bathroom because there were three switches on the outside.

I went straight ahead and then stopped at the door that was ajar and peered inside. The strip of light from the hallway indicated it was a large room. Under the right-hand window was a large wooden desk with a monitor rising in the middle. As I slowly opened the door, the opposite wall entered my field of vision. It was completely lined with books except for the lower middle part taken up by a three-seater upholstered in dark-pink plush.

I entered the room and turned on the lights. This time I did not have to search for the switch. It had to be on the left because the door opened to the right. The light bulb in the yellow ceiling fixture was weaker than the one in the hallway. I turned around slowly. The layout on the right-hand wall was similar to the one facing me. Since it was shorter, a two-seater of the same color was all that interrupted the background of floor to ceiling books.

Bookshelves filled every free space on the wall with windows. The only place where there were no books was under the left-hand window. That space belonged to music: a stereo system and two speakers in the middle with a row of CDs above it and old-fashioned gramophone records below.

A large printer stood on the far right-hand corner of the desk and behind it on a wide board above the radiator was a brass flower pot resembling a pail. A rubber plant with large leaves blocked at least a third of the window. On the opposite end of the desk, a thin goose-necked metal lamp rose straight up from a round base and then arched forward so that its light fell upon the keyboard. Between the monitor and the printer there was just enough room for a white fixed telephone. I did not see the cellphone until I went up to the desk. Small and black, it was inconspicuous next to the equally black keyboard. I put my hand on the lampshade: it was cold.

The fourth wall had the fewest books. Two rows of shelves extended just below the ceiling. The door I had entered was the smaller of the two on that wall. The other was more than twice as big with a folding door that connected the study to the smaller room I had first seen from the entrance. Now I could see a wall of books rising proudly beyond the glass table. The only thing that interrupted it was a closed sliding door on the left. Kitchen cabinets could be seen in the gloom through the glass of the upper half.

Before I went in that direction, I paused to consider the central part of the study's fourth wall between the two differently-sized doors. Eight paintings in four rows completely covered it. They were in thin rust-colored frames with wide light-brown *passe-partout.* The painter had used only two colors on a white background. A preponderance of black only gave way to bright red in the middle. The arabesques did not depict anything recognizable, but they seemed familiar nonetheless. As my eyes passed from one painting to another, it struck me where I had seen them: the drawings in the corridor came from the same brush.

I entered the smaller room through the open folding door and turned around. The space above the door also had eight paintings, but what they depicted was quite clear. If I'd had a chance to see the enlarged covers of Miss Jakovljević's books before going to the teashop, I would have remembered at least one of the titles and would not have been caught off guard when the shot putter asked which novel I liked best.

I barely pushed the sliding door and it moved to the right smoothly and without a sound. It was less than two meters to the opposite wall. Cabinets covered its entire length, narrowing the space even more. Nothing about the kitchen indicated that it had been used. Here, as in the rest of the apartment, everything was neat and tidy. So much so, actually, that it almost seemed like no one lived there.

The windowsill, level with the kitchen workspace, extended into a little counter and next to it was a wooden chair with a back. The only thing on the counter was a book-stand.

I turned on the light next to the door and went inside. On the left, across from the refrigerator and sink, rose a wide, two-sectioned closet. I approached and opened the lower, larger part first. It was filled with women's clothing and there were several pairs of shoes underneath. Then I opened the upper part. It contained neat piles of bed linen. I stood there indecisively for a moment after closing the closet and then opened the refrigerator. It was empty except for a large green apple on the middle shelf.

I turned off the light and closed the sliding door behind me as I left the kitchen. Only one room was left. I turned right into the hallway and stopped in front of the bathroom. The indicators above the three switches were small, so I had to move closer. I pushed the right one and started to open the door, but it was still dark inside. As I looked at the switch, puzzled, the lights flickered and went on. The neon light in my bathroom also has this short delay before it goes on. The all-encompassing whiteness dazzled me; there seemed to be no other color in the bathroom.

To the left were the sink and a towel bar with two towels. There was nothing on the little shelf under the large oblong mirror. Next to the far edge of the mirror was a round metal holder fixed to the wall for the ceramic beaker with a tube of toothpaste and a toothbrush sticking out of it. To the right was a washing machine with a small cabinet above it and beyond it was the toilet with the lid lowered.

A white plastic curtain was pulled over the bathtub that stretched from one lateral wall to the other facing the door. Even though it was opaque, I stopped in front of it briefly, trying to catch sight of something. Finally, I took hold of the left edge of the curtain, pulled it slightly and peered behind it.

The bathtub was not completely empty. I pulled the curtain halfway, squatted down and looked at the yellow rubber ducky on the bottom. A good minute passed before I finally stretched out my hand and picked it up. It was almost weightless. I held it for a moment and then put it back in the same place. I got up and pulled the curtain closed, left the bathroom, closed the door and turned off the light.

As I walked toward the study to turn off the light, out of the corner of my eye I caught sight of something gleaming on the floor near the bottom of the coat rack. I shook my head. This should have been taken care of as soon as I'd entered. I bent down and picked up the key that Inspector Vesić had pushed out of the lock. I started to put it in my pocket along with Miss Aksentijević's keys, but then stopped. I would need it soon.

Standing at the door to the study, I scanned it once again, then turned off the light. Just as I reached for the switch in the hall, there was a sharp "ping" behind my back. It confused me at first. My cellphone has that same ring, but it was in my inside pocket, not somewhere behind me.

I turned around and went back to the study. There was no need to turn on the light again. I would have been able to find Miss Jakovljević's cellphone even without the light from the hall, with only the faint external glow from the window. I remembered its location next to the keyboard.

"New message" was written on the illuminated blue background under the number 23:01. I picked up the black telephone, but before I had time to do anything, the screen went dark. I turned toward the hallway. I could handle my cell even in the dark, but not this one.

Pushing a button at random, I brought the blue screen back to life. Then, following the instructions at the bottom of the screen, I pushed another button. The "new message" notice faded but the message did not appear right away. First the blue turned white and then two words slowly formed as though emerging from below the surface.

"*Find me.*"

7

I STARED AT THE writing for about ten seconds until the screen went dark. Then I continued to look at the telephone in my hand, musing. Finally, instead of putting it back by the keyboard, I slipped it into my pants pocket.

Before leaving the gloom of the study, I looked around it one more time. When I turned off the light in the hall, the darkness around me grew deeper. The window at the bottom of the small room had metamorphosed again and become the source of weak illumination.

Miss Aksentijević was standing right by the door, a clenched fist by her mouth and her eyes filled with fear. Inspector Vesić had an inquisitive look on his face.

I inserted the key in the lock, turned it twice, then took it out and put it in the pocket with Miss Jakovljević's cellphone.

"Why did you do that?" asked Miss Aksentijević in

bewilderment as I put the latex gloves back in my inside jacket pocket.

"Because there is no reason to leave it unlocked. There's no one inside."

"How can that be?"

I shrugged my shoulders. "I don't know."

"But there must be someone. The door was locked from the inside."

"That's right," I replied.

"Then how is it possible that no one's there?"

"I don't know," I repeated.

She shook her head. "You want to spare me, don't you? You don't want to tell me . . . the truth . . . about Jelena?"

"The truth is that Miss Jakovljević is not in the apartment. And neither is anyone else."

"That's impossible." Her voice became shrill. "I don't believe you. I want to see for myself. . . ."

She took a step toward the door but I blocked the way.

"Miss Aksentijević. . . ." I started, but her shout cut me off.

"Let me by!" She raised her hands to get me out of her way. "You have no right . . . I must go in. . . ."

I grabbed her by the wrists, holding them tighter than I would have liked because she started to put up a fight. I was spared from further difficulties when the lights went out. She stopped resisting as soon as we were plunged into darkness. I waited a little and then let go of her hands. Everything was quiet for a while and then the sound of the switch broke the silence.

"Please forgive me," she said, her head bowed. "I'm a nervous wreck. This is all too much for me. I thought you were lying to me. . . ."

"There would be no sense in lying to you. If something had happened to Miss Jakovljević inside . . . anything at all . . . I would have had to call a doctor right away. Those are the regulations. And I won't be doing that. There's no work for a doctor here."

"So why won't you let me go inside and see for myself. . . .?"

"Because no one is allowed to enter an on-site investigation without authorization."

"Investigation?"

"Yes. An investigation will have to be conducted. The case has become more complicated than it seemed at the outset."

"That might take some time. . . ."

"It might."

"But there is no time. . . ." She glanced briefly at Inspector Vesić. "I explained it to you. . . ."

"Are you thinking of the deadline? On Monday?"

"Yes," she replied as though making her case.

"There are two whole days until Monday. Quite a lot could happen in the meantime."

She looked at me for several moments without speaking.

"One thing could be settled right away."

I knitted my brows. "What?"

"If I could just use Jelena's computer for a few minutes . . . Even an unfinished novel might do the trick . . . I wouldn't touch anything else. . . ."

"I told you why you can't go inside."

"All right, all right. But perhaps you could. . . ."

Now I fixed my eyes on her.

"You don't seem too worried about Miss Jakovljević anymore."

"Of course I'm worried. But if she isn't in the apartment, then there's probably no reason to worry."

"Do you have any idea where she might be?"

She shook her head.

"I haven't a clue. But if she's pulled this stunt on purpose, which now seems the only explanation, then your efforts to track her down will be in vain. She's very clever. As befits someone who writes detective novels."

"I have no doubt that she's clever. But it takes more

than cleverness to leave an apartment locked from the inside. Isn't that right, Inspector Vesić?"

The Inspector looked at Miss Aksentijević carefully for a moment before replying.

"Quite a lot more. You need magic for that."

"Wouldn't you be able to do that?"

"I am only an ordinary locksmith, Miss, not a magician."

She opened her mouth to reply, but we ended up in darkness again. I was the first to speak when the lights came back on.

"Why would Miss Jakovljević pull a stunt? Particularly when pressed by a deadline?"

"Oh, you'd better not try to figure out what makes a writer tick. She could have come up with all kinds of things. To make me suffer, let's say."

"Why would she torment you?"

"Because that's what writers do to their agents. You had no idea, did you?"

"No, I didn't."

"Forget the idealized notions you have about writers. They're all sadists who take particular pleasure in torturing their poor agents."

"Who would have thought?"

"So, will you help me?"

"Do you mean, will I check Miss Jakovljević's computer to see if there is a file with the new novel?"

"Not just check but copy it for me. I would be greatly in your debt. Here, I have a flash drive. . . ."

She started to rummage through her large briefcase.

"I'm afraid that's impossible. I have no right to enter Miss Jakovljević's apartment and even less to copy something from her computer."

She stopped searching and looked at me archly.

"Didn't you already go in?"

"The first time it was feared that something had happened to her. Now the only justification would be the assumption that she has decided to torment her agent. A sadistic relationship with one's agent, however, is by no means sufficient reason to raid a writer's apartment."

"What about the investigation? Isn't there going to be one in there?"

"I have nothing else to investigate in the apartment. I have assured myself that it is empty."

"So where will you conduct the investigation, then?"

"I will try to find Miss Jakovljević. She, above all, could tell us how she left an apartment that was locked from the inside."

"If she's decided to hide, you'll never find her. I warned you."

"We'll see."

She gazed at me briefly in silence.

"So you can't do anything for me?"

"I will be doing a lot for you if I find Miss Jakovljević by Monday. She is the only one who can give you the manuscript of her new novel."

She glanced at Inspector Vesić and then turned her eyes back on me. Her pursed lips indicated she was racing to think up something else to try, but before she could get a word out the lights went off again.

"We have no reason to stay here anymore," I said, once she had banged on the switch. "Let's go."

I gestured toward the corridor. Inspector Vesić put an end to Miss Aksentijević's hesitation by waving his hand as well.

"After you," he said with a smile.

I opened the elevator door for Miss Aksentijević, then moved aside to let Inspector Vesić pass, but he shook his head.

"It's my turn to take the stairs, dear colleague. And I'll find my way better in the dark if I don't go down fast enough."

He passed round me and started swiftly down the stairs. I sighed and then joined Miss Aksentijević in the elevator. I expected her to push the ground floor button, but she just kept her finger on it. I looked at it questioningly.

"No one has to know that I went into Jelena's apartment," she said softly. "I will be very discreet. Just give me back my keys." She paused and a smile spread over her face. "I'm sure I can find a way to repay you for this service."

I reached inside my pocket and removed the set of keys. As she stretched out her hand to take them, I pulled out the latex gloves, put them on and then took the key I'd picked up from the floor of Miss Jakovljević's apartment out of my other pants pocket. Miss Aksentijević's hand fell again as she watched me compare the key to those on the key ring. It matched the third one I'd tried. I had some trouble taking it off because the ring was stiff. The latex on the tip of my forefinger and the nail underneath were torn in the process.

"I will pretend you haven't spoken," I said, putting the two identical keys into different pants pockets and removing the gloves. "I will return the key ring to you downstairs after I remove the key to the front door of the building."

Her narrowed eyes gave me a drop-dead stare and then she turned her head away. When it became clear that she did not intend to push the button, I did it myself. The lights in the corridor went out as the elevator doors were closing.

"Regardless of how discreet you tried to be, you would not escape Mr. Teodosijević's attention. And Adam's even less. I advise you not to try anything. You'll only get into trouble."

She did not reply and continued to look askance. We spent the rest of the ride down in silence. It was only when the doors opened at my back that I became aware of something strange. Being surrounded by mirrors had not made me ill at ease this time. No illusion had threatened reality.

"This is already worrisome, esteemed colleague," said Inspector Vesić who was waiting for us on the ground floor. "I understand why I reached the fifth floor by elevator faster than you did on foot, but why would I go down faster on foot than you did by elevator. . . .?"

"You never know what might slow you down."

"I hope you didn't run into ghosts again."

"This time it was something more innocuous. Isn't that right, Miss Aksentijević?"

She let out something that sounded like a snarl, then passed between the two of us and headed towards the exit. Opening the glass door briskly, she stepped outside and stood near it with her back turned. I preceded Inspector Vesić, held the door for him and then went out.

The wind had died down a little. There were not many whirlwinds of dust on the ground and the top of the linden was rustling more softly. Nevertheless, Miss Aksentijević drew the poncho around her, head bowed, as she stared at the tips of her shoes. She did not seem inclined to cooperate so I had to find the key to the front door by myself. After my second failed attempt, Inspector Vesić joined in.

"Allow me."

I thought he would keep on trying the keys, but all he did was lift up the set, shake it a little, causing it to jingle, then single one out.

"This is what you're looking for. Shall I take it off?"

I felt my torn nail. "Please do."

He placed his briefcase on the ground and took the keys in his cupped hands. For five or six seconds he seemed to be making a wad out of them, and when he opened his hands the set was in one hand and the key to the front door was in the other. Nothing was torn. I looked at them for a short time in disbelief, shaking my head, before taking them. He bowed with a smile. I did not have to check whether the key was the right one, of course. That would have been insulting. I put it in the pocket with the key I had removed and then handed the key ring to Miss Aksentijević.

"Here you are."

She almost yanked it out of my hand, but I had crooked my forefinger into the ring.

"I'll do my best to find Miss Jakovljević by Monday."

We stayed there joined by the key ring for several moments, eye to eye. Finally, I released the ring.

"Good night," she said coldly after throwing the keys in her briefcase. The hint of a smile softened her angry expression as she nodded to Inspector Vesić.

"Good night, Miss Aksentijević," he replied, removing his hat and bowing once more.

We watched in silence as she walked to the parking area, searched a while for the keys in the abyss of her briefcase, backed out a small red car and quickly drove off with a screech of tires.

"It's not easy with agents," said Inspector Vesić when the car's tail lights had disappeared at the end of the short street.

"Particularly not with literary agents." I paused. "Did you mean that seriously?"

"What?"

"About magic."

"Oh, that." He paused as well. "Unless it's a hoax, it must be magic."

"A hoax?"

"We're talking about the greatest challenge for all those who . . . have a special interest in locks. No one has yet managed to lock a door from the outside with a key that is located inside. Whoever succeeds will see their reputation soar. Unofficial reputation, of course, but no less desirable for that. So it's no wonder that people have resorted to various hoaxes."

"For example?"

"Usually there was another way out of the premises that were locked from the inside."

"There's no other way out of Miss Jakovljević's apartment. There are four windows but they are all closed."

"Maybe there's another exit that you didn't notice. You have to know what you're looking for in order to find it."

"But where could that secret exit lead? Certainly not into the apartment next door. That would already be a conspiracy. And who would hatch a complicated plot just to play a trick on a literary agent?"

"There's the roof too. No conspiracy would be needed if the exit led there."

I shook my head. "Some sort of hole would have to be visible on the ceiling, but I didn't notice any."

"Secret openings are the hardest to find."

"Even if I missed it, let's go back to the question of why. Who would go to the trouble of making a secret exit onto the roof just for the fun of it?"

"From what I understand, writers are rather eccentric."

"They are, for the most part. But not quite that much."

"Then all that's left is magic. I'd like to meet Miss Jakovljević when you find her. If she really did the impossible, she's worthy of my admiration."

"If I find her. . . ."

"You'll find her. Who else if not you? Writers are your specialty."

I smiled. "Thanks for your help, Inspector Vesić. I'm sorry to have bothered you this late."

"You did me a favor. The case could be quite interesting. I'd like to follow your progress."

"I'll keep you posted."

He pointed down the street.

"I'm parked nearby. There was no room here when I arrived. Good night, Inspector Lukić."

He put out his hand.

"Good night," I replied, shaking it.

Before I got into my car, I raised my eyes to the façade again. Only a few windows were still alight, but none of them was in the upper left-hand corner of the building.

8

I DIDN'T LEAVE RIGHT away. I put the gloves back on again and took Miss Jakovljević's telephone out of my pants pocket. I didn't have a spare pair, but there was just a little tear on the tip of the forefinger that I rarely use when handling a cellphone. I hit a button at random with my thumb and the screen turned on.

I went into the main menu and then messages received. But nothing was there. I stared at the screen in bewilderment until the blue glow faded. I went back to the menu and into the call register that recorded all the communications.

That screen was empty too, even though there should have been evidence of considerable activity. The agent, if no one else, had frequently called the writer on this telephone over the past two days. Even if someone had erased everything, no one could have removed the record of the last two calls. About an hour and a half ago Miss Aksentijević had let the chirping ring a long time to convince me that the cellphone was in the apartment. And then a little less than half an hour ago a message had arrived in my presence and then somehow disappeared, even though the telephone had been with me the whole time since then.

I kept my eyes on the screen even after it soon went dark again, until I finally figured out a possible explanation. The phone was set so it didn't record any calls, and messages were erased after they were read. This hadn't occurred to me right away because I never used this feature. Miss Jakovljević clearly had a reason not to allow anyone to trace her calls and messages if the cellphone were to fall into the wrong hands.

Luckily, evidence of this telephone's use was recorded in other places. I had reached for my cell to call the Communications Department at police headquarters, when I suddenly realized I didn't know Miss Jakovljević's phone number. My first thought was to ask Miss Aksentijević, but I didn't take out her business card. Bearing in mind her mood when she'd left, I could hardly count on her obliging me.

Then it dawned on me that I didn't need her help. The number had to be somewhere on the phone's menu. I spent a good minute going through it, but finally gave up. Either the number wasn't there or I simply didn't know how to find it. If it was the former, then the owner of the phone had taken great pains to prevent any possible misuse.

I felt out of my depth and defeated, and then I realized there was a simple solution. I should have thought of it right away, but it seemed that fatigue had got the better of me. There was no need at all to search for the number. I would call my own phone with Miss Jakovljević's. Actually, it would be better to call the Communications Department directly. As, evidently, an extremely cautious person, the writer had probably turned off the identification of her number along with the other measures she'd taken. Nothing would appear on my screen. But she couldn't hide from the Department.

I looked at the contact list on my cell and punched the number of the Communications Department on the other phone with my thumb. After the fifth ring, I thought something strange was going on. Indeed, it was rather late, but the duty officer always answered promptly.

Someone finally picked up after the eighth ring, but didn't speak. Silence reigned for several moments.

"Hello?" came from the other end just as I was about to speak. The unfamiliar youngish male voice sounded surprised and cautious.

I must have hit the wrong number in the dark car, I concluded. Just in case, though, I asked, "Communications Department?"

This was followed by another brief silence.

"Yes," said the voice in the same tone.

"Hello, this is Inspector Dejan Lukić. I need some information about the phone I'm calling from."

The hesitation was repeated a third time.

"Where did you get that telephone, Inspector Lukić?"

Now it was my turn to pause slightly before answering.

"I was given a new case tonight. I found it in the apartment of the missing person. Why?"

For a moment I had the impression that the duty officer was talking to someone in a low voice. He cleared his throat before replying, ignoring my question.

"Could you come to the Communications Department right away? Don't use that telephone anymore."

I knew there was no point in repeating "Why?" I curbed my curiosity, replied, "I'm on my way," and ended the call.

As though Miss Jakovljević's telephone was breakable, I put it in the right inside pocket of my jacket. In my rush to get moving, I didn't take off the latex gloves.

9

THE COMMUNICATIONS DEPARTMENT WAS located on the top seventh floor of Police Headquarters. The display above the elevators indicated that both of them were up there. It seems something unusual is happening in Communications tonight, I thought as I waited for one of the elevators to reach the ground floor. As the doors closed behind me and the elevator started up, a feeling of slight discomfort set in. I had already reached the fourth floor when I realized what was causing it. I turned my back to the small mirror where my reflection gazed at me and the unease disappeared.

I expected to come across someone in the long corridor, but it was empty. There was no crowd in the central room of the Communications Department either. The middle of the large, round windowless room was filled with a massive curved control panel and row of monitors. Seen from the back, they looked like some sort of rampart. With the exception of a table lamp with a bell-like shade in one corner of the panel, there was no other light. The duty officer's face looked spectral in the grayish glow of the screens. Behind him by the opposite wall stood another man, but I couldn't get a good look at him in the gloom.

"Inspector Dejan Lukić," I said as I approached the control panel.

I thought I knew everyone who worked in the Communications Department, but I had never seen this man before. He couldn't have been more than twenty-five. His unkempt hair, stooped shoulders, hooded sweatshirt and conspicuous earring in his right ear were much more characteristic of a hacker, at least as I imagined them, than a police officer. I had never come here at this hour. The dress code seemed more relaxed on the night shift.

"Good evening, Inspector. Stanislav Mirić."

It was the voice I'd heard on Miss Jakovljević's telephone. He hadn't mentioned his title after his name, as was customary. I guessed he didn't think it necessary. Who else could he be but the Communications Department duty officer?

He got up from his office chair and extended his hand over the control panel. His long limbs made this an easy matter. It hadn't appeared so while he was sitting, probably because of his hunched posture, but he must have been a good six feet two. I was just about to shake his hand, when I became aware of the latex gloves. I quickly took off the right one, held it in my left hand and we shook hands.

"Sorry to ask you to come right away this late."

"There certainly must be a reason for it," I replied.

"I'd like to take a look at the phone you used to call me."

He stretched out his hand again, palm up. I put the glove I'd taken off into my right hand and with my left took Miss Jakovljević's cell out of my inside jacket pocket. But I didn't give it to him.

"There was no chance to check for fingerprints," I explained.

The young man nodded his head. He glanced around the control panel and found what he was looking for near the lamp. He had trouble putting the latex gloves on his large bony hands. As though they were not his size.

When he sat down again, his shoulders and head were visible above the rampart, but his hands were hidden. He did something briefly, looked up at me and then glanced behind him.

"Did you open the phone after we talked?"

"No, I didn't. I just put it in my pocket and drove over here. You told me not to use it."

Officer Mirić got up and headed for the wall behind the control panel. His tall frame completely concealed the man standing there. They spent about a minute whispering to each other. The young man shrugged his shoulders twice and once turned his head briefly toward me. Then he moved aside and a short, balding, corpulent man in his fifties stepped out of the shadows. His thumb and index finger were holding the top of a little transparent plastic bag containing Miss Jakovljević's cellphone.

"Our paths cross again, Inspector Lukić," he said.

I stared at him for several moments before replying.

"Good evening, Commissioner Milenković."

"It was good until you called the Communications Department. Which phone did you use?"

"Why, that one," I said in bewilderment, motioning to the little bag with my chin.

"Perhaps there's an error. Do you have any other?"

"Yes, my service phone."

"That's it?"

"That's it."

"You certainly must have a private cellphone."

"I certainly do, but I don't carry it with me when I'm on duty. It's at home. What's the problem, Commissioner?"

He ignored my question.

"Would you please let me see your service phone?"

I took it out of the left inside pocket of my jacket. The commissioner nodded to the young man, who went back to the control panel, took my cell and sat down again. As he was examining it, Commissioner Milenković came up to the control panel. He looked older in the subdued light. Or at any rate exhausted.

We spent about two minutes in silence. The commissioner first watched Officer Mirić as he worked and then raised his eyes to me. We stared at each other until the cellphone examination was over. The long-limbed officer raised his head toward his superior. Neither one spoke, nor did I notice them exchange signals. Nevertheless, the next moment my phone was given back to me.

It should have occurred to me earlier, I thought, reproaching myself. I had not met this young man before because he didn't work here. He was a member of Commissioner Milenković's team. But why had the National Security Agency taken over the Communications Department tonight?

"Where did you get this telephone?" asked the commissioner, raising the plastic bag a little.

"I already told Officer Mirić," I replied. "I'm on a new case. I took it from the apartment of the missing person."

"Who's the missing person?"

"Miss Jelena Jakovljević. She's a writer. Perhaps you've heard of her?"

The commissioner sighed instead of replying. "Literature again."

"It can't be helped, those are my kind of cases."

"We seem to share the same fate. Although literature's not my profession."

"Why would the National Security Agency be interested in a missing writer?"

"Because she has an unusual cellphone."

"Unusual?" I repeated after a short pause.

"Very. In particular, it doesn't leave any identification. And that can't happen here." He swept his outstretched finger over the monitors on the control panel. "But if it does happen, then it's a case for us."

"So, how's that possible?"

The commissioner shrugged his shoulders.

"It's possible. New things are being invented all the time in communications technology. If you don't keep an eye on developments, you fall behind before you know it and then you've got no protection whatsoever. But the lack of identification is the lesser of the two mysteries."

"What's the greater one?"

He eyed me silently for a moment before he spoke again.

"Are you quite certain that you didn't open the telephone after calling the Communications Department?" he asked in return.

"Quite. I had no reason to."

"Were you alone or with someone else?"

"Alone."

"I hope you're not hiding anything from me. Our cooperation was a bit flawed last time."

"I agree. It was rather one-way."

He seemed about to reply to this, but just looked at me again without speaking for several moments.

"If what you say is true, then the second mystery is really a whopper. There's no SIM card or battery in Miss Jakovljević's phone."

Now it was my turn to stare at him.

"But that's impossible," I said at last. "How . . . could I have talked to Officer Mirić?"

I hoped he hadn't noticed my hesitation. I decided at the last moment not to mention the message. The last time I'd worked with him had taught me not to reveal more than was necessary.

"Not even he knows how. And there's no one better in communications and information technology. Don't let appearances deceive you."

"I'll go through the phone with a fine tooth comb once again," interjected the young man, grinning awkwardly at the compliment. "But the SIM card and battery are definitely not where they should be and there's simply no other place for them." He rubbed his earring absentmindedly between his thumb and index finger. "I'll check the fingerprints too, if there are any."

"Of course," continued Commissioner Milenković, "great mysteries sometimes have simple, even commonplace solutions. Occam's razor. It might turn out that someone here is pulling our leg."

"Who would pull the National Security Agency's leg?"

He shook his head. "I don't know. Some joker. They crop up here and there."

"They would be a very stupid joker."

"I'm glad that you, as an intelligent man, realize that, Inspector Lukić. Well, let's leave the jokers alone for now. What did you find out about Miss Jakovljević?"

"Mostly what her agent Miss Aksentijević told me. She called the police tonight because she hadn't been able to contact the writer since Wednesday night. She was afraid that something had happened to her in her apartment. She couldn't go in and check because the door was locked from the inside."

"You broke into the apartment?"

"No, I didn't. There was no need. We have an expert who delicately opens any lock."

He knitted his brow.

"Vesić?"

"Vesić."

"He's got talent. Too bad he doesn't come and work for us. Did you find anyone in the apartment?"

"No."

"And it really was locked from the inside?"

"That's right."

"Was there any other way to get out?"

"If there was, I didn't notice it. All the windows were closed."

"Another mystery," he said in an even voice. "Did anything catch your eye in the apartment?"

"Nothing special. It was spic-and-span. Writers' apartments usually aren't like that."

"I had no idea."

"That's because you don't have much to do with literature."

"What little I have is quite enough. Please give me the address."

"Number 12 Oak Street. Apartment 19."

Although the young man had received no orders, he quickly typed the data on one of the keyboards.

"All right," said Commissioner Milenkovć. "That's all for now. Keep working on the case. If you track down the missing writer, I'd appreciate being informed without delay. I'd like to talk to her. Somewhere she got hold of a very interesting telephone."

"Cooperation goes without saying," I said flatly.

"I'm sorry I can't say I look forward to working with you again. Goodbye, Inspector Lukić."

"Good night."

I turned and headed for the door, but the commissioner's voice stopped me before I got there.

"Did you take anything else out of Miss Jakovljević's apartment?"

I turned around and shook my head.

"No, I didn't."

"So why did you take her cell, of all things?"

We stared fixedly at each other for a long moment. Finally I shrugged my shoulders.

"I thought it would be more useful with me than in an empty apartment. Now it isn't anymore."

The commissioner nodded his head slowly.

"Good night, Inspector."

10

I HAD JUST GOTTEN out of the elevator on the ground floor when my cellphone rang. As I took it out, I thought that it was Commissioner Milenković with a few more questions. But I saw on the screen that it was Inspector Prvoslav Bobić, the duty officer in my Investigations Department. As I'd entered the elevator on the seventh floor a few moments ago, I had briefly considered going down to my office on the fifth floor. One look at the clock had made me change my mind. My shift had ended at midnight, four minutes ago, and I had no other business to take care of there.

"Hello," I said.

"Mr. Branislav Teodosijević would like to speak with you. He says it's urgent."

"Please transfer the call to my office. I'm on the ground floor. I'll be up shortly."

"All right."

I re-entered the elevator, as the doors hadn't closed. I heard the telephone ringing in my office as soon as I stepped onto the fifth floor. It sounded piercing in the quiet corridor with its subdued lights.

I picked up the receiver without turning the light on.

"Inspector Dejan Lukić."

"I'm sorry to disturb you so late, Inspector. But I thought you might be interested. There's someone in Miss Jakovljević's apartment."

I wanted to ask three or four questions all at once, but had enough presence of mind to refrain. They would keep.

"I'm on my way," I replied.

Driving quickly to Oak Street, I concluded that I had probably achieved nothing by not talking to Mr. Teodosijević on my cell. I had started working with Commissioner Milenković again, which meant that they were checking all my telephones. And probably my movements. Even if Officer Mirić was not the wizard his superior made him out to be, he could have planted some monitoring device in the short time he was supposedly checking out my cellphone. Indeed, they must have realized I hadn't overlooked this. They couldn't have underestimated me. We had played this game before. . . .

As soon as I got out of the car in the parking area, I looked up at the façade of the building at number 12. Only three windows were still lit up and they were all quite far from the upper left-hand corner. I hastened toward the entrance, unlocked the door and entered the building. I didn't push the light switch in the foyer and headed for the elevator in the gloom.

The elevator was on the fourth floor. I pushed the call button and as it slowly descended I realized that I actually should have taken the stairs. If someone had really gone into Miss Jakovljević's apartment, they might not have left the building. I would miss them if they went down the stairs just as I was going up in the elevator. In the stairwell, though, I would have heard the elevator.

Although there was no need, I waited for the elevator

to reach the ground floor. The doors opened, revealing the empty interior lined with mirrors. I hurried back to the foyer, turned on the lights and then ran up the stairs. I tried to be as quiet as possible, my ears pricked, but there was no humming of the elevator. Nothing disturbed the building's nocturnal peace.

As I reached the fifth floor, my panting broke the silence. I was already heading down the corridor when, just like last time, I stopped in mid-step and turned towards the stairs. My internal counter seemed to be seriously out of whack. Now there were only sixty-nine stairs. At some point I would have to go up—or even better, go down—when I wasn't agitated and taking two or three steps at a time. Just to see if I could count them correctly.

I paused briefly at the end of the corridor, my breathing subdued. Although it was just my imagination, I could almost feel Mr. Teodosijević and Adam standing behind the right-hand door. When I turned towards the door on the left, I had the impression that a silent void was gaping behind it. I went up and pressed my ear to the wooden surface.

I stayed that way against the door but didn't hear anything. Finally I stepped back and took out Miss Aksentijević's key. Had I needed latex gloves again I would have been in a fix. I'd taken off the other one as soon as I'd left the central room in the Communications Department and thrown both into a waste basket in the corridor, considering that I wouldn't need them anymore that night.

As I took the elevator back down to the ground floor of Police Headquarters after talking to Mr. Teodosijević, it had dawned on me that I might need them. I briefly considered going back to my office for a new pair of gloves, but then I would have lost several possibly vital minutes.

I inserted the key in the lock, turned it twice, pulled

it out and put it back in my pocket. I did all of this very quietly, at least as far as my ears were concerned. The lights went out just as I pulled down on the handle.

I didn't open the door right away, wondering whether I should first turn on the lights in the corridor again. No, it was better not to be seen. If someone was still inside, there in the dark they would have an advantage over me if I was in the light. I waited briefly for my eyes to adjust to the darkness, then opened the door just wide enough to slip inside.

I paused as soon as I had stepped inside the apartment and stood stock-still for several moments, listening. As there was no sound or movement, I groped for the handle behind my back and slowly closed the door. Everything was still. Finally I pushed the light switch. The radiance that filled the hallway, pouring out of the rectangular ceiling light, forced me to squint.

I stopped in front of the door leading to the larger room. It was ajar at the same angle as when I'd left there a little over an hour ago. I opened it slowly to my right until it reached the shelf. Behind it was a triangular space, large enough to hold a slender person. I entered the room and returned the door to its original position. There was no one behind it.

I didn't have to turn on the light to determine that the rest of the room was also empty. I entered the smaller room as far as the sliding door that led to the kitchen. I peered left and right through the upper part of the door and then turned on the light, pushed the door aside and entered. I went up to the closet and opened it. No one was hiding there either. I had suspected such an outcome, but verification takes precedence over suspicions in an investigator's job. Nevertheless, there are limits. I didn't check the refrigerator.

I closed the closet, pulled the sliding door shut and turned off the light. As I headed toward the bathroom, I figured that if I were to discover no one, there were only two possibilities left. Either Mr. Teodosijević was mistaken or whoever had been in Miss Jakovljević's apartment had left before I got there.

I waited two or three seconds for the neon light to go on before opening the bathroom door. The whiteness of the empty room blinded me again. Everything was just as I had left it. I was about to close the door when my duty to verify made me stop. I went over to the bathtub, grabbed the left edge of the plastic curtain and pulled. The yellow ducky was just where I'd left it.

I studied it briefly and then pulled the curtain closed. I exited the bathroom, shut the door and turned off both lights. As I stood in the darkness only slightly softened by the streetlight outlining the window, I thought with a sigh that I had come back in vain. My hand was already heading for the knob on the front door, when a sharp "ping" came from behind me.

Shivers began crawling down the back of my head and neck. I quickly turned toward the large room from where the noise had come, but all I could see was the upper contour of the desk. I shook my head, angry at myself. Of course, I should have turned on the light when I went into the main room a moment ago. Then I probably would not have overlooked what was on the desk, even if it was small. But I had been looking for something larger that could be seen in the gloom. . . .

I stopped at the door and hit the switch. Even though I knew what I would see, I stared nonetheless in disbelief at the small black object next to the keyboard. The last time I'd seen it was about half an hour ago in Commissioner Milenković's little bag. How had it got back here?

As I walked toward the desk, I realized that this was the wrong question. There might be cellphones that don't leave any identification in the Communications Department and even work without a SIM card and battery, but they certainly aren't magical. This could not be the same telephone that I had taken with me. Someone had indeed been in the apartment after my departure and had left an identical cellphone in the same spot where I'd found the first. And now they had sent a new message on it.

I reached for the little device, but stayed my hand. I needed those latex gloves after all. Well, since I don't have them, I'll have to make do without, I thought. I reached into my pocket for my handkerchief, but then concluded that the precaution was unnecessary. I didn't have to take account of the fingerprints. Officer Mirić would look for them on the first telephone. I suspected, however, that his efforts would be in vain. Whoever was behind this seemed to me cautious enough not to allow such a commonplace mistake.

I picked up the cellphone. Even though I knew it had to be just an illusion, I couldn't get rid of the impression that there was something special about the way the smooth metal back of the phone touched my palm. I hadn't felt that with the previous phone, as though the thin latex of the gloves had insulated me from the unusual effect, if it had been there too.

I remembered which button to push. The New Message notification disappeared, the blue turned white and the same two words came up just like the last time.

"Find me."

I stared at them, deep in thought, until they disappeared. This was indisputably meant for me. One message could accidentally arrive when I was leaving Miss Jakovljević's apartment, but two such incidents within a short time ruled out any coincidence. Someone was determined to play tricks on me and I had no idea who, why or how.

I saw only one way to try and find out. My thumb hovered above the little buttons once again, but I didn't touch any of them. I would answer the message a little later. In another place, not here. And when I didn't have my service cellphone with me. In any case, I was in no hurry. Let whoever wanted to play stew in their own juices for a while, if they expected me to reply right away.

I put the phone in the right inside pocket of my jacket and headed out of the apartment.

11

I FELT FOR THE lock in the dark corridor, locked the door and turned around. I could not even make out the entrance to the apartment across the way. I thought of feeling along the wall to find the doorbell too, but concluded that it would be better to turn on the lights. Otherwise I would have trouble seeing where to enter Mr. Teodosijević's apartment. I stretched out my hand and walked toward where I thought the switch should be, but a light flashed on before I touched the opposite wall.

"You'll have no trouble seeing without that, Inspector Lukić," said the tall man in a black robe. He was standing at the open door with bright illumination behind him. Adam was by his left foot. The dog just looked at me inquisitively, making no sound.

"I thought you didn't turn the lights on in your apartment," I said as though justifying myself.

"There's no reason to when we are alone. But we must make allowances for the special needs of our visitors."

"Sight might even turn out to be a drawback," I said, hoping he could tell by the tone of my voice that I was smiling.

"It's certainly not an advantage in the dark." He returned my smile more with his lips than his tone. "Please come in."

He moved aside and motioned for me to enter. Adam also retreated from the entrance.

As soon as I entered, I realized that the apartment

was identical to the one I had just left. Actually, its mirror image. The bathroom here was on the right and the large room was on the left. The small room in front of me contained a square table with one chair. Piles of books were stacked on the table and the empty wall behind it framed the window.

Mr. Teodosijević closed the door. Moving with confident steps, he circumvented me and entered the large room. Adam went into the smaller room and joined him from that direction.

"Please come in," he repeated.

I stopped at the entrance to the room and looked around. What I saw was quite different from Miss Jakovljević's apartment. Indeed, the walls here were also completely covered, but not with bookshelves. The large room resembled an art gallery closely hung with paintings. Although they were of different sizes, their thin frames fit together nicely, creating a mosaic without any unused space. The effect was harmonious, almost like wallpaper, because the white canvases contained only red and black brush strokes, and the rectangles were separated by rust-colored wooden borders.

In the middle of the room under a blazing ceiling light stood an easel. The tall round stool in front of it had a palette and two brushes on the seat. A dark-blue cloth had been placed over the large canvas on the easel. The entire floor was lined with newspaper spattered here and there with paint, particularly around the easel.

There was almost no furniture. A narrow cot extended under the two windows and a plaid blanket had been thrown over the unmade sheets. On the opposite side of the room, centered against the wall, was a worn and cracked brown leather armchair.

"Take a seat," said Mr. Teodosijević, indicating the armchair. Then he approached the bed, grabbed hold of the metal frame and sat down. Adam followed him and dropped to the floor by his side.

"I won't keep you," I said. "It's late."

"Not for me. I do most of my work at night." His lips curved into a smile again. "That's the privilege of a painter who doesn't depend on daylight." This time his tone of voice was fitting. "Please," he added, motioning to the armchair once more.

As I sank into it, the springs creakingly complained. I waited for him to speak first, but he remained silent. I had the uncomfortable feeling that blind eyes were examining me.

"There is no one in Miss Jakovljević's apartment," I said, breaking the silence.

"I know. You were too late," he said with a tinge of reproach. "They left just before you got here."

"You didn't do anything this time." I hoped he had not missed the reciprocated reproach in my voice.

"Because I would not have had the advantage of the dark. Whoever was in Miss Jakovljević's place did not turn on the lights in the corridor."

"Perhaps they had a flashlight."

"Perhaps. But maybe they didn't need one."

"Why do you think so?"

"This was no amateur burglar who would be bothered by the dark. Everything was done quite skillfully. And silently."

"But you heard them nonetheless. How else would you know that they'd entered the apartment next door?"

"I wasn't the one who heard them. Although my hearing is very keen, I would have missed them. But not Adam."

He lowered his hand unerringly to the dog's head and patted it lightly.

"Perhaps Adam made a mistake."

The corners of his mouth turned up briefly.

"Adam never makes mistakes."

"We all make mistakes sometimes. For example, you

claimed that Miss Jakovljević was in the apartment and there's no one there."

The green jade seemed to flash for a moment.

"Jelena did not come out of there," he said softly.

"In any case, we have a new mystery before us. Why did a professional break into Miss Jakovljević's apartment? There are no signs of a break-in. Everything is just the same as the first time I went inside."

"Of course there's no sign of a break-in. What the burglar was looking for did not require a search or any unnecessary noise."

"How do you know what the burglar was looking for?"

His expression turned sneering.

"You don't have to be particularly insightful, Inspector, to figure that out. There's only one thing of value in the apartment across the way that would warrant a burglary."

I eyed him dubiously.

"I found nothing there more valuable than books. Indeed, I didn't have a chance to examine them in detail. Is there an old and expensive edition on the shelves?"

"Expensive yes, but it's not old and it's not on the shelves."

"Are there expensive new editions?"

"Yes, if there's only one copy."

"I didn't know that books were printed in only one copy."

"This one isn't printed. That's why it's not on the shelves."

"How can it be a book if it isn't printed?"

"I didn't say it was a book. It's a manuscript. Actually, a computer file. Miss Jakovljević's new novel. *Find Me*."

I scrutinized him again briefly in silence.

"I thought that only Miss Aksentijević considered

the manuscript valuable. Why would a burglar be interested in it?"

"Miss Aksentijević is certainly not the only one trying to get hold of it. Might I ask—what did she tell you, why does she need it?"

"She has to submit it to the publisher on Monday. And she is personally quite keen to do so, even though she's only her agent."

"Double agent."

"Double literary agent?"

"That's right. Miss Jakovljević caught on to her double game. That's why she was avoiding her. Miss Aksentijević would have submitted the manuscript, indeed, but certainly not to the publisher."

"To whom else?"

"To the highest bidder. A lot of people are after it."

"A lot of people?"

"You can't imagine how many want to read it, particularly if it's finished."

"Miss Jakovljević must write really exciting novels if her readers don't have the patience to wait for the book and break into her computer to get hold of the manuscript. She would be the envy of every writer."

Mr. Teodosijević stroked Adam before he replied.

"These are not ordinary readers."

"Burglar-readers certainly aren't ordinary."

"That's not what makes them exceptional."

"So what does?"

"They'd give anything to be the first to read the manuscript."

"I don't understand. Why do they care so much about being the first?"

He did not reply immediately. When he spoke, his voice was hushed.

"Because this might be the Grand Manuscript."

"Grand Manuscript?" I repeated.

"Haven't you heard about it?"

I shook my head. A moment later I realized that this was not enough and hastened to say, "No, I haven't."

"Those awaiting its advent believe that the first reader will become immortal."

We sank into silence. I knew I should say something, but nothing appropriate came to mind.

"No less," I said finally.

"Although this must seem like pure superstition to a police inspector, I don't recommend that you underestimate the adherents of the Grand Manuscript. These people will do anything to reach their goal."

"It's no wonder, if they really believe the reward is immortality. But immortality is usually connected to serious literature, not detective novels."

"Literary quality is not decisive in this regard."

"I see you are well-informed about the Grand Manuscript's state of affairs."

"Only so-so. All I know is what Miss Jakovljević told me."

"So that means she knew she was writing the Grand Manuscript?"

"She knew that something strange had been happening ever since she started working on the novel *Find Me*. Odd characters kept importuning her with bewildering bids and unbelievable stories about the Grand Manuscript. She didn't take them seriously at first, but as her writing progressed they became increasingly insistent. That's why she had to withdraw completely from the public eye."

"She did a splendid job. But now that it's all over, she can resurface."

"All over?"

"Well, if the burglar got hold of the new novel's manuscript from her computer, then no one will harass her anymore. All that's left is to see which lucky person becomes immortal after reading it first."

"The burglar left empty-handed, of course. Don't

forget that Miss Jakovljević writes detective novels. A computer is the last place she would leave a manuscript she wanted to hide."

"Then it's strange that the burglar didn't look for it somewhere else. If they did, they left no traces."

"Of course not. This was not an ordinary burglar. Nevertheless, I doubt that they found anything."

"Miss Jakovljević is the only one who could tell us that. And we don't know where she is."

"She did not leave her apartment," repeated Mr. Teodosijević like a mantra, after a brief hesitation.

I didn't know what to say to this. The armchair creaked beneath me again as I got up. On the other side of the room, the man and his dog rose in concert that same moment.

"It's time for me to go," I said. "There's nothing more I can do here and I have to get up early in the morning. I'm on duty over the weekend."

I was already at the door to the small hall when something crossed my mind.

"Those pictures of yours in Miss Jakovljević's apartment are interesting. Those are her eight books, right?"

He nodded his head and gestured broadly towards the walls.

"Those are all books. That is my library."

12

I CLIMBED INTO BED and then took the cellphone from the bedside table where its ebony color seemed to absorb the glow of the green-shaded table lamp. When I had it in the palm of my hand, once again I seemed to feel an eerie prickle.

The precautionary measures I'd taken now seemed excessive. It's easy, however, to fall prey to paranoia when the National Security Agency complicates your life. I left my service cellphone in the kitchen all the way on the other side of the living room. If it was set to serve as a microphone, it would have a hard time picking up anything through two doors.

And what was there to pick up, anyway? My bedroom is quiet at night, particularly when I'm alone. I don't snore, as far as I know. At least none of the ladies who have spent the night with me there have ever complained about it. Indeed, they may have avoided mentioning the little nocturnal annoyance out of consideration. . . .

The telephone had a camera too, although I doubted that even a real wizard could have set it in less than a minute to send pictures. But just in case, I'd covered the phone with a cloth.

In fact, the simplest course would have been to remove the battery. Then there would be no way to misuse the device. But I didn't. Disabling it would only indicate that I was on to them and intended to do something I didn't want them to see. This way, everything would appear normal.

There could be other cameras though. What if someone had been here after my run-in with Commissioner Milenković and now they could watch a live broadcast from my apartment? I winced at the possibility. After giving it some thought, I concluded nevertheless that this was going too far. Even the National Security Agency would have to get a court order for something like that and it would take quite a while to do so during the night.

No authorization would be needed, however, if they placed the camera somewhere outside my apartment. For example, in the foliage of the oak tree next to my bedroom window. I'd drawn the drapes before going to bed, something I rarely do because it makes me feel confined. But they didn't know that. If they really intended to spy on me through the window, it would be natural for them to assume I pulled the drapes every night, not just because I wanted to thwart them.

It was not until I lay there staring at the little black

cellphone in my hand that I realized I'd given paranoia free rein and feared those who might not be threatening me at all, while disregarding the real danger. Suddenly I felt stripped bare before the mysterious telephone that seemed to return my gaze from the dark screen, penetrating deep inside me.

Wanting to chase away this uncomfortable feeling, I raised my thumb to call up the message. All at once I was struck by the realization that I should not have postponed my reply. If the second cell was the same as the first, the message had been erased after I'd read it and the number would be impossible to find.

I wouldn't hesitate to disturb Miss Aksentijević in the dead of night, regardless of how she felt about me, but it had just become clear that this would be pointless. The number she had given me would certainly not belong to either this telephone or the other one that was now with Commissioner Milenković. There must be a third cellphone in the writer's apartment—an ordinary one with a SIM card and battery. I hadn't found it because I hadn't looked for it after taking the first one, considering it to be all there was.

The thought about the SIM card led me to turn the telephone over in my hand. I fumbled a bit until I discovered how to open the cover, then raised it and saw what I had expected. The place for the SIM card was empty. Soon my other suspicion was also confirmed. There wasn't any battery. I replaced the cover, turned the phone over again and stared in frustration at the front of it for several moments.

As I was about to put it back on the bedside table, I thought, why not give it a try? One should never take anything for granted about a device that stumped even the National Security Agency. My thumb danced about the buttons. I sighed in relief when Messages showed one was there. I pushed another button and two words appeared once again on a white background: *"Find me."*

I gazed at them for a while, uncertain what to reply. A multitude of ideas swarmed in my head, jockeying for precedence. In the end I decided to start with the basics. Although it appeared obvious, I had to establish who had sent the message.

"Miss Jakovljević?" I typed.

Even though the cellphone had neither a SIM card nor a battery, confirmation appeared on the screen that the message had been sent. I did not fear that sending this message would let the National Security Agency know I had another unusual telephone. They already knew I had it. If they'd wanted to take it away from me, they would have done so immediately after the last time it had been used—when the message appeared on it while I was in Miss Jakovljević's apartment the second time. They would most likely have come for it themselves instead of asking me again to take it to them.

But they hadn't done anything, which could only mean that they'd decided to let me use it so they could monitor me through it. Very well, I would keep that in mind. Then it dawned on me that there was another possibility, although highly improbable. What if even the National Security Agency couldn't see when this phone was used?

There was no time to dwell on this matter because a "ping" rang out. It sounded thunderous in the quiet of the night. It might even have reached the kitchen. I hastened to open the message.

"Good evening, Inspector Lukić. How are you?"

I smiled and quickly replied:

"Fine, thanks. How are you?"

As soon as I had pushed the Send button, I searched through the menu to turn down the volume. Before I could figure out how to do it, there was another "ping". I stopped what I was doing to open the new message.

"Wonderful."

I didn't reply immediately and continued to examine the menu, fearing it might not be possible to adjust the volume. That would be troublesome. Luckily, however, it could be done. Instead of turning it down, I switched it off and turned on the vibration.

"That's nice to hear. So this means we can close the case."

Moments later, the little device trembled in my hand. She was clearly more skillful than I at texting.

"Does it seem over to you?"

"The police case, yes. Someone is reported missing. They are found. In good shape, by their own statement. The investigation is called off."

"Has everything really been resolved?"

"What hasn't been resolved is not within police jurisdiction. No one has broken the law."

"There are some peculiarities, though. Will the police turn a blind eye to them?"

"The police are not interested in a writer's private life, regardless of how peculiar it is."

"And you personally?"

"Me?"

"You have a degree in literature, don't you?"

"You are well-informed."

"It comes in handy. One would expect you to be interested in a writer's private life. Unless your studies left you with a bad opinion of detective novels and you carry prejudices against their authors. . . ."

"My studies taught me that every prejudice in literature is wrong. And that the main division is into good novels and bad novels. Regardless of whether they are detective stories or any other."

"If this were a detective story, it would be wrong to end it here. Many questions would go unanswered."

"But it's not a detective story and reality is under no obligation to provide a satisfactory ending."

"Who knows what obligations reality has? Let's not go into that now. So you're giving up?"

"As I said, there is no reason to continue with the investigation now that you have told me you are fine."

"A police inspector should not be so credulous. What proof do you have?"

I felt this was a trap, but there was no retreating.

"Your statement. These messages."

"You would use messages exchanged with a telephone that has no SIM card or battery?"

Before I could think of an answer, a new question arrived.

"Even if you use them, are you sure they will still be there when you need them?"

Of course I wasn't sure, but I was spared the embarrassment of having to admit it by the fourth question that soon followed.

"Finally, even if the messages are saved, do they prove that you were actually in contact with Jelena Jakovljević?"

"Aren't I?" I answered at last.

"Maybe you are and maybe you aren't. That remains for you to establish beyond reasonable doubt. As you see, the case is still open. You still haven't found the missing person. We are far from a satisfactory ending."

"Like in a detective novel?"

"Like in a detective novel. Good night, Inspector Lukić. Sweet dreams."

13

THE DOORS STARTED TO close as soon as I stepped inside the elevator. That was strange. I hadn't pressed any button. I looked to my left where the panel of buttons was located but there was nothing there. I thought I must be mistaken and it was on the right. But nothing troubled the glass surface there either.

I turned in bewilderment toward the doors just as the two sides touched and joined the halves of my face together. Staring into my own wide eyes, I felt trapped.

Even though I was not claustrophobic, an unbearable feeling of confinement swept over me. I had to get out of the elevator as soon as possible.

I did the only thing that crossed my panic-stricken mind—I tried to dig my nails into the barely visible gap between the two doors to separate them. A moment later, however, I jumped away from the doors; the elevator had started and it was moving in an impossible direction. Even though I was on the top floor, the elevator began to ascend. I could clearly tell that I was going up—and much faster than the elevator's usual speed.

Feeling unsteady, I looked reflexively for something to hold on to, but all I could do was place my hands on the smooth wall in front of me. Instead of anchoring me, however, staring at my equally unsteady reflection only increased my instability.

As I took my hands off the glass, I had the impression that the reflected hands would not let go of me. With a yank, I backed away to the middle of the little compartment. I no longer dared to go near any of the walls. I had the impression that my replicas from all sides, even from above, were reaching out to me for support.

Not from all sides, however. There was no threat from the red carpeting under my feet. The thick weave did not reflect anything. I quickly squatted, placed my fists on the floor and bowed my head, looking between my shoes. This position made it easier to bear the elevator's rapid speed as it continued inexplicably upwards.

The change began as I was feverishly trying to figure a way out of my predicament. Even though I could still feel the rough texture of the carpeting under my clenched fingers, what I saw clashed with it. The red changed to light blue, then lost its solidity and quickly dissolved. If I dared believe my own eyes, I was squatting on the gently rippling surface of the water.

A new panic attack was blocked by my sense of touch that still informed me I had a solid floor beneath me and there was no risk of sinking. But something was rising slowly from the depths. Even before it reached the surface, I detected an enormous human face. Not until it was directly beneath the soles of my shoes did I finally recognize it. Constructed solely of water, it appeared diffuse and unstable.

Miss Aksentijević started to say something, but nothing could be heard. Then her distorted voice reached my ears as though muffled.

". . . .Because Jelena has recently started to lose faith in what she writes, even though it has made her famous. And rich. It's as though she's had enough of detective novels. . . ."

The mouth kept moving but the voice fell silent as the face began to sink. As it sank, the color of the floor beneath me started to change again. At first I thought the water would turn back into carpeting. The blue changed to red, not a darker shade but the red of a brightly flaming fire.

Considerable willpower was needed to regain confidence in my sense of touch and not jump away from the fire that was raging on the elevator floor. The absence of heat was also inconsistent with the roaring flames. Quite the contrary, I started to shiver as though engulfed in cold air.

The fiery tongues were at first chaotic and then started to entwine, creating a form. Sculpting in fire was no easy matter. Just as the facial features stabilized, they melted away. Finally, they settled long enough for the teashop proprietor to speak in a crackling voice.

". . . .There you have three musicians, two painters, a sculptor and a writer. . . ."

As soon as this was said, the face deconstructed and the fire quickly subsided. The flames dwindled and went out. Several glowing spots lasted a little longer before they too disappeared. Finally all that remained was pitch blackness.

The new change in color was the most subtle. I barely noticed that the darkness had grown slightly paler. I had to strain to make out the rectangular hole gaping in the floor.

The clay packed hard in the bottom suddenly became loose and swollen as though something was trying to emerge. First a forehead was formed, then eyes, cheeks, a chin. It was not until the mouth appeared that I recognized the earthen face of Inspector Vesić. The mouth opened but no sound was heard until lumps stopped falling inside it.

"You have to know what you're looking for in order to find it," said my colleague.

His cheerful tone seemed to induce the next change in the elevator floor. The dark grave quickly dissolved and welled blue, no longer the turquoise of the deep sea but the diaphanous hue of a sunny sky.

Several scattered clouds were the only blemish on the overall brightness. As though set in motion by an imperceptible wind, they started to gather and lose their amorphousness. When the downy montage was composed, I recognized the face now being shown to me by the two cloudless jade spaces in place of the eyes.

The swollen lips of white diaphanous matter uttered a divine proclamation in a slow, deep voice.

"Those awaiting its advent believe that the first reader will become immortal."

Mr. Teodosijević's words still filled my ears as the montage broke up. The clouds did not scatter but dispersed, leaving no trace behind them. Nothing disturbed the blue anymore.

The splendor of the day did not last long, however. The square frame of the floor filled first with crimson and then darkness. This time pitch blackness was honeycombed with a multitude of twinkling points.

Although it was quite obvious, the realization took a while to reach my consciousness. I was squatting on stars.

This seemed rather unbecoming, so I stood up hastily. In the process, I realized that the elevator was not moving. It was no longer going up. In all the commotion I had failed to notice when it stopped.

I wondered in bewilderment where it had reached and my eyes, still looking downward, provided the answer. This would surely have alarmed me were it not for the much greater fear that swept over me that same moment.

Despite all the floor's changes, it had been my sole support since entering the elevator. Now it had magically disappeared and I started falling out into the cosmic void. My hands flailed about, trying to hold on to something, but my fingers only slid down the smooth surface of the mirrors. I opened my mouth to scream, but no sound arose in airless space.

14

My panic intensified when the stars suddenly went out. I stared wide-eyed at the impenetrable darkness around me. Several terrifying moments passed before it slowly dawned on me. I couldn't scream, but I was still breathing, actually panting with excitement. And there would be no breathing out in space. . . .

Even without light, I finally figured out where I was: sitting in bed. I'd just snapped awake from a nightmare. I was surrounded by darkness because I'd drawn the drapes. I shook my head to scatter the last remnants of the dream before placing my feet on the floor. I felt for my slippers, put them on, got up and headed for the window, arms outstretched.

When I pulled the drapes open, I was dazzled by the sun. I closed my eyes reflexively and turned my head.

When I reopened my eyes, a bright white circle still flickered before them for a while. I'd been certain for some reason that the sun wasn't up, yet here the morning was well under way. The agitation that had subsided now returned. I'll be late for work.

As I rushed back to the bed and grabbed the cellphone from the bedside table to see what time it was, I remembered that my service phone was in the kitchen. It made no difference, this one probably had a clock too. It vibrated the moment I picked it up.

I glanced at the four numbers in the corner—08:14—before opening the new message.

Didn't sleep well? We overslept too. . . .

I pushed the button angrily to remove the message from the screen. I had left my innocent cell in the kitchen just because it had spent a few moments in the hands of one of Commissioner Milenković's men and had left this mysterious device in the bedroom that could do who knows what. Take pictures in the dark, let's say. Otherwise, why the allusion to my not sleeping well?

There was no time to go into that now. I looked around, trying to find a place to put the black telephone while I got dressed. I stuck it under the pillow and then hurried into the bathroom. I'm no fan of reality shows and would be quite unhappy to take part in one. . . .

At 08:42 I was ready to leave. I hesitated briefly about which cell to take. It seemed safest to take only my private phone, but I couldn't do without my service phone at work. In the end I decided to take all three. I put my private and service phones in the inside pockets of my jacket. The telephone from Miss Jakovljević's apartment vibrated so softly that it would be inconspicuous in my pants pocket.

Traffic is light on Saturday, so I quickly advanced toward police headquarters. I was not far away when the phone in my left jacket pocket started to ring. I don't like to talk on a cell while driving, but now I was in a hurry. Holding the steering wheel with one hand, I took out my service phone and saw the name of Inspector Ognjen Prokopović on the screen. I was on duty with him today.

"I'll be up in three minutes," I said without preliminaries.

"Maybe you won't, Inspector Lukić. A break-in was reported at 12 Oak Street. I thought you'd be interested. I see in the record that you were there last night."

"Yes, I was. Which apartment was broken into?"

"Let me see . . . number 19. An on-site investigation team has already been sent."

"I'll go there right away."

I was already well on my way to Oak Street when I realized there was no reason to rush, so I slowed down. It made no difference if I got there sooner or later. The police were already on the site, so the damage could not be any greater than it already was.

A patrol car was parked in front of the entrance. I left my car in one of the two available spots. As I got out of the car, I looked once again at the upper left-hand corner of the five-story building. All the windows were still closed. As I drew near to the building, I recognized the heavy, mustachioed policeman standing in the foyer where Miss Aksentijević had been waiting for me the night before. He wasn't at all bothered by the wind, particularly since it had died down considerably during the night. He'd probably gone inside so as not to appear unnecessarily conspicuous.

"Good morning, Inspector," he muttered, opening the door for me.

"Good morning, Vranešević."

"Fifth floor."

"I know."

"Inspectors Kostić and Zarić are up there."

I nodded and continued on to the elevator, then

called it. Just as it started down from the top floor, my dream came vividly to mind. If I'd been alone in the foyer, I would have taken the stairs. Since there was no reason to hurry, I could finally count them carefully. But if I avoided the elevator, Vranešević's suspicions would be aroused. I didn't have to explain anything to him, of course, but rumors about me would soon start to spread. Policemen are much more inclined to gossip than people think. And not much is needed to get them started.

I looked down at the floor as soon as I got inside and pushed the button. As the doors met behind me, I waited in dread for the elevator to shoot upward. I felt no relief, however, when this failed to happen, since the ascent took the opposite extreme. The elevator seemed to climb considerably more slowly than before. After some time, the ride should already have been over, but it seemed never to end. I wanted to check our progress on the display, but was afraid of confronting my reflections in the mirrors. Finally, just as I was starting to get jumpy, the elevator stopped. I exited backwards without waiting for the doors to open all the way.

In front of Miss Jakovljević's apartment stood Inspector Zarić and a middle-aged woman in dark-blue overalls, a kerchief tied around her head. The tall, lean, balding inspector was holding a notepad and pencil. Next to the cleaning lady was a red plastic bucket with a long handle of the same color sticking out, its tip leaning against the wall.

"Hello, Inspector Lukić," said Zarić when I reached them. "This is Mrs. Sokolović. She's been working here for 17 years. She's the one who reported the break-in. Inspector Kostić is inside, taking pictures." He shook his head. "I've never seen such a . . . mess."

"The door was ajar. All I did was peek inside," said the cleaner, as though defending herself. "Poor Miss Jakovljević. Everything's ruined. It's awful. . . ." She stopped for a moment. "I didn't touch anything. I called you right away."

She patted the large pocket of her overalls, showing the contours of a cellphone.

"You did the right thing," I replied with a smile. "We won't keep you once you have made a statement. Please don't clean on the fifth floor anymore today."

She nodded quickly. Obviously she could barely wait to get out of there.

I raised my elbow to push the door all the way open, but before doing so I turned to Mrs. Sokolović.

"Did you see anyone in the corridor?"

Zarić answered for her. "No, she didn't. I asked." He tapped on his notebook with the end of his pencil.

"Not a soul," she replied hastily. "I rarely run into anyone on Saturday. People sleep in."

Now I nodded, with another smile.

Even before I entered Miss Jakovljević's apartment, I could tell from the entrance what awaited me inside. When the door opened, before me lay the exact opposite of the excessive tidiness I'd found the night before. Inspector Zarić's hesitant description of it as a "mess" was a gross understatement.

There was not a single book on the shelves next to the window at the end of the small room. They had been thrown onto the round glass table, the chairs and the floor. I entered the short hall and looked with foreboding through the right-hand door into the large room. Burglars leave a variety of scenes behind them. With some there is not the slightest trace, as though they haven't been there at all. Others, on the contrary, seem to take great pains to cause as much damage as possible, either from the frustration of leaving without the expected booty or just as a prank. This, however, looked like the work of a psychopath who really hated books for some reason.

Had I not been a book lover, I wouldn't have been

so affected by what I saw. As a policeman I'd come across considerably worse sights, but as a professional I had not let them affect me personally. The emptied shelves here seemed eerie and when I lowered my eyes to the literally hundreds of books scattered about the three-seater, desk and floor, something tightened in my chest. The square rug that covered the center of the room was barely visible beneath the pile of books.

I heard footsteps in the small room. Inspector Kostić appeared in the opening that connected it to the large room, holding a camera. He was short and stout, with a thick red beard and round wire-rimmed glasses.

"Hello, Inspector. What do you have to say about this jumble?"

I shook my head. "Appalling."

"Odd kind of burglar. Looks like the only thing he pounced on were the books. Didn't seem to be interested in anything else."

"Have you been in the kitchen and bathroom?"

"Yes, I took pictures of everything. Seems tidy enough. But there weren't any books there."

"How did they get in? Are there any traces of the break-in?"

"None at all. They must be good at picking locks."

"Burglars usually are."

"What were they looking for in the books? Seems like they leafed through them before they were tossed."

He pointed at the tallest pile in the middle of the rug. Several of the volumes were lying open somewhere around the middle.

I shrugged. "What do burglars usually look for that can be put inside a book? Probably money."

"Who keeps money in books anymore?"

"Writers, for example. They think something is safest when they hide it in a book."

"Writers, sure. Your specialty. You were here last night, weren't you? What happened?"

"Nothing. Suspicions had been aroused that something was wrong with the woman who lives here. Apparently she was in the apartment, locked in from the inside, but was not answering the interphone or telephone. I didn't find anyone here."

"Had the door really been locked from the inside?"

"That's right."

"But how. . . .?"

I shrugged again.

"It looks like we won't know until we find the woman."

"How did you get in?"

"Inspector Vesić opened it for me."

"Of course. Nothing stands in his way." He hesitated a moment as though uncertain and then asked, "Are you sure you locked it on your way out?"

I nodded. "Quite certain. Inspector Vesić would have told me if I hadn't. He would not have allowed such an oversight."

"This doesn't seem to be an ordinary break-in. If the burglar really was looking for money, as you say, they were certainly counting on a tidy sum, what with all this effort. They would've had to have been here a long time to check each book. When did you leave here?"

"A little after eleven." I decided not to mention my second visit. Further explanation would be required and I didn't feel like going into the details right then.

"They probably had enough time the rest of the night. But there's another problem. Judging by the disorder," his free hand swept over the scattered books, "they didn't take much account of the noise they made. Like they didn't care if the neighbors heard. There's nothing quiet about throwing heavy books on the floor. But no one heard anything. Inspector Zarić went one floor down and checked it out."

"Maybe they're sound sleepers."

"No one sleeps that soundly. You'd have had to be deaf not to hear this."

I snapped my fingers when the word "deaf" reminded me of something.

"I know someone who would have heard even much softer sounds. He has a perfect sense of hearing."

Without any more ado, I turned around and left Miss Jakovljević's apartment. Inspector Zarić was now standing alone in front of it. He gave me a puzzled look as I silently took two steps to the other side of the corridor and raised my hand to the doorbell, thinking how much easier life was during daylight than at night.

Before my index finger reached the button, the door started to open. The person who appeared was not Mr. Teodosijević, however, but the one I least expected. Although, naturally, I should have.

15

"Good morning, Inspector Lukić," said Commissioner Milenković. "You overslept."

He looked like he had not slept a wink. There were visible circles under his eyes and his tie was a little crooked. But he was freshly shaven.

"Good morning," I replied after a brief pause. "I didn't oversleep. My shift began at nine."

"If you stick to shifts you miss a lot in a policeman's line of work. And if you get a lot of sleep. While you were resting, things here were jumping."

He motioned his head toward Miss Jakovljević's apartment.

"It seems that even a service without shifts that never sleeps was unable to prevent the break-in."

"We don't cover break-ins."

"Not even when it's the apartment of someone you're interested in?"

The commissioner glanced over my shoulder at Inspector Zarić and, moving aside, opened the door fully.

"Come on in."

There was a young woman in the large room who could not have been more than twenty-six or -seven. If I had run into her in the street I would never have thought that she worked for the National Security Agency. Her dark hair was shaved above her ears and the rest of her head was covered with multicolored streaks. She had little rings in the middle of her lower lip and on the edge of her left nostril, and two more larger rings hung from her earlobes. She was wearing skin-tight jeans that were ripped in a few places, a colorful knit vest that barely reached her navel and a white wide-collared shirt with sleeves rolled up to just below the elbow.

Judging by this girl and the young man I had met the night before in the Communications Department, one would say that the Agency had brought in fresh blood and changed style. I did not recall anyone younger than forty among Commissioner Milenković's earlier associates, and you could more or less tell what they did for a living by their conduct and dress code. Compared to this new generation, the commissioner alone gave this impression now, although he was still quite inconspicuous as someone whose main concern was national security. Perhaps it was time he retired. Or perhaps he was one of those irreplaceable people who keep on working even after they retire.

The girl was taking photographs of the framed paintings that densely covered the walls. As I entered the room she turned, quickly raised her camera and took my picture.

"I didn't have time to smile," I said with a belated smile.

"I already have a picture of you smiling," she replied, also smiling, then went back to her work without offering any explanation.

Everything in the large room looked the same as it had the night before: the cot under the window, the brown armchair facing it, and the tall round stool next to the easel in the middle with a covered painting on it. The easel no longer stood out because the bright ceiling light was off. The apartment faced northwest so it did not get much morning light. I walked toward the large opening in the partition wall and looked into the small room.

"We're alone, Inspector Lukić," said Commissioner Milenković behind me.

"What about Mr. Teodosijević?" I asked, turning to face him.

"He's on a trip. Abroad."

I gazed at him, mystified. "He left this morning?"

"No. He's been gone for three weeks and will stay at least another three."

"How's that possible? I talked to him last night."

Commissioner Milenković took a large cellphone out of his inside jacket pocket, punched some buttons and then raised it toward me.

"Is this the person you talked to?"

I moved my head a little closer to get a better look at the photograph on the screen. The man bore no resemblance to the one I had seen the night before. His eyes were even more different than his facial features. They were muddy-brown and watery, the exact opposite of sparkling jade.

"Who is that?" I asked, although there was no need.

"Mr. Branislav Teodosijević. Artist. The owner of this atelier. They are three hours ahead of us where he is so we didn't wake him when we called this morning to ask permission to enter here."

"I don't understand," I said, shaking my head. "Then who was the man who introduced himself as Teodosijević?"

"I'd like to know that too. No one in our database matches his description."

I wrinkled my brow. "How do you know what he looks like?"

"That at least was not hard to find out. You weren't the only one here last night."

"Miss Aksentijević. . . ."

The corners of Commissioner Milenković's lips turned up almost imperceptibly. "She was very willing to cooperate, even though we did wake her up."

"Why did you wake her up?"

"To check whether you might have neglected to tell us something about what happened here last night. For example, you made no mention of meeting the painter."

"I didn't consider it important. I didn't think it had any connection with the telephone that made our paths cross again."

Commissioner Milenković sighed. "In this work it's always wiser to assume there's some connection. In any case, Miss Aksentijević mentioned him right away and helped us determine what he looks like. It turns out she has an excellent eye for detail. Here, see for yourself."

His fingers danced over the buttons on the cellphone's little keypad once more, then he raised it toward me. If I didn't know it was a computer-generated composite portrait, I would have sworn I had a photograph of the alleged Mr. Teodosijević in front of me.

"Does it bear a resemblance?" said Commissioner Milenković, more as a statement than a question.

I nodded. "Very much."

"Miss Aksentijević said she immediately distrusted him. One might say she was more astute than an inspector."

"Is that so? What was it that raised her suspicions?"

"The fact that he was blind, of course. Or even that he was impersonating a blind man and introduced himself as a painter."

"If there have been deaf composers and illiterate writers, why not a blind painter?" I stopped for a moment and looked around the large room. The girl was still hard at work taking pictures, paying no attention to us. "If I had any doubts like Miss Aksentijević, they disappeared when I saw these paintings. This is exactly how I imagined a blind man would paint. . . ."

"That's not much of a compliment to the real Teodosijević. Well, let's not go into that right now. As you know, art is not my forte. I'm more interested in what else you can say about the man you met here last night. Miss Aksentijević saw him only briefly, and you met him one more time, right?"

We looked at each other in silence for a few moments.

"You are well informed, even without a cooperating eyewitness," I said.

"I have traces that, as a rule, are more reliable than eyewitnesses. Last night, just after you left the Communications Department, Mr. Teodosijević called you through your duty officer to tell you that someone was in Miss Jakovljević's apartment. You stayed in the building over half an hour. You didn't need that long to inspect the little neighboring apartment. It doesn't take much hard thinking to realize that you spent most of the time talking to the alleged blind painter. That must have been in here, right? Why would you stand in the corridor?"

"I see you know how long I was in the building."

"Of course I know. Did you expect me not to put an immediate tail on the man who had such a strange cellphone?"

"Even when he's a fellow inspector?"

"Especially when I've already had unforgettable experience with this same fellow inspector."

"Bearing that experience in mind, I'd say it would be useful for both of us if we cooperated. This time, however, not one-way. . . ."

We looked each other in the eye again briefly. Two clicks of the camera were all that disturbed the silence.

Finally, Commissioner Milenković gestured toward the armchair.

"Take a seat," he said and then headed for the cot. He sat down next to the metal frame where Adam's owner had been the night before. He waited for me to get settled and then asked: "What would you like to know?"

"I assume you had the building under surveillance the whole night. What happened while I was peacefully asleep?"

"Nothing."

"What do you mean, nothing?"

"No one went in or out of the building after you left at 00:52 until this morning at 07:26 when the cleaning woman arrived."

"Is there any other way out except the main entrance?"

"There's one in the back." He pointed his thumb over his shoulder at the window behind his back. "There's a little park. No one was there either."

"So where could the false Teodosijević be?"

"Not only him but his dog too. The simplest answer is that if they didn't leave the building then they must still be in it. But that doesn't seem very probable."

"Why not?"

The shadow of a smile crossed Commissioner Milenković's face again. "How about if I do the asking for a bit? We've done away with the one-way cooperation if I'm not mistaken."

"Go ahead," I replied contritely.

"What did you find when you visited Miss Jakovljević's apartment the second time?"

"The same as the first. No one was there."

"What did the allegedly blind painter say about that?"

"He said I was too late. The visitor had purportedly left before I got there."

"Was there any trace of them?"

"Not that I noticed."

"Did you take something with you again, by any chance?"

I shook my head and replied with a question: "What would I take?"

Before I finished my sentence I felt a vibration in my pants pocket announcing that I had received a message. I knew it could not be seen and would stop very quickly, but even so I interlaced my fingers more hastily than I intended and put both hands over my pant leg. As though things were not tense enough already, the girl turned toward me suddenly and took another picture. Once again her only explanation was a smile.

"I don't know," said Commissioner Milenković, shrugging his shoulders. "I thought there might be other unusual devices such as a cellphone without a SIM card and battery."

"I didn't see anything unusual. Everything looked the same as the first time."

"Then the mysterious visitor was incomparably more discreet than the one that came afterward and made that mess with the books. If, of course, there was any visitor."

"What do you mean?"

"Perhaps the impostor in Teodosijević the painter's apartment used the excuse of a nonexistent visitor to lure you back here again."

"Since he was an impostor, wouldn't he rather see the back of a police inspector instead of luring him here again?"

"That would be more natural, I agree. Unless he had some special reason to see this very same police inspector in private."

"What might that reason be?" I asked after a brief hesitation.

"I can't imagine. Something, however, certainly kept

you talking for almost half an hour. What did you talk about?"

I gazed at him again without speaking.

"I think my turn has come to ask questions," I replied at last.

Commissioner Milenković seemed about to protest, but then he just nodded.

"Go ahead."

"What are you doing here in Mr. Teodosijević's apartment?"

"Is it hard to guess? There's no better stakeout for Miss Jakovljević's apartment. It's a shame we didn't come last night, things would probably be much clearer now. We entered as soon as the cleaning lady reported the break-in. If we'd found someone in the apartment, we would have talked them into cooperating. It turned out simpler this way, even though a new mystery cropped up. But at least we established that the Teodosijević here was a fake. And the real one's mind is now at rest. He would have a hard time finding a better guard for his apartment than the National Security Agency."

"Have you been to Miss Jakovljević's?"

"Just briefly." He nodded toward the girl. "There was only enough time to take a few pictures. Your colleagues got here quickly."

"The cleaning lady must have seen you."

"Yes, but we had no trouble convincing her that she hadn't."

I smiled. "She's quite credible when she says she didn't see anyone."

"All right," said Commissioner Milenković, keeping a straight face. "Let's get back to my question. What did you talk about?"

I pressed my interlaced fingers more firmly over my pants pocket.

"The Grand Manuscript," I said in a low voice.

He grabbed the root of his nose between his thumb and index finger, closed his eyes and bowed his head a little. As I looked at him in that position, he seemed like an old man for the first time. An old man surrounded by adversity. He sighed noisily through his nose, then spoke softly as well, without raising his head.

"I'm listening."

"It's a twisted story. Everything revolves around Miss Jakovljević's new novel. She writes detective stories. It seems that some people believe it is a . . . special . . . book. Apparently, the first one to read it will become—immortal."

Commissioner Milenković let go of his nasal root and raised his head.

"Immortal?" he repeated without any special emphasis.

"I told you it was twisted. Literature sometimes has peculiar side effects. . . ."

"You're telling me. . . ." he mumbled with another sigh.

"I don't think anything . . . out of the ordinary . . . is about to happen. Last night you mentioned Occam's razor. The simplest explanation is that Miss Jakovljević has gone somewhere to finish her new book in peace so the weirdos don't bother her. She didn't even ask us for protection. If someone hadn't been searching her apartment last night, the police would have had no reason to get involved."

"If only Occam's razor could always be applied. How, for example, did Miss Jakovljević leave an apartment that was locked from the inside? By the way, what did Inspector Vesić have to say about that?"

"He was impressed."

Commissioner Milenković nodded.

"There, you see. But a cellphone that works without a SIM card and battery is an even greater mystery."

"Didn't you say that communications technology is coming up with new things all the time?"

"I did. This, however, would be a real communications revolution, and I doubt that the first we heard of it would come from a woman who writes detective books and is being hounded by weirdos. But there's a third mystery that's giving me the biggest headache."

"Third mystery?"

Frowning, Commissioner Milenković rubbed his temples with the tips of his fingers and turned his head toward the girl.

"Officer, if you please. . . ."

The photographer lowered her camera, went up to the easel and with a sharp jerk removed the cloth covering the painting.

16

If it had been anyone else, I would have recognized him at once. Provided, of course, that I knew him. As it was, it took at least two seconds for me to realize that I was looking at my own smiling face. The photographer must have had this in mind when she'd said she already had a picture of me smiling.

Incredulous, I got up from the squeaky armchair and went to the easel in the middle of the room. It was a sketch on a large square piece of paper pinned to the frame. Drawn in short strokes with charcoal, I would say it had been done in a hurry, but that was only a guess. In any case, it had been made by someone very skilled at drawing. Although just an outline, it was a perfect likeness. I didn't have a single painting or drawing of myself, so I would have loved to frame this one and put it in my study, but it would do no good to ask Commissioner Milenković. Even if the case were quickly closed, the National Security Agency would never part with evidence.

Instead of going back to work, the girl remained next to the easel and took pictures of me staring at myself. I turned toward her; I could tell by the upturned corners of her mouth that she was amused by my confusion.

I looked at Commissioner Milenković. "Who drew this?"

"Not Mr. Teodosijević."

"Did you ask him?"

"Yes. He was almost insulted."

"Why?"

"First of all, he's never seen you. At least that's what he claims. And then, it seems he's not a fan of figurative painting. To put it mildly."

"Is that so?"

"Why does that surprise you?" His hand gestured toward the walls covered with black and red arabesques. "It was to be expected."

"So who drew it if he didn't?"

"The choice is not very wide, at least as far as we know."

"The false Mr. Teodosijević? Even if he had a talent for drawing, he couldn't have made my portrait because he couldn't see me."

"Are you certain?"

"What? He was blind so he couldn't have made my portrait or he was blind so he couldn't see me?"

"The latter. The former would not surprise me. There is little that can still surprise me so far as artists are concerned. Who knows, maybe a blind painter would be able to draw you based on your voice."

"You overestimate artists. If he relied solely on my voice, the result would be something like the paintings on the walls. If, however, he was only pretending to be blind, then he was very convincing."

Commissioner Milenković nodded his head. "He is without doubt a master of deception."

"Judging by that, it seems that not even you know what happened to him after we said goodbye last night. Where are he and the dog if your people didn't see them leave the building? Does it have anything to do with the break-in at Miss Jakovljević's apartment?"

"Those are all very interesting questions, Inspector Lukić. One of them, however, intrigues me more than the others. And worries me too."

He got up, went to the easel and gazed at the drawing. In the meantime, the girl had gone into the small room where clicking could be heard from time to time.

"Which one?" I asked to snap him out of his musing.

The commissioner knocked with his index finger on the edge of the drawing paper.

"Why is it a portrait of you?"

I shrugged. "I have no idea."

Just as I said this, the cell in my pants pocket started vibrating again. I barely stopped myself from reflexively covering the pocket with my hand. But it was even harder to bear up under the commissioner's inquisitive look.

"Absolutely nothing comes to mind?"

We were standing less than a meter apart, looking each other straight in the eye. The clicking stopped in the small room.

I shook my head. "Nothing."

The commissioner examined me again briefly, then sighed audibly through his nose. He took the cloth from the easel trestle and covered the drawing.

"I expect you to call me if you think of anything. Now we're cooperating fully, aren't we?"

"To be sure. I hope that you will contact me in the same spirit if something comes up. For example, if you get onto the alleged Mr. Teodosijević's trail."

"To be sure, to be sure," replied Commissioner Milenković with a tinge of impatience. "Cooperation above all."

I motioned my head toward the front door. "I don't suppose you have anything against us sealing Miss Jakovljević's apartment. Those are regulations, as you know, although the measure is not necessary, of course. The writer, along with the painter, currently has the safest apartment in town."

"Goodbye, Inspector Lukić."

Inspectors Kostić and Zarić were waiting for me in the corridor with questioning looks, but they didn't ask anything. I went to the door of the neighboring apartment, took out the key and locked it twice. The key moved smoothly in the lock.

"Seal this, please," I said to Inspector Kostić.

He turned briefly toward the door to the painter's apartment, as though in a quandary, then nodded. He opened his equipment bag, having already placed his camera inside, squatted by the door to Miss Jakovljević's apartment and got to work. It took him less than three minutes to finish.

"There's not enough room for all three of us," I said when we were in front of the door to the little elevator. "I'll take the stairs."

Kostić and Zarić exchanged quick looks and then headed after me. I had hoped they would take the elevator. This was a new chance to count the steps at my leisure, in daylight. But it didn't work. I doubted they would keep quiet until the ground floor.

Inspector Zarić was the first to speak, softly, when we reached the fourth floor.

"This must be something big if Commissioner Milenković is here in person."

"Must be," I replied in a low voice.

"He kept you a long time," said Inspector Kostić, half as a query.

"He wanted to know what happened here last night."

"Who would think," said Zarić, "that the Agency would be interested in . . . an authoress. . . ."

I would not have responded if the last two words had not been spoken derisively.

"That's because they've brought in new blood. The

old guys aren't readers, while these younger ones are well-read. They won't hire them otherwise. Rumor has it that being well-read will soon be a requirement for us too. Haven't you heard? How's your reading coming along, you two?"

The inspectors exchanged glances again.

"So-so. . . ." replied Kostić.

"My advice is that you get cracking right away. It doesn't have to be serious reading matter. Take detective novels, for example. That's something you know. You could even start with Miss Jakovljević. If the Agency finds her interesting, I'm sure you will too."

"What would you recommend?" asked Zarić.

Serves me right, I thought. The predicament I'd gotten myself into only worsened when the cellphone started trembling in my pocket again. This was getting stressful. As I pretended to mull it over, we reached the ground floor. Officer Vranešević rushed out of the foyer and held the door open for us.

"Whichever of Miss Jakovljević's eight books you choose, you won't be wrong," I said in front of the building. "They are all excellent."

They nodded and then climbed into the back seat of the patrol car. Vranešević got behind the wheel and had already started the car when I remembered something and knocked on the window. Kostić opened it.

"Send those pictures you took upstairs to my computer right away, please."

"All right."

I took a look around after the patrol car left. Even though it was almost ten o'clock, the short street was empty. Heading for my car, I closely examined Miss Jakovljević's apartment along the way. Not only her windows, but all those on this side of the building were full of brightly reflected sunlight. Just as I inserted the key in the car door, barking disrupted the calm Saturday morning. I raised my head in the direction from which it had come and caught sight of a large dog at the far corner of the street. It looked at me and continued to bark, as though wanting to draw my attention. As soon as it was certain I had seen it, the dog turned and disappeared down a side street.

I quickly took out the key and started running. This certainly must have confused Commissioner Milenković's invisible people, assigned to monitor my every move, but that was not important just then. I had to double check. All German shepherds look more or less the same to me, particularly when seen briefly and from a distance. It was probably just a stray dog, but it might have been Adam.

I reached the corner in a jiffy and looked down the street, which was longer than Oak Street. Out of five pedestrians, the two closest to me turned around, attracted by the sound of my running, and looked in bewilderment as I stood there turning my head left and right, clearly searching for someone. I was bewildered too. There was no dog anywhere in sight.

I waited for the curious pedestrians to continue on their way and then carried on down the street at a normal pace, looking all around. The dog had to be nearby, out of sight somewhere. This would have been easier, of course, had the dog been smaller. There were not many places where a big dog could fit. And why would it first lure me this way and then hide, as though we were playing hide-and-seek?

I didn't feel like playing, so I stopped after five or six steps, determined to go back. That's when I caught sight of the wrought iron fence several buildings away. The dog might be there. Three tall steps led down to the teashop's below-level entrance—quite enough space for even a person to take cover if they crouched low.

Approaching it cautiously, I looked down through the railings. There was no one in front of the entrance. I shrugged my shoulders and turned to go back, then thought, why not stop by, since I was already there. The shot putter had invited me to come back when I was not with Miss Aksentijević. Here was that chance. I was not in a hurry to go anywhere.

17

As I DESCENDED THE steps, it crossed my mind that the teashop might not be open this early on a Saturday. There was no sign on the door with its opening hours. I pulled down on the massive iron handle and at first thought it was locked, but then the door started to move and, as on the day before, herbal fragrances greeted me from the semi-darkness. Even on a bright day not much sunlight penetrated; the lower halves of the two windows were always in shadow.

I remained in the entrance for several moments, waiting for my eyes to adjust to the subdued light. Even then all I could really see was the illuminated wall opposite me with the bar. Next to it stood a middle-aged man with luxuriant curly hair in a white shirt and brown vest, busy with the cups and saucers. The muted music was drowned out by the sound of water running in the sink. He raised his head toward me and nodded with a smile.

"Good morning," he said in a soft voice, turning off the water.

"Good morning," I replied. "I hope I'm not too early."

"Certainly not. We open at nine. Every day. Please take a seat, sir."

As I looked around the teashop, I realized it was not empty as I had first thought. On the left, approximately in the middle of the wall, someone was sitting on the dark-brown leather banquette, but I could not tell whether it was a man or a woman. The contours of a cup were on the table.

I headed for the little round table where I had sat the night before with Miss Aksentijević. The waiter wiped his hands and then approached me, smiling all the while. He minced his steps as though wearing high heels, even though his shoes were flat. There was a brass pin in the shape of a teapot on the lapel of his vest.

"Tea against illusions is to your liking, sir, if I'm not mistaken?"

I looked at him warily. "Does it show?"

"No, it does not show, but we know. We keep track of our customers. That's the tea you had last night. I hope that it helped you."

I shook my head. "I'm afraid not. I'm still plagued by illusions. I just had one a few minutes ago."

"Then we'll have to add something to your tea." His smile broadened. "Sometimes we don't get the remedy right the first time."

He hastened back to the bar, swinging his hips.

Watching as he prepared the tea with theatrical movements, I wondered what the Agency people tailing me thought about everything that had happened in the past ten minutes. First I had run after a dog, then the dog had disappeared without a trace and I'd ended up in the teashop where they had no surveillance. More customers could be expected at any moment. What tea would suit them? What would be their complaints?

A thought suddenly struck me and I looked over my left shoulder at the middle of the wall that was now behind my back. My vision had improved somewhat, but I still could not make out the person sitting there. I was certainly more visible to them because I was close to the window. I faced forward again so my staring would not be conspicuous.

Nevertheless, no, I concluded. Even though Commissioner Milenković was certainly not to be underestimated, that would be going too far. They had no reason to keep someone in the teashop. Nothing had indicated that I would stop by. I had not even known it myself. If I let paranoia get the upper hand, I would end up seeing Agency people everywhere. Even the waiter who was just bringing me my tea.

He placed the cup in front of me.

"This should get rid of your illusions."

"The woman who served me yesterday must have given you a good description if you recognized me so easily."

"There was no need to describe you. I had a good look at you last night. I was really curious to see what the customer looked like who asked for tea against illusions. It's not ordered very often." He swept a curl off his forehead. "And one does not forget such a nice manly face. . . ."

"You see quite well in this dim light. I can barely make things out. And Madam was truly admirable in that regard."

"Miss, actually. My sister."

I looked at him closely.

"I might be wrong, but I wouldn't say you resemble each other very much."

"We don't resemble each other at all. As you know, she is quite. . . .butch."

"I thought she did athletics. Some throwing event. . . ."

"She's done different jobs. Mostly men's. Now she's settled down here. Teas are her strong suit. It's a family trait."

"Last night we started an interesting conversation, but didn't have a chance to finish it. When will she be in the teashop again?"

"From five in the afternoon to one in the morning. We will be pleased to see you again. Me in particular . . . And we have to check whether the illusions are gone. Enjoy your tea, sir."

The tea now seemed a deeper red. That might have

been owing to the new ingredients or the influence of spare daylight. I brought the white bell-shaped steaming cup to my lips and sipped the hot liquid carefully. A sweetish taste now joined the bitter and sour that I remembered from the night before. As I lowered my cup, vibrations filled my pocket once again.

I hastened to take out the black cellphone. Finally I had a chance to read the messages. This was the fourth. Coming to the teashop had turned out to be rather a good idea. Reading the messages in the car, office or any other public place would not have been wise; that would not have escaped the attention of those who were tailing me. Then I would have had a hard time explaining to Commissioner Milenković which cell I had used when there was no trace of my service or private phone. I turned briefly once again to the invisible person behind my back. I should be safe here.

I pressed a button on the keypad and the last message appeared on the screen.

"If this were a detective novel, Inspector Lukić, it would be high time you checked the messages you receive on this special telephone. There is no compelling narrative coherence that could explain your ignoring them."

I wanted to reply at once, but opened the three previous messages first.

"What should we do now?"

That was the first one. I had received it after Commissioner Milenković asked whether I might have taken something else from Miss Jakovljević's apartment.

"You really have no idea? Pretty poor intuition for a police inspector. . . ."

The second message had come after I replied to the Commissioner's question as to why my portrait had been drawn that I had no idea.

"It's certainly no compliment when someone recommends a writer without reading a single one of their books. . . ."

The third message had come after Inspector Zarić's awkward question regarding which of Miss Jakovljević's books I would recommend.

I thought things over for a few moments and then opened the last message again, chose Reply and started to write.

"If this were a detective novel, the writer would not complicate the inspector's life by sending unimportant messages at the most inconvenient times. There is certainly even less compelling narrative coherence for her playing tricks."

A new message arrived just a moment after I had sent mine.

"If you had read any of the writer's books you would know that playing tricks is her distinctive trait. And it has excellent narrative coherence."

"Coherent or not, it's an obstruction. I'm tempted to turn off this cell."

"It isn't easy to turn off a cell without a battery. . . ."

"Maybe so, but I could stop taking it with me."

"Under no circumstances would I advise that you stay out of contact with the writer. Her help might come in very handy."

"Is it commonplace in your novels for the writer to help the inspector?"

"No, it only happens when the inspector can't find his bearings. Like you, for instance."

"I can't find my bearings?"

"That's what it looks like. You're trying to find the writer's trail, aren't you?"

"Yes."

"And you don't even know what she looks like. Isn't that indispensable? You might run into her without realizing who she is. . . ."

As I feverishly considered what to reply, the service phone in my jacket started ringing. Rattled, for a few moments I did not know what to do with the phone in my hand. I finally put it back in my pants pocket and reached into my left inside jacket pocket.

"Hello!" I said, almost shouting.

"Is everything all right?" asked Inspector Prokopović, mystified.

"Yes, yes," I hastened to assure him. "Just a little . . . hitch. . . ."

"Do you plan on coming over here soon?"

"Yes, I was just getting ready to go. Why?"

"You have a visitor."

"Who is it?"

"A lawyer from Search Publishers."

"Since when do lawyers work on Saturday?"

"I don't know, but if I were you, I wouldn't waste a moment."

"It's that urgent?"

"No, that's how good she looks. It's almost a sin to make such a pretty woman wait. . . ."

Just like the night before when the alleged painter Teodosijević had called about the break-in at Miss Jakovljević's apartment, I wanted to ask at least three questions at once, but instead I just replied: "I'm on my way."

I put my service phone back in my jacket pocket and finished my tea as I got up. It had cooled while I was exchanging messages. The ones I received had come in a split second, unlike the ones I composed that were so frustratingly slow, even though I wrote quickly. I headed for the bar with long strides, taking change out of my pocket along the way.

"It's not a good idea to let tea go cold and then drink it all at once," said the tea maker reprovingly. "It has the best medicinal effect while it's hot. Besides, tea should be a pleasure." He stopped briefly and his seemingly stern expression turned into an impish smile. "As should life. . . ."

I sighed. "Obligations spoil pleasure. With tea and with life. . . ."

"You must be swamped with obligations. Being an inspector isn't easy, I imagine."

I looked at him askance. "Is this another family trait—guessing your customers' profession—or is it just your sister who is endowed and you found out from her?"

"I found out from my sister, although I could have guessed by myself. We both have that skill. And I'm sure you have it too. How could a police inspector not be well-endowed. . . .?"

We looked at each other for a moment in silence. A curl had fallen on his forehead again and he twisted it around his index finger.

"You overrate police inspectors," I said. "You and your sister, for example, might have an easy time guessing the profession of your other customer, but I couldn't do it at all."

"What other customer?"

I motioned with my head to the left. "That one."

The tea maker looked in that direction and then questioningly at me. I turned around quickly and stared at the place where I had seen someone sitting. The light was still dim over there, but the banquette along the wall and the chairs next to the little round table were definitely empty. I looked around the teashop in bewilderment.

"It seems we'll have to add something more to your tea against illusions, Inspector," said the tea maker with another grin. "I look forward to seeing you again tonight."

18

It was not customary for an unannounced visitor to wait in an inspector's office. There was a common waiting room on the ground floor, but the duty officer at the entrance probably thought it was not elegant enough for such a lady. Her looks even made me ashamed of my office, which had never happened before. Perhaps not even the chief inspector's office would have suited her.

She was sitting in the armchair facing my desk with her long legs crossed. Everything about her was stylish: black pants and a blazer with discreet pinstripes, a dark-red wide collar blouse, open to the fourth button, shoes of the same color with a medium heel and a row of decorative little straps. The handkerchief sprouting like a bouquet from the left breast pocket of her blazer matched her blouse.

High cheekbones made her large blue eyes look a little slanted. She did not require a toothy smile to appear cheerful. Her coal-black hair was luxuriant, straight, parted in the middle, reaching just below her ears. She was barely over thirty so there was almost no need for makeup.

"Sorry to keep you waiting," I said, pausing before her. No apology was called for, but that's how it sounded.

"It's no problem. You didn't know I was coming."

She held out her hand. Her handshake was firm despite her seemingly delicate hands. Then she reached into the inside pocket of her blazer and handed me a business card.

"Jovana Timotijević, attorney at law."

"Inspector Dejan Lukić," I replied, putting the card on my desk. "What business brings you to the police station on a Saturday morning, Mrs. Timotijević?"

"Miss. . . ." she said, correcting me.

"Excuse me . . . Miss. . . ."

"Urgent business, Inspector. I hope that you can spare me a little of your time."

"With pleasure."

She gave me a smile but did not continue, and looked at me as though expecting something. I returned the look, perplexed.

"There's no need for you to stand while we talk," she said at last. "It won't be quite that quick."

"Of course," I said with a nod, feeling foolish.

As I hastened around the desk to take my seat, Miss Timotijević opened the large black briefcase she had placed on the floor next to the armchair. She took out a piece of paper and handed it to me.

"My power of attorney."

"Thank you." I skimmed over the short text and gave it back to her.

"I have been informed that you are in charge of Miss Jakovljević's missing person case."

I shook my head. "You have been incorrectly informed. I am in charge of no such case."

Now she looked at me in bewilderment.

"You're not?"

"The police are not investigating Miss Jakovljlević's disappearance."

"Didn't you . . . break into . . . her apartment last night?"

"Your source is unreliable. There was no break-in."

"What would you call it, then, when the police enter a private apartment without authorization?"

"No authorization was required. Your source was the one who reported that Miss Jakovljević was locked inside her apartment and something might be wrong with her. As someone well-acquainted with the law, you undoubtedly know that in such cases the police have the right to enter an apartment without a court order. Even by force. Luckily, that was not necessary last night."

"Be that as it may, you didn't find Miss Jakovljević in the apartment?"

"No, I didn't."

"And the door was locked from the inside?"

"That's right."

"Isn't that sufficient grounds for the police to investigate her disappearance?"

"No, it isn't. The police are not interested in whether apartment owners lock their doors from the outside or inside when they leave, or where they go afterward."

I could tell by the movement of her blue eyes that she was thinking quickly.

"So does that mean that as far as the police are concerned, there is no Miss Jakovljević case?"

"There is, but only as of this morning."

"This morning?"

"Last night, actually. During the night someone really did break into her apartment and ransacked it. We found out this morning."

Her eyes were now calm as she surveyed me in silence.

"Did they steal . . . anything?"

"I don't know. Only Miss Jakovljević would be able to say."

She lowered her eyes so I could not see them during the brief silence that followed.

"What about you?" she said, suddenly raising her head. "Did you find . . . anything . . . when you entered the apartment last night?"

"Such as what?" I retorted.

"Anything at all."

"I didn't find anything."

"Did you turn on her computer?"

"I had no reason to. Miss Jakovljević could not have been hiding inside it."

She seemed tempted to say something about my sense of humor, but held back.

"Did you go into the apartment after the break-in?"

"Yes."

"Was the computer still there?"

I thought for a moment and then nodded my head.

"Yes."

"Was it turned on or off?"

"Off." I stopped for a moment. "You certainly are interested in Miss Jakovljević's computer. . . ."

She did not reply at once. Her deep-blue eyes scrutinized me. Then she reached into her briefcase again. This time she took out a sheaf of papers stapled together.

"It's not the computer that interests me but what's inside it. The file with Miss Jakovljević's new novel. It is the property of my client."

She folded back the first sheet and handed me the document. It was some kind of contract. Parts of the text were redacted.

"Article Four," said Miss Timotijević. "The manuscript is the sole property of Search Publishers."

I quickly read the three paragraphs of Article Four.

"Does this cover just the finished manuscript?" I asked.

"It covers any form of the manuscript, particularly when it's finished. Please understand the circumstances. My client paid Miss Jakovljević a very large advance. . . ."

"That's what's been blacked out, right?" I said, interrupting her, and handed her back the document.

"Yes. It's confidential information that concerns the contracting parties alone and is not for other eyes. But believe me, it's truly enormous."

"I never imagined that truly enormous sums were part of the local publishing industry."

"Miss Jakovljević is a very popular writer. In any case, the publisher is extremely interested in protecting his highly paid property. He definitely does not want anyone else to get their hands on the manuscript. Even briefly. It would cause inestimable damage."

"What kind of damage?"

She looked at me as though I'd asked a stupid question.

"It's not hard to divine. It's a detective novel. If someone malicious read the dénouement, they might leak how the book ends. On the internet, for example.

Then no one would want to buy it. That would be a real catastrophe for the publisher."

"Couldn't they do same thing after the book comes out?"

"Yes, but then it would be too late. The major part of the print run is sold soon after the book hits the stores."

"Everything would be simpler if Miss Jakovljević didn't write detective novels."

"What do you mean, simpler?"

"Readers have yet to change their minds about buying serious literature because they know how the book ends."

"Perhaps. The publisher, however, makes his living selling detective novels, not serious literature. That's the only place where big money is at stake. And a possible big loss that we would consider the fault of those who should have prevented it, and didn't. The police, for example."

"The police cannot be expected to protect something if no one knows where it is."

"No one knows where it is? It has to be in the writer's computer. Where else would it be?"

"I have no idea, but it doesn't necessarily have to be in her computer. The mess in Miss Jakovljević's apartment confirms that."

"How?"

I returned her look of a moment ago.

"It's not hard to divine. If, as you think, last night's burglar really was someone malicious who did this just to damage your client, where is the first place they would look for the manuscript?"

"In her computer," she replied somewhat hesitantly, sensing trouble.

"That's right. But if they found it, they'd have no reason to ransack the apartment."

Her blue eyes started dancing again.

"Maybe they wanted to throw you off the scent. . . ."

"There was no need for that. If they'd got hold of the file, the smartest thing would be to leave as soon as possible and not draw attention with the noise that necessarily accompanies a ransacking. No, the file was not where you assumed it would be, and I'd say it wasn't anywhere else in Miss Jakovljević's apartment either. Judging by how the burglar left the apartment, they went away empty-handed."

"Maybe the file is somewhere in the apartment, but they didn't find it. . . ."

"Then you have no reason to worry. But the whole idea seems rather shaky—an ill-intentioned person pulling a risky break-in just to harm a publishing house. It's hard to imagine such a fanatic. This was much more likely an ordinary break-in. Writers who receive enormous fees have more chances of being robbed than mere mortals."

"It wasn't some fanatic or ordinary thief. Don't be naive. The burglar was hired to do it."

"Who hired them?"

"It's not hard to divine. Do you really know so little about how things work in the publishing world? Lots of publishers would loosen their purse strings to hurt the competition."

"I know so little because the publishers of the books I read have no need to resort to mafia tactics. . . ."

By the look on her face, she was hesitating whether to continue this battle of wits with me over highbrow and lowbrow literature. Finally, the attorney's expediency prevailed over her bruised ego.

"Shouldn't you be looking for Miss Jakovljević to tell her about the break-in at her apartment?"

"We have no idea where she might be and there are no grounds to issue an APB. She has committed no crime. All we can do is wait for her to turn up. That's how most such disappearances end anyway."

"If she turns up, please let me know immediately."

She motioned her head toward the business card on the desk. "My client is very anxious to get hold of his property before other interested parties. Furthermore, please bear in mind how important it is that no one look at the manuscript." She paused briefly, then added with a hint of reluctance: "Not even you."

I smiled. "Don't worry, I certainly won't. I'm not a fan of novels that lose all value once you find out who did it."

Miss Timotijević took hold of her briefcase and stood up. I rose too. She was almost my height. The pants emphasized her long legs. She stretched out her hand across the desk. This time her firm handshake lasted a while.

"It was nice to meet you, Inspector Lukić." Her full lips turned up into a smile. "I'll find a way to personally repay you if you help me discover the file with Miss Jakovljević's new novel. As soon as possible."

Without waiting for me to reply, she finally let go of my hand, turned around gracefully and headed for the office door.

19

Before Miss Timotijević got to the elevator, the cellphone in my pocket started to vibrate again. I reached to take it out, but stopped at the last moment. Standing at the desk with my hand in my pocket, I looked around the office. There was no reason for those who had me under surveillance to be suspicious about my hand in my pocket. But this looking around would draw their attention. They might wonder what had led me to look for their surveillance camera at that particular moment. Good, let them rack their brains over it a bit.

They knew, of course, that I was on to them. Just as I knew that there was no sense in finding and disabling the hidden camera, because they would quickly install a new one in the same or another place, and my action would only increase their suspicions unnecessarily. Our cards were on the table. I knew they were watching me, they knew that I knew, and both sides knew that we would not stop trying to outwit each other in spite of our newly established two-way cooperation.

As I left my office, the elevator door was just closing after my visitor. I headed down the other side of the corridor. It was probably covered by cameras too, but not the place where I was going. Not even the National Security Agency would have the audacity to invade the privacy of the police men's room.

Everything in the stall was dark-green: the door, partition walls, tiles, toilet bowl. Even the lowered lid I was sitting on was a matching color. Before I took out the phone, I looked up briefly at the ceiling. It was predictably green too. No, even had they wanted, there was no way to hide a camera here. And they would need one for each of the six stalls. . . .

"So?" was the message.

"So?" I repeated.

"Stop pretending. How did the lady strike you?"

"She's pretty."

"That's all, pretty?"

"What else do you expect?"

"She usually leaves men breathless."

"This man held onto his breath. She's not my type."

"What is your type?"

"My current location is not exactly the right place to discuss that."

"You didn't have to go there. We could have freely exchanged messages even if you had stayed in your office."

"No we couldn't. There are too many curious eyes even when I'm alone. . . ."

"Let me worry about that. . . ."

"Oh, yes, I almost forgot. The almighty writer manip-

ulates the world of the detective novel as she sees fit. But doesn't such meddling disrupt the narrative coherence behind the work?"

"It is less disruptive than an inspector going to the men's room all the time. Not to mention that the very next time might arouse the suspicions of curious eyes."

"Then the best thing is to spare the inspector from having to go to the men's room all the time. Everything would be fine without your messages."

"Am I forcing you to read them? Who's to blame for your own curiosity?"

"I could stop."

"That is what would endanger the narrative coherence. The inspector is given an exceptional telephone and then for no reason disregards the messages he receives on it."

"I don't have to take narrative coherence into account. I'm not a writer."

"But you are a smart inspector. Would you refuse the only trail that might lead to solving the case just out of a capricious desire to show that you can curb your curiosity?"

I stared at the message on the screen until it started to fade.

"I've already been here too long. The curious eyes will become suspicious."

"Just one more thing. If it had been Miss Jakovljević who just visited you, she would not have impressed you, then. . . ."

"It was Miss Timotijević, not Jakovljević."

"Are you sure? Any woman at all could show up with a false business card, power of attorney and contract. Should a police inspector be so credulous?"

I sighed before starting to write again.

"Now is the time to establish what the mysterious Miss Jakovljević looks like."

"Best of luck. . . ."

I put the phone back in my pants pocket and was just about to leave the stall when something occurred to me. There might not be hidden cameras in the men's room but why not a microphone? It would not be an invasion of privacy, and conversations sometimes took place there that might be of interest to the National Security Agency. I raised the lid and flushed the toilet. This should be sufficiently audible confirmation that I had come here for the usual reasons. I waited about half a minute, emerged and stopped briefly at the sink, washing my hands.

I sat down at my office desk and turned on the computer. The first thing it did was tell me that Inspector Kostić's photographs had arrived. They could wait. I opened my browser and wrote "Jelena Jakovljević" in Google. There were more than 150,000 hits. All of them certainly did not refer to the Jelena Jakovljević who interested me. It was not exactly an uncommon name. But a quick inspection revealed that the great majority were nonetheless about her. She seemed truly popular.

The writer's official website was at the top of the long list. I clicked on the link and entered the site. The first thing I expected to see was her picture, but it was missing. I went to the bottom of the page. Nothing there either. I went back to the beginning and after establishing that there was no picture anywhere, started to read the introduction. The very first sentence explained the absence of a photograph, but this only increased the mystery.

"Jelena Jakovljević" was a pseudonym. Since the real identity was not divulged, the lack of a picture was not surprising. The real author of eight detective novels had to hide their appearance so no one would recognize them. I stared pensively at the screen where shades of brown prevailed. Then I put the cursor back in the Google field in the upper right-hand corner of the screen and added "pseudonym" after "Jelena Jakovljević".

The number of hits this time was much smaller, but still rather large. Readers were clearly intrigued as to who was hiding behind the pseudonym. I visited several of numerous forums that discussed this topic. Excluding the frivolity characteristic of anonymous collocutors exchanging ideas on the internet, the prevailing belief was that the pseudonym belonged to a reputable author of highbrow literature who was embarrassed by their forays into detective fiction.

It was interesting to see that by far the majority of candidates proposed were male. The assumption of such literary cross-dressing made me smile, particularly when I saw the names most mentioned. But whoever had resorted to the pseudonym was not a man. Miss Aksentijević spoke of the author she represented as a woman, and there would be no sense in doing so if the person was of the opposite sex. Why would she needlessly confuse the inspector she expected to find her client?

It was not clear, however, why she had called her by her pseudonym. Did she count on the police doing their job without learning the real identity of the missing writer? The fact that they would see her did not have to mean that they recognized her. She might not be a public figure at all. The other possibility would be that Miss Aksentijević did not even know who was hiding behind "Jelena Jakovljević". Yes, but then there were the contracts. Her real name probably had to be written there. Or did it? It was a shame I hadn't looked in more detail at the document Miss Timotijević had briefly shown me. Unless, of course, the name had been also censored as confidential information.

In either case, Miss Aksentijević might not know who Jelena Jakovljević was, but she certainly knew what she looked like. And she had proved talented at describing someone she had seen briefly only once. Commissioner Milenković might have asked her to describe the writer, but I doubted it. He had no grounds. Nothing had led him—or me, for that matter—to suspect that her identity was shrouded in mystery.

I searched through my pockets until I found the business card that Miss

Aksentijević had given me the night before and then took out my service cellphone. As I pressed the buttons, I had a notion that this was not going to be an easy conversation, bearing in mind her mood when we had parted. But I had no choice. Who else could describe the person who presented themselves as Jelena Jakovljević the writer? The fake painter Teodosijević claimed that he had talked to her, but it was hard to believe him in any regard, and he had disappeared so masterfully that not even the Agency could find any trace of him.

The telephone started to ring. If it turned out that Miss Aksentijević was still peeved with me, all I had left was Miss Timotijević, although she did not raise my hopes very much. Judging by what I had learned in the teashop the night before, the writer's agent was the primary contact with the publisher. If Miss Aksentijević was authorized to sign contracts or if she took them to her client to be signed, it was possible that Miss Timotijević had never seen the person who had made a name for themselves as Jelena Jakovljević.

Just when I thought she wouldn't answer, after the seventh ring I finally heard her groggy voice.

"Hello."

"Hello. Inspector Dejan Lukić speaking."

Silence reigned for several long moments.

"Good morning," she said like it was the last thing she meant.

"Did I wake you?"

"This is the second time the police have wakened me on a Saturday morning. The secret police did it at the crack of dawn. It wasn't even eight. I barely got back to sleep after they left and now you've done your best to ruin that. I'll be good for nothing all day, drowsy like this."

"Should I not have called with news for you?"

"If your news is as bad as this morning's, you'd have done better not to call. I almost fainted when they told me about the break-in. Great damage. You have no idea how great. And it's all your fault. . . ."

"Mine?"

"That's right. But let's put that aside for the moment. What news do you have? Did you find out something about Jelena?"

"Yes . . . something interesting."

She waited for me to continue, but when I didn't she said impatiently, "Let's hear it."

"It's not for the telephone. Could we meet somewhere?"

She was about to object, but fell silent. Her encounter with Commissioner Milenković had clearly left an impression.

"I hope you're not thinking of that awful teashop."

"No. You choose the place."

It took her some time to decide.

"Café Mocha. On the corner . . ."

"I know where it is. When can you be there?"

"What time is it now?"

I looked at the corner of the computer screen.

"Eleven eighteen."

"Already? I'll be there at twelve thirty."

"Fine. See you then." I turned off my cellphone and put it back in my jacket pocket.

If I hadn't been counting on Miss Aksentijević's assistance, I would have been tempted to ask why she needed more than an hour to reach Café Mocha which, as I saw from her business card, was in her neighborhood. Fair enough, she was still in bed, but did she really need so much time to get ready after learning that

I had news about her client? I supposed, however, it wouldn't be wise to annoy her further with such questions. And perhaps she could not get ready any faster in the morning after all, regardless of the urgency.

20

THIS WAS A CHANCE to look at the pictures of Miss Jakovljević's apartment and to try and sort out my thoughts without being disturbed. I had not had time to catch my breath properly since everything had started the night before. Events had closed in on each other just like in a detective story. Before opening the photograph file, I called Inspector Prokopović. We were having a quiet Saturday morning so I did not have to be in the duty room. I told him I was still working on the break-in and would be going out in about half an hour on a case-related job. I did not expect to be very long. If something urgent came up, I could be reached on my cell.

A slide show of scattered books began on the monitor. Something tightened in my chest just as it had that morning when I'd been there in person. Only someone without the slightest respect for books would do something like that. I could just imagine some vandal snatching books off the shelves, riffling through them and then throwing them all over the place, but why were they doing it? And this was by no means the only mysterious aspect of the break-in.

The ransacking clearly seemed to have some connection with Miss Jakovljević's disappearance, but this did not necessarily have to be true. It might have been an ordinary robbery. This assumption, being the simplest, was not to be disregarded. Commissioner Milenković was right, of course. Occam's razor could not be applied in every situation, but it must always be taken into account. In an inspector's line of work it was advisable to be wary of accidents and coincidences, but they should not be ruled out completely.

Everything, for example, could have taken place like this: not suspecting what had happened in the apartment last evening, some burglar decided to break into it last night. Even if they were watching the apartment, they could easily have missed the two occasions when I briefly turned on the lights. The windows were not lit up for the most part, leading to the conclusion that there was no one inside. They waited until the middle of the night, entered the building without being seen and broke into the apartment. They would have been unpleasantly surprised to find the door locked from the inside, but Inspector Vesić had removed that obstacle.

Up to this point everything seemed plausible, but now the trouble began.

First of all, what plunder was the burglar hoping for? It would not have been hard to find out that a wealthy woman writer lived there, but did they expect her to keep money in her apartment? And what writer would keep it in a book? That would be a sacrilege. I had only been joking with Inspector Kostić when I said writers considered something safest when they hid it in a book.

The same thing was true of valuables, although they would not fit unless the book had been violated like in some third-rate spy movie by hollowing out the middle to make a repository. Such a cliché, however, would be the last resort of a detective story writer.

Indeed, the burglar did not have to be aware of these writerly taboos, but on the other hand, robberies like that are not undertaken without preparation. Break-ins are only made when plunder is assured. And if, perhaps, they had not been counting on money and valuables, what would they be looking for in the books?

As far as I could tell from the pictures, nothing else had been touched. The paintings had not been taken down, for example, in search of a hidden safe. Everything in the kitchen seemed in place. There was nothing to search in the bathroom. Of the items with any value, the computer could have been taken, but the burglar had shown no interest.

Then there was the noise that throwing the books must have made. Even burglars who don't care about leaving a trail behind them are always quiet, because noise gives them away the easiest. What was even more inexplicable about the noise was the fact that the neighbors in the apartment below had not heard a thing. And there was no way to check whether the alleged painter Teodosijević had heard anything.

By all accounts, the idea of an ordinary break-in, although the simplest, had to be rejected. Something more complicated was going on. And the false Teodosijević was certainly involved.

Everything about him was a question mark. Who was he, anyway? Was he really blind? Why had he gone into the apartment of the real Teodosijević? Why had he called me back under the pretext that someone was in Miss Jakovljević's apartment? What did he actually know about her? Was he the one who drew my picture? If he was, when had he done it and why? Was he the one who broke into the apartment next door after I left, since it was no longer locked from the inside? What had he been looking for in the books? How could he have thrown them like that? How had he done it without being heard? Had he found what he was looking for? And finally—how had he disappeared from a building that was under Agency surveillance?

I was already well along with my examination of the pictures when something finally caught my eye. If I hadn't been deep in thought, I probably would have noted it earlier. Actually, I should have done so during my two visits to apartment number 19 the night before, but my attention had been directed at something else.

The pictures showed the books up close so I was

able to read their titles. The person writing detective novels under the pseudonym Jelena Jakovljević had a discriminating taste in literature. There wasn't a single work that would be out of place in my own library. Furthermore, they were all hardback editions, some even leather bound. This seemed to confirm the internet conjecture that the real author came from the world of highbrow literature.

The fifty-some photographs ended with two extremely white ones that Inspector Kostić had taken in the bathroom. The first was taken from the door with the curtain pulled over the bathtub. In the second one the curtain was pulled aside; all that disturbed the uniformity of the bathtub was a small yellow object at the bottom, zoom-magnified. Who knew what had led the photographer to single out the rubber ducky in this way.

I reached for the mouse and closed the window with the pictures, then moved the cursor to the lower left-hand corner and turned off the computer. I pushed the button to turn off the monitor and had already started to get up from my desk when a sudden thought made me sit down again. It seemed to come out of the blue. Certainly nothing in the photographs had instigated it.

I wondered: could the man I had met as the painter Teodosijević, whose true identity I still did not know, be hiding behind the pseudonym Jelena Jakovljević?

At first glance, this assumption had a large drawback. It contradicted what Miss Aksentijević had said. She had presented her client as a woman and there was no reason to deceive the inspector she expected to track her down as soon as possible.

Or perhaps there was a reason. . . .

I felt a tingling sensation at the top of my spine. What if everything from the very beginning had been a performance intended to deceive the inspector? Not just any inspector, of course, but one who could be perfectly used in an original ad campaign for Jelena Jakovljević's new novel, *Find Me*.

I should have seen through them the night before as soon as the would-be painter started that twisted story about the Grand Manuscript, but fatigue seemed to have already taken its toll. Plus, I could not imagine that someone would be bold enough to try and manipulate me. But why not? As I had recently learned, lots of money was at stake and in such cases few holds are barred.

It was hard to think of better publicity for a new thriller than the writer's mysterious disappearance just after she had finished it, with the inspector trying to find her the same one who had already conducted an extremely unusual literary investigation—a case that, at least officially, had not been solved because neither the regular nor the secret police would accept an increase in the number of realities, so everything had been put *ad acta*. The Grand Manuscript had been concocted to tie into the inspector's case of the "Last Book".

The tangle of knots surrounding the false Teodosijević suddenly started to loosen. He was, of course, in collusion with his agent, Miss Aksentijević. It could not be any other way. Both of them had proven skillful actors and had succeeded in deluding me. Her anxiousness at the possibility that something had happened to Miss Jakovljević and her anger at not getting hold of the manuscript had been convincing, as was his performance as a blind painter, something obviously calculated to confuse me. The absence of the owner of the neighboring apartment had only played into his hands.

He had called me back, lying that someone was in Miss Jakovljević's apartment, just so he could mention the Grand Manuscript. He wanted to make me think that something extraordinary was happening again. He had probably commissioned my portrait from someone. The drawing was intended to confirm my connection to the case.

After I left, he had gone back into his apartment and ransacked it to make it look like someone had broken in for mysterious reasons. There was no need to make any noise if Miss Aksentijević helped him. The books gave the impression of having been tossed about, but they could have been quietly positioned that way. Lastly, someone who was familiar with the building could have left it at night without being seen, even with the Agency keeping an eye on it, just as they could have stayed hidden somewhere inside.

Indeed, all that had to be proven was the initial premise that the detective story writer was an unknown person who had posed as a blind painter, but the consequences were so elegantly simple they seemed made to measure for Occam. Even so, I had to stifle the excitement that came over me. There were still several questions awaiting answers.

For example, how could they be certain that I would be the one to come last night? It could have been some other inspector. Even if they found out that I was on duty, it was still no guarantee that I would come and not the other person on duty with me.

Then, how had they managed to lock the door from the inside without being inside? According to Inspector Vesić it was impossible, at least for that type of lock, and he was the greatest expert around.

Then, why had Miss Aksentijević given Commissioner Milenković such a good description of her client? Shouldn't she have kept his identity hidden? Had she been frightened, not having counted on the National Security Agency getting involved in the whole thing? Or had she realized there was no sense in describing him otherwise since I had seen him too, and the other tenants in the building must have seen him from time to time? And what if that was not his real appearance? What if he had been in disguise last night?

Finally, there was the greatest enigma—two extremely unusual cellphones. If the publisher was ready to invest the wherewithal to promote his new edition, an explanation could be found for all the rest, but not for this gadget. I had taken to it so effortlessly, even though it was impossible in all respects. It worked without a SIM card and battery, it closely monitored me even when inside my pocket, and I received messages as though my unknown collocutor was writing them instantaneously.

Just as this thought crossed my mind, vibrations started in my pocket again.

21

I HESITATED JUST A moment and then took out the cellphone. Did it have another impossible characteristic—the ability to be invisible to Commissioner Milenković? The person I was exchanging SMS messages with had said *"Let me worry about that. . . ."* and I was convinced she was Jelena Jakovljević. If she had underestimated the commissioner, I would be in double trouble. I would have to explain why I had kept this other telephone secret, and he would certainly take it away from me. I didn't want to break off contact with this mysterious individual, of course, and I felt she was equally anxious to stay in contact with me. And I supposed she knew what she was doing when she wrote that. . . .

Before I opened the new message, I glanced up at the ceiling. It seemed probable that the hidden camera was up there somewhere, although that did not have to be true. The smile trembling on my lips was an oxymoronic combination of apology for being disloyal to our cooperation and defiance for staying outside the National Security Agency's field of vision, as I hoped. This hope would be in vain if the service phone in the inside pocket of my jacket started ringing in a few moments. I waited briefly, but when no sound disturbed the silence in my office, I pushed the button on the black phone's keypad to open messages.

I expected another derisive remark—this had already become a disagreeable habit of my unknown collocutor—but for the first time there was no text. I looked in bewilderment at the last picture I had received from Inspector Kostić: the yellow ducky parading on the bottom of the bathtub.

The first thing I should have wondered, of course, was how the sender had got hold of this picture. Kostić had no reason to send the on-site investigation photographs to anyone else, and it was impossible for someone from the outside to enter the closed police communications system and get them that way. But this issue seemed less important than another one. Why had I been sent this of all pictures? Most likely it had not been chosen at random just to show me that our communications system was not as impenetrable at it seemed.

I was tempted to reply with a message containing just a question mark, but then thought better of it. This was clearly some sort of riddle and a question mark would mean that I was unable to solve it and was asking for help. My pride would not let me. Also, there was no time for a new chat session. These would have been shorter if I could master the skill of instantaneous texting, but unfortunately I was far from it. And it was already seven minutes after twelve, as I saw on the cell's screen before returning the phone to my pants pocket.

I had spent more time than I realized looking through the photographs and would have to hurry to get to Café Mocha before twelve-thirty. Even though it was Saturday, traffic was doubtless lively by now and the café was in a different part of town.

As I drove the car out of the police headquarters underground garage, I suddenly found myself in a predicament. The natural thing would be to take the shortest route, but I would have preferred a more roundabout way even if it meant being a little late, just so I could avoid a street that I had not taken for a year and a half.

I lingered at the garage exit trying to make up my mind until another car emerged. The flashing high beams forced me to decide. You can't run away from the past by refusing to face it.

Even though neither of the two places that tied my memories to that street still existed, I felt a thrill when I turned onto it. I knew what stores had replaced the old ones. The Mandarin Teashop was now the Lucky Hand second-hand shop. As I passed by, I saw it was closed. It was nondescript from the outside, like most such stores, I supposed.

The Oriental teashop proprietor and his twins had disappeared without a trace as soon as the "Last Book" case had ended. Even though I tried, I had not succeeded in finding out what happened to them. Had they fled somewhere to elude the unpleasant investigation or was the National Security Agency behind their disappearance? Commissioner Milenković could have told me, but he had no reason to do me any favors. Besides, last night was the first time I had seen him since that case.

I had not been able to dodge the investigation, but it had been short and without consequences, contrary to my expectations. I told them what I knew without concealing anything or presenting things in a different light. My story was duly noted with no astonishment as though the case, while indeed unusual, was certainly not outlandish. Ultimately, all I had to do was pledge that I would never reveal anything about the Last Book. I continued doing my job as though nothing had happened. It seemed that my colleagues had been ordered to stifle their curiosity. No one tried to ferret anything out about the case.

A Fragrance high-end cosmetics chain store now

stood in place of the Papyrus Bookstore. It was all metal and glass, illuminated by bright lights even in the middle of the day. I slowed down a little as I passed by. I saw a crowd of customers through the large display window but not a single armchair. No one had any reason to stay there longer than they needed to buy a quick body beautification product. Slow beautification of the soul definitely did not go along with cosmetic glamour.

Vera had closed the bookstore just two weeks after the "Last Book" case was brought to a conclusion. She had tried briefly to run it herself, but it was too much responsibility for one person. She hired an assistant, but that hadn't worked either. She missed Olga in many respects. Furthermore, the bookstore had become a hangout for annoying curiosity seekers. It was not books that interested most visitors but recent events; their mysteriousness had only increased with the official hush-up and unrelenting articles in the tabloids. Even organized tourist groups had started coming.

The bookstore was supposed to be closed only temporarily until the dust settled, but weeks passed and Vera showed no desire to go back to selling books. When the Fragrance chain made an offer to buy the store, she accepted it without a second thought. The offer had indeed been high, probably owing to the popularity of the location. She kept the books and furnishings in order to open a new bookstore somewhere else. At least that had been her intention.

We kept on seeing each other, but only at her place. She never came to mine. I invited her, of course, until I realized where the problem lay. She had an aversion to my study. It was identical to the other study from the other reality where the novel *The Last Book* had been written. And the cost of writing that novel had been the death of six people in our reality.

I too had trouble accepting the existence of two realities, but it helped that they were no longer crossed. I could pretend that ours was the only one. It was harder for Vera. Whenever she opened her eyes she saw a reminder from the other reality—colors. That weighed her down the most. *The Last Book*'s writer had made amends, but the gift she received had become a mark of culpability. She had not been able to refuse it and that seemed to make her an accomplice in six-fold murder. She would gladly have become color blind again if that would bring back the dead. Or at least one of them—Olga.

By tacit agreement we avoided talking about it. That had seemed best. Soon, unfortunately, we stopped talking about almost anything. Vera withdrew further and further into silence and I could not find a way to break through her shell. I might have succeeded if I'd spent more time with her, but a police inspector's job devours time relentlessly. . . .

On the thirty-seventh day after the "Last Book" case was closed, I received a brief, vague SMS from Vera. *"I'm leaving. Don't look for me. I'll be in touch."* Of course I didn't listen to her. I used every means I had at my disposal as an inspector to find her, but the earth seemed to have swallowed her up.

When it was clear that I would not succeed, in my despair I was tempted to turn to Commissioner Milenković for help. If anyone could track her down, it was the National Security Agency. But I didn't do it. Not because I doubted that the commissioner would be willing to help, as I had not helped him in the case that became a stain on his service's otherwise spotless history. I held back because I suspected that Vera would not forgive me for finding her through the Agency. She would have considered it my ultimate betrayal.

And so all I could do was put my trust in the promise from the last sentence of Vera's message. A year and a half had passed since she'd disappeared, however, and she still had not gotten in touch. There was no sense in waiting any longer. The time had come to surrender one chapter of my life to the past. There was no reason to avoid this street anymore.

I stepped on the gas so I would not be late at Café Mocha.

22

I WAS IN FRONT of Café Mocha a little before twelve-thirty and then lost ten minutes parking. I cruised around looking for a free spot, but they were all taken. In the end I left the car in an unauthorized place. I used this privilege reluctantly because it singled me out. An illegally parked car without a ticket under the windshield wipers told someone with an attentive eye that the police were nearby. Perhaps I should have a ticket ready for such occasions. Funny that I hadn't thought of it before.

The crowd inside the café reflected the one in front of it. Nice weather on a Saturday had lured people out of their homes. I saw at a glance that all the tables were taken and so were the stools at the bar. Moving a little to the side so as not to block the entrance, I began searching for Miss Aksentijević in the large room. But she had not yet arrived.

I raised the left sleeve of my jacket a fraction. Twenty to one. She would probably get here at any moment, and then what? We had nowhere to sit and would have to go somewhere else. Better to wait outside in the sun, I thought. Just as I began to turn toward the exit, a young couple got up from a round table nearby.

He was burly with short hair, wearing sports clothes, and had a striking tattoo on his left earlobe. She was small and plump with straight, long, dark hair, flashily dressed. There was a tiny mole on the tip of her nose. They were holding hands. As they passed by, the girl smiled at me.

"For you, Inspector," she said softly, motioning her head toward the table.

They did not turn around to see my reaction. I waited for them to go out and then sat on the closest chair. Commissioner Milenković had clearly taken our cooperation seriously. I would have to find a way to repay him for this service. I looked around the café again, hoping to catch sight of him in a corner, but he wasn't there.

Then I noted five of his possible associates at two tables. Provided, of course, I was not wrong about the Agency bringing in fresh blood and its new members' informal dress and adornment code. If I was right, the commissioner had some reason to consider my upcoming meeting very important, judging by how many people he had deployed.

A waitress in a brown uniform soon came over. She put the previous customers' barely touched soft drinks on a tray and asked me what I wanted. I hesitated briefly over whether to wait for Miss Aksentijević before ordering, and then asked for a cappuccino. There had been no chance for a cup of coffee since morning, and Café Mocha was filled with fragrant caffeine.

The cappuccino seemed to have an enlightening effect on me. The very first sip brought a thought that made me wonder for the second time that morning why it had not occurred to me before. I sat there stock-still for several moments, holding the cup to my mouth.

I was there to coax Miss Aksentijević into describing the person who wrote under the pseudonym Jelena Jakovljević. I did not expect her to capitulate just like that because she had no reason to be accommodating. I could warn her about refusing to cooperate with the police, but even if I frightened her in that way, I was not certain to get what I wanted. This might not happen even if I promised in return to give her what she coveted, although I didn't have it—the manuscript of the novel *Find Me*.

If she was determined to hide the identity of her client, she could put me on the wrong track with a phony description. There would be no way to confirm what she said. Nevertheless, I had to try. The only thing I knew for sure about her was that she had seen the mysterious writer. I counted on being able to tell whether she was lying.

But what if she had to keep the description secret regardless of the cost, not to protect her client but so she wouldn't describe herself? It should have occurred to me first that she, and not the alleged painter Teodosijević, was Jelena Jakovljević. Everything that concerned him could apply even more to her.

With her in the main role an ingenious ad campaign for the new novel also stood behind it all and I was to have an important, although unwilling, bit part too. The false Teodosijević had been Miss Aksentijević's assistant in last night's performance that had been calculated to involve me in a sophisticated game. She had enticed me to the building, pretending to be a panic-stricken agent, and then the blind painter had come onstage, increasing the aura of mystery.

First he had persistently maintained that Miss Jakovljević was still in the apartment even after I had established that it was empty. Then when I came back because of the so-called break-in, he had passed off the story of the Grand Manuscript that was intended to convince me that the case was similar to the "Last Book". Finally, he had helped Miss Aksentijević quietly set the scene of disorder in the writer's apartment. That was the end of his role and he could disappear without a trace. This would have been all the easier if he'd been in disguise the night before, so Miss Aksentijević would have nothing to worry about when she described him in detail to Commissioner Milenković.

Search Publishers most likely did not know the agent was hiding behind the pseudonym, otherwise the information would have been leaked by now. The competition would have had no trouble finding someone to reveal the secret for the right sum. Part of Jelena Jakovljević's popularity lay in the enigma surrounding her identity. The publisher did not necessarily have to know it if Miss Aksentijević had authorized herself in her capacity as an agent to sign contracts with them.

Nevertheless, the premise that Miss Aksentijević was the detective story writer came up against the same unanswered questions as the premise about the man who pretended to be Teodosijević the painter. How could they be sure that I would come last night? How had they been able to lock the door from the inside without being inside? Where had they got a telephone that worked without a SIM card and battery?

I was really interested to hear what Miss Aksentijević had to say about these riddles. The best thing would be to tell her straight out, as soon as she sat down, that I had found Miss Jakovljević. She would be unprepared for such a move. If she was the one, it would show on her face.

I finished my cappuccino, put down the cup and looked at my watch again. Seven minutes to one. I sighed. Some writers had a bad reputation for their easy-going attitude toward time, but I had imagined that agents were more responsible. Did she need an hour and a half to get ready? And after I'd said I had news for her?

A sudden thought cut into my meditations. What if she had sensed I was on to her and decided not to come? No, that was impossible. Nothing I'd said could have led her to that conclusion. After all, when we'd talked I hadn't suspect her at all. The possibility had just crossed my mind there in the café.

I took out my service phone and called the last number again. After a brief silence a mechanical female voice said the person who had been called was unavailable at the moment. I put the phone back in my pocket. I sat there a while longer, deep in thought, and then opened the brown menu to see how much a cappuccino cost. I put some money next to the saucer and got up. There was no reason to keep waiting.

I left the Café Mocha with the eerie feeling that eyes were drilling holes in my back. I squinted in the bright sunlight and then headed for my car. Just before reaching it I stopped and took out Miss Aksentijević's business card to check the address. I was sure she would not be at home, but why not try since I was already in the neighborhood?

The old four-story building somewhat farther down the street had large balconies and a steep roof. My eyes slid down the row of names on the intercom next to the glass front door. I would have found what I was looking for right away if I had started at the bottom. The next-to-last name at number 11 said "Ljubica Aksentijević, literary agent".

I pushed the gray button. The reply was almost instantaneous, as though someone had been standing next to the intercom at the other end.

"Please come in, Inspector Lukić."

I recognized the young female voice immediately, although I had only heard it once before.

23

As I CLIMBED TO the fourth floor, I remembered Miss Aksentijević complaining the night before that she was not in shape because she smoked. It must have been hard living on the top floor of a building without an elevator where the stairs were so steep. Even I was a bit out of breath.

The girl with a mole on the tip of her nose was standing at the door to apartment 11.

"Fifty-four stairs," she said with a smile.

"Good count," I agreed gloomily.

"I only counted to the second floor. Then I multiplied by three."

"You shouldn't always depend on stairs being the way you expect them to be."

"I intended to double check on the way down." Her smile broadened. "Now I don't have to."

She opened the door all the way and closed it after I entered. "This way," she said, leading me toward the other end of the short hall.

The scene awaiting me in the study did not affect me as much as the one that morning because the proportions were smaller. Of the two narrow shelves, the one with books had been almost emptied, while the other one full of large black file folders was untouched. The contents of the four desk drawers had joined the fifty-some books scattered on the floor. The drawers had clearly been tossed after being emptied because two of them lay there in pieces.

The young man with the tattooed earlobe was crouched down by one of them. He was wearing white latex gloves, and a large black bag with equipment for collecting forensic samples was open next to him. From where I stood I could not see what he was examining, but I assumed from the pipette he was using around the bottom of the broken drawer that there was a bloodstain there. The girl who had greeted me put on gloves too and joined him.

The woman photographer I had already met was taking pictures of the desk, where everything was in disorder as well. The keyboard was awry, the monitor upside down, the receiver was off the telephone hook, felt-tip pens and paper clips were scattered all about, a vase of flowers had been knocked over next to the edge, and yellow juice had spilled from a tall glass. The girl raised her head briefly toward me and smiled. I replied with a short nod.

"We've started seeing more of each other, Inspector Lukić," came the voice of Commissioner Milenković from behind my back.

I moved aside to let him into the study from the hall. He was holding the upper edge of a steaming plastic cup between his left fingers, a tea bag string hanging over the top.

"That's in the spirit of two-way cooperation."

"Ah, yes, cooperation. It almost slipped my mind. All right, shall we cooperate a little more?"

"Excuse me?"

"You know, like last time. First one asks a question and then the other."

"All right."

"I'm listening."

I thought for a moment. "When did you enter the apartment?"

"At 12:35. While you were looking for a place to park."

"Did you have a reason?"

"We wanted to see why Miss Aksentijević was not on her way to meet you. First we called her cell, but it had been turned off. . . ."

"What would you have done if she had answered?" I said, interrupting him. "Reprimand her for being late?"

He raised his eyes over the plastic cup as he started blowing into it.

"If she had answered, we would have excused ourselves for dialing the wrong number. And if she had answered the intercom that we then rang, we would not have said anything, leaving her to believe it was a childish prank. But since there was no answer, we entered the apartment."

"Did you have the building under surveillance?"

"Of course. No one went in or out after 11:47."

"I assume you didn't find her here . . . injured?" I

nodded toward the young man and girl who were still examining the broken drawer.

"No, we didn't. There was no one in the locked apartment. We still don't know if that is her blood."

"It looks like we now have a kidnapping along with a break-in."

He took a cautious sip of tea from the cup. "Yes, that's what it looks like. Although they don't really go together. Burglars mostly try to avoid the people they burgle. If their paths do cross, they might even resort to murder, but not kidnapping."

"Do you mean to say that the ransacking is fake? A front for kidnapping?"

"It might be."

"Even if that's what happened, how could the kidnappers get out without being seen by your surveillance?"

"You're asking me a lot, Inspector Lukić. I still don't have all the answers. But another question plagues me more than that one right now. What is the connection between the kidnapping and your meeting with Miss Aksentijević?"

"Why would those two events be connected?"

"Because it would be naive to assume that their chronological concurrence was accidental. Kidnappings don't happen in the middle of the day under the National Security Agency's nose unless they are absolutely necessary. For example, to make sure that two people don't see each other. Who knew about your meeting?"

"No one. Except you, of course."

"You're certain you didn't tell anyone?"

"You would know if I had. You keep an eye on me all the time. In the spirit of two-way cooperation."

"You can't keep your eye on someone all the time. Particularly if they know about it. And if they have a reason to hide something. In the spirit of two-way cooperation."

We looked at each other in silence for several moments. I broke the silence first.

"No one else knew about the meeting. I told Inspector Prokopović, who is on duty with me today, that I would be going out to do something for the case I was working on, but didn't give him any details."

"Someone found out anyway."

"How?"

Commissioner Milenković slowly took another sip of tea.

"Maybe they tapped your conversation with Miss Aksentijević," he said in a lower voice.

"You can't tap a police service phone."

"Every telephone can be tapped. All you need is the proper equipment. And I know who has that equipment. The problem is that no one used it. I checked."

"So how could someone have tapped me?"

"That's another question I can't answer. There are too many of them already. Ever since that impossible cellphone turned up last night my life has become very complicated."

I smiled in commiseration. "Mine too, if it helps any."

He tried to return my smile, but all he managed was a grimace.

"What was the news you wanted to tell Miss Aksentijević?"

"There was no news."

"Inspector Lukić!" he said in a raised voice, looking at me reproachfully. "We're cooperating, remember?"

"How could I forget? I really didn't have anything to tell her. It was just an excuse to get together."

"As far as I remember, she's not exactly your type."

The girl, who was now photographing the books and contents of the drawers on the floor, cleared her throat. The commissioner turned his head toward her briefly.

"She's not. I was interested in another woman. Miss

Aksentijević is the only one who can tell me what Miss Jelena Jakovljević looks like."

"Oh, yes. The mysterious Miss Jakovljević. You were surprised when you discovered it was a pseudonym, weren't you?"

"Was my surprise so obvious?"

"Not at all, but I've become skilled at detecting the unobvious. By the way, that's not her biggest surprise."

"There's an even bigger one?"

"Yes, but you won't find anything about it on the internet. It's a highly guarded secret. I had no idea that publishers were such tough nuts to crack. Even I had to use some elbow grease to get hold of it at Search."

"You found out her identity?"

Commissioner Milenković took another sip from the plastic cup. The tea was no longer steaming.

"Which of the eight identities were you thinking of?"

I stared at him for several moments in silence.

"Eight?" I repeated at last.

"Yes. It's a collective identity. As someone well-versed in literature, you certainly know about that. But for an ignoramus like me, it was completely new."

"You mean to say that several writers are hiding behind the pseudonym Jelena Jakovljević?"

"Eight. Every novel written under that name came from the pen of a different author."

"Do you know who they are?"

"I do, but I have to keep it to myself. It is highly confidential business information. The Agency would be in hot water if it was leaked."

"All right, all right. Those eight don't interest me, but the ninth one does. Did you find out who wrote the new novel that will be published under the pseudonym Jelena Jakovljević?"

"No, unfortunately. We would have found that out too, but not even they know. The author's anonymity was a key item in the contract this time. It seems that the writer of the ninth novel is a really great name in literature. They suspect two authors that even I have heard of." He paused for a moment. "If you ask me, it's pure hypocrisy. The kingpins from highbrow literature will do their best to hide any involvement with detective novels, but won't be the least bit appalled by the big money that goes along with them. I never imagined that books about our profession were so well paid. It's much more profitable to write about detectives than to be one."

I smiled. "It's still not too late to change your profession."

"That's not for me. I'm better at solving cases than making them up. All right, now it's back to work. We've had enough cooperation this time. We'll have occasion, I hope, to see each other again soon."

I nodded my head and the inspector's two female associates replied in kind. I was already in the hall when the commissioner's voice stopped me.

"I forgot to ask, Inspector Lukić." He raised his plastic cup. "Are you still fond of tea?"

I hesitated a moment before answering. "I am."

"It's an excellent drink. I myself have become an enthusiast. Sometimes it seems to have a miraculous effect."

24

I TOOK THE STEEP stairs down from the fourth floor.

Everything that Commissioner Milenković had just told me was consistent with my assumption that Miss Aksentijević was the ninth writer to use the pseudonym Jelena Jakovljević. This would have been all the easier to pull off if she did not have to tell Search whom she was representing. The publishers must have had great confidence in her if they'd agreed to such an unusual arrangement—not knowing whose work they were publishing. This probably came from her being the agent of the previous eight writers too.

This would also explain the eight paintings in the small room of apartment 19 on Oak Street. Otherwise it would make no sense for the author of the ninth novel to have the framed covers of the earlier works by other writers. Only one person had a reason: the only real person who connected all the books. The same agent.

Over time she had probably given her role in the success of the detective series too much credit and thought it was time finally to have a go as Jelena Jakovljević. She knew, however, that she would never be accepted as the author, so she concocted the story of a great writer who insisted on remaining anonymous, even to the publisher.

Search had no reason to suspect anything. It suited them to get a top literary name even if it was only under such conditions. And what was more fitting for a top name than the same kind of ad campaign—full of mystery, just like Jelena Jakovljević's books? Miss Aksentijević had certainly been willing to take part in it.

It was not hard to establish why her alleged kidnapping had come about. Our meeting had nothing to do with it. Search Publishers had called to tell her about the visit of a National Security Agency commissioner and she was afraid they might soon come to see her again to inquire about the identity of the person writing the ninth novel. This would let the cat out of the bag.

She had staged the ransacking and then left the apartment. She might still be in the building or might have left it without being seen, like the phony painter Teodosijević, in the morning. She had taken care to damage her apartment as little as possible. Books were scattered so they resembled the break-in in the other apartment, but also because they could be easily put back in place. The same was true of the contents of the drawers, and even the disorder on the desk was not really very great.

The blood would probably turn out to be hers, but it could have come from a harmless little cut, not a serious injury. The files, however, had not been touched. If someone had really been searching for something well hidden in her apartment, they would have looked there first. And putting the files back in order would have taken the longest time.

How wise was Commissioner Milenković to all of this? Not very, I'd say, but that might just be appearances. The fact that we were now cooperating meant nothing. He would never tell me everything he knew and it was always better to assume that he knew more rather than less. This was confirmed by his allusion to tea at the end of the conversation.

He had seemed sincerely worried about the possibility of someone completely unknown to him being able to tap police cellphones. If the assumption about Miss Aksentijević being the ninth Jelena Jakovljević was true, he could rest at ease. The Agency had no competition. No one else had tapped me. There had been no need.

All I could do was hope to find an elegant solution for what worried me too. But I was still not one step closer to answering those three questions: how could whoever had devised this be certain that I would be the one to appear last night; how could they lock an apartment from the inside without being inside; and where did that impossible telephone come from?

Without those answers my assumption was not worth much, so the danger still loomed that someone was tapping my service telephone. I would have to be careful when I used it, just in case.

I left the four-story building and headed for my car, but stopped after only three steps and quickly went back. I tried to open the door, but it was already too late. I remained there several moments staring through the glass at the staircase, then headed for my car once again. I could have rung the bell at apartment 11 and asked to be let back into the building, but what explanation could I offer? That I wanted to count the stairs again because the automatic counter inside me had reached only fifty-two as I walked down, deep in thought? They would think I had lost my mind, and nothing more convincing occurred to me.

As I walked down the sunny street, I wondered how to proceed now that Miss Aksentijević had decided that the safest thing for her was to disappear. I could look for the answers to my questions at Search Publishers. If I was not mistaken, that's where the intricate and expense ad campaign for *Find Me* had been worked out.

That would have to wait until Monday. I doubted I would find anyone in their offices over the weekend, particularly after the Agency's unexpected visit. Commissioner Milenković had ways to convince publishers to get together on a Saturday morning so he could question them, but I was just an ordinary police inspector. Indeed, I could have tried something through Miss Timotijević, but I had no reason to hurry. On the contrary. If I had indeed been forced into a bit part in this show, I didn't have actually to identify with it.

I was already close to my car when ringing reverberated from my jacket pocket. It took a few moments to realize it was my private cell. The last time I'd heard it was before this case began. I took it out and looked at the screen. I didn't recognize the number.

"Hello?"

"Inspector Dejan Lukić?"

"Yes."

"Hello, Inspector. Jelisaveta Šumanović from the *Evening Courier* speaking. Would you give us a statement?"

"Where did you get my private phone number?" I replied with a question.

"You know that we never disclose our source of information."

"And you know that the police spokesperson is the only one authorized to make statements."

The line was briefly silent.

"You won't believe me if I tell you."

"It's that unbelievable?"

"It's that stupid. You'll think I have absolutely no imagination for not coming up with something cleverer."

"I would never think that a lady had absolutely no imagination."

"I'll take that as a compliment."

"You would be correct."

"I was given your number in an email," she said after another brief pause.

"Who sent it?"

"It was anonymous."

"Was there anything else in the email besides my cellphone number?"

"Yes. Shall I read it to you?"

"Please do."

"Call Inspector Dejan Lukić and ask him what he has to say about last night's break-in at writer Jelena Jakovljević's apartment."

"I have nothing to add to what you will get in the regular police bulletin at two o'clock. A routine break-in case."

The journalist cleared her throat.

"Excuse me. There's more in the email."

"Let's hear it."

"If the inspector says it is a routine break-in, ask him what the door of an empty apartment locked from the inside has to do with it."

Now I was silent for a moment.

"Do you expect me to believe it really says that?"

"Word for word. If you want, I can forward the email to you."

"I think it would be best to say goodbye. Being without imagination is not good, but overdoing it is even worse."

"Please don't hang up. Let me at least read you the end, it's the most imaginative part. Aren't you interested?"

I hesitated a moment.

"I'm listening."

"And ask him about the telephone that works without a SIM card and battery."

She stopped, clearly waiting for me to say something.

"Is that the end now?" I asked.

"No. There's one more sentence. Finally, ask him about the connection between the break-in and the 'Last Book' case."

When I did not say anything, the journalist spoke up again.

"Would you care to answer these questions, Inspector Lukić? Was the door really locked from the inside? What kind of cellphone works without a SIM card and battery? Is the 'Last Book' case being reopened?"

"I do not answer questions from anonymous messages, but I believe you."

"What do you believe?"

"That you really did receive an email with the contents you read to me. I even know who sent it."

"Who?"

"Someone who was convinced you would take the bait. That you would report on all of this."

"Maybe I wouldn't if you told me a bit more. Alluding to some sort of bait is not really enough. . . ."

"I told you as much as I could, Mrs. Šumanović."

"Miss . . ."

"Miss, excuse me. It should be enough for an imaginative lady. Goodbye."

I ended the call and sighed. I should have expected the dust being raised around *Find Me* to start in a tabloid like the *Evening Courier.* Miss Šumanović would certainly not be deterred by my vague warning and flattery. What she had been offered was inflammatory enough for her to take no consideration of what I thought. The publisher had immediately pulled out the three strongest trump cards that were still a puzzle to me.

I put the phone back in my jacket pocket and then took out my car key. I turned off the alarm and sat behind the wheel. I had to do a bit of maneuvering to get out because in the meantime my space had been narrowed by another illegally parked car.

The ringing started just as I entered Chestnut Boulevard. I thought it was the phone in my pants pocket ringing for the first time because the ring tone differed from my private and service phones. I almost lost control of the car when I realized that the ringing was coming from the back seat.

25

Holding the steering wheel firmly, I glanced over my shoulder and saw a cellphone on the seat behind me. It was the same gray color as the seat cover. I quickly faced front again and barely suppressed the urge to grab the phone to stop the piercing sound as it intensified. If I had tried, however, I probably would have caused an accident. Traffic around me was lively and the cell was hard to reach.

I started looking for a place to stop and soon realized it would not be easy. I could not give in to psychosis, however, and do something rash. The initial surprise had already subsided so I was able to think more clearly. There was actually no reason for haste.

Indeed, why should I rush to answer the phone, apart

from the ringing that was grating on my nerves? Even if it stopped ringing, there would be a trace of the missed call's number. And if there wasn't, the person would call again. They certainly had not taken the trouble to leave the phone in a police inspector's official car just to give up after the first attempt to reach him failed.

I couldn't imagine how they had pulled it off. Not only was the car alarm on, but Commissioner Milenković's people must have been keeping an eye on the whole stretch of street from Café Mocha to Miss Aksentijević's apartment, including my car. That was customary procedure even for ordinary police during an operation. The surroundings are always monitored, just in case. And I could see no reason for the commissioner not to inform me that someone was fooling around my car or not to prevent it.

A free spot suddenly appeared. My abrupt braking without a signal caused a chain of squealing tires, honking and angry shouts behind me. I had to unbuckle my seat belt and get up off my seat in order to reach the cellphone that was ringing without letup, but at least the unpleasant sound had stopped getting louder.

I did not recognize the number on the screen. I took a look at the gray phone before answering. From the outside it appeared to be a simple model.

"Hello," I said.

"Hello, Inspector Lukić," replied a young female voice. "Thank you for answering."

"Who are you?"

"Someone who has a good reason to talk to you."

"Is this the simplest way for us to talk?"

"No, but simpler ways are not reliable. Our conversation needs to be confidential."

"And that justifies breaking into a police car? Are you aware that it is a serious offence?"

"Are there any traces of a break-in? Did the alarm go off?"

"The phone did not appear on the back seat all by itself."

"Why don't you ask the National Security Agency how the telephone got there? They had your car under surveillance and they videoed it the whole time too."

I fell silent for a few moments.

"What do you want to talk about?"

"About the novel *Find Me*. We are interested in the file of the final manuscript."

"Why don't you talk to the publishers? They own it."

"Yes, but they don't have it. They didn't get it from the author."

"Then see with the author."

"Do you know where she is?"

"No, I don't. And I don't know why you called me about it, either."

"Because we think you might have the file."

"Me? How could I have the file?"

"You were alone in Miss Jakovljević's apartment twice last night, right?"

"You are well informed."

"Even better than you think. That was your chance to get hold of it."

"I was looking for Miss Jakovljević, not some manuscript."

"That still doesn't mean you didn't take it."

"Why on earth would I do that?"

"Because you knew how much it was worth."

"All I knew was that she received a large advance from the publisher. But what kind of motive would that be for taking it?"

"I wasn't thinking of that kind of worth."

"What kind were you thinking of?"

A hint of impatience appeared in the otherwise composed voice.

"Let's not waste valuable time needlessly, Inspector Lukić. You know perfectly well what worth I have in mind. We are talking about the Grand Manuscript."

"Oh, that. The first time I heard about the Grand Manuscript was not until after my second visit to Miss Jakovljević's apartment last night."

"You don't expect us to believe that, do you?"

"Believe whatever you want. In any case, I don't have the file with the novel's manuscript. But even if I did, what would you want?"

"For you to give it to us, of course."

"Why would I give it to you? It doesn't belong to you."

"Because you would get the most from us. Far more than from the others."

"What others? There are no others."

"There were, but they bluffed you to get hold of the manuscript for free. Soon, however, you will be showered with offers. The Grand Manuscript is a very hot property."

"Trying to bribe a police inspector is a considerably more aggravated offence than breaking into his car."

"With what we'd give you, you could leave your poorly paid police inspector's job and spend the rest of your life in luxury."

"Something doesn't add up here."

"What?"

"If you really believe the story about the first person who reads the Grand Manuscript becoming immortal, then if I did have it why would I sell it and not use it myself? Nothing you offer me could be greater than immortality."

"We believe in the Grand Manuscript, but you don't. You think it's preposterous, so why not sell the file for a high price?"

"Even if I don't believe it, what would it cost me to read it first, just in case?"

"It would cost you dearly. Immortality does not mean an easy life forever. You can be immortal in hell too. And we would do our best to arrange a suitable never-ending hell. I heartily advise you not to open that file, let alone start to read it."

"Thank you for your advice. It's easy to accept because I have nothing to open. Let me repeat—I have never had possession of the file."

We sank into a brief silence.

"Too bad, Inspector Lukić. If you'd been reasonable, everything would have worked out to the advantage of us both. This way, we have no choice but to see for ourselves whether or not you've read the Grand Manuscript."

"How will you do that?"

"It's simple enough. If you've become immortal, you'll have no trouble passing a test that mere mortals fail."

"Test?"

"Yes. We've already had one today. We suspected one other person of having read *Find Me*, but it turned out they hadn't. Unfortunately they did not survive. Such is the nature of the test."

"What person? What was the test?"

"You'll soon find out."

I sighed.

"How about cutting this show short? Things have really gone far enough. Tell your employers at Search not to string the police along like this. It's deplorable to abuse us like puppets in an ad campaign for Jelena Jakovljević's new book. Someone will be held criminally responsible."

My unknown collocutor suddenly seemed at a loss for words.

"What ad campaign are you talking about, Inspector?"

Just as I was about to reply, the phone in my jacket pocket started ringing.

"Wait a moment." I put the gray phone on the seat next to me and took out my service phone. "Hello," I said promptly without looking at who was calling.

"Inspector Lukić," said Inspector Prokopović, "we've received a report about a woman who was found in the elevator at 12 Oak Street. She seems to be dead. I just sent an on-site investigation team."

"I'm not far, I'll be there right away."

I put the service phone back in my pocket and then picked up the gray one.

"Hello?"

In return came the silence of a disconnected line.

26

I WAS MOMENTARILY UNCERTAIN what to do with the gray telephone, then put it in my left pants pocket. Never before had I had four cellphones on me. The next time one of them rang, it was unlikely I'd be able to tell which one it was right away. As I watched for a chance to pull out of my parking spot, glancing over my right shoulder, I wondered why they had left the little gray phone on the seat behind the driver and not, for example, in the glove box in front of the seat next to me where it would be better hidden.

In all probability, they had not wanted me to notice it too soon. The chances were much greater of my looking for something in the glove box than on the back seat. Although in plain sight, the cell behind me had blended like a chameleon with the seat cover. I'd had no reason to look on the back seat when I entered the car, but even if I had it would have been easy to overlook. If it hadn't rung, who knows how long it would have ridden around with me.

A sudden thought made me sit upright behind the wheel. Maybe the same thing applied to the past. I could not rule out the possibility that the cell had been in the car with me for some time, but had not caught my eye. They might have put it in earlier and not now while the car was under Agency surveillance.

They would still have had to take care of the alarm, but that was an easier hurdle for someone determined to outsmart the police.

I looked over my shoulder again and realized it would be some time before I pulled out into the street. I didn't like to use the rotating light, but now I had no choice. I took it out of the glove box and put it on the roof. I had to turn on the siren too before I finally moved out.

I had the right of way, but it was hard to use it on the congested boulevard. I was only able to drive faster when I turned off it. Then I didn't need the rotating light and siren anymore, so I turned them off.

The production concocted by Search was reaching its dénouement. The woman in the elevator who seemed to be dead would, of course, turn out to be alive. Publishers had indeed lost all sense of proportion in their ad campaigns, but no one would be bold enough to kill. I couldn't figure out who the alleged victim was, the one they suspected of reading *Find Me*. Who had had access to the manuscript? As far as I could tell, no one had seen it yet.

I reached the building at 12 Oak Street first. Traffic had clearly slowed down the on-site inspection team and Commissioner Milenković. There was no place to park, so I stopped at the entrance. A long-haired young man in worn-out jeans and a thin brick-colored sweatshirt was standing in front of the glass door. His running shoes were loosely laced.

"Hello, Inspector Lukić," he said. "Commissioner Milenković will be here any moment. He ordered that nothing be touched. We are taking over the case. Your investigation team has been told not to come. The commissioner asked for you to wait for him."

I nodded. "Where is the elevator?"

He pointed over his shoulder with his thumb. "On the ground floor. It's blocked. An elderly woman who lives on the fourth floor found the body. The elevator was on the fifth floor when she called it down from here. It was a shock when the doors opened, but she had enough presence of mind to call the police. We helped her climb up to her apartment."

"I'll just take a look," I said.

He unlocked the door to the building, opened it and moved aside. It was darker inside, making me pause to let my eyes adjust. I remembered awkwardly colliding with Miss Aksentijević there the night before. I had not forgotten where the switch was located. I pushed it and looked across the foyer.

At the other end, near the open elevator, stood a girl with unruly dark hair and a round face. She was wearing a short yellow t-shirt and tight black corduroy pants, low on her hips, baring a rather wide strip around her waist with her navel in the middle. Commissioner Milenković might have had too much understanding for the informal way his young colleagues dressed.

Without uttering a word or changing her expression, the girl just moved away, revealing the scene behind her.

At first it seemed there were several bodies on the elevator's red carpet. The three mirrors multiplied the face of the woman lying on her left side in a fetal position. She would not have fit in the small elevator stretched out. Her loose dark-green short-sleeved dress covered her completely like shroud. Her head was resting on her left biceps, the upright forearm leaning against the glass wall opposite the doors. Her hand was hanging like a large drooping flower. Red hair enveloped her face.

"Miss Ljubica Aksentijević, literary agent," said the girl, confirming what I already knew.

"Is she dead?" I said, not realizing until afterward how pointless it was to ask.

The girl eyed me guardedly before answering.

"There's no carotid pulse. We checked."

I crouched down by the entrance to the elevator and looked intently.

"Did you establish the cause of death? I don't see any external wound. At least not with the body in this position."

"We are not to move her."

"I know. If there is a wound, it certainly isn't big. Otherwise there would be blood."

"People die even without spilling blood."

Just as I was gazing inquisitively at the girl, there came the sound of the front door being unlocked and then opened. I turned around and saw Commissioner Milenković entering with a short, spare, middle-aged man with a receding hairline, wearing a dark-blue linen suit. He was carrying a large medical bag. I quickly got to my feet.

As they reached the elevator, the commissioner just glanced at me. The doctor crouched right down where I had been a moment before. He placed his bag on the floor, opened it, took out latex gloves and started putting them on. The commissioner exchanged a brief look with the girl and then signaled me with his head to follow him up the stairs. Not a word was spoken.

We continued in silence as we went up. I took advantage of the unexpected opportunity to count the steps for the first time during the day and in peace. I did not rely on my automatic counter but consciously counted them. If I had been alone, I would have done so in a low voice.

"Seventy-two stairs," gasped Commissioner Milenković, the first to break the silence as we got to the last floor, confirming the number I had also reached. "This is wearing me out."

We continued to Teodosijević's apartment. I glanced at the door to the neighboring apartment. The lock seemed properly sealed. The commissioner gave a short knock and the young man I had met the night before in the Communications Department appeared at the door almost at the same moment. He would have had to bow his head a little if he'd wanted to go out. He moved aside so we could enter, greeting me with a slight nod.

I followed the commissioner into the large room. He passed by the covered easel and sat on the edge of the cot where he had sat that morning. He rubbed his forehead with the tips of his fingers for several moments. Then he sighed and motioned toward the brown armchair. I sat down there.

"I'm listening, Inspector Lukić," he said in a tired voice like a man who did not feel at all like talking.

"What do you want to know?"

"Who did you talk to after stopping on Chestnut Boulevard? And more importantly—what phone did you use?"

I reached into my left pants pocket and took out the gray cellphone.

"It rang on the back seat after I started driving. I assume they left it there earlier. Otherwise they would not have escaped your attention if they'd tried while my car was parked near Café Mocha."

Commissioner Milenković raised his eyes toward Stanislav Mirić who was standing at the entrance to the room. It suddenly occurred to me that the tall young man was the only associate who had ever introduced himself to me. He came and took the telephone from me, then headed for the window in the small room.

"Someone you knew?" asked the commissioner.

"No. A young woman's voice. I'd never heard it before."

"What did she want?"

"Jelena Jakovljević's new novel."

He stared at me briefly.

"The Grand Manuscript?"

I nodded.

There was another pause. "Are they behind the body in the elevator?"

"That's what they indicated."

"Why did Miss Aksentijević . . . die?"

"They wanted to establish whether she had read the novel. They put her to some test that, it seems, only the immortal can survive."

This time Commissioner Milenković rubbed his temples.

"Why is it that literature attracts so many lunatics?"

"There are quite a lot of them in the other arts too, but they stay below the National Security Agency's radar."

"I'd be happy to let you handle this too if it wasn't for that damn telephone without a SIM card and battery. And not just the phone. . . ." He turned toward the small room. "What do we have this time?"

Mirić went up to him holding the cellphone in his outstretched hand.

"A cheap model. No modifications."

The commissioner motioned his head toward me. The young man came up again and handed me the telephone, then went out into the small hall.

"I thought you would hold onto it," I said.

"Why take away your only contact with them? It's in everyone's interest to maintain it. And even if we took it away from you, before long you'd find a new one in your car or some other place." He paused. "We're dealing with serious lunatics here. They should not be underestimated."

"I would have expected them to use better equipment. If it's possible to tap police cellphones, what's to be said about such toys?"

"They don't care if we tap them. They feel they have the upper hand. They killed Miss Aksentijević right under my nose. Or they brought her body here without being seen. It was in the elevator on the fifth floor and none of my people noticed it."

As I put the telephone back in my left pants pocket, my right pocket vibrated. In my confusion I almost reached for it.

"Why did they call you?" asked the commissioner.

"They're continuing their search for the manuscript after it turned out that Miss Aksentijević didn't have it. Now they think it's with me."

"Is it?" he asked in a softer voice.

"No."

I held out under his long inquisitive look.

"We must have true cooperation, Inspector Lukić. Otherwise I will not be able to protect you. And you need my protection. These lunatics are not only serious, they're dangerous too, as we have just seen. They will not be deterred at all by the fact that you are a policeman."

I felt like putting Commissioner Milenković's mind at ease. A ruthless publisher, not dangerous lunatics, was behind it all. I did not mention this hypothesis, however, because the cracks in it were getting too big. It was no longer about just three unanswered questions. Miss Aksentijević's murder certainly did not fit into the idea of an ad campaign. Publishers were indeed ruthless, but there's a limit to everything. Something quite different was going on, something that could definitely be dangerous.

"Of course we will cooperate," I replied with a nod, then got up and headed for the front door that Mirić had already opened for me. I was stopped by the commissioner's voice. What he said was the last thing I expected to hear from him.

"Take care of yourself." The tone was gentle, paternal.

Puzzled, I just smiled and went out. In the corridor my conscience bothered me for not saying anything in return.

As soon as I was in the stairwell, I took the cellphone out of my right pants pocket. Again there was no written message. The same picture as last time was on the screen: the yellow ducky on the bottom of the bathtub. But there was no time to go deeper into this riddle because my inside jacket pocket started ringing. I only realized it was my private cell when I took it out. No call number was given.

"Hello?"

"Hello, Inspector Lukić," said a voice that I had been firmly convinced I would never hear again.

27

"HELLO," I REPLIED IN confusion, although that was surely not the correct response to the man who had almost killed me. There was no doubt in my mind. His deep voice was as distinctive as fingerprints.

We had met twice before but I still didn't know what he looked like. Both times his face had been concealed by the hood of his white robe—the regalia of the Last Book secret society's Grand Master. Our paths had crossed first in the underground amphitheater of a villa and then in the corridor that connected two realities. Commissioner Milenković's sudden arrival had saved me at the last moment in the amphitheater, while I had been in no danger in the corridor. Although seen just briefly, the tableau of fifteen motionless figures in brown robes sitting at a long table with one in white at the head was etched in my memory forever.

I had heard nothing about the secret society since the end of the "Last Book" case. The investigators had not seemed very interested in it even though I'd described in detail what I'd gone through in the amphitheater and corridor, and the members I had met. Vera told me that none of them had dropped by the Papyrus during the short time the bookstore was still open.

"I hope you remember me," said the Grand Master.

"How could I forget the man who tried to kill me?"

He laughed resoundingly. "Kill you? How did I try to kill you?"

"You know perfectly well. You lowered *The Last Book* open toward my face."

"Yes, I lowered an open book, but why do you think it was *The Last Book*?"

"You said it was." I stopped, realizing this was not enough, and added, "It had a blue cover."

"Lots of books have a blue cover."

"It had to be *The Last Book*. You would've been in a tight spot if it had been any other book. If you'd managed to bring it close to my face, what would you have said to the secret society members when the book didn't have the effect everyone expected, announced by none other than you?"

"There was no danger of my bringing it close to your face. I knew that the arrival of National Security agents would get me out of that tight spot."

"You could not have known that they would turn up, let alone when."

"Do you think so? You underestimate me, Inspector Lukić."

"And you underestimate me if you expect me to believe the unbelievable."

"But you did believe that an unbelievable coincidence took place—the agents arrived just as I was lowering the book toward you. Rescuers appear at the last moment like that only in second-rate detective stories."

"And *The Last Book*, of course, is not that."

"Of course it isn't, although the main character turned out to be rather credulous."

"Did you call me to tell me that?"

"No, something else. I did not try to kill you; on the contrary, your safety has always been uppermost in my mind. You are extremely important for our society. If it were religious we would have already proclaimed you a saint. Without you *The Last Book* would not exist."

"That's not exactly how it looked to me down in that amphitheater."

"Nothing was as it seemed there. But let's not talk about the past. Your safety is in much greater jeopardy now than it appeared to you to be in the villa."

"You don't say."

"Are you really so credulous? Even after Miss Aksentijević's murder?"

I thought of asking him how he knew about the murder, but I was sure he wouldn't tell me. Then I would have looked naive indeed.

That's when I reached the ground floor. No one was there. I looked across the foyer. The long-haired young man was no longer standing in front of the door. The display above the elevator indicated that it was still down there. I stopped beside the closed door. It would be better to remain inside the building until I had finished the conversation.

"Perhaps you would enlighten a credulous inspector. Why would his safety be jeopardized after Miss Aksentijević's murder?"

"Your sarcasm is out of place. You know the answer perfectly well. You have something that many people are looking for. They will stop at nothing to get hold of it."

"And that is . . . ?"

"What's the purpose of this game, Inspector Lukić? We don't have time for it. You are in serious danger. You have the Grand Manuscript, of course."

"No, I don't."

A few moments passed in silence before a loud sigh came from the phone.

"All right, you don't, if that's the way you want it. But it actually makes no difference. What's important is that they are convinced you do. Miss Aksentijević didn't have it either, but she paid for it with her life anyway."

"They?"

"The people who believe in the Grand Manuscript."

"Just like you believe in the Last Book?"

"More or less."

"So that's another secret society devoted to a book? You've got competition."

"It's not a good idea to take secret societies lightly. I thought you already realized that. Our belief has turned out to be true."

"Maybe it escaped my attention, but I don't see any end of the world."

"It escaped your attention because the end can come in various forms. The world is certainly not the same since the advent of the Last Book."

"You should do your competition a favor and tell them about it. They are confident that the first person to read the Grand Manuscript will become immortal. And what's the good of being immortal if the end of the world is nigh?"

There was a moment of silence. When the Grand Master spoke again, his voice was hushed.

"Immortality is the only way to survive the end of the world."

"So that's it. Then the Grand Manuscript has even greater value. It's no wonder so many people are interested in it. How about you? Are you interested in it too?"

There was another brief silence.

"We are only interested in protecting you."

"I've never heard of a saint being offered protection. Usually it's the other way around. Saints are the protectors."

"I won't hold this mockery against you. Not all saints are wise. They include the naive who don't realize what danger looms ahead and so they make fun of it instead of eagerly accepting the protection they are offered."

"What kind of protection are you offering me?"

"It's certainly better than what the police would provide. Even the secret police. We would take you somewhere safe. Beyond the reach of people looking for the Grand Manuscript. Only a secret society can save you from another secret society."

I sighed.

"You really do think I'm naive if you expect me to swallow that story. What you're interested in, of course, is not my safety but the Grand Manuscript. You're convinced I have it and you want to get your hands on it before the others do. But you're wasting your time. As I told you, I've never set eyes on it. It makes no difference whether you believe me or not. Thank you for your offer of protection."

He sighed in return.

"I'm sorry it turned out like this. It would be much easier if we cooperated. But there's nothing to be done. We'll have to protect you even against your will. Regardless of what you think about our motives, your protection is a priority for us." He paused and then added on a lighter note, "I look forward to seeing you again soon, Inspector Lukić."

The line went dead before I could say anything. How strange, I thought. The secret police and a secret society have offered me protection at the same time, and both are dissatisfied with my cooperation.

I put the phone back in my jacket pocket and headed for the exit. On emerging I squinted at the bright sunlight. I unlocked the car door but did not get inside. I checked the back seat and then looked all around me. I didn't notice anything suspicious, least of all Commissioner Milenković's people. I knew, however, that they were somewhere nearby, keeping a close eye on me. For the first time, I was pleased about it.

I got in behind the wheel. Just as I turned on the engine, my jacket pocket rang again. How much simpler my life had been when I had had just one cell with me. With four, I would spend most of the day on the phone.

28

"Chief Inspector Đorđević" was written on the screen of my service cellphone.

"Hello."

"Hello, Inspector Lukić. Can you talk?"

"Yes, go ahead."

"What's this murder we've got?"

"Miss Ljubica Aksentijević was murdered, a literary agent."

"Agent? What do literary agents do? Forgive my lack of knowledge."

"No problem. They represent writers as a go-between with publishers."

"Oh, I see. Is a literary agent's work also so dangerous that they could lose their life?"

"Not usually. This is actually the first such case to my knowledge."

"The case file says she called us last night and you went to do an on-site investigation. What was it about?"

"She suspected that something had happened to the writer she represents . . . Miss Jelena Jakovljević. She couldn't enter her apartment because it was locked from the inside. But the apartment turned out to be empty."

"How's that possible?"

"Not even Inspector Vesić could explain it. He opened the door for me."

"So where's the writer?"

"She's disappeared."

"Interesting. And then there was a break-in at the same apartment, right?"

"That's right. They searched it thoroughly."

"Very thoroughly indeed. I saw the photographs. What were the burglars looking for?"

"By general consensus, the manuscript of Miss Jakovljević's new novel."

"Is it that important?"

"Big money is at stake."

"I never imagined there was big money in literature."

"Usually there isn't. Detective novels are the only exception. Our profession."

"You don't say. Nice. Does Miss Aksentijević's murder have anything to do with the manuscript?"

"It seems so. Someone is very anxious to get hold of it."

"Do you have any indication as to who it might be?"

"No one specific, although they made contact with me. Anonymously. Miss Aksentijević didn't have what they were looking for, so they can be expected to continue their search."

"Another murder?" asked the chief inspector after a slight hesitation.

"It shouldn't be ruled out."

"We've got to do everything we can to prevent that. You'll get reinforcements right away."

"That might not be necessary. The National Security Agency has taken over the forensic examination of Miss Aksentijević's body and just might take over the entire case."

"Oh, yes. I almost forgot about them. They joined in last night, right? What caught their attention? The case is unusual, but it's certainly not the type that interests the Agency. At least apparently."

Now I was the one to hesitate.

"I have no idea what caught their attention. They didn't say. As you know, they're not inclined to explain."

"Yes, they're not inclined at all. Although it would be easier for everyone if we cooperated. Well, we can't do a thing about it. In any case, if you need any help, let me know right away. And keep me informed of any new developments."

"By all means."

I waited for him to hang up first, but he had something more to say.

"Take care of yourself, Inspector Lukić. The Agency has a reason for getting involved, and literature isn't harmless, as you know."

"Everything will be fine," I replied, trying to sound self-confident.

Before returning the cell to my jacket pocket, I looked at the clock in the upper right-hand corner of the screen. Twenty-five to three. It was later than I had thought.

As I drove to police headquarters, I glanced at the rear-view mirror repeatedly. Traffic had lightened up a bit so it was easier to check behind. No one seemed to be following me, but I knew that was a false impression. Commissioner Milenković's people were certainly around. If anyone else was there, they would have to be really adept to dodge both my attention and theirs.

After getting out of the car, I looked around the garage, flooded by bright neon lights. It would not have crossed my mind before, but now it was obvious: I was alone. There were only a few parked cars in the large space with its rows of square pillars. My steps echoed hollowly as I made my way toward the elevator.

I had the impression that someone was stealthily watching me—and not just the cameras that covered the whole garage. In the past I had ridiculed such B movie clichés, but that didn't ease the anxiety that filled me now. It was not until the elevator was taking me to the fifth floor that I breathed more easily.

After sitting down at my desk, I turned on the computer and called Inspector Prokopović. I told him I was back and did not expect to go out again, and would soon be coming to the duty room. He briefly informed me that there were still no emergencies. If it weren't for the case I was working on, it would have been a very calm Saturday.

I opened the message that Inspector Kostić had sent that morning and a chessboard of little pictures filled the screen. I clicked on the last one and its enlargement replaced the grid of thumbnails. Bringing my head a little closer, I stared at the ducky on the bottom of the bathtub. I stayed that way around half a minute and then my right pants pocket started vibrating.

I hesitated just a moment and then took out the cellphone and pressed the button that opened messages.

"*Well?*" was what the new one said.

"*Well, what?*" I replied.

"*Haven't you seen it yet?*"

"*What?*"

"*Does famous Inspector Dejan Lukić need help seeing the obvious?*"

"*Did I ask for help? Why on earth did you send me a photograph of the ducky? And not only once but twice?*"

"*Because the novel can't wait for you to figure it out for yourself. Someone might come to harm because of your poor insight. Even twice was not enough for you.*"

"*If you care so much about the novel, doesn't its narrative coherence suffer when the writer openly helps the main character?*"

"*It suffers, but there's nothing to be done. Of two evils, I accepted the one that seemed lesser to me. If at least I had been of some help . . .*"

"*A good writer would not be in the awkward position of choosing between two evils. . . .*"

"*That was low.*"

"*That bit about my poor insight was not very high either.*"

For the first time since we started exchanging messages, I did not receive a reply almost immediately. A good fifteen seconds passed before it came.

"*You're right, Inspector Dejan Lukić. The novel has to*

be my top priority. I must not subordinate it to a main character. So the best thing is to stop helping you. From now on you'll have to manage on your own as best you can."

"That's what I've been doing. You just said that you haven't really helped me."

"Please don't cry for help when you get in trouble. And you will for sure."

"Rest assured there will be no cries for help. I'm in the habit of getting myself out of trouble."

I expected another message, but the seconds passed and nothing appeared on the screen. My eyes remained fixed on the clock in the corner. Two minutes later I put the phone in my pocket and sighed.

Perhaps this should have been avoided, but now it was too late. That's the usual outcome when two egos collide. Very well, let's see how an inspector with poor insight manages on his own. I returned my gaze to the ducky on the large screen.

Ten minutes later I reached for the mouse to close the photograph's window. It made no sense to keep on staring. I would not see anything because there was nothing to see. I had naively let my mysterious SMS collocutor trifle with my pride. She must be gloating now.

The cursor was already on the x-spot when my hand suddenly stopped. I looked at the same picture on the screen, but as though with different eyes. All at once I clearly saw what had persistently eluded me before. It was indeed obvious, just as she had said. So obvious that instead of being thrilled, I felt a twinge of frustration.

29

THE DUCKY WAS STILL where I'd seen it the first time, but was not looking in the same direction. Like a little arrow, its beak now pointed right, not left. The difference became evident just a moment before I closed the window, when the picture on the screen overlapped with the one that finally surfaced from my memory. I might not have the fastest recollection, but it was reliable and had never let me down. Someone had turned the yellow rubber toy around.

Who could have done it? And no less important, why? After my two visits, there had been the burglar—or several of them—and then inspectors Zarić and Kostić. The cleaning lady had found the door ajar, which would have made entry easy after the burglar's departure. But I didn't think anyone else had entered, and it was unlikely that Mrs. Sokolović had lied when she said she'd just peeked inside.

The burglar was primarily interested in books and there weren't any in the bathroom. If they went in there at all, they didn't move the curtain. The first picture that Inspector Kostić took in the bathroom showed it was pulled over the bathtub. Whoever had made such a mess in the rest of the apartment certainly would not have been careful to pull the curtain closed after pulling it aside, let alone waste time turning the ducky around.

I could have called my two colleagues and asked whether anyone had touched the rubber ducky—or just Kostić, who had taken the picture, since Zarić had only been inside the apartment for a brief time. But I didn't have to; both were experienced inspectors who would never slip up and move something on the site of an investigation. Let alone photograph it afterward.

None of those who could have turned the ducky around had any reason to do so, and yet there it was, turned around. This was a new riddle. Had I noted it by myself, I might have put it aside temporarily. It would seem less important than the larger riddles whose resolution had precedence. But the mysterious person I had exchanged SMS messages with over an impossible cellphone didn't think so. The riddle of the rubber toy was clearly very important to them since they had broken off contact with me because of it, rightfully accusing me of poor insight.

Was it nonetheless possible that someone had entered the apartment after the burglar had left? There certainly were candidates. Many parties were interested in Jelena Jakovljević's ninth manuscript. Their job would have been easier because they wouldn't have had to break into an unlocked apartment, and their traces would be invisible in the chaos left behind by the previous visitor. But even if that were so, there was no answer to the key question: why would anyone touch the yellow ducky?

My eyes were still trained on the large photograph on the screen. Something else started wriggling in the depths of my memory. I made a concerted effort, but what emerged was something I already knew: the picture I was looking at and the one I remembered overlapped each other, creating a two-headed ducky.

Something, however, was different, but it took some time before I realized what it was. The first time they overlapped, the head on the photograph was sharper than the other one, as recollections tend to be hazier. Now the heads were equally hazy as though both had come from my memory.

And that's when it hit me. Both overlapping pictures had truly come from my memory. I had seen the ducky with its head turned left when I first entered the apartment of the person masquerading as Jelena Jakovljević. The first time I saw it turned right was not on Kostić's photograph but during my second visit, when I entered the bathroom briefly. I would never have noted this by myself had I not been put on the right trail.

So someone had turned the ducky around much earlier, between my two visits, not during the night after the burglar had left. That meant that the alleged Mr.

Teodosijević had not been lying when he told me there was someone in the apartment next door. It had not been just an excuse to lure me back.

Who could it be? Who had unlocked the door and entered the apartment so silently that even Adam had almost missed it? Who had frightened the fake painter so much that he'd had no other choice than to call the police, even though their presence was not the least in his favor? And above all, who had turned the yellow toy around in the bathtub in order to leave a trace of their visit for those skilled enough to detect it?

I felt my hackles rise when the realization struck me. It was not smug excitement that filled me, however, but disquiet at the terrible possibility that it had come too late. Part of the message from my anonymous SMS collocutor flashed before my eyes:

"Someone might come to harm because of your poor insight."

30

I REACHED FEVERISHLY INTO my jacket pocket and took out my service cellphone. My thumb danced about the keypad searching for Inspector Vesić's phone number. It soon appeared on the screen, but I didn't push the call button. A sudden thought stayed my finger at the last moment.

I had to assume that whoever killed the literary agent was able to tap police communications. Regardless of how they did it. Let Commissioner Milenković tackle the problem. I didn't dare say anything to Inspector Vesić that would make him look suspicious in their eyes.

Judging by our only conversation, they didn't realize that Vesić had been in Jelena Jakovljević's apartment between my two visits. If they had, they would have tried to get hold of him before Miss Aksentijević. They had put her to a lethal test because she might have had something to do with last night's break-in. But he had entered the apartment much earlier, so the prospects were greater that he was the one who had gotten hold of the *Find Me* file.

They did know, however, that three visits had taken place before the break-in and that I was not there all three times. The young woman who had called while I was driving down Chestnut Boulevard mentioned the two times I went in. The only witness to Vesić's visit was the alleged painter Teodosijević and he—it was now certain—was a member of the Grand Manuscript secret society.

Blind or not, he could not have seen Vesić because the inspector did not turn on the lights when he went back into the building after the two of us parted. He got along equally well in the dark and had wanted to stay hidden. So the secret society was searching for the mysterious second visitor. They might subject them to the test even before me owing to the mystery cloaking them.

If the phony painter wasn't blind, however, then he'd seen Vesić the first time he was in the building with Miss Aksentijević and me. He had probably been watching us the whole time through the peephole and seen the inspector's skill for himself: using just two little picks, he had quickly handled the front door that was locked from the inside. Sooner or later he was certain to connect Vesić to the second visit. It was actually strange that it had not yet happened.

I pushed the call button. My conversation with Inspector Vesić had to be as innocuous as possible so that the inquisitive ears most likely listening would not suspect anything. The phone started ringing. When no one answered after the fourth ring, I felt tightness in my chest. The call was finally answered after the sixth ring, and I let out a sigh of relief.

"Hello, Inspector Lukić," said Vesić.

"Hello, how are you?"

"Very well, and you?"

"My shift is almost over and then I'll be very well too."

"An exhausting Saturday?"

"Unusual. Nevertheless, I managed to get hold of what you asked for."

A short pause followed.

"You did?"

"For your collection."

"Ah, my collection."

"The yellow rubber ducky that you're missing."

Again there was a lapse before he spoke.

"Was it hard to find?"

"It wasn't easy, but anything for an esteemed colleague. Shall we meet for a moment so I can give it to you? Then you won't have to wait until Monday."

"Sure. I have to go downtown anyway. Where would you like to meet? And when?"

I looked at the clock at the bottom of the monitor.

"Now it's seventeen minutes to four. How about if we meet at four-fifteen at the same place we parted last night?"

"In front of the entrance?"

"Yes."

"I think I can make it."

"Wonderful. See you there."

"See you soon, Inspector Lukić. And thanks for the ducky."

"You're welcome."

I expected Commissioner Milenković to call me as soon as I put my service cell back in my pocket, but none of my telephones rang. He had certainly been listening to our conversation and easily caught on to the fact that it should not be taken literally. He also knew that the photograph of the ducky in the bathtub had been on my monitor for some time. It would not be hard for him to make the connection and realize that Inspector Vesić had been in apartment 19 last night too.

On second thought, the commissioner had no reason to call me. All he could do was rebuke me for not calling him first to report what I had discovered about Vesić, but he would just be wasting his time. Taking care of Vesić's safety was his most urgent issue now. If members of the Grand Manuscript secret society had also tapped my service cell, they might have come to their own conclusions about the identity of the mysterious second visitor. In that case, Inspector Vesić would indeed be in great danger.

I nevertheless trusted this was not the case. Without the photograph of the ducky, they didn't have the key to our coded conversation. They might have found it unusual, but it would stay covert. And they had no access to the photograph in the closed police communications system. I had to believe that, otherwise we would be in a quandary that greatly surpassed this case.

Perhaps I really should have called the commissioner first, but I had been seized by the fear that something had already happened to Inspector Vesić. I'd been under the influence of the insinuation in my unknown collocutor's SMS. In my excitement, it had not occurred to me that another untapped phone could be used to check whether the inspector was all right.

Well, that could not be changed. I would soon be seeing Vesić, and the commissioner would be there as well with his people, so we would get the inspector to safety right away. Members of the Grand Manuscript society would probably be in the vicinity too. They would have had no trouble figuring out where we were meeting, even though no place was mentioned. But their hands would be tied with the National Security Agency there. This was all I had left to hope for.

Before turning off the computer, I glanced at the clock in the lower right-hand corner of the monitor again. Nine minutes to four. I needed about ten minutes to get to Oak Street. I would go there at once, finding it easier to wait in front of the building than here. I called Inspector Prokopović again and told him that I would not be seeing him today after all, and then headed for the elevators.

My jacket started ringing just as I entered the empty garage.

31

As I RUSHED TOWARD my car, I took out my private cellphone with a frown. With four telephones in my pockets and the way things were going, it was a real wonder that no one had called me since Chief Inspector Đorđević more than an hour ago. But whoever was calling this phone had chosen the wrong moment. I was not at all in the mood for a private conversation.

I didn't recognize the number that appeared on the screen. I was just about to push the answer button when a thought cut me short: perhaps they were trying to distract me. They were calling me while I was in the garage to put me off my guard. If a trap had been set for me there, I would fall into it more readily if I was preoccupied with telephoning.

I stopped and looked around me as the sharp ring continued to reverberate in the large echoing space. Just like the last time, it seemed no one was there. I tried to remember the parked cars I'd seen. I would have said there weren't any new ones, but I might have been wrong.

I continued cautiously toward my car and finally answered.

"Hello?"

"Inspector Dejan Lukić?" asked a female voice. The

only people who spoke so cordially were telemarketers trying to sell me something I had no desire to buy.

"Yes," I replied in a voice that was the exact opposite of hers.

"Nice to meet you!" continued the woman, who sounded of indefinite age. My icy tone had done nothing to decrease her friendliness. "My name is Leposava Žutić. I'm from Magnifying Glass Press."

She paused as though waiting to see what impression her words had made.

"That's nice, Miss or Mrs. Žutić, but right now I don't have time to talk about publishing. I'm in a terrible rush."

"Of course, Inspector. I understand you completely. So I'll be quite brief. I'm calling about the manuscript of the novel *Find Me*. Magnifying Glass is very interested. . . ."

"I will be even briefer," I said, interrupting her. "I don't have the manuscript."

"You haven't heard our proposal. . . ."

"And I won't hear it either."

I turned off the phone with a sharp jab and put it back in my jacket pocket, then reached for the car keys. I felt bad about cutting her off so rudely, but I'd had no choice. Regardless of whether the conversation was polite or impolite, it would have ended the same way. There was no reason for it to go on for ten minutes.

Before getting into the car, I checked the back seat. This had already become a conditioned reflex. As I unlocked the door, my private cell started ringing again. I took it out, ascertained that it was the same number as before, then turned off the call. If she persisted, I would have to caution her. I would be reluctant to resort to this, but with some people you had to take off the kid gloves. Luckily, she seemed to realize it was pointless to insist.

Once behind the wheel, I hesitated a moment about

using the rotating light, then decided not to. It would make me unnecessarily conspicuous and I would not get there much faster. It was lunchtime, so rush-hour was probably over.

The thought of lunch reminded me of what I'd been pushing to the back of my mind for some time. I had barely put anything into my mouth that morning and had skipped dinner the night before. This case really had no consideration for hunger. My stomach had growled two or three times since I'd gone back to the office. Even though there'd been almost no letup, I would have found at least the time to pick up a sandwich in the second-floor restaurant. Unfortunately, it didn't open on Saturday. Under other circumstances, I would have asked Inspector Vesić to have lunch with me, but Commissioner Milenković would be unlikely to go along with it. Forget it, I thought, I'll have to eat alone, as usual.

I concentrated on getting there as soon as possible and didn't pay much attention to whether anyone was following me. It wasn't even necessary. Traffic had indeed lightened and someone tailing me for any length of time would easily have caught my eye. In any case, even if I had noted someone, I wouldn't have done anything. They all knew where I was headed, so it made no difference if I was being followed.

I reached Oak Street at 16:07. This time I found two free parking places. I parked in one, got out of the car and headed for the entrance. The front of the building was still in sunlight, but it was not as bright as before. I stood beside the door and scanned the surroundings. Several passers-by were going their own way. The calls of children came from somewhere. Nothing seemed out of the ordinary, but I hadn't expected it to be.

I thought of calling Vesić to see how far he'd gotten, but it would not have been wise. He would get there all the more safely the less we were in contact. Furthermore, Commissioner Milenković was surely keeping an eye on him. I would have to be patient a little longer.

I hated admitting it, but my mysterious SMS collocutor was right. I should have been more insightful. Even without their help I should have deduced that Inspector Vesić had gone into apartment 19 last night after my first time there. He'd had an excellent motive for doing so.

He had not been enticed there by the same thing that interested the others, ranging from the secret society to this Magnifying Glass Press that was clearly ready to loosen its purse strings to get the better of the competition. He had known nothing about the novel *Find Me*. Neither Miss Aksentijević nor I had mentioned Jelena Jakovljević's new book in front of him, and when the two of us were together not even I had known anything about the Grand Manuscript.

He'd taken advantage of the fact that his car was parked slightly farther away, had headed toward it but had not left. He had waited for me to drive off and then gone back inside the building. He'd had little trouble entering the apartment without being seen. What compelled him was the urge to decipher something far more important to him than any manuscript, the greatest enigma for those who "have a special interest in locks," as he had nicely put it: how could an apartment that was locked from the inside be empty?

Had he discovered something there? If he had, he would not have called to tell me because he would have wanted to hide the fact that he'd been in the apartment. Well, almost. He'd left the trademark of his visit—the turned around ducky. He would tell me whether he had solved the mystery if I discovered his trademark. He had always been inclined to such games. Well, I had discovered his trademark. Not exactly on my own, but that was of no consequence. Soon I would find out whether the empty apartment locked from the inside was the result of a hoax or magic. And also whether Inspector Vesić had possibly found something else that had escaped my attention.

I looked at my wristwatch—16:19. He should be there any minute. Last night it had taken him about forty minutes. It suddenly occurred to me that I'd taken it for granted he was leaving from home, which wasn't necessarily the case. The problem with cellphones was that you never knew the other person's whereabouts. Indeed, he'd said he thought he could make it by 16:15, so it was probable that I'd found him at home after all. I stayed there waiting by the entrance, periodically shifting my weight from one foot to the other. Everything around me still seemed ordinary.

At 16:26 I finally lost patience, hounded by a sense of foreboding. I would call Commissioner Milenković. If he rebuked me for calling him, I would reply that I'd imagined cooperation meant his not keeping me on tenterhooks in this way. If he wanted to avoid any telephoning, there were other ways to let me know discreetly what had happened to Inspector Vesić, and not leave me to wait indefinitely. Several of his people had to be in the vicinity.

Just as my hand started for my jacket pocket to take out my service cell, the telephone in my left pants pocket went off. It didn't sound like it had on the back seat of the car, however. What came out was like a muted gong. I quickly lowered my raised hand toward my pants.

It took a few moments to figure out what to press to open the SMS message. There was no text and I had to bring the gray phone a little closer to get a better view of the photograph. Even so, I couldn't tell what it was right away. At first it appeared to be an abstract picture full of straight lines and symmetry. It took a good fifteen seconds before I finally realized what I was looking at.

On the floor of the elevator in the building behind my back lay Inspector Vesić's briefcase in triple reflection. Open and empty.

32

I PUT THE GRAY telephone promptly back into my left pants pocket and started feverishly searching through the others for the key to the building's front door. This would ordinarily not be necessary because I prided myself on my keen memory. With just a fraction more self-possession I would have immediately remembered which pocket it was in, but I seemed to have suddenly lost my presence of mind.

When I finally found the key, I couldn't get it into the keyhole because my fingers refused to obey. This hadn't happened to me in a long time. Luckily there was no one nearby to see a police inspector barely keeping his trembling under control. When I finally got into the foyer, I didn't waste even the moment it would have taken to turn on the lights in passing, even though I knew it would take a little time for my pupils to adjust to the weak light inside. Heedless of the noise I made, I ran the short distance to the elevator.

First I banged unnecessarily hard on the call button, and only then raised my eyes to the display. The elevator had just started down from the fifth floor. Although it traveled at its normal speed, it now seemed unbearably slow to me.

I had never thought I would ever see Inspector Vesić's briefcase open. Had circumstances been otherwise, my chief interest would have been to know what was in it. It was known to contain something heavy, but no one had any idea what could be so important for him to carry it with him at all times. Certainly not burglary tools, because two little picks were all he needed to take care of any lock.

Right then, however, what interested me was not the contents of the mysterious briefcase, but the fate of Inspector Vesić himself. The picture of the empty briefcase sent to the gray telephone clearly indicated who had hold of him. How was that possible? How had they outwitted the National Security Agency? Commissioner Milenković knew he was facing a serious and dangerous opponent, but still it shouldn't have happened. No secret society should be a match for the secret police.

There was yet another puzzle. Even if they had managed to outsmart the Agency, how had they reached the building and unlocked the three security locks so as to take the picture of the empty briefcase in the elevator? I had spent most of the past half-hour in front of the building. In all that time only one elderly couple had emerged. True, they could have entered by the back door, but presumably it was under surveillance.

A thought suddenly crossed my mind that made possible all that was seemingly impossible. The secret society could easily have gotten hold of Vesić, reached the building in time and effortlessly unlocked the three locks that had given many people a headache—provided that nothing had to be done by force. If they could count on Vesić's cooperation.

There was no chance to give this crazy idea more attention, however, because the elevator had almost reached the ground floor and squealing tires could be heard behind me. Swiftly, I turned my head, in time to see a light-red car stop in front of the entrance. Car doors started opening even before it had reached a standstill and four young people quickly got out. If I hadn't recognized them, I might have thought they were rushing to an afternoon party in the building.

Unlocking the front door, the first to enter the foyer was the long-haired young man in a brick-colored sweatshirt, followed by the girl photographer and the couple I had first seen in Café Mocha.

"Don't touch anything, Inspector Lukić," said the lad in loosely laced trainers at the forefront, almost shouting.

I was about to reply that I had no reason to touch an empty briefcase, when I looked round again—and was at a loss for words. The elevator had meanwhile reached the ground floor. The noise from the entrance had drowned out the already soft sound of the doors opening. Lying on the floor of the elevator was not the briefcase but its owner.

He was curled up, like Miss Aksentijević. Nor was his face visible—a hat covered it instead of hair—but there was no doubt as to who it was. The elegant black suit and large dark-red bow tie that had distinguished his appearance now seemed somewhat grotesque on the elevator's dark carpeting.

Uncertain what question to ask first, my eyes slid in confusion over the commissioner's four young associates who had gathered around the entrance to the elevator.

"Let us take care of this, Inspector Lukić," said the photographer. "Commissioner Milenković is waiting for you in the car." She nodded toward the foyer.

Instead of leaving, I looked at the elevator again. Something deep inside me fought against leaving just like that, turning my back on my dead colleague. My conscience stung me with an almost physical pain. How could I have thought for a moment that Inspector Vesić was in collusion with the secret society?

I felt a hand touch my shoulder lightly. This time the photographer did not say anything, but her smile expressed more than condolence. Slowly I made my way to the exit.

33

The forensic doctor in a dark-blue linen suit, whom I'd met there a little over two hours ago, appeared at the entrance just as I was leaving. He thanked me with a brief nod for opening the door and holding it for him, and then hurried past me toward the elevator.

I squinted again when I got outside. Shading my eyes with my hand, I stooped slightly to look inside the light-red car. It didn't surprise me that the Agency had started using such flashy cars. Everything was upside-down with them. They had been most conspicuous when trying to be least so. Instead of the somber colors that used to catch everyone's eye, these bright hues matched the Agency's fresh blood and did not stand out at all.

Commissioner Milenković was sitting on the right-hand side of the back seat. I opened the left-hand door and got in next to him. We regarded each other for several moments without speaking.

"It is extremely important that you tell me everything you've left out, Inspector Lukić," said the commissioner, breaking the silence. "I mean everything." He spoke in an even tone as though we were making small-talk.

I pointed at the building's entrance. "A police inspector is lying in there dead, Commissioner Milenković." Even though I tried to speak calmly too, my voice trembled. "How about if you tell me why you let it happen?"

"I could ask you the same thing."

"How could I have prevented Vesić's murder?"

"You should not have telephoned him. You've been going it alone since the beginning instead of cooperating with me. We might have been able to save him if you'd contacted me as soon as you found out he'd been in that apartment upstairs last night." He paused. "Although I doubt we would have succeeded."

"You doubt that the National Security Agency is capable of handling a secret society?"

"The Agency is powerful but not almighty. The secret society probably suspected that Vesić was in the apartment between your two visits. Your unnecessary call only confirmed that. They had a big advantage. Obviously they'd been keeping an eye on him for some time and had no trouble getting hold of him before us. We found out where he was through his cell, but didn't get there in time. By the way, he was here in the vicinity."

"In the vicinity? Then why did he tell me he thought he could get here in half an hour?"

"Who knows? Maybe he realized they were closing in on him and tried to confuse them."

"Let's say it was like that. Then how did they bring him . . . or carry him . . . into the building? As you know, I've been here since seven minutes past four, and I'm sure you still have both entrances under surveillance. Did you see anything?"

"No, we didn't, but that's of lesser importance. There must be another entrance, a secret one perhaps."

"What do you intend to do now? Are you going to catch these lunatics or will you hand the case over to us? They've already committed two murders and it's quite possible they won't stop there."

Just then two young men in jeans and orange teeshirts moved toward the entrance. They looked like repairmen who had come to fix something in the building. One was carrying a large black plastic box resembling a toolbox and the other was holding something upright that looked like two poles wrapped in olive-green cloth. Only an expert eye could recognize a folded stretcher. They knocked on the door and the girl with a mole on the tip of her nose soon opened it.

"We'll take care of the lunatics, Inspector Lukić," said Commissioner Milenković after the young men had gone inside. "But a much bigger problem has cropped up. Everything else is now secondary. Even the murder of a police inspector."

"What problem?" I asked, bewildered.

"The telephone has disappeared."

"Which telephone?"

The commissioner sighed like a teacher questioning a dim-witted schoolboy.

"The telephone that works without a SIM card and battery. The one you claim you found upstairs in the apartment. The damn telephone that got me into all this."

"What do you mean—disappeared?"

"Disappeared. Vanished into thin air. From a place where nothing can disappear. There is no safer repository in this country than the National Security Agency's safe."

I looked at him in disbelief.

"That's impossible. Nothing can disappear from your safe."

"No, it can't."

"So how . . . ?"

The commissioner shrugged his shoulders.

"I don't know. I'm hoping that you'll be able to tell me."

"Me? How in the world would I know?"

"I've run out of both the time and patience to play hide-and-seek with you, Inspector. I want a plain answer to the question I'm about to ask you. Is this another case like that?"

"Like what?"

"Like the 'Last Book.' Crossing realities. I see no other explanation for the appearance or disappearance of that impossible telephone unless someone from another reality is behind it. Another wizard-like writer playing irresponsibly with our reality."

We sat there in silence for about ten seconds.

"I don't think Occam would have liked that explanation," I said at last.

"Leave Occam out of it. It was a lot easier for him than it is for me. He had a much simpler world in mind. Well?"

"Why do you think I have the answer to that question?"

"Because everything revolved around you the first time too. Because as soon as I saw you in the Communications Department last night, my intuition told me that something exceptional was in the works. Because I have an unmistakable hunch that you've been hiding something from me from the beginning. What haven't you told me, Inspector Lukić? We've played at cooperation long enough. This is the last chance to take it seriously."

The door to the building opened and the forensic doctor came out followed by the two girls. Then came the young men in orange teeshirts carrying a large black bulging plastic bag with closed zippers on the unfolded stretcher. The lads with short and long hair were the last to come out.

They all headed to the parking area. I felt a lump in my throat and rose up on the seat, leaning on my right hand so I could see out the back window. A van decorated with colorful flowers was parked next to my car.

The girl photographer opened the back door and the stretcher was placed inside. One of the young men in an orange teeshirt hopped into the back and the other sat behind the wheel. The forensic doctor got in on the other side. Before they left, the doctor had a short conversation with the long-haired lad. I watched the van until it turned at the end of the street. The commissioner's four associates did not approach the car where we were sitting, but stayed in the parking area. They looked like a group of young people cheerfully chewing the fat. If anyone had observed them just then, there would have been nothing to indicate what they'd been doing a little while ago.

As I sat back down on the seat, I slid my hand over my pants pocket, hoping this inconspicuous movement would escape the commissioner's attention. The little black telephone was still there, although in terms of security, my pocket could not be compared to the Agency's safe.

"That reminds me," said the commissioner, motioning his head in the direction the van had taken. "There's something else besides the telephone's disappearance that leads to the conclusion we're facing crossing realities again. An autopsy was performed on Miss Aksentijević's body. What do you think was the cause of death?"

I shook my head. "I don't know."

"There was no medical cause. I'm convinced it will be the same with Inspector Vesić. We'll know soon enough."

"How can there be no cause?"

"Just like there wasn't in the 'Last Book' case. Not a single secret society, regardless of how powerful, would be able to kill without leaving at least some trace."

"But there's no mysterious book here."

"Everyone is looking for a mysterious manuscript."

"No one's found it yet."

"Who knows? That's my main problem. I don't know enough. I would certainly have an easier time if you told me what you're hiding."

He looked me straight in the eye. Just as on that morning when we stood next to the easel, it wasn't easy to bear up under such close scrutiny.

"Why would I hide something from the only person who can protect me now that I'm in the greatest danger? I'm the only one left of the three suspected of getting their hands on the Grand Manuscript."

The commissioner sighed again. "All right, if that's the way you want it, then I have no choice. The best way to protect you is to take you off the case."

"Only my superior can do that." I knew, of course, that this was useless, but frustration made me talk back.

"Don't be ridiculous. I'll take your superior off it too. This is no longer a case for the police. Actually, we should have taken it over last night as soon as the telephone appeared, and not allowed someone to nose around the Agency's safe. It was a mistake to believe that we would cooperate this time."

"You'll be making an even bigger mistake if you keep me off the case. You said just a moment ago that everything might be revolving around me again. Remember the drawing."

"That might be true, but I can't take the risk. Regrettably, I don't have full confidence in you. Good-bye, Inspector Lukić."

"Good-bye," I replied gloomily after a slight pause. I turned and started to open the door, but was stopped by his voice.

"If you want, we could take you somewhere secure until this is over."

"Thank you, but I wouldn't be secure with you even if you locked me in your safe."

Without waiting for his reply, I got out quickly and slammed the door harder than necessary.

My leaving the car seemed to be a signal for the commissioner's four associates. They left the parking area hurriedly. As they were getting into the red car, the photographer flashed me a smile. In my dismal mood, I couldn't smile back at her.

I remained beside the building entrance after the Agency car's rapid departure. The tranquil summer afternoon that suddenly reigned around me was exactly contrary to everything that had happened since I had first arrived there the night before. This peace, however, was not destined to last long. My service cell rang in my jacket pocket.

"They just called from the Agency," said Chief Inspector Đorđević. "I'm really sorry about Vesić. Did he have any close relatives?"

"Not as far as I know."

"A blessing in disguise. The hardest thing for me is notifying the family."

"Are our hands completely tied? Vesić deserves better than to have us sitting on the sideline just watching."

"I'm aware of that. I'll try to work something out. Don't do anything until I contact you. The best thing would be to come to headquarters. We've got to devise a plan and you shouldn't be alone after what just happened."

"All right."

Just as I started for the parking area, I suddenly felt weak. I turned around in confusion, but everything still looked normal. If my stomach hadn't started growling, something might have crossed my mind that was not in the least to Occam's liking.

I consulted my wristwatch: three minutes to five. It was Saturday, so it would certainly be some time before Chief Inspector Đorđević got in touch with the people who could give us back at least partial command of the investigation into Inspector Vesić's murder. For the first time since the previous night, I was not in a hurry. Finally I had opportunity to catch a bite to eat.

But where should I go? I didn't know the neighborhood well enough and there was no one around to ask. Then it dawned on me that I did know of a place. Indeed, they wouldn't serve me lunch, but I dared to hope for a sandwich. In addition, someone I would enjoy chatting with was supposed to be there from five onwards. Unofficially, of course, since the case had been taken away from me.

I headed for the teashop at a slow pace.

34

I STOPPED WHEN I reached the streetlight next to a linden tree. The night before, heading to the teashop for the first time accompanied by Miss Aksentijević, that's where I'd glanced up at the four windows of the apartment in which the writer Jelena Jakovljević had allegedly been locked. There had been a weak glow in the second window from the end. Later, as we were coming back from the teashop, none of the windows had been alight.

If that had been the end of it, I would have trusted Occam. No one could have entered the apartment until Inspector Vesić removed the key from the front door lock that had been locked from the inside. The weak glow that seemed to come from the large room was probably the reflection of some light in the street that had disappeared in the meantime. Nevertheless, it was only one in a series of illusions that Occam had not properly explained to me.

It had all started in the elevator. I had ridden in elevators lined with mirrors before, of course, but never felt as disconcerted as in this one. Its effect on me the night before had been so shattering that I dreamed about it. What had upset me the most, however, was that morning's illusion as I went up by myself to the on-site investigation after the break-in. The elevator seemed to move so slowly that I thought I would never reach the fifth floor.

And then there was the stairwell. My automatic counter had never let me down, but now it appeared to be broken. Not once had it counted the number of stairs correctly. Not only in this building but in the one where Miss Aksentijević lived as well. I had not reached the right number here until I counted the stairs to myself, accompanied by Commissioner Milenković, after the literary agent's body was found.

The most unusual illusion had taken place in the stairwell too, but it had nothing to do with counting. Miss Aksentijević and Inspector Vesić were taking the elevator up to the fifth floor and I was going on foot so we would not be too cramped together. The lights had gone off between the third and fourth floors. In the darkness I'd had the almost palpable impression of someone passing by me on their way down. But when I'd rushed to the ground floor no one was there.

Probably under the influence of my dream where everything that happened the previous night seemed strangely connected, when the elevator finally stopped on the top floor after its seemingly endless ascent that morning, I'd wondered whether something connected these illusions too. I could not detect any link between them and there had been no time to go into the matter in detail. I was still haunted, however, by the feeling that some connection existed and was even simple, and yet it continued to escape me.

I raised my head again toward the windows in the upper left-hand corner of the building. Just as in the morning, they were filled with brightly reflected sunlight, except it was now coming from the western half of the sky. As I started to lower my eyes, I thought I caught a glimpse of light movement. It was the second window again. I quickly reexamined it, but everything was now at rest.

I stood there staring a little longer, then shook my head. The play of sunlight on glass is capable of creating such chimeras, particularly if a person is inclined to see them. I headed toward the teashop, but had barely taken a few steps when I stopped dead in my tracks. That which had been persistently evading me suddenly exploded before my eyes.

The connection between the illusions was indeed quite simple, but, just as with the ducky, I had missed the obvious. They were linked by the fact that only I had seen them. There was no other eyewitness, even when someone was next to me, like Miss Aksentijević the night before on this very spot.

I had been alone in the elevator that went up at a

snail's pace, alone on the stairs as my automatic counter wrongly counted them, alone in the darkness between the floors when I clearly felt someone pass by me. And I was alone right then, when something had seemed to move briefly behind the window up there.

Occam would have declared this pure coincidence. That would indeed be the simplest explanation. There was, however, another more complicated one that was not to be rejected simply because it was not to Occam's liking. A year and a half ago this world had stopped conforming to his principles and I was the last person with the right to close his eyes before the possibility that realities were in fact crossing again.

That possibility had plainly to be taken into account from the moment I, of all inspectors, stood in front of the door to an empty apartment locked from the inside, and particularly after the appearance of the telephone that worked without a SIM card and battery and that had until recently been receiving impossible SMS messages sent to me—both in terms of the speed of reply and their content.

I'd refused to accept that possibility, even though it had inevitably crossed my mind right away. I'd been devising increasingly intricate hypotheses, rejecting the one that, in spite of its complexity, was the most elegant and fully explanatory. I had even let Commissioner Milenković take the case away from me just so as not to corroborate what he had also realized—that the writer of *The Last Book* was magically influencing our reality once again.

I'd acted that way because I trusted the writer's promise that he would never do it again. The six corpses in our reality that *The Last Book* had left behind were too heavy a burden on his conscience and he could find no redemption. In addition, there was a secondary reason for not returning to our world. He never wrote sequels to his works.

Well, I could avoid it no longer. I finally had to reconcile myself to the fact that he had broken his promise; the writer was back, he was pulling strings from behind the scenes and his impact was leaving behind more corpses. I could not imagine why he was doing it. I'd been convinced that I knew him well, almost as well as I knew myself, but I had clearly misjudged him.

First of all, it was not like him to treat me this way. He had given me a thoroughly hard time in *The Last Book*, but I'd still enjoyed his goodwill. Now, however, he had started playing with me. Not out of ill will, admittedly, but he certainly must be taking pleasure in it. My conviction, for example, that I was exchanging SMS messages with a woman must have greatly amused him. Even now, considering who was the person I had taken to be Jelena Jakovljević, it was still hard to believe that I had spoken to a man.

The illusions were playing with me too. All of this was a novel to him, a novel that would be lacking nothing if he left out the illusions that I alone knew were there. He had nevertheless introduced them to confuse and bewilder me, to put me in an awkward position. He had clearly enjoyed this, not caring whether it would confuse his readers as well. This, too, looked to me more like a female than a male trait.

I was yanked out of my musing by barking somewhere in front of me. I glanced toward the corner where I had seen a German shepherd similar to Adam that morning, but no dog was there now. I looked around me. The short street was still empty. I stood there perplexed for a moment and then it dawned on me. Another illusion! It was the right moment. I was all alone.

Or maybe not. Maybe this was a call to hurry to the teashop. There was no more time for games. The illusions were over. The novel's dénouement could not be far off. The only thing left to explain was why the writer had returned to this world.

35

I WAS GREETED BY the teashop's habitual gloom, so I stayed near the door until my eyes had adjusted. It took some time for my pupils to dilate, since they had completely contracted in the bright afternoon sun. Gradually I could make out parts of the underground room filled with densely interwoven herbal fragrances and the muted sounds of a stringed instrument.

Just as in the morning, the man in a white shirt and brown vest was working behind the bar. Even though the entrance was poorly lighted, he recognized me at once. He waved coquettishly. I replied by raising my hand briefly and then looked over to the other side. The patrons' contours were outlined on the banquettes along the window wall and on the nearby chairs. It seemed quite full. The only free table was the one where I had sat the previous two times.

Before heading there, I looked around the rest of the teashop, my eyes having finally adjusted. Almost all the places were taken along the two side walls as well. This time it certainly could not have been an illusion because the crowd of customers was audible as well as discernible. The din overpowering the soft music had seemed to subside for a moment as I entered.

As soon as I sat down, the curly-headed proprietor came up to me, swinging his hips.

"Welcome, Inspector! How nice to see you again."

"I didn't expect there to be such a crowd already at five."

"It's always like that on Saturday. You need a reservation." He smiled. "But that, of course, does not apply to you. Whenever you come, this table will be at your disposal."

I had to smile in return.

"Might I ask you one other favor?"

"Whatever your heart desires, dear Inspector! Just say it!"

"I'd like a bite to eat. Would you be so kind and make me a sandwich?"

"But of course! With pleasure! What kind of sandwich would you like?"

"It makes no difference. . . ."

"Come, now. Your kind of man must not be indifferent about what he eats. You could ruin yourself with the wrong food. Would you let me prepare you a special tailor-made sandwich?"

"I didn't know there were tailor-made sandwiches too."

"That's because we haven't spent much time together. Otherwise you'd know that a lot of other things are tailor-made. Particularly for you."

I cleared my throat. "Is your sister here? I can't see well in such dim light."

"Not yet, but I expect her any moment. There's just enough time for you to have a snack."

I nodded. "Very well. Thank you."

"By the way, when I talked to her on the phone, I told her that even the tea I made for you this morning hadn't got rid of your illusions. She sent word not to worry. As soon as she comes, she'll make you some tea that will get rid of all your troubles, not only your illusions."

"Tea like that would be very useful to me right now. Although the only thing she won't have to get rid of is the illusions. They're gone."

"What's that you say? So that means my tea did the trick after all, although with some delay. That's wonderful! Just leave things in my capable hands, Inspector. You have no idea how pleased you'll be."

I cleared my throat again. "What would please me the most right now is a sandwich."

"Oh, how thoughtless of me!" He tapped his forehead lightly with his fingertips, throwing his head back a little. "Here I am talking on and on, and you're dying of hunger. I'll get right to it. In a jiffy. Would I let my favorite inspector suffer?"

He turned on his heel and hastened friskily to the bar.

As I watched him busily making sandwiches, I wondered whether there were any people from the Agency among the indistinct figures in the gloom around me. The fact that the commissioner had taken me off the case did not have to mean he was no longer interested in me. He could use me as bait.

When the mysterious telephone disappeared from the Agency safe, it had become a much greater problem than the Grand Manuscript secret society. The awareness that realities were crossing once again had taken the limelight away from the fact that we were also dealing with a group of dangerous and very skilled lunatics who had already killed two people.

In the red car Commissioner Milenković had told me he would take care of them, but I thought he underestimated them. They had already outwitted him several times. If he wanted to beat them at their own game, he had to keep me in sight because he knew the secret society would be looking for me.

I was the only one left of the three who had been suspected of getting hold of the *Find Me* manuscript. If something happened to me too, the commissioner might lose his last chance to strike back at those who'd had the audacity to ridicule the Agency. And his pride.

No one had entered the teashop after me, but that didn't mean anything. The commissioner knew that I'd been here before and might even know that I'd said I would be back again after five, and sent his people in advance. They would not have needed a reservation. I started looking around slowly, hoping to make out younger, casually dressed customers, but couldn't see through the semi-darkness.

"Here's your pick-me-up!"

I turned back swiftly. Had it been the proprietor's

sister, I certainly would have heard her approach, but his soft footsteps were almost inaudible. He set down a plate in front of me with two large sandwiches and a brown napkin.

"Thank you."

"But I must warn you. Once you've tasted my sandwiches, you will never think of any other."

I waited a while for him to go away, but he was clearly determined to wait and see how delighted I was with the sandwiches. I smiled graciously, picked up one and took a bite. Since I was hungry, it did me good, of course, although it did not seem out of the ordinary. I recognized the flavors of tuna, mayonnaise, hard-boiled egg and lettuce. Had I been allowed to choose, I would certainly have left out the mayonnaise and added a bit of lemon juice, but nit-picking was clearly out of the question.

"Excellent," I said, after chewing and swallowing my first bite. I hoped my voice sounded sufficiently delighted. His face lighted up in return. I once more waited briefly, but I seemed fated to have an audience until I finished my meal. I sighed and picked up the sandwich again.

I had almost brought it to my open mouth, when my hand froze. I didn't understand what was happening at first. I wanted to finish the movement, but someone seemed to be preventing me, holding back my hand. There was no one next to me, however, except the teashop proprietor who was watching me, a smile glued to his face.

I did my utmost to get my hand moving again, but it was no good. It hung stiffly in the air, holding the sandwich next to my mouth. I was filled with confusion, having no idea what had come over me or what to do. Great willpower was needed to maintain even a little composure. First I tried to help myself with my other hand, but it lay there in my lap, also inert.

That's when panic seized me. The urge to jump headlong away from the table overcame me and when I realized I couldn't move a single part of my body, I became frantic with fear. All I could do was sit there, paralyzed, staring straight ahead while my heart pounded in my ears.

Several eternally long moments passed in this way, and then the teashop proprietor leaned toward me and stroked my cheek.

"I warned you, my dear Inspector, that after my sandwiches there would be no others."

36

THE TEASHOP PROPRIETOR LOOKED at me for a moment, smiling triumphantly, then moved to the left and disappeared from sight. My hearing was still good, but his movements were so quiet that I couldn't tell whether he had moved off or was still close by. I sat facing a corner of the teashop so my field of vision was quite narrow. Most of the underground room was behind my back.

The first thing I did was swear at myself for having ordered a sandwich. Even though I'd been really hungry, I should have waited a little longer. And then I realized that it really made no difference what I ordered. Whatever was in the sandwich could have been put into anything else. Into tea that removes all troubles, for example.

I had acted incautiously even though alarm bells should have gone off the night before as soon as this turned out to be a teashop and not a café, as I'd first thought. Being wary of all places like this just because of what had happened to me in the Mandarin Teashop would be paranoid, but I should not have been completely nonchalant either, particularly since I had reason to be suspicious.

First of all, such gloom where the other guests are barely visible is not the customary atmosphere for a teashop. In addition, I had been recognized as an inspector with an affinity for literature, allegedly by the way I drank tea. Finally, mentioning Jelena Jakovljević's new novel led to an invitation to come here again.

The night before I had not succeeded in talking to the woman who owned the place about these things and today I had only come across her brother. If he was her brother. And if he was the type of person he was making himself out to be. If he wasn't, then he was an excellent actor. The goodwill he showed me had appeared quite genuine. So genuine that I had actually made his job easier. Instead of refraining from ordering anything, it was I who had asked him for a sandwich—and given him a chance to put in it what they had previously given to Miss Aksentijević and Inspector Vesić.

It had probably not gone as smoothly with them as it had with me. Signs of resistance had been found in Miss Aksentijević's apartment and Inspector Vesić was not the type to give up without a fight. I, however, had played into their hands. It was almost as though I'd been cooperating. I'd already been reproached several times that day for being credulous and here I was doing it again. And at the most badly chosen moment.

Whatever they'd given me had caused no more than complete paralysis for now. There was no pain or even discomfort. After the initial shock had passed, my heart beat normally again and my breathing was regular. Nevertheless, I had no idea what might happen next. Would the effects of what I'd been given stay painless until the end? Judging by the appearance of those who had not survived the test, they hadn't seemed to suffer, but the death mask could have erased their final agony.

Although it should have been the last thing on my mind, it occurred to me that Commissioner Milenković had wrongly concluded that crossing realities were to blame for the two new deaths. The secret society had outsmarted him there too. They had clearly found some substance that kills without leaving any trace. Or at least the very sophisticated equipment at the Agency's disposal had been unable to find any trace.

Someone approached me on my left. From the heavy footsteps I knew it was the shot putter before she entered my field of vision. She paused and examined me briefly.

"I'm sorry, dear Inspector, that you didn't have a chance to try my tea against all troubles. Miss Aksentijević and Inspector Vesić were delighted. Now they no longer have any worries. But sandwiches provide much the same relief. It just takes them a little longer to kick in. I hope you'll be patient."

She turned around and headed back the way she'd come and another woman appeared from the same direction. I had to make an effort to recognize her. Although only eight hours had passed since I'd seen Mrs. Sokolović, so many things had happened in the meantime that it seemed our sole encounter had taken place long ago.

"If it made any difference, dear Inspector, I would advise you not to take at face value what the support staff say. Be wary in particular of harmless-looking cleaning ladies. You have no idea what they're capable of doing. Not just cleaning up messes, for example, but making them too. Without a sound."

She giggled and left my field of vision. Jovana Timotijević, attorney at law, entered it.

"If you could only see yourself, dear Inspector. You've gone terribly downhill. And everything could have been so different. Didn't I promise to repay you personally? If you'd just handed over what I asked for, I would have given you pleasure you'd never experience with any other woman. But you craved immortality. And this is where it brought you. It serves you right for not knowing your limits. As though immortality were for everyone."

She left, shaking her pretty head reprovingly, and made room for a girl I hadn't seen before. She was short with dark-blond hair and an oval face, wearing jeans and a checked cotton short-sleeved shirt. Everything was consistent with the look of Commissioner Milenković's new associates.

"Hello, dear Inspector," said the voice that I had previously heard through the gray cellphone. "We didn't necessarily have to meet under such circumstances, but you left us no choice. We had to put you to the test. For your sake, I hope you haven't read *Find Me*. In that case, you will die soon, quickly and easily, like the other two. Otherwise you'll see for yourself—as I warned you—how unbearable hell is when it lasts forever."

She walked beyond my sight, but no one took her place. My heart started pounding again. So all that remained was a quick and easy death. I should have been happy with such an outcome, considering the alternative prospects, but somehow I was not overwhelmed with joy.

And then a new, tall figure began to fill my field of vision, this time from the right. It was completely covered by a white robe, the head bowed under the raised hood. It did not remain standing like the four women, but sat down on the chair across from me. After remaining motionless for several moments, it raised its left hand finally to the hood and pulled it back.

37

Had my facial muscles not been inert, they would have formed an expression of amazement. As it was, I just stared deadpan at the Grand Master whose face appeared from under the hood.

When he'd called me earlier that day on my private

cell, I'd thought I still didn't know what he looked like, even though we'd met twice. I'd been mistaken, however, in both respects. We'd met more than twice and I knew what he looked like. I just didn't know that I knew it.

His thick salt-and-pepper hair was still pulled back in a ponytail, emphasizing his high forehead and bony face. This, along with his height, would have been enough to lend him a striking appearance—which was probably expected from secret order grand masters. But it was the bright green jade of his eyes that provided his true charisma.

His gaze appeared even more surreal thanks to the fact that even now, when he no longer had to pretend he was a blind painter, I couldn't tell for sure whether or not he could see. His eyes didn't seem perfectly focused on mine, but at the same time they seemed to penetrate much deeper than I found comfortable.

"Dear Inspector Lukić," he said in the voice that I'd first heard the night before in the dark corridor outside the painter Teodosijević's apartment, after Adam had growled at Miss Aksentijević and me.

I was unable to respond to his words with a bewildered expression, but this wasn't necessary. Even without it he knew he had bewildered me, so he repeated himself.

"Dear Inspector Lukić." This time his voice had the distinctive depth that I remembered quite well from the amphitheater underneath the villa where the Last Book followers had gathered. He'd spoken to me in the same voice on the telephone around three hours earlier.

"Which one do you prefer?"

He waited a bit.

"Please don't hesitate. Even though I personally like this deep voice better, I'll be happy to use the other one if you prefer."

He fell silent again for a moment.

"Oh, yes, I almost forgot. How thoughtless of me. You're not in a position to reply. You are completely paralyzed. Not much fun, is it?"

He frowned and shook his head, ostensibly sympathetic.

"Nevertheless, since it doesn't hurt, it's not so terrible over the short haul. But just imagine having to stay in that position for a long time. A very long time. Forever. Soon you'd want only one thing—for death to come and put an end to your suffering. And there is no death in deathlessness."

He paused as though wanting to let me imagine this as vividly as possible.

"And then again, perhaps you aren't facing that ghastly end at all. Perhaps you weren't lying when you said you hadn't even seen the Grand Manuscript. Ah, if only I dared trust your word. Or if another test existed, just as reliable as this one, that you would be able to survive. There is none, unfortunately. I know you'll have a hard time accepting death if you told the truth, but it is the only thing that can get you out of this paralysis. Nothing else. The immortal would envy this privilege."

He raised the left sleeve of his robe and looked at his watch.

"Just a little longer and we'll find out whether you read *Find Me*." He smiled. "It's too bad you can't speak. I'm sure that even now you'd like to satisfy that inspector's inquisitiveness of yours. It's not hard to guess which questions intrigue you. What, for example, did we give the three of you that leaves no trace? How did we intercept police communications? How were the two bodies put into the elevator? How did I disappear from a building that was under Agency surveillance? And you might also be interested in some questions that Commissioner Milenković doesn't care much about. What, for example, was in Inspector Vesić's briefcase? Do I know who the ninth Jelena Jakovljević is? Or am I really blind?"

Just then the jade needles that were aimed a little below my eyebrows seemed to plunge into my pupils.

"But we don't have time for the answers, dear Inspector. Only a few moments are left. And what would be the sense in replying if you are just about to die? If, on the other hand, it turns out that you're immortal, I'll have plenty of opportunities to reveal all the secrets to you. You'll have far more time on your hands than you want."

A veil of silence, heavy with expectation, seemed to fall over the teashop.

If I hadn't been completely paralyzed, I would have jumped up from my chair when a vibrating suddenly started in my right pants pocket.

38

If only I were able, I would have laughed at my predicament. There could hardly be a worse moment for a message to arrive. Just a few instants separated me from death and I couldn't move a finger. The writer had clearly lost control of what he was writing if, under the circumstances, he expected me to take out my cell and read his SMS. To say nothing of the fact that I was surrounded by an entire entourage of unkindly disposed Grand Manuscript adherents. As if I were standing in front of a firing squad just waiting for the order "Fire!"—and asked them to delay the barrage a moment or two so I could check the writer's important message.

That's when the ringing started. It didn't sound muffled in the dead silence of the teashop, even though it was coming from one of my pockets. I couldn't tell which one right away or recognize the telephone by its ring. Another amusing thought crossed my mind. If all four telephones sounded at the same time, the situation would become really grotesque. If the writer had decided to rescue me and this was all he could think of, then I didn't stand a chance and neither did his book.

The other three cellphones kept silent, however, while the fourth one rang without letup. I finally realized what would never have escaped my attention if I'd had the slightest presence of mind. But who can keep their cool when they are about to die? I didn't recognize the sound because I'd never heard it before. That telephone had only received SMS messages until now.

This realization was accompanied by another, also belated. The vibrating of the small telephone in my pants pocket had been inaudible and imperceptible to other people, but everyone had to hear the ringing. I didn't know, admittedly, about those outside my field of vision, but the Grand Master seemed completely unaware of it. Or, if he was, he was totally uninterested. His eyes were fixed on me, his expression unchanged.

And then I did notice a change. It was elusive, but certain. The green jade had lost its brightness. The needles were still there, but dulled. They could no longer penetrate inside me. It was like having a picture of the Grand Master in front of me instead of himself in person. And that's when it struck me what had happened.

No one but me heard the ringing because time had stopped for everyone else just before the first ring. Just as it had stopped for the Grand Master and the Last Book adherents, and for Commissioner Milenković and his people, in the two rooms off the corridor that linked realities. Just as it had stopped for Vera in the Mandarin Teashop as she was raising a cup to her lips from the saucer on the table.

So the writer had not lost control of what he was writing after all.

And yet, why had he let time flow for me alone when I was hopelessly paralyzed and it served no useful purpose? What was the sense of me alone hearing the ringing when I couldn't answer the telephone? None, of course, but the cell rang another three times before the scales suddenly fell from my eyes.

The first thing I did when I realized I was no longer immobile was to throw away the sandwich that had almost cost me my life. It was a reflex; I didn't intend to hit the Grand Master, although I certainly had reason enough. The sandwich hit him in the chest and fell apart, leaving a large stain on his immaculate white robe.

Then I got up briskly from the table, causing the chair to overturn behind me. I reached for the telephone as I rose, but the ringing stopped just as I stuck my hand in my right pocket. I muttered a curse and then took out the cell. There was no sign on the screen that someone had just called. My thumb hastily pushed the button to open SMS messages.

"Left of the bar. Behind the plush curtain. Door. Hurry!"

Clutching the telephone in my hand, I turned around without a moment's hesitation—and came face to face with a forest of tightly packed statues. The brother and sister, cleaning lady, lawyer and girl who called me on the gray cellphone were in the front row. Their empty eyes were trained on the place where I'd been sitting. Behind them, around thirty figures in brown robes filled the central part of the teashop. All their hoods were raised. I hadn't heard when they'd got up and gathered behind my back.

I couldn't make my way through this crowd, so I circumvented it, going between the now empty banquettes along the right-hand wall and the little round tables. No one was sitting in the chairs around them either. On reaching the bar, I ran to the other end. I didn't see the plush curtain until I got there. Even though this part of the teashop was slightly better lit, the dark-brown drape was hard to detect because it blended in with the wall of the same color.

I had already stretched out my hand to pull it aside, when I saw that not everyone was gathered in the middle of the teashop. A young couple was seated in the last two places in the left-hand corner. Peering through the semi-darkness wasn't easy even from this close. I recognized the young man first by his long hair. I had to take a step forward to make sure that the girl next to him was the photographer. And another to identify what was on the plates in front of them.

Two sandwiches. With bites in them.

Blind with rage, I spun around toward the statues. Everything suddenly left my mind except the desire to grab the remains of the sandwiches, go back to the table where I'd sat and stuff them into the Grand Master's and brother's mouths.

The telephone's sharp ring snapped me out of my rage. Biting my lower lip until it hurt, I pulled the curtain, took hold of the doorknob, opened the door with a jerk and walked through it.

39

The ringing stopped the instant I closed the door behind me. I was in a narrow passage that curved to the right after six or seven meters. The walls, floor and ceiling were lined with the same dark-brown plush as the curtain. The lighting was muted, with no visible source, as though the plush itself was shining.

The SMS had given no instructions about what I should do once I got there, but this wasn't necessary. There were only two possibilities—stay by the door or head down the passage. The former seemed pointless, so I started to run, although I didn't actually know why I was in such a rush.

The message had said "Hurry!" I'd even been warned

by renewed ringing not to dawdle when tempted to retaliate for the murder of Commissioner Milenković's two young associates. Particularly the photographer. But no explanation had been provided.

After the curve, the passage ran straight for a dozen meters, followed by another bend, this time to the left. After I'd run along that part, I saw that the passage didn't turn anymore. It stretched out before me straight as an arrow. I might have been able to make out the end if the lighting had been better, but as it was, it seemed to stop somewhere in the distance in an indistinguishable dark point.

After I'd run another thirty meters, a door appeared on the right. Were it not for the round doorknob, I probably would have missed it because it looked like part of the wall. I didn't become aware of the rectangle, its edges barely outlined, until I stopped.

Suddenly knocking was heard. I stared at the door in confusion, not realizing at first that the sound was coming from the inside. When it was repeated, something tempted me to open it, but another sharp ring from the cellphone put me off. One ring was enough to get me running again.

I came across another door about thirty meters further on. I could hear music before I reached it: a violin, double bass and oboe. The music grew louder and the beat quickened. As I reached the door, the composition was rising to a crescendo. I had slowed down a little before, but this spurred me to go faster.

After another thirty meters the phone in my hand suddenly rang again. I stopped and looked in bewilderment, first at the right-hand wall, then at the left. I couldn't see the outline of another rectangle or anything else unusual. The ringing didn't stop, however, until my thumb almost pushed the call button.

In the silence it left behind, I first heard a commotion from somewhere behind me and then rapid movement. People were rushing toward me from that direction. The chase was joined by a dog, who barked angrily. So that was the reason to hurry. The writer hadn't been able to keep the Grand Manuscript adherents paralyzed in timelessness for long. I ran as fast as my legs could carry me.

I didn't turn around to check and the sounds didn't confirm it, but I had the impression that they were gaining on me. I thought of drawing my gun, but it wouldn't have done much good. Even if I were to shoot the dog and hit the legs of the five or six who were heading the chase, the others wouldn't be discouraged, but enraged even further. I was being hounded by more than thirty fanatics and I didn't have enough bullets for them all.

When the end of the passage finally came in sight, panic seized me. I'd had no idea what I would find there, but it hadn't crossed my mind that there would be nothing. The passage seemed simply to end in a bare wall.

Having no choice, I kept running frantically in that direction. It was only after I'd covered half the distance to the end of the passage that I detected something on the wall after all. A black iron ladder was attached to the middle, reaching from floor to ceiling. I couldn't see where it led, but it certainly had to go somewhere. I didn't suppose it would be there otherwise.

I couldn't figure out what was on the ceiling even when I reached the bottom of the ladder. Raising my head apprehensively, all I made out was a square outline measuring one meter at most. Regardless of what was up there, it was the only place I could hope to find refuge, so I grabbed hold of the rungs.

I reached the top in an instant and did the only thing I could. Holding the highest rung with my left hand, I placed the palm of my right hand in the middle of the square and pushed as hard as I could. At first it seemed as hopeless as trying to move the entire ceiling.

Then the side next to the wall budged a tiny bit, so I quickly moved my palm to that side—and everything became easier. The hatch swung upwards. Without a second thought about what was above me, I scrambled up the last rung, climbed through the opening and stepped aside to lower the hatch as quickly as possible.

Once the hatch was in place, I almost jumped on it, convinced that no one down below could handle my eighty-five kilos, even with the strength that fanaticism gave them. That didn't seem enough, however, so I crouched down, as though this would increase my weight.

As soon as the hatch covered the opening, I was hemmed in by darkness. When weak light had shone from down below for a moment, I'd been completely preoccupied with trying to thwart my pursuers and hadn't looked around to see where I was. Now I had no chance. All I could do was breathe heavily and stare into the impenetrable darkness, trying to figure out what to do. I kept my ears pricked too, but there was nothing to hear. The silence seemed more ominous than if a noisy crowd down there was striving with might and main to get through.

Suddenly I realized that the solution lay in my hand. All I had to do was push a button on the black cellphone. The screen would turn on and lessen the darkness somewhat in my immediate vicinity. But my thumb was not destined to complete the movement this time either. Before it could reach a button, I felt that whatever place I was in had started moving upward. And that's when I knew where I was, even though I still couldn't see.

I should have figured out where the passage was heading, of course, but the circumstances had disconcerted me completely. A mere ten minutes ago I'd been about to die, and had then rushed headlong before my pursuers. Commissioner Milenković was right.

There was a secret entrance into the building at 12 Oak Street. The Grand Master had used it last night to leave without being seen. Miss Aksentijević's and Inspector Vesić's bodies had been taken from the teashop, where they hadn't survived the test, along this underground passage about 150 meters long and finally through the opening in the elevator floor, hidden by thick carpeting, where I was now crouching.

I had no time to wonder why the elevator had started moving because the carpeting began to shine at the same moment. The radiance was blue and wavering, as though I were standing on rippling water, but the unchanging firmness of the floor told me this was just an optical illusion. It lasted just as long as it took to go from the ground floor to the second floor, then was transformed into the lively glow of a fire. For a moment I had the eerie feeling that intense heat had erupted down there. But the third floor soon arrived with a new change. The fire seemed to go out and I was surrounded by darkness again, but when the flames faded from my eyes, I became aware of a weak brown glow, as though loose soil under my soles had just been touched by the dawn. The floor began to shine once more after the elevator left the fourth floor. The blueness seemed again to announce water, but it thinned and acquired a celestial translucence before the fifth floor.

Lights came on as the elevator stopped, bringing relief. Even though I knew that it had been just a chimera, the final change in the floor had frightened me. Neither water, fire, nor earth had been as scary as the abysmal empty air beneath me. The firmness of the floor had no longer been able to assure me that I wouldn't plunge from the sky.

The lights returned the carpeting to its dark-red color, but brought a new nightmare as well. I became aware of it as I rose from my crouch. I was facing toward the wall right of the door. I should have seen my reflection, but it wasn't there. As though I wasn't in the elevator, it reflected nothing but the opposite mirror, creating the illusion of infinity.

Terrified, I turned left to the wall facing the door, but I didn't see myself there either. I already knew the same thing would happen with the other two mirrors, but even so I made a quick semicircle in disbelief, stopping in front of the door. Nothing I'd seen earlier in the elevator, whether awake or asleep, had filled me with such horror as this absence of any reflection whatsoever.

If the doors hadn't opened, I wouldn't have been able to stop myself from screaming. As it was, I burst into the corridor but didn't have the courage to turn around even when I clearly heard the doors close behind me. I stood there a little longer to pull myself together. Then I put the black cellphone in my pants pocket and headed down the corridor to the right.

I was already at apartment 19 when I had the funny feeling that I'd missed something. I looked back over my shoulder. A good half-minute had to pass before I finally noticed what had changed. The four drawings on the opposite wall were no longer red but black, on a white background.

My heart jumped for joy as I pressed down on the door handle.

40

WHEN I OPENED THE door, my first impression was that I was looking at an enormous black-and-white photograph of the short hall and part of the small room with its window in the background. The wealth of colors had disappeared, but not of shades. Between black and white stretched a magnificent spectrum of gray. I hesitated briefly and then stepped into the world as seen by the colorblind.

The photograph took on depth at the same moment, as though I'd entered the three-dimensional version of an old black-and-white movie. It all seemed unreal until I saw my hand on the handle of the door as I closed it behind me. Although its color was unnatural, it was no less real. No less mine.

I heard Vera before I saw her. She was sitting in front of the keyboard and monitor in the large room, typing. She must have known I'd come in, but she didn't turn around or stop writing. Her typing even seemed to speed up as I headed toward her. And my heart started pounding more quickly as I drew closer to her.

I'd imagined a reunion with Vera for an entire year and a half, but nothing like this had ever occurred to me. Not knowing what else to do, I stood behind her and gazed at what was closest to me—her hair, its length unchanged. I never would have guessed what shade of gray corresponded to red. It was the same with her clothes. I recognized the cut of the tweed suit she had been wearing the first time we met. Now it looked almost black and I'd remembered it as dark blue.

The typing slowed and then stopped. Everything stood still for a few moments. Then I did what I'd been yearning to do for a long time. I touched Vera. I placed my right hand on the top of her head. It was a light, soft, hesitant, quizzical touch. Not until my fingers and palm felt the familiar cascade of thick hair was the doubt dispelled that my eyes had raised. Even though it was ash-colored, it was her red hair. My sense of sight was still able to deceive me, but not my sense of touch. It remained in the world of colors.

My hand slid all the way down her smooth hair, stopping on her shoulder. I squeezed it a little, wanting to let her know that it was me behind her even though, of course, this wasn't necessary. She raised her left hand and placed it on mine, as the fingers of her right hand quickly danced about the keyboard.

This didn't last long, and she finally turned her head toward me. The swarm of pale gray freckles joined together into a smile, lighting up her face. I returned her smile, but had no chance to bend down and kiss her because she turned her attention back to the keyboard and continued typing with both hands.

She soon finished and turned toward me again, motioning her head at the monitor. I looked at her confusedly for a moment and then over her shoulder at the big screen. She had used a font large enough that I didn't have to move closer in order to read the last paragraph that she wanted me to see.

> *She soon finished and turned toward me again, motioning her head at the monitor. I looked at her confusedly for a moment and then over her shoulder at the big screen. She had used a font large enough that I didn't have to move closer in order to read the last paragraph that she wanted me to see.*

"We're still in the novel?" I asked.

She started typing as soon as I spoke. My words appeared on the monitor as soon as I said them. Then she hit the enter key and answered me in italics in a new line.

"Of course we're still in the novel. I have to finish the fortieth chapter. The dénouement is missing and it won't be a detective story without it."

"*The Last Book* ended in the fortieth chapter too."

"This is its sequel, so it's fitting for them to be the same."

I pondered this briefly. And she immediately wrote that on the screen.

"Are you just going to write? Aren't you going to say anything to me?"

"What writer talks while they're writing? But here, I'm talking to you through the monitor. I'm next to you. It's as though we're talking"

"It's not quite the same. I miss your voice." I paused,

feeling a lump in my throat, then added softly, "I haven't heard it in a long time. . . ."

She raised her left hand again to mine on her shoulder and stroked it, while her right hand quickly wrote this very sentence.

"You'll hear it in a little while, as soon as the last chapter is finished."

"When I give it some thought, though, there's justice in this."

"Justice?"

"Yes. I was the one doing the writing for a long time."

"Are you thinking of The Last Book?"

"I'm thinking of all those SMS messages I sent you from this cellphone." I patted my right pants pocket and then put my hand back on Vera's shoulder. "The writer arranged it so her messages arrived momentarily, as though she was saying them, while she had me write mine slowly like some simpleton. It's only fair that we change roles for a bit. Am I talking too fast? I'll be happy to slow down if you can't catch everything I say. . . ."

This time Vera slapped my hand.

"Don't you worry about whether I can catch your words. I don't type with just my thumb, like some people. . . ."

"Actually, that should have made me realize who I was dealing with. Only you would think of tormenting a poor inspector in that way."

"I hoped you would figure it out even earlier. But, as we know from other situations, it turned out that our poor inspector lacked insight."

"Like when?"

"Like when you received the first message. 'Find me.' *That might have been the title of Jelena Jakovljević's new novel for other people, but I expected you to connect it to what I wrote you a year and a half ago, before I left. Do you remember? 'Don't look for me. I'll be in touch.' Well, I got in touch with a message that would have been perfectly clear to an insightful inspector. Unfortunately . . ."*

"Luckily. . . ."

"Luckily?"

"If the uninsightful inspector had figured out who he was dealing with back then, the novel would have ended just after it began. It's unlikely there would be any novel at all. This way you reached the dénouement in the fortieth chapter. And the dénouement has to begin precisely with that message of a year and a half ago that you mentioned. I think you owe me an explanation about it."

"I'm sorry everything turned out that way, Dejan. I knew our parting wouldn't be easy for you. It was even harder for me. But I had to go."

"I almost asked Commissioner Milenković to track you down."

"Not even he would have found me. The other reality is not in the jurisdiction of the National Security Agency."

"You've been here the whole time? In the writer's reality? For a year and a half?"

"That's how long it took me to write Find Me. *It might have taken less time if I'd had any writing experience."*

"Where did you get the idea to write a book? Let alone a sequel to *The Last Book*?"

"I asked the writer to do it, but he turned me down."

"You asked the writer? How?"

"He visited me."

I took my hand off Vera's shoulder.

"Why? What reason did he have to visit you?"

"Out of compassion. Kindness. A guilty conscience. He did me wrong in The Last Book. *He knew how I felt, and he had time for me. Work wasn't the most important thing for him, like it is for you. That's when I saw you very rarely."*

"Unlike police inspectors, writers are known for being laid back. And cunning. He refused to write a sequel to *The Last Book* just so he could entice you here."

"You have no reason to be jealous."

"I don't? He arranged it so you spent a year and a half with him here."

"Nothing happened."

"Is that so?"

"First of all, the writer isn't my type, and he's well along in his years. In addition, there's a technical barrier. You looked at yourself in the elevator mirrors on the way up. What did you see?"

"Nothing. . . ."

"Me neither. Visitors from the other reality are as real here as characters in a book. I've spent a year and a half in this world like a ghost. Visible only to the writer. But intangible even to him. And how can you make love to someone you can't touch?"

"It's not entirely inconceivable. . . ."

"Maybe not, but there's a third reason, the most important one. I love you."

My hand went penitently back to Vera's shoulder.

"I missed you terribly all this time. . . ."

"I missed you too. . . ."

"Why did the writer refuse to write the sequel?"

"Among other things, because he's never written a sequel to his works."

"Some pretext. . . ."

"In any case, in the beginning he was vehemently against my coming here and writing it myself. We almost had a falling out. But the sequel had to be written, so in the end he had no choice if he wanted to help me."

"Why did it have to be written?"

"To show that there can be detective stories without killings. That was the only thing that might assuage the guilty conscience plaguing me. The writer maintained that such a book was impossible. I had to try and write it."

"It seems he was right. *Find Me* has just a few less killings than *The Last Book*—four."

"Four?"

"Well, Miss Aksentijević, Inspector Vesić and Commissioner Milenković's two associates—the photographer and the long-haired young man."

"Why do you think the photographer and long-haired young man are dead?"

"I saw them paralyzed in a corner of the teashop. They'd been served sandwiches, like me."

"Their sandwiches didn't contain the same thing as yours. They didn't have to be tested. It was known they'd never even been close to the Grand Manuscript. It was enough to incapacitate them temporarily until they were through with you. They might kill a police inspector, but they wouldn't have the audacity to harm Agency staff. As powerful as the secret society might be, it would not be spared Commissioner Milenković's wrath."

"That's good to hear. The death of those two young people would be senseless. Particularly in a novel that was not supposed to have any victims."

"The death of those two young people, and particularly hers . . ."

"Excuse me?"

"Cut the act. You don't care a bit about the long-haired young man or whether the novel has any corpses. The photographer is the only one who means anything to you. You never stopped smiling at each other from the moment you first met. I just watched you flirt with her."

"What was I supposed to do—frown in return for her smiles? You leave me without a word of explanation. I have no idea where you are or whether you ever intend to come back. And you expect me to behave like a monk. Now I'm sorry for having lived the last year and a half like that."

Vera raised her left hand from the keyboard again and placed it on mine upon her shoulder. She didn't stop typing with her right hand.

"I should have suspected who was behind the whole thing when so many women started hanging around me," I continued. "You surround me with enterprising single young women and then accuse me of flirting because of two or three innocent smiles."

"Which one did you like best?"

I gave it some thought. "The only married one among them."

"Married?"

"Mrs. Sokolović."

"The cleaning lady?"

"Why are you surprised? You're in the best position to know what strange taste I have in women."

Her hand slapped me again and then returned to the keyboard.

"All right, there aren't four dead, but there didn't have to be even two. Inspector Vesić's death was completely unnecessary."

"I did everything I could to save him. I was really fond of him. It was your fault."

"My fault?"

"We've already talked about that. If you had solved the riddle of the ducky in time, Inspector Vesić would be alive. But your insight failed you there too, even though I almost ruined the novel's narrative coherence to give it a boost. I even sent you the photograph in the bathtub twice, and I shouldn't have done it at all."

"It's not fair to lay the blame on me. If you'd wanted me to be insightful, I would have been. But it suited you when I wasn't, because it's not good for inspectors to be too insightful in detective stories. The key secret must not be disclosed too early. And sometimes that comes at a high price. . . ."

"So now I'm to blame for Vesić's death. . . ."

"No you're not. I wasn't being fair to you when I said that a good writer would not be in an awkward position like you—having to choose between two evils. You were right to be offended by that. I should have said—an experienced writer. And this is your first novel. An experienced writer, however, was by your side the whole time as your mentor. He brought you into his world so you would write under his supervision and then he let you get tangled up with no way to resolve things. All we can do is speculate as to why. In any case, he's to blame for Vesić's death."

"Poor Inspector. . . ."

"By the way, what was in Vesić's briefcase? As you know, that rascal of a Grand Master didn't tell me."

"I have no idea."

"You have no idea?"

"I'm not an omniscient narrator. The novel is told in your voice. I know as much as you do."

"The readers will be disappointed. . . ."

"Whose fault is that? Why do they read detective stories where everything isn't explained in the usual way?"

"Some things have to be explained, though. Why didn't you show the writer that he was wrong to think it's impossible to write a detective story without any killings? Why did you go ahead and kill Miss Aksentijević when there was no need?"

"Yes, there was. She knew who was the ninth Jelena Jakovljević. She was the only one to see the person hiding behind that pseudonym. If she'd revealed it to you, the novel would have ended too early as well."

"She was removed so I wouldn't recognize you in her description?"

"Not me. Miss Aksentijević and I never met. She knew nothing about me or what I looked like, so she couldn't have described me."

"Then whom could she describe?"

"Come on, dear Inspector Lukić, put your insight to work. If it wasn't me, who else is left?"

I was silent for a few moments, my eyes fixed narrowly on the back of Vera's head.

"The writer?"

"The writer, of course. From the very beginning he engineered everything in our world so it conformed to my

novel. First he rented an apartment on Oak Street that was almost identical to this one. For some reason that was important so that the two apartments from the two realities could be connected."

"Connected?"

"I'll get to that in a minute. Then he contacted Miss Aksentijević. He had an irresistible offer for her. He would be the author of Jelena Jakovljević's new novel. He didn't mention me so things wouldn't get too complicated, plus I'm a beginner while he is a reputable writer, and from another reality to boot. He promised her that this could be disclosed after the book came out. She was utterly delighted. What a bestseller it would be once it was made public that the book was by the author of The Last Book*."*

"How did the secret society find out about it?"

"The writer took care of that. He had to involve them because that's how it was in my novel. He even arranged for the real painter Teodosijević to go on a trip so the Grand Master could use his apartment. He brought your drawing there to emphasize the relationship to the 'Last Book' case."

"He did a good job of drawing me."

"Not him. He's extremely untalented at drawing. He ordered the drawing to be made based on a photograph he took a year and a half ago."

"The drawing looks like I posed for it recently. It seems I haven't changed very much in the meantime. . . ."

"You haven't, thanks to your monastic life. Once the preparations were made, all that remained was the final act. The writer was allegedly writing Find Me *in the apartment on Oak Street, and his agent visited him from time to time. The manuscript was supposed to be finished on Friday evening, but when Miss Aksentijević appeared, she found the apartment locked from the inside and was unable to contact the writer through the intercom or telephone. She panicked and called the police."*

"There's something I don't understand. She presented the writer to me the whole time as Jelena Jakovljević. Wasn't she afraid I might find a man inside?"

"No, she realized that you wouldn't find anyone. That the writer was playing a game, regardless of what it was. All she cared about was getting hold of the manuscript, the rest was play-acting. She thought that the police would break into the apartment and she would be able to find it."

"While we're on the subject of Jelena Jakovljević's gender, the Grand Master made a slip-up. In front of Miss Aksentijević he said he'd seen the woman writer often. I didn't find that strange, but the agent realized at once that he wasn't who he pretended to be."

"That bought her a little time. If she hadn't been afraid of the fake painter, she would have gone back during the night to try and get into the apartment, and the secret society members would have been waiting for her and given her the test on the spot. This way, she lived several more hours."

"The Grand Master was nonetheless right when he maintained that Jelena Jakovljević hadn't left the apartment, even though it was locked from the inside. How did the writer pull that off?"

"Through the bathroom. It was one of the connections between the two realities. He went from this bathroom to the other one, and vice versa."

"How?"

"I don't know. He didn't tell me so I wouldn't be tempted to go back. I went through crises during that long year and a half. Being a writer is a very lonely job, particularly when you're in someone else's reality. But I think that the passage had something to do with the ducky. I didn't suspect that until I saw Inspector Kostić's photograph. The bathtub here has a ducky just like it."

A thought suddenly flashed through my brain that forced me to squeeze Vera's shoulder.

"Did Vesić find it out somehow . . . ?"

"Wouldn't he have told you if he had?"

"He didn't have a safe way. If realities had crossed again, every contact with me would be under surveillance. Nevertheless, he sent me a message, except I was blind to it at first, and afterward, until now, too dim-witted to interpret it properly. Turning the ducky around was not his customary sign that he'd broken into some seemingly inaccessible place, but a message about what was behind it all."

"If that's true, then we don't have to speculate as to why my mentor, as you say, let me get tangled up without a good resolution. He had to remove Inspector Vesić before the two of you met so you wouldn't find him out too soon, and I had to do the dirty work for him."

"So the writer was to blame for both murders in your novel and if we accuse him he'll invoke the book's narrative coherence, which would be jeopardized without those two violent deaths."

"I still think it's possible to write a detective story without a single murder, but also without jeopardizing its narrative coherence. If I decide to try it again, it will certainly be without a mentor. And in my own reality."

"The one mistake in narrative coherence is nevertheless your fault."

"Really? What's that?"

"Saving the main character in the teashop."

"Would you have preferred for me to let you die just for the sake of the novel's narrative coherence? In any case, there's narrative coherence of a higher order here. This novel is intended to be a melodrama, and they are the best when they have happy endings."

"So what happy ending awaits us?"

"An original one. As far as I know, there has yet to be a story written that ends like that. I was inspired by your jealousy. You suspected there was something between the writer and me. There wasn't, but at the end of this novel the writer and the main character will make love."

"The writer and the main character?"

"That's right. In this reality I'm a writer and you are a character in my novel."

"And we're going to make love in front of all the readers?"

"Don't be silly. That would be lowbrow literature. Pornography. This is a serious melodrama. We will soon exclude the readers. I can hardly wait to stop writing. It's really tiring like this."

I looked around the large room.

"Well, I don't know. I've never made love in black-and-white. . . ."

"Oh, in the end you'll see what real colors are. . . ."

Compendium of the Dead

Translated from the Serbian
by
Vuk Tošić

It was just past nine as I drew up in front of the entrance to the City Cemeteries Administration Building. I had not expected to find a free space so easily. Having passed from time to time, I remembered that it was rather busy with people trying to park their cars nearby. The rush was understandable bearing in mind that on average around a hundred people died every day in the city, and that in the majority of cases funerals were scheduled here. However, it seemed too early still for the business of death.

The squat bungalow was surrounded by a narrow garden full of well-tended greenery, and separated from the street by a cast-iron fence. The old-fashioned building was likely a private villa originally. Its façade did not provide any hint as to which department was housed there. The mosaic of bright yellow and red bricks and the tall windows would have better suited the services related to entrance into the world, rather than departure from it.

As I got out of my car, it occurred to me that I had never set foot in this house, even though death was an integral part of my job as an inspector. There had not yet been any reason for me to come. Now there was a reason, although I had not quite understood what was the matter. It was also unclear to my colleague Bumbaković, who had called me from the switchboard just as I was headed towards my office at the Police Headquarters, twenty minutes earlier.

"You should go over to the City Cemeteries Administration, on. . . ."

"I know where it is," I said, interrupting him. "What's happened?"

There was a short pause.

"I'm not sure. The woman who called was excited and mixed up. She said something about some books. . . .that they were amiss. . . ."

I sighed. Why did everyone on the police force immediately think of me the minute anybody mentioned books?

"If it isn't anything more serious than something being wrong with some books, just send the nearest patrol. Let them see what exactly it's about. The City Cemeteries Administration isn't on my way. It might take me as much as half an hour to get there in this traffic."

There was another pause. Bumbaković coughed before continuing.

"I would have sent a patrol already, but the woman asked for you specifically."

"Me?" I asked, slowing down a bit. "Why?"

"I didn't understand that either. Do you want me to play back the recording of our conversation?"

"There's no need. I'm on my way."

I returned my cell phone to my jacket pocket and stepped on the gas.

I HAD TO PUSH quite hard in order to budge the gate in the cast-iron fence. The short gravel path led up to three wide steps at the entrance to the former villa. The doors were tall, as were the windows. Above the upper left corner a small camera blended into the yellow brick background like a chameleon.

I reached for the door handle, but someone on the inside beat me to it. The door opened towards me halfway and the space was filled by the figure of a short, bald, stumpy man with watery eyes. He looked like he was well into his fifties. His dark blue guard's uniform was rather wrinkled. Blinking, he began speaking rapidly before I had even had a chance to introduce myself.

"I didn't close an eye all night, I swear. They just keep on accusing me of sleeping on the job. And that I drink. No one came in. You can check the recording." He glanced up towards the camera. "It's all a frame-up, so I. . . ."

"Mr. Rabrenović!" A sharp female voice from within interrupted him.

Flinching as though caught in the act, he hastily opened the door wide, and scampered into his glass booth across from the entrance.

The broad corridor was covered with thick red and yellow carpeting. A tall woman dressed in a dark gray suit and a lighter blouse of the same color approached me from the left. She was closer to fifty than forty. Her shoulder-length dark hair, with ends curling toward her chin, framed her long sunken face. Large glasses hung on a dark cord around her neck, resting on a mere hint of a bosom. She wore almost no makeup, and had on low-heeled shoes.

She raised her eyebrows slightly as she stood in front of me.

"Inspector Lukić?" Her voice had become softer, but was still brusque.

"Dejan Lukić," I responded with a nod, holding out my hand. "Good morning."

Before accepting it, she sized me up me once more, as though in slight disbelief; she must have imagined police inspectors differently. Her grip was firm.

"Good morning. Hristina Leleković, Head of the City Cemeteries Administration. We have been waiting for you, Inspector. The police should arrive faster in such extraordinary cases."

"The police are always fast, except when a specific inspector is requested. Then it inevitably takes a little time."

"Well, let's not go into that now. Before we proceed

any further, I have to tell you that your investigation must not jeopardize the normal functioning of our service. Any interruption or obstruction is out of the question. The City Cemeteries Administration does not suspend its operations even in times of war. Other affairs can be postponed, but not burials. Nothing is more important. I hope this is clear to you."

"Absolutely. However, I still don't know what I'm supposed to be investigating."

"Didn't your colleague inform you? I explained everything to him clearly."

"From what he conveyed to me, I only understood that something unusual had happened, involving some books. Could you please explain it to me too?"

She sighed, shook her head, and motioned me towards the stairs next to the guard's booth. "Please follow me," she said as she passed me by. I thought she would be taking me upstairs, but instead she headed into the basement.

The downstairs corridor was covered with the same red and yellow carpeting, but it seemed shabbier, perhaps because of the slightly weaker lighting. We headed right. Large black and white photos of cemeteries hung on the walls between the office doors. The inscriptions on the plates beneath the black frames were too small to read in passing.

The administrator stopped in front of the last door on the left. Before knocking, she glanced past me down the corridor. As though waiting right inside the door, someone instantly unlocked and opened it.

A thin middle-aged man, slightly hunchbacked, moved aside to let us enter, then closed and locked the door again. He wore a dark suit and vest with a gray striped tie. He had a high forehead, thick sideburns and glasses with round metal frames. Without saying a word, he walked to the large desk in the middle of the room and remained standing next to the chair.

I looked around the room. Even though it was not small, it seemed cramped because the walls were covered with bookcases filled with large volumes of equal height and thickness. They were almost the identical dark gray color as the administrator's suit. Walking up the gravel path I had noticed barred basement windows along the entire width of the building. They were not visible here, which meant that the bookcases covered them. Someone considered storing books to be more important than daylight. The only lighting in the room was provided by a square ceiling light.

A large volume lay open on the desk, and alongside it a bundle of documents. In front of the book was something that I hadn't seen in a long time—an inkwell. The bottle stood on a black metal stand with arched supports, the pen shaft sticking out. A round vase with a single yellow flower had been placed behind the writing set.

The administrator moved away from the door a little and gestured vaguely to the bookcases.

"This is perhaps the most important office in our Administration. The Archive. And this is precisely where someone chose to harm us."

"Are the archives still kept the old-fashioned way?" I asked. "I thought that all departments had gone digital long ago."

"This one has too, of course. Modernization cannot be avoided, although our experiences with it have been rather traumatic. On two occasions we almost lost our entire database. Computers might speed things up, but they are not at all as reliable as is generally believed. Can you imagine what a disaster it would be if we were to lose what is kept here?"

She looked at me questioningly, as though expecting me to answer, but as I did not say anything, she continued.

"We keep the only trace that most people even existed—information on where and when they were buried. Everything else has been forgotten, lost. As though they had never even lived. We cannot surrender such a treasure to the imperfections of digital storage alone. That is why, in addition to computer archiving, we have also resorted to the old-fashioned system. We keep records of burials as has been done since ancient times. Here it cannot happen that someone mistakenly or intentionally presses a few keys on the keyboard—and destroys everything. The dead are safe this way."

"It seems that in fact they are not. Why else would you have called the police? What happened?"

The administrator looked briefly at the clerk before answering. Her voice became more subdued.

"Last night someone broke in here and scoured through the books. We discovered it this morning."

"Scoured?"

"Moved them. As you will see, the books are arranged neatly. By number. In the first bookcase," she pointed at the first bookcase on the wall across from the door, "we discovered as many as seven volumes in the wrong place."

I walked up to the bookcase and looked it over from top to bottom. There were twelve books in each of the five rows. The only inscription on the spines was a gold-embossed Arabic numeral at the bottom. The volumes were moved around in all the rows, at first glance—randomly. I tried to open the glass doors, but they were locked.

"Who has the keys to this room and the bookcases?" I asked.

"Only Mr. Trpimirović, the archivist." She turned her head toward the clerk for a moment. "No one else has access here."

"Is there a spare key? With the guard, for example?"

"There are no spares. And even if there were—the guard would certainly not have them." She just waved me away, without adding anything, as though everything was clear.

"These are not exactly locks used to protect treasures," I said, pointing at the door and the first bookcase. "Anyone with any skill at all could open them even without a key."

"They were quite all right until now. Nothing like this has ever happened before. At least, not in the twelve and a half years that I have been administrator." She sighed. "All right, we'll change them. We'll install better ones. We cannot allow this to happen again."

"You should probably upgrade this old-fashioned archive a bit. Install video surveillance. Cameras would be more useful here than in front of the entrance. Had you had them, we would have identified instantly the prankster who decided to play a joke on you."

"Prankster?" she said, the pitch of her voice rising. "This is no prank. It must be taken quite seriously. . . ."

"As far as I can see, no harm has been done. Nothing was stolen or destroyed. Several volumes were just moved. Return them to their places—and everything will be as it was. There is no work here for the police."

"I insist that you conduct an investigation. You have to determine who did this."

Now I sighed. First she had made me come over in the worst morning rush-hour traffic, and now she was insisting that I carry out an investigation into someone's juvenile behavior. That is not how you treat a police inspector, no matter how important all this seemed to her.

I walked up to the desk, slightly raised the volume that lay open and read the number on the spine: 3584.

"Perhaps you wouldn't like what an investigation could uncover."

"What do you mean?"

"You see, in investigations we rely on one rule, which has almost no exceptions: the simplest solution is the most likely one. We can imagine that behind all this is someone from the outside, who crept into the building in the dead of night, past the sleeping or intoxicated guard, while remaining invisible to the video surveillance; or that it was someone on the inside who is adept at burglary. However, why should we resort to such complex explanations when we have at our disposal a significantly simpler one?"

"A simpler one?" she repeated questioningly.

"Yes. There is someone who could very easily pull this off without any nighttime sneaking around and breaking in; someone who could have unlocked both the door and the bookcase without any difficulty, because he is the only one who has the keys to them."

It took her several moments to understand who I was talking about. She opened her mouth to protest, but I beat her to the punch by turning to the archivist.

"Mr. Trpimirović, you discovered that the books had been moved, right?"

"Yes," he answered evenly.

"How did that happen? What led you to pay attention precisely to the first bookcase? The volume that you are working on was not in it. Judging by the number, it is from a completely different part of the room. And if you were not standing in front of the bookcase and staring right at it, you could not have noticed that the books had been rearranged."

For a moment we fell into silence. The administrator's gaze slipped from me to the archivist. His face remained expressionless. He cleared his throat before finally speaking.

"I would like to ask you something, Inspector Lukić."

"How do you know my name? The administrator did not introduce me."

"No, she didn't. But she insisted that you come in particular. And since we waited for a long time for the police to arrive, then it had to be you. What do you think, why did she ask specifically for you?"

I shrugged. "I have no idea. I was leaving that question for the end. I am very interested in why out of all the inspectors she chose me."

"You will get your answer right away."

He leaned over, opened a drawer on the left side of the desk and took out a large yellow envelope. It contained something firm, with a regular shape. He approached the first bookcase, removed a small bunch of keys from his jacket pocket, searched through them briefly, set one aside, and unlocked the glass door. He placed the envelope upright in front of the books in the middle row, then closed the door, without locking it. He left the key in the lock.

"This is how I found it when I came in at eight o'clock. Is it conspicuous enough to attract your attention?"

The yellow rectangle stood out prominently on the dark gray background. One could not overlook it if one's gaze were to rest there for even a brief moment.

"What is it?" I asked, realizing that same instant what a stupid question it was.

A smile passed across the archivist's lips.

"An envelope," he answered matter-of-factly, just as my question merited. He opened the bookcase again and took it out; he then closed and locked the door, and returned the bunch of keys to his pocket. He came up to me and handed me the envelope. "It is addressed to you. That is why we asked for you specifically."

I hesitated a little before accepting it. I turned it right-side up and was presented with four words written across the middle in red pencil "For Inspector Dejan Lukić." I didn't recognize the handwriting.

My eyes moved from the administrator to the archivist. Then I slowly removed the two brass clips from one end, spread out the stuck edges, and peered into the envelope.

2

I REMAINED STARING FOR a moment, then briefly raised my eyes once more to Mrs. Leleković and Mr. Trpimirović. I reached for the thing that was inside, but stopped halfway. I set the envelope down on the desk and took out a pair of plastic gloves from my inside jacket pocket. I put them on hastily and picked up the envelope again.

It took some effort to remove the book whose corners kept getting caught on the plastic lining. Whoever had placed it inside had doubtless had similar difficulties. I put the envelope back on the desk and examined the volume in the palm of my hand. It was approximately a B5 format, rather thick. There was no lettering on the leather cover.

I turned the book over, expecting it to be face down, but there was no inscription on that side either. I looked at the back once again, then at the spine. Nothing interrupted the monotonous whiteness of the cover.

I opened the book and started leafing through it. At first I turned one page at a time, but I quickly realized that there was no reason to make slow progress, so I quickly flipped through to the end. The plastic glove didn't hinder me much in doing this.

Like the cover, the book was also empty. The snow-white surfaces had only the page numbers in the outer corners at the bottom. Printed on the last page before the endpaper was the number 2048. I was convinced that paper that thin was used only for Bibles.

I closed the white book and took a look at the archivist. He looked back at me, still with an expressionless face.

Not knowing about the envelope addressed to me, I had rashly concluded that it was a case with a simple explanation. Whoever had pulled this off, it was not mere juvenile behavior. One does not obtain such an unusual book and get a specific police inspector involved just to play a prank on the administrator.

"What is it?" Mrs. Leleković broke the silence, while pointing at the volume in my hand.

"A book," I answered, also matter-of-factly. "Why didn't you tell me immediately about the envelope?"

"Because it isn't the most important thing," she responded irately. "We are deeply honored that it occurred to someone to leave packages for you precisely here, but we are very concerned that this jeopardizes the safety of our archive. And it worries us even more that you have no intention of carrying out an investigation."

I sighed again, then said apologetically: "There will be an investigation, of course."

"Very well," she said with a light nod. "I hope that you haven't forgotten what I first drew your attention to: your investigation cannot interfere with the running of our administration."

"There will be no interference. I am just leaving."

I picked up the envelope from the desk. I hesitated briefly over whether to replace the book inside so that I could remove the plastic gloves. But that would undoubtedly have taken time.

"But you haven't . . . investigated. . . ." the administrator protested.

"On the contrary. I have seen everything there is to see. I have even spoken to everyone that I need to speak to. There is no more work for me here. For now."

"Won't you look for some . . . traces . . . of who broke in here?"

"It wouldn't do any good. Whoever did this certainly made sure not to leave any traces."

"You can take a look at what the camera in front of the entrance recorded. . . ."

"There is no need. The guard has already looked at it. He didn't see anything unusual."

"And you trust him?"

"I have no reason not to trust him. He could have been drunk as a skunk all night, but he was definitely sober when he looked at the recording this morning."

I could see by the administrator's wavering eyes that she was frantically thinking what else she could propose, but nothing was coming to mind. I started towards the door, stopping after two steps. I returned to the desk and looked at the open book. Mr. Trpmirović's handwriting was significantly different from that on the envelope.

"What kind of an investigation will it be, then?" asked the administrator as I started back once more towards the exit. "What will you investigate?"

"The only lead that I have," I answered, rapping the knuckle of my index finger on the white book.

I unlocked the door and went out into the corridor. She joined me hastily. A moment later the door closed, followed right away by the sound of the key turning in the lock.

Halfway to the stairwell I stopped in front of one of the cemetery photos. I drew closer and read the inscription on the brass plate, then looked closely at the picture.

"Nice cemetery," I said after we had continued on.

"The others are also nice." The administrator pointed down the corridor. "Unfortunately most people don't realize that. They stay clear of cemeteries, even though it is only in them that they can find complete tranquility."

"Perhaps that is precisely what puts them off. They lack a little vivaciousness. There will be plenty of time for complete tranquility. . . ."

"Vivaciousness!" the administrator grunted. "Those who care about vivaciousness remain unprepared, and one needs to prepare. . . ."

She left the sentence unfinished because we had reached the ground floor. There were people in the corridor now. The guard's booth was empty.

"We'll stay in touch during the investigation. Please let me know immediately if something out of the ordinary happens. Have you written down my cell phone number?"

I was sure that she would pull out a notepad and pencil from one of her suit pockets, but a cell phone appeared in her hand. She skillfully pressed several buttons and entered the number that I dictated to her.

"Goodbye, Mrs. Leleković." The gloves spared me another handshake with her.

I had half-turned towards the exit when her voice stopped me.

"I have to tell you something, Inspector Lukić. It wasn't at all nice that you suspected Mr. Trpimirović. He is the best clerk in our administration."

"It's his own fault. He should have told me everything immediately, and not put the envelope away in the drawer."

"In any case, you could apologize to him, now that you no longer suspect him."

For a long moment I just looked at her.

"The envelope didn't change anything in that regard. It was still simplest for him to pull it all off."

"But why? What reason would he have to move the books, and then to involve a police inspector as well? That would be quite irrational, and Mr. Trpimirović is the embodiment of rationality."

"Even the most rational people are sometimes led to take unreasonable steps. Perhaps he could no longer take the years of being denied daylight for the sake of storing records of burials. . . ."

Before she had to time to respond, I completed my interrupted movement and left the building of the City Cemeteries Administration.

I was two steps from the gate when my private cell phone rang.

3

I STOPPED, TOOK IT out of my inner jacket pocket and looked at the screen: Vera.

"Are you busy?" she asked after I had picked up.

"Not any more. I was just leaving the City Cemeteries Administration."

There was a brief silence. When Vera spoke again her voice had a different tone.

"What are you doing at the City Cemeteries Administration?"

"Someone decided to toy with the necrophiliac administrator. They rearranged the records of the burials in the archives."

"They could have come up with something more original. They were imitating our patients."

"That crossed my mind too. Mrs. Stojanović, right?"

"Yes, poor Mrs. Dragana Stojanović. But we didn't call the police because of her harmless fiddling with the books."

"I gave the administrator a piece of my mind for having to come over here in the rush-hour traffic. It took me almost half an hour."

"Couldn't someone closer have gone?"

I looked down for a moment at the white volume and envelope under my arm.

"As soon as it turned out that it was a problem involving books, anyone else was out of the question."

Vera giggled.

"That's the way it goes when a person has a reputation of being well-read."

I cleared my throat. "What's new with you?"

"I just got an unusual offer."

She stopped, so I asked: "I hope it's not an indecent one."

"No, unfortunately. . . ."

"Unfortunately?"

"Indecent ones are the most profitable. Although this one isn't bad either."

"A decent offer that is not bad?"

"Alright, I won't exactly be fabulously rich, but my overall financial situation will certainly improve if I accept it."

"What could it be?"

"Try to guess. Let's see whether your inspector's insight has improved. You've grown a bit rusty in that department lately."

I pondered for a moment.

"You have been offered to write a book entitled *How I Seduced an Uninsightful Police Inspector*?"

"I seduced you? The inspector isn't only uninsightful but his memory is also failing. Not to mention how indecent that book would be."

I had to move to the side of the path to let pass five or six people, who had gathered in front of the gate while I was standing there. Suddenly it was like someone had fired a gun that only they had heard, and the race was on. They rushed into the yard, almost running the short distance to the entrance. I looked at my watch: 09:30. The business of death had started.

"Alright, the dimwitted and senile inspector gives up," I said while walking out into the street, after the last person in the group had passed. "What kind of an offer did you get?"

"To sell the inventory and books from the Papyrus." Vera's voice had become serious.

"To whom?"

"I don't know. I got a call from the Samardžić Law Offices. They represent the buyer, who wants to remain anonymous. They only hinted that it was a wealthy collector."

"They really offered you a good price?"

Vera was silent for a few moments, then told me the amount in a muted voice. I whistled in awe.

"That's a lot more than the inventory and books are worth, right?"

"At least fifty times more than the market value."

"Why would he offer you so much?"

"He obviously cares strongly about including what remains of the Papyrus in his collection."

"What collection? What is it that this anonymous wealthy collector collects?"

"I have no idea. I recently read a book about outlandish collectors. You'd never guess what all they collect. . . ."

"Still, fifty times more. . . ."

"Things don't have just a market value. The Papyrus was certainly not an ordinary bookstore. That is how much the books and inventory from it are worth to the collector. Who knows, perhaps he is counting on them being worth even more in the future, and he sees this as a good investment."

"How much is what you kept of the Papyrus worth to you?"

Vera didn't answer right away. Her voice again grew soft when she continued.

"I would never sell it at market price."

"And for a price fifty times as much?" I asked, also quietly.

"I don't know," she answered, after a fresh hesitation. "I would have to think about it. Unfortunately I don't have much time. The offer stands only until eleven o'clock."

"Today?"

"Today, yes. I have to make a decision in the next hour and a half."

"Why in such a short time?"

"I didn't get an explanation for that either. The law office believes that the syntagma 'wealthy eccentric collector' is a sufficient answer to all my questions."

I sighed. "That's tough."

"It is. What do you think, what should I do?"

Now it was my turn to pause.

"I don't know, but whatever you choose—I will support you."

"You're not of much help in making decisions, but it still feels good."

"Did you expect more from an uninsightful inspector?"

"I didn't, but I still love him."

"I love you too. Let me know when you reach a decision."

"No one will know before you."

I returned the telephone to my jacket pocket and took out my car key. I placed the envelope on the passenger seat, removed the plastic gloves and laid them over the white book. I still hadn't pulled the car out completely when I heard the angry honking of two competitors for the empty parking space right in front of the entrance to the City Cemeteries Administration.

4

AFTER PARKING THE CAR in the underground garage at the Police Headquarters, I first put on the plastic gloves again, then took the envelope and the book. I did not go immediately to my office on the fifth floor, but rather towards the entrance to the basement area, near the elevator. A corridor illuminated by neon lights extended beyond the metal door. It was here that all the technical services were located, with the exception of the Communications Department, which was on the seventh floor.

Walking towards the opposite end of the corridor, I greeted two colleagues in passing. The last door on the right had a sign with the legend "Laboratory." I knocked and entered.

Workstations with a number of apparatus were arranged along the walls of the room. Some were working, and one made a muffled humming sound. The upper space contained several metal shelves with glass dishes of various sizes and shapes, plastic containers, tubes, measurement instruments, utensils, and the occasional book or folder. The whiteboard across from the door was partially filled with chemical symbols. A slender vase with several yellow flowers stood in the right rear corner, in contrast with everything else.

The central part of the room was filled by a spacious rectangular table. It was covered with laboratory equipment, as well as two large computer monitors.

"Hello, Ms. Mirković," I said to the girl in a white lab coat sitting on the left-hand side of the table. She was using an instrument that looked like a microscope with two eyepieces. There was no on else in the lab.

Ana Mirković had been hired by the police department a few months earlier, straight out of school. She was short, round, with cropped brown hair and high-set cheeks. She kept to herself, and seemed skilled despite her young age. We had collaborated on several occasions and every time she'd exceeded my expectations. The praise I gave her appeared to cause problems for her.

Our relationship strayed beyond the professional on only one occasion. Our last conversation had not ended with her wordless, bashful smile, which was how she usually responded to my praise. She just looked at me without any expression for several moments, then with a hint of reluctance she asked me an unexpected question.

"Could you recommend a good novel?"

I sighed. Police officers are no less prone to gossip than the rest of the world. Quite the opposite. Who knows what they had told this innocent girl about me.

"It would be my pleasure," I responded. "However,

I don't know anything about your literary taste. What topics appeal to you?"

"Death," said Ms. Mirković without hesitation.

"Death?" I repeated in disbelief.

Seeing my expression made her smile widely for the first time.

"Death that is told as comedy," she quickly added, as though wanting to justify herself.

"Ah, so . . . That's better," I said, also with a smile.

We were silent for a moment while I searched my memory. She waited patiently, with her eyes fixed on me.

"Have you read anything by Saramago?" I finally asked.

She shook her head. "I haven't, but I've been planning to."

"Excellent. Then first take his novel *Death with Interruptions*. I think that it will suit you."

"Is it funny?"

"Irresistibly."

She nodded. "Thank you for the recommendation."

It had been about three weeks since that chat. We had not worked together in the meantime, but we did meet several times in passing and exchanged a few words. However, she had not mentioned the book at all. Perhaps she still had not read it, or perhaps she did not find Saramago's dark humor amusing, but didn't feel comfortable saying so.

"HELLO, INSPECTOR LUKIĆ," SHE responded with a smile, looking up from the eyepieces.

"Everyone has deserted you?" I pointed to the empty seats at the table.

"That's my karma."

I looked at her suspiciously. "You don't expect me to believe that, do you?"

"Believe it or don't. Alright, they also leave for other

reasons, not only to desert me. It's like everyone is just waiting for an excuse to go somewhere outside, or at least where there are windows. They feel claustrophobic here."

"And you?"

"I don't mind the underworld, at least not yet, but I've only been here a short while. Perhaps I will start to feel stifled here after a bit as well."

"And perhaps the laboratory and other technical services will be relocated somewhere higher up. There has been talk of it."

"So I've heard. My colleague who has been here the longest says that there was also talk about it thirty years ago, when he first arrived."

"I don't think you will have to wait that long."

She smiled again. "You've comforted me. What can I do for you, Inspector?"

I approached and handed her the envelope and the book.

"Would you be so kind as to check this for fingerprints? There's no hurry. Finish what you are doing first."

"That isn't urgent either. I'll check right away. Besides, I am in your debt."

She removed a pair of plastic gloves from a drawer, put them on and took the envelope and the book. She kept them in her hands.

"In my debt?" I asked, as I took off the gloves.

"Saramago, remember?"

"Ah, that. I was just wondering whether you had had the opportunity to read the funny novel about death."

"I read it over the first weekend after you had recommended it."

"I hope it didn't disappoint you."

"On the contrary, it captivated me. I occasionally laughed out loud."

"It's Saramago's unique skill, laughter that stems

from the morbid. It is even more prominent in *Blindness.*"

"Thank you for the new recommendation. However, there is something in *Death with Interruptions* that scared me."

"Was there? What was it?"

"The idea that there is no more death."

"That scared you?" I asked in puzzlement.

"Very much. I once even dreamed that I found myself in such a world. I woke up terrified."

"What is so terrifying about that? Wouldn't you like never to die?"

The girl looked at me piercingly for a moment before shaking her head.

"It isn't about dying but about growing old. Imagine getting older and older, and there being no death to put an end to that agony."

"That never occurred to me. All right, perhaps the world without death would also be a world without aging."

"You have consoled me yet again, Inspector." She nodded towards the envelope and the book. "This will be done quickly. Should I bring the items and the report to your office?"

"I would appreciate it. It would also give you reason to leave the underworld for a little while."

5

Ms. Mirković knocked on the door of my office about twenty minutes later. She entered, approached the desk I was seated at, and placed on its edge the envelope, the book and two pieces of paper.

"There wasn't much work, Inspector. I found fingerprints only on the envelope. In addition to yours, just one other person touched it with their bare hands."

She picked up the top piece of paper, which contained her report, then rapped the knuckle of her index finger on the black-and-white photo that took up a quarter of the bottom piece of paper. The archivist from the City Cemeteries Administration looked several years younger in the picture.

"A certain Tihomir Trpimirović. I barely found anything on him. An impeccable citizen, one might say. We don't have any information about him in the database. He has actually never had any dealings with the police. This is from the general birth records. Even there he appears quite inconspicuous. He has lived at the same address since birth, single, no children, just one job—at the City Cemeteries Administration." She stopped and smiled. "It is as though he stepped out of *Death with Interruptions*."

I responded with a smile of my own. "Reality and literature have more in common than is believed."

Watching me carefully, she waited for me to say something more, but since I did not, a shadow of disappointment passed over her face as she continued.

"I also googled him. There is no mention of him. Not a single hit. As though he doesn't even exist. Being so digitally inconspicuous is extremely rare."

"It doesn't surprise me. I met with him this morning. Computers have been banned from his workplace. He uses a nib pen and inkwell. Apparently that is what he is like privately too."

"Not everyone lives in their own era," she said with a shrug.

"In any case, thank you for your efforts. You have done an excellent job once again."

She gave me her usual bashful smile, but didn't walk away as on previous occasions.

"Regarding the book. . . ." she said and then stopped.

"Yes?"

"It has absolutely no fingerprints. Albeit, that is how most books are when they come off the printing press.

Machines have been doing all the work at printing houses for some time now. Copies don't pass though human hands at all. However, someone had to place this one in the envelope. Machines still don't do that. If it was Mr. Trpimirović, why did he avoid leaving prints on the book, but didn't care about leaving them on the envelope?"

It was I who shrugged now. "I have no idea."

"And there is the book itself. I have never heard of one that has no lettering. Even if this weren't a book at all, but for example a luxurious diary or notebook, there would be some writing, right?"

"I guess."

"Someone sent it to you?"

"Obviously." I pointed towards the envelope.

"You weren't expecting it?"

"No, I wasn't."

I saw in her sparkling eyes that she wanted to continue asking questions in this direction, but she was discouraged by the brevity of my answers. It was clear to her that I did not wish to discuss it.

We were silent for a while.

"Just one more thing. That paper. . . ."

"Paper?"

"It's strange. . . ."

"In what sense?"

"I don't know . . . I'd like to test it. I was rushing to finish the fingerprint analysis, and there wasn't time to look into it. Would you give me the book again? I'll keep it for no more than half an hour."

"How about I bring it to you in half an hour? I'd like to look at it a bit first. I haven't had an opportunity yet."

She nodded. "Of course, Inspector. I'll be in the lab."

"Ms. Mirković," I said, stopping her after she had already opened the door.

She turned around and looked at me inquisitively.

"I hope that *Blindness* will not frighten you like *Death with Interruptions*. It's not as funny, and it is more morbid."

She smiled. "It isn't easy to frighten me twice. Not even Saramago could manage that."

I went to reach for the book when the girl had left, but my action remained incomplete. My private cell phone rang from my inner jacket pocket.

"Do you have a little time?" Vera asked.

"A lot, if needed."

"A little will be enough. I've reached a decision."

"You'll sell the Papyrus inventory."

"How did you guess?"

"It wasn't a guess. I relied on my famous inspector's insightfulness."

Vera laughed. "Just don't become arrogant. It didn't exactly require any special insightfulness."

"It didn't," I agreed.

"It doesn't make any sense to keep the remains of the Papyrus. I will never go back to that business. That is quite certain now. Those things are just a painful memory. Not to mention the rent for the storage unit where I keep them. That is a significant expense for an unemployed former bookstore keeper."

"The unemployed former bookstore keeper will now become nearly a fat cat. A pitiful police inspector will hardly be a match for her any longer."

"Well, my dear pitiful police inspector, work on your insightfulness, and perhaps you will earn a promotion and greater benefits. Just hurry up—it is a known fact that wealthy bachelorettes are besieged by suitors. . . ."

"Does that mean that the wealthy bachelorette will not be engaging in anything other than choosing the best suitor? I can hardly imagine you as such an easy-going person."

"Oh, no, the suitors will only be my hobby. Wealth will finally allow me to do what I've always dreamt of."

"And that is. . . .?"

"I won't tell you just yet. Not to jinx it. Wait until I actually become wealthy first. I've told the law office about my decision. We will meet there at half past eleven to sign the contract. Everything should be over by noon. They will pay me the money as soon as I hand over the keys to the storage unit."

"Why are they in such a hurry?" I asked, after a short hesitation.

"You know their wild card answer—'the wealthy eccentric collector.' Well, now I'm in a hurry too. I need to get ready and get across town. I'm already running late. Kisses."

She hung up before I had time to say "Kisses to you too."

6

I PICKED UP THE book and stared at it in my open left hand. There was something sensual in the touch of the leather cover. I had not experienced it holding the white volume while wearing gloves. Previously it had only been an object, and now for an instant I had the deceptive impression that something living was in the palm of my hand.

I opened the book and flipped through several pages. I then took one between my thumb and index finger and rubbed it slightly, the better to feel its texture. Nothing seemed unusual. What did Ms. Mirković mean when she said that the paper seemed strange?

I raised the book towards the window, without letting go of the page. The thin paper became semitransparent under the strong daylight. The shadow of my index finger was clearly visible from the other side. I put the book down and leafed through it again. The quick succession of more than two thousand empty pages flipped past my eyes.

I shut the book and then examined the thick volume from all sides some more. However, there was nothing to see. The only obvious thing was that such a book had to be expensive even without being printed, especially since it existed in only one copy. This was what made it stand out, that and the way it had been delivered to me. What I usually got was significantly cheaper and reached me by simpler means.

It was inevitable that I would be marked out by the role that I'd played in the cases of the "Last Book" and the "Grand Manuscript." The full contingent of weirdoes, paranoids and conspiracy theorists saw me as the person with whom they had to get in contact right away. They had to inform me of the discoveries they had made, and which mainly concerned the fate of the world.

I usually received the messages by email. They somehow found my address. When the number of emails exceeded ten per day I changed my address, but the lull was short-lived. They would find the new one too, and the torrent of messages continued unabated. I changed addresses three more times, and then I finally gave up. I didn't pay attention to such emails any more. I simply deleted them. The record was a hundred and thirty-seven deleted messages, which is how many had accumulated between two Saturdays.

While deleting them, now and then I would read the beginning of an email, and sometimes even a longer passage. Occasionally I would laugh heartily at the incredible ideas these people had come up with, and I was tempted several times to propose that they try to turn them into prose. They would make excellent detective novels.

I also received letters in envelopes, as well as packages, although not as often. The senders preferred to leave them personally in my mailbox, convinced that email and postal communication were being monitored. The messages were no different from those in the emails, and the packages mainly contained books. They were mostly amateur and self-published, but I also received official publications, with an appropriate short or longer text on how one should read them in order to uncover their hidden meaning. These books even included several great works of world literature.

Occasionally I received publications with jackets that didn't belong to them. The work would have its own title, while the added jacket would have the inscription *The Last Book* or *The Grand Manuscript*. On one occasion someone wanted to be funny and put *The First Book* and *The Minor Manuscript* on the jackets. I threw away the letters, as I did the emails, but I kept the books. In time a rather large collection of these works accumulated, and it eventually got its own bookshelf.

It was most uncommon for them to call me on the phone. They would get in touch with me through the police switchboard, and only once did someone get hold of my work cell phone number. The calls did not last long. All it took for them to hang up was for me to tell them the number from which they were calling. I imagine this left a particular impression on those who believed that they were invisible if they switched off the caller identification.

This morning's attempt to get me involved in some weird business was the most complex one so far. Not only was the person behind everything willing to go to considerable expense for what they had set out to do, but they had also pulled it off very skillfully. My main suspect was still Mr. Trpimirović, but I didn't have any evidence that would incriminate him.

If it really was him, he'd made sure not to overlook any of the details that amateurs always miss. He hadn't left any fingerprints on or in the book, and he'd found someone with different handwriting to write the four words on the envelope. I picked it up off the desk and looked at the red lettering. The letters were round and upright, unlike the archivist's elongated and slanted script in the burial records.

Well, he was doing well so far. Nevertheless, we'd see how he would do next time. And there would certainly be a next time. One does not invest this much in a single performance—where among other things the police inspector is being pulled by the nose—only to end it with the volumes that were moved around in the underground bookcase being put back in their places and me adding another book to my odd collection. The main event was yet to come.

I had just placed the envelope back on my desk when my work cell phone rang.

"Inspector Lukić," my colleague Bumbaković called from the switchboard. "You are being requested by the National Library."

"I'm in my office. Patch them through to my landline."

"All right."

I picked up the receiver as soon as it rang.

"Inspector Dejan Lukić."

"Inspector, you have to come to the National Library immediately." The young female voice sounded rather excited.

"To whom am I speaking?"

"Please forgive me. I didn't introduce myself. It's because I'm excited. Olivera Šuvaković. Deputy Head of the Department of Old and Rare Books."

"Pleased to make your acquaintance, Mrs. Šuvaković."

"Miss. . . ."

"Miss. What has happened?"

There was a moment of silence.

"I can't tell you, Inspector. I mean, not over the phone . . . Only when you get here. . . ."

"Has someone . . . been injured?"

"Oh, no, worse than that. . . ."

"Killed?"

"No, no, even worse, I tell you."

What could be worse than that? Nonetheless, there was no sense in asking Miss Šuvaković, who was obviously beside herself. Arguing with her would only be a waste of time.

"I'll send the nearest patrol immediately."

"No! You have to come personally! It concerns you too. . . ."

I fell silent for a moment.

"I'll come right away."

"Inspector!" she shouted. "Don't use the main entrance, please! We have to be discreet. It's very important. I'll wait for you by the staff entrance. In the rear of the National Library building. Do you know where it is?"

"I'll find it, don't worry. I'll see you in about fifteen minutes."

I hung up the receiver and hurried towards the door. Going around the desk I grabbed the book. It would take only a minute to drop it off at the lab.

I almost ran down the basement corridor, and entered without knocking. Mr. Grubijanić, the head of the laboratory, was the only person seated at the large table.

"Ms. Mirković isn't here?" I asked, pointing towards the place where she had been sitting.

"She wasn't here when I came in a little while ago. She must have popped out. Should I call her?"

He reached for the upper pocket of his white lab coat and pulled out his cell phone.

"No, thank you. It's not urgent. I'll leave this for her. I saw her earlier. She knows what to do."

I walked up to the left-hand side of the table and placed the white book next to the instrument with two eyepieces. Then I hurried to the garage.

7

I HAD TO SHOW the guard my badge for him to let me into the small parking lot behind the National Library building. Of the forty or so spaces only two were unoccupied. As I approached the staff entrance I saw a female figure standing behind the glass doors. She was of average height, slightly portly, with long red hair, wearing a dark red suit and a beige blouse. She was still in her thirties.

She opened the door when I was two steps away from it.

"Mr. Lukić?"

"Dejan Lukić." I held out my hand. "Hello, Miss Šuvaković."

"Hello," she responded in a rush.

She pulled my hand slightly as we shook, as though she wanted me to enter as soon as possible.

"This way, please."

She pointed towards the elevator opposite the door. As we quickly crossed the lobby, she glanced to the right. An older lady in a light-gray uniform watched us curiously from the reception desk.

As we waited for the elevator, Miss Šuvaković played nervously with a small bunch of keys. She kept her head down, staring at the floor in front of her, obviously avoiding conversation. I was silent too.

As soon as we entered the elevator she separated one of the keys in the bunch. She placed it in the opening at the bottom of a vertical series of small square numbered boxes, and turned it a quarter-turn clockwise. There was no inscription next to the keyhole, and above it was "–3."

"We're going down deep," I said with a smile as the elevator started to move, just to dispel the silence.

"The greatest treasures are always the deepest." She tried to return the smile, but it came out as a grimace.

When the elevator doors opened, there was no corridor in front of us. It gave straight onto our destination. There was no need for an ante-room because one could only get there by using the elevator key. This was also the key to the Department of Old and Rare Books.

The room was about fifteen meters long and five meters wide, but it seemed cramped because of the low ceiling. There were only slightly more than two meters separating it from the floor. And just as at the City Cemeteries Administration, the walls were covered in bookcases. However, these were not mere storage for uniform volumes, but genuine works of art. The hand-carved walnut must have been extremely costly, but nothing cheaper would have been fitting for these books.

The conditions in the room were also in keeping with their preservation. The temperature was slightly lower than regular room temperature, and the humidity had been completely removed, although the dry air did not seem stale. Wide lights along the spine and edge of the vault cast a soft bluish light.

As I stepped inside I looked behind me. The view of the exceptional books and shelves was not spoiled by regular metal elevator doors. They too were lined with walnut on the interior.

Along every wall a brass ladder on guide rails extended the entire height, even though a person slightly taller than average could easily have reached the top row of books without their aid.

There were five horizontal hand-carved bookcases in the center of the room, resembling pool tables. The upper portions were made of glass, which allowed only visual access to the most valuable and sensitive editions beneath.

The sixth element in the row, nearest to the door, was a massive desk. It was surrounded by eight chairs, and on it were as many desk lamps. The center of the desk was given over to flowers. In a shallow porcelain flowerpot there grew a low green bush with a sprinkling of small yellow blooms. These plants obviously didn't mind the absence of sunlight deep underground.

At first glance it seemed to me that there was no one in the great hall, but then a small figure emerged from behind a green screen and walked towards us. The woman was barely one meter sixty tall. She was already nearing retirement age, with short dark hair, a suit and a slightly lighter turtleneck, whose exact color was difficult to make out in this lighting. She wore a large oval brooch on her left shoulder.

Miss Šuvaković stepped aside and waited for the older woman to approach.

"Mrs. Evgenija Ognjanović, Administrator of the Department of Old and Rare Books," she said, introducing her. "Inspector Dejan Lukić."

"Pleased to meet you," I said, holding out my hand. She held it slightly longer than necessary in a soft grip, sizing me up, although not in the same way that Mrs. Leleković had done. Her eyes were not filled with distrust or reproach, but rather curiosity and relief.

"Dear Inspector, thank you for coming so quickly. Olivera and I are completely beside ourselves. We have no idea what to do."

"It is extremely important that you understand," the deputy intruded before the administrator had the opportunity to continue, "that this must remain in the strictest confidence. No one besides the three of us can know what has happened. There would be immeasurable consequences if word got out. Immeasurable . . . You have to promise not to say a word to anyone."

"I cannot promise anything until I know what has happened. You indicated that it is something worse than violent death, and that can hardly be kept secret. I can only promise that I will be very discreet."

Miss Šuvaković had already opened her mouth to say

something, but Mrs. Ognjanović interrupted her with a raised hand.

"You must forgive Olivera, Inspector. She was very wound up when she said that. Of course, that is not what she meant. All this has been a great blow to her; to me too, after all. Both of us are very concerned with the reputation of our department. I have spent decades building it up, and she will soon take over, since I am retiring. This is the first time that this reputation has been seriously compromised."

I glanced over the lavish shelves full of even more lavish books.

"It is difficult for me to imagine what could compromise the reputation of this place. Perhaps something has been stolen, despite all the security measures?"

The two women exchanged glances, and then the administrator coughed lightly.

"Precisely the opposite, Inspector," she said in a somewhat softer voice.

"The opposite?" I repeated in confusion.

"Something has been brought in that has no right to be here."

I stared at her, expecting her to continue, but she fell quiet. We passed several moments in silence.

"I'll show you right away," she said finally, "but first I have to prepare you. Olivera said that this also concerns you. Do you recall?"

"How could I forget?"

"It wasn't only one . . . thing . . . that was brought in, but rather two. The second is addressed to you."

Now she stared at me, waiting for me to respond, but I remained mute.

"Come!" she said, again speaking first, and took me around the large desk.

The part concealed by the plants was not empty. There was something covered with a large white scarf-like cloth, between the two central lamps. Mrs. Ognjanović glanced at me, then pulled away the cover with one swift movement, as though performing a magic trick.

8

My eyes first came to rest on the larger and more prominent of the two objects that had been under the scarf. The yellow envelope seemed to be the same as the one at the City Cemeteries Administration archive. Judging by the silhouetted contours, it too contained a book. Even the red inscription was no different: the same four words, the same rounded upright script.

I was aware that the two women were gauging me, but I disappointed their expectations and again remained silent. I only approached the desk to get a better view of the second object. As I leaned over the small, but very thick antique book with a dark red cover, a shout rang out behind me.

"Don't touch anything!"

I straightened up and briefly turned to Miss Šuvaković. "I had no intention of doing so."

Placing my hands behind my back, I returned to my observation of the book and tried to make out the title, albeit in vain. What was once an inscription could only be made out by the remaining specks of unpeeled gold embossing. The shapes of two letters that were only slightly more visible led me to the conclusion that the title might be in Gothic script.

This time I turned to the administrator and looked at her inquiringly.

"*Das Buch der Auferstehung*," she replied to my unspoken question.

"*The Book of Resurrection*," I heard from behind my back.

"Danke," I responded, without turning around.

"Anonymous author," Mrs. Ognjanović continued. "Printed in Mainz in 1488."

"An incunabulum," I muttered to myself.

"That's right. And a very special one at that. This is the first banned printed book. It's no surprise. Over more than seven hundred pages the unknown author provides short entries about people who he believes deserve above all to be resurrected after the Second Coming of Christ. These are primarily historical persons, but there are also those who were the author's living contemporaries. Trouble occurred when it came to the living contemporaries whom he left out. He was convinced that those who were included would offer sufficient protection, but it turned out that a wounded vanity was much stronger than a satisfied one. Those who had been left out made sure that the book was banned. They did not discover who the author was, so they couldn't burn him at the stake, but they destroyed all the copies they could get their hands on. As far as we know, only one copy remains."

I nodded towards the desk in front of me. "This one?"

She shook her head. "The only copy of *The Book of Resurrection* officially in existence still belongs to one of the most reputable collectors of old books. I've checked. It wasn't easy to pull it off. I couldn't call him and simply ask whether someone had stolen the crown jewel of his collection. I actually had to put on a little performance. Luckily, we've known each other for a long time so I didn't make him suspicious."

"So what is this?"

"There is only one possibility: a second copy that somehow escaped being burned in the late fifteenth century."

I bent over again to take a closer look at the book.

"Are you certain that it is . . . an original?"

"Completely. That was the first thing that we checked. We have an excellent laboratory. The verification lasted a good hour and a half. That is why we didn't call you this morning as soon as we found it. We had to be sure that it wasn't a hoax. That was also a possibility. There is great money at stake in this business."

"So where did the second copy come from? You said that only one remains."

"I said—as far as we know. And you never know everything when it comes to old books. It isn't exactly a rarity for a book that no one was expecting to suddenly turn up out of somewhere. Who knows what else remains hidden in private collections and various depositories of antiquities, that no expert has seen yet. Some owners have no idea how rich they are."

I straightened up again and pointed at the two items on the desk.

"How did these get here?"

The administrator and her deputy exchanged glances again.

"If we knew that, Inspector Lukić, we wouldn't have called you," Miss Šuvaković responded. "We thought that you might have some idea." She looked at the envelope.

"Who exactly found these this morning?" I asked, ignoring her remark.

"Olivera did," Mrs. Ognjanović answered. "She comes in first, shortly before nine o'clock."

I stepped back from the desk a little so that I would not have to keep turning my head towards the women, who stood on each side of me.

"You found the book exactly in this place? Beneath the white cover?"

The deputy nodded.

"Did you immediately lift the cover or did you wait for the administrator?"

"I lifted it immediately, but didn't touch anything until the administrator arrived. When we realized what the book in question was, we took it to the laboratory. We did everything in gloves, of course."

"Of course," I repeated, with a smile. "Who did the testing at the lab?"

"The two of us," Mrs. Ognjanović intervened. "That is one of our duties. It isn't very difficult. We have excellent equipment. You place the book in one instrument and it does everything for you. The only thing that remains is to interpret the results properly."

"Did anyone touch the envelope?" I addressed the deputy again.

She glanced at the administrator, then shook her head.

"Who has the key to the elevator that leads to this department?"

"Only the two of us," said Mrs. Ognjanović. "In the morning, when we come in, we each take our key from the library's main safe, and we return them before leaving. No one else is authorized to take them. There is a third key, a spare, in the safe, in case of an emergency."

"There must also be an emergency exit, in addition to the elevator, right?"

The administrator looked at me briefly, without saying a word. "Only the director of the National Library is authorized to give you that information."

"I thought you wanted everything to stay within the smallest circle. . . ."

The mute stare lasted a bit longer this time. It was apparent from her eyes that she was thinking frantically.

"Please believe me when I say that no one uninvited could have come in that way. . . ."

"I believe you," I said with slight hesitation, then raised my head and scanned the low-lying ceiling. "Do you have video surveillance?"

"Of course," the deputy responded.

"Did you check last night's recordings?"

"There was no recording during the night."

"Why not?"

"The system is set up so that the cameras go on only when something moves in the room. Since nothing moved, nothing was recorded."

"And yesterday's footage? Did you look at it?"

"If you mean the time when the department sees visitors, from 9 a.m. to 5 p.m., there is also no footage there."

"Do your visitors not move when they are here?"

"They most certainly do," Miss Šuvaković retorted angrily. "What do you think they are, statues? And the two of us also don't sit still for eight hours. Nonetheless, it would be an unforgivable insult if we were to record our guests while they are working in our department. Do you have any idea who has access to this place? This isn't some village library where anyone can just walk in off the street. Only the most select individuals come here: academics, university professors, respected researchers. And even they have to get special permission. How could we suspect them of doing something inappropriate?"

I was tempted for a moment to respond to this, but I refrained. The conversation would be needlessly prolonged if we were to get into a discussion about the rectitude of the most select individuals, especially when confronted with the temptation of such treasures.

"I didn't have anything inappropriate in mind. In any case, there has been no theft here or any other violation of the law. I only asked whether any of your dignitaries could have perhaps left these two items here last night. Had there been any recording, we could easily have established that."

"No one left anything. I carefully inspect the entire department after the visitors leave. This was not here last night."

Silence took over the room. The two women looked at me fixedly, expecting me to say something, since we had apparently exhausted all possible explanations for the mysterious appearance of the enigmatic objects in the most secure room of the National Library. I would have said something, but I was impeded by my recent experience. I had already acted rashly once that morning by relying on Occam.

Occam offered a simple solution here too. It was easiest for Miss Šuvaković to carry all this out. She had been first to come in this morning, bringing the book and envelope with her. At that point the nighttime video surveillance was already switched off in the department. She had placed the two items on the desk, covered them with the white cloth, and assumed the role of the bewildered deputy.

However, I could not accuse her of this because I didn't have any evidence, nor did I have any clue as to what her motivation might be. Furthermore, if I were to leave the envelope aside for the moment—the issue of the book remained. Where did she get it? Why would she bring it here at all? If moving around volumes at the City Cemeteries Administration archive was only an opportune game when compared to the envelope, at the National Library this could not be the case. Who would leave behind an extremely expensive incunabulum for the sake of playing games?

All I could do was resort to the same tactics as at the City Cemeteries Administration—buy time.

"We have to carry out an investigation into how this appeared." I pointed towards the book and the envelope. "That could take a while. . . ."

"You don't understand. . . ." said Miss Šuvaković in a raised voice, interrupting me. Nonetheless, she didn't have the opportunity to continue because she was in turn interrupted by Mrs. Ognjanović, who lifted her hand again.

"Allow me, Olivera. I will explain it to the inspector. The investigation cannot take a while. We have very strict procedures in place. Not only is it prohibited to take the books from our collection out of here, there is also a careful procedure for bringing in new ones. Among other things, the origin of each edition must be precisely known. This is the basis of the Department's reputation. It would be destroyed if word were to get around that we have an exceptionally rare incunabulum with an enigmatic origin, which apparently materialized on this desk."

"Word doesn't need to get around. Only the three of us know about it, right? I will personally carry out the investigation as discreetly as possible. In the meantime, you should move the book somewhere. Perhaps it is best that you remove it from the department, since its presence here. . . ."

"Are you insane?!" shouted the deputy, again not allowing me to finish my sentence. "You don't know what you are saying! To remove an incunabulum. . . ."

"Olivera, Olivera, calm down. The inspector didn't have any bad intention. We won't remove it, of course. We'll hide it somewhere here. But this can only be temporary, a day or two at the most. I beg you to clarify everything that has happened as quickly as possible, Inspector. As quickly as possible."

"I'll do my best."

"Well, and what about this other one?" She jerked her chin in the direction of the envelope. "Is that a book inside there too?"

I shrugged. "How could I know?"

"It's addressed to you."

"You don't think that I expected a package delivered here, do you?"

She scowled at me. "It looks like a book. Would you like to check?"

"I'd rather not. Not everything that looks like a book is a book. My colleagues from the anti-terrorist department should check it first."

The two women simultaneously stepped back from the desk.

"Take that out of here," Miss Šuvaković squealed instantly.

I nodded. "Right away."

I took out a pair of plastic gloves and put them on, then lifted the envelope extremely carefully. Carrying it with my arms held out, I moved towards the elevator. I had to wait in front of the doors for the deputy to muster the courage to come and open them. She stepped aside to let me through. Standing as far back from the elevator as she could, she pressed the box with the zero, then retreated hastily.

9

As SOON AS THE elevator doors closed, I lowered my hands and put the envelope under my arm. Even though I didn't feel like laughing, I couldn't hold back a smile. Miss Šuvaković's terrified face was irresistibly comical. I was still smiling when I passed through the lobby. I glanced left and nodded to the receptionist, who looked on in confusion.

When I got into my car, I placed the envelope on the passenger seat and took off the gloves. On my way out of the parking lot, the guard waved to me as though we were old friends. In front of the ramp three cars waited for a space. Through slightly lighter traffic than on the way over, I headed back to the Police Headquarters.

What had started out as a simple case had now become complicated. True, Mr. Trpimirović was not exactly the usual weirdo, the likes of which occasionally beleaguered me. If nothing else, he would have had to make a considerable investment in order to procure the strange white book. However, I had no clue as to why he had done it, what his ulterior motive was. If the purpose was to get me involved, he had only partially succeeded. To be precise, nothing was stopping me from simply removing myself from the entire affair. Since there was no violation of the law, what had occurred at the City Cemeteries Administration was no longer any of my concern. There were no grounds for an investigation.

The appearance of the second envelope, most likely with a new white volume, at the National Library Department of Old and Rare Books primarily meant that Mr. Trpimirović was not alone in all of this. He certainly was not among the dignitaries who had access. He had to have an accomplice, and that could only be the deputy administrator. No one else had had the opportunity to bring in the envelope unnoticed.

Deep underground, however, it was not only the envelope that was left, but also the incunabulum, of whose existence nobody knew. Plotting with Miss Šuvaković, Mr. Trpimirović could have procured two white books—but not such an exceptional volume. Even if they could have acquired it in some miraculous way, would they simply squander it like this? Being a weirdo has its limits too. Whatever they may have contrived, the gains they expected had to be negligible compared to such a treasure.

A sudden thought made me raise my foot off the gas pedal. The sound of hard breaking and angry honking came from behind me.

Was the thick dark-red small-format volume actually what I had been led to believe? The inscription had faded from the cover, and I wasn't permitted to open the incunabulum and see for myself the title that was printed inside. I had taken for granted what Mrs. Ognjanović had told me—that it was *The Book of Resurrection*.

However, if this wasn't true—if it was an ordinary old book—then a number of difficult questions would simply disappear. Where did the second copy of the incunabulum come from? Why would someone give up ownership of it? Finally, why specifically that book?

On the other hand, the circumstances were growing more intricate because Miss Šuvaković could not have pulled off the underground performance on her own. The administrator had to take part in it, and that already meant a genuine conspiracy. At least three people had conspired to involve me in an intrigue the sense of which completely eluded me.

Fortunately, there was a simple way to eliminate at least one perplexity. I would return to the Department of Old and Rare Books and demand to see for myself whether it truly was a 15th century edition of *The Book of Resurrection*. If it turned out not to be, I would threaten them all. Actually, the best thing would be for me to appear down there again holding the envelope at arm's length. . . .

I had already started to look for the best place to turn the car around and go in the opposite direction when my work phone rang.

I took out the telephone and looked at the screen: Mr. Grubijanić, head of the lab.

"Hello?"

"Inspector Lukić, can you stop by the lab again? It's urgent."

I wanted to ask at least two questions, but I just answered: "I'll be there in a few minutes."

10

IN ADDITION TO MR. Grubijanić, a stocky balding man in his early fifties, I also found Vesna Uskoković, the new chief inspector, in the lab. They were sitting at the table across from the entrance.

Someone who didn't know her would never think that this fragile woman, with straight blond hair and small light eyes, nearing the age of fifty, even worked for the police, let alone that she held such a high position. She looked more like a humble solfeggio teacher.

Her soft, quiet voice contributed to such an impression. Nevertheless, unlike most police officers she didn't need a strong voice in order to act authoritatively.

She had been appointed head of the city police eight months earlier, after Chief Inspector Đorđević took early retirement, immediately after the conclusion of the "Grand Manuscript" case. Even though he was not criticized officially for anything related to the case, it appeared that he was in fact advised to step down, to which he gladly acceded, all the more so because he would reach mandatory retirement in a few years' time.

His office trademark, the large aquarium, had disappeared along with him, and the new chief inspector had brought her own—a large cage with two white parrots. I'd expected her to call me in for a lengthy one-on-one talk, but she was satisfied with a short conversation that we had during the meeting where all the inspectors were introduced to her. At the time she didn't mention the two cases that set me apart from my other colleagues. She had probably learned elsewhere everything that she wanted to know.

The "Grand Manuscript" case had been concluded in the same manner as the "Last Book." My report, in which I faithfully recounted everything, was simply acknowledged. No clarification or supplement was requested. I had once more to vow that I would keep in the strictest confidence everything that I knew. I went back to my regular duties as inspector.

No one even interviewed Vera, even though I had not kept her role a secret. In any case, how could I?

"Hello, Inspector Lukić," the chief inspector said quietly. "Please, have a seat."

She indicated the chair on my right, in front of one of two large monitors. The other was between the two of them. I sat down and placed the envelope on the table. For a moment I thought about whether to remove the plastic gloves, which I had put back on after parking the car in the garage minutes earlier, but I left them on. My eyes lingered on the monitor which displayed a mosaic of images. I didn't realize right away that they were from cameras installed throughout the Police Headquarters building.

"You met with Ana Mirković twice today," the chief inspector said, getting right to the point. "Here and in your office. Did she seem upset or unusual in any way?"

I reflected for a moment, then shook my head. "No, she didn't."

"Did she perhaps say something about herself?"

"What do you mean?"

"Anything at all."

"With the exception of work, we only spoke briefly about literature. If that counts. . . ."

"About literature?" she repeated inquisitively.

"About Saramago. Perhaps you've heard of him. The Portuguese Nobel laureate who. . . ."

"I've read everything by Saramago. Did our colleague perhaps mention that she had to go somewhere? Outside of Headquarters building?"

"No, on the contrary. She said that she would be here, in the lab. Why are you asking me all this?"

The chief inspector looked at the head of the laboratory.

"Because we don't seem to be able to find Ms. Mirković. She's disappeared."

I shook my head. "How could she disappear?"

"That's precisely what we are trying to determine."

Mr. Grubijanić cleared his throat.

"I called her about fifteen minutes after you left. She would always let me know when she would leave the lab for any longer period of time. However, her phone was out of service."

"I don't understand. You don't switch off your work cell phone during office hours."

"It wasn't just turned off. I asked our colleagues from

the Communications Department for assistance. If she had only switched off her telephone, they would have gotten through to her. They told me that the cell phone is dead; as though its battery has been removed."

"Why would she remove the battery?"

"Perhaps she didn't," the chief inspector interjected. "Cell phones also appear dead when they sustain serious damage."

"You think. . . ." I started, then stopped, ". . . .that something has happened to her?"

"We don't know. However, if it has—it happened here, at Headquarters."

"How do you know?"

"We've checked footage from all the exits. She didn't leave the building. So, she's still in here, and we have no idea where."

I slapped the side of the monitor in front of me.

"You can check the recordings from the other cameras too. The entire building is covered. You'll surely get a lead on her."

"We've already checked, Inspector Lukić. This is what we've learned."

She leaned towards the monitor and her fingers danced across the keyboard. Instead of a mosaic, the monitor in front of me displayed the image of an empty corridor. It again took me a little time to recognize the view—the fifth floor. The upper right-hand corner displayed the time—10:41:26.

The image was frozen briefly, but then came to life when Ana Mirković emerged from my office. She went to the right-hand one of the two elevators and pressed the call button. The doors opened immediately and she stepped inside. As soon as they closed, the shot changed.

This time I immediately realized what I was looking at, because I had just passed by that place. The camera covered the entrances to the two elevators in the garage. Everything was still except the clock in the corner. Less than half a minute later the doors to the right-hand elevator opened, where the girl was supposed to be—but the car was empty.

I raised my puzzled gaze from the monitor. "How is this possible? Judging by the time stamp, the elevator arrived directly from the fifth floor."

"That's right. If the elevator doesn't make any stops, the descent to the basement lasts twenty-six seconds," the chief inspector said.

I stared at her bleakly. "So where is the girl?"

"We too would like to know that."

"There are no cameras in the elevators, right?"

"No, unfortunately."

"What now? What will you do?"

"We will conduct an investigation. I will personally head it. We have to find Miss Mirković as soon as possible. She can't simply disappear from the elevator at the Police Headquarters." She stopped for a moment. "Just one more question, Inspector Lukić. What was Ana doing for you this morning?"

"She was checking a book for fingerprints." I looked across the table, then nodded towards the white volume, which was still where I had left it, next to the device with two eyepieces. "That one."

"The book has already been to the lab. We saw that on the recordings. Why did you bring it again?"

"Miss Mirković did not find any fingerprints, but she wanted to run some other tests. She didn't tell me which ones. I'd like to take it with me, if you don't have any objections."

"Do you perhaps want someone else to take a look at it?" the head of the lab asked me.

"There's no need," I said as I rose and picked up the envelope. "I was only interested in the fingerprints. I'll wait for Miss Mirković to return, then I'll bring her the book again."

I took the large volume and headed towards the

door, but the chief inspector's voice stopped me. "Does that one also need to be checked for fingerprints?" she asked, pointing towards the envelope in my hand. "I see that you're wearing gloves."

"Perhaps later," I responded. "I'd first like to take a look at it."

11

I CALLED THE ELEVATOR in the garage. One of the two cars was already there and the doors opened immediately. Deep in thought, it wasn't until I had already set a foot inside that I realized that it was the right-hand elevator. I hastily pulled back my foot, and flipped the switch on the left wall of the car. The elevator was now blocked with the doors open. Without entering, I looked around the inside.

Everything seemed normal. On the opposite side was a small mirror with my reflection in it. For months following the misfortune in the elevator at 12 Oak Street I had kept my back to this mirror, as I did to mirrors in other elevators. Even though there was nothing mysterious any more about the "Grand Manuscript" case, I couldn't shake a certain uneasiness. In order to lessen it, I would keep my eyes on the floor, especially if I was alone in the elevator.

The anxiety, which had in the meantime finally receded, now had a sudden resurgence. What had happened to Ms. Mirković during the twenty-six second ride down from the fifth floor? Generally, there were only two ways to escape from a moving elevator: up and down. I remembered the hatch in the elevator floor that the disciples of the Grand Manuscript had used. Here, however, there was no carpeting that would conceal it. The floor was covered in solidly attached tiles. I looked upward. The ceiling and the lighting fixtures also looked firm.

Even if there was a secret hatch, how could a girl who had only recently started working for the police know about it? And why would she leave the elevator that way in the first place? The investigation that the new chief inspector would be heading would have to deal with a series of difficult questions.

It was odd that Chief Inspector Uskoković had not ordered the right-hand elevator to be shut down. Perhaps she wanted to avoid creating a panic at the Police Headquarters, and believed that there was no threat here because undoubtedly many people had ridden the elevator after the girl had gone missing—and nothing had happened to them. Was it prudent to take the left-hand elevator, just in case? I had to make up my mind quickly because I had been holding the elevator for quite a while. When I once again stepped into the right car, it was with the conviction that the impending uncertainty was a lesser evil than my elevator phobia kicking in again.

As the ascent started, I hastily placed the envelope and book under my arm, then crouched and started touching with one hand the edges of the floor, along the walls. Having bare hands would have improved my sense of touch, but there was no time to remove the gloves. Next I stood up, raised my free hand and passed my fingers along the edges of the low ceiling. As expected—I didn't find anything. If there was a hatch, it was concealed perfectly.

There was no need to carry out this inspection since the colleagues sent by the chief inspector had indubitably done a thorough job. Had they discovered anything, she would have told me. However, my efforts were not in vain. I was preoccupied with something and the anxiety of the ride on an elevator where one could disappear without a trace did not have the opportunity to take hold. The car came to a stop just as I lowered my hand. Twenty-six seconds had truly passed quickly.

I nodded to my colleague who was waiting for the elevator on the fifth floor, then proceeded to my office. I put the book down on the desk and opened the new envelope. Once again it was difficult to remove the thick volume. When it was finally in my hands, I briefly inspected its exterior, quickly flipped through it, then placed it next to the first one. The two white books were absolutely identical.

It crossed my mind that this could be a problem. If for any reason I needed to know which one I had received first, I wouldn't be able to identify it. The same applied to the envelopes. It was necessary to label them somehow. I glanced across my desk and concluded that sticky notes were best suited for the task. I wrote the number one on two on them and the number two on two of them, and then stuck them on the two books and the two envelopes.

Then I wondered where to put them. They could stay on the desk, since the door was locked when I was out, but there would be issues while I was in the office. Visitors would be curious, and I didn't feel like explaining how I had come by them. My first thought was to put them in one of the four drawers, but I finally concluded that it would be best to place them in the safe; it was sitting there empty anyway.

I had just locked the safe and returned the bundle of keys to my pocket, when my private cell phone rang. I removed the plastic gloves and answered.

"Do I have the honor of speaking to an actual rich person?" I asked Vera.

"Genuine and tangible."

"Tangible? What do you mean?"

"I mean that the wealth can be touched—not the rich person, if that's what you were thinking. I was given the money in a leather briefcase. All new bills. Like in the movies."

"In the movies such payments are usually illegal."

"You will not have the satisfaction of arresting me, dear inspector. The lawyers assured me that everything is perfectly legal."

"You're still at the law office?"

"I was just getting ready to leave."

"With all that money? Should I come pick you up?"

"You amaze me, inspector. Offering a rich person private protection while on the clock. Are you aware how illegal that is? No, thank you. I'd rather take a taxi. Perhaps it's not as good as police protection, but at least it is completely legal."

I coughed.

"All right, so. . . .?"

"So?"

"What is it that you can finally do, now that you're rich? What is it that you've always dreamed of?"

"You don't cease to disappoint me, inspector. What about your insightfulness? You really can't figure it out?"

"I didn't know I was suppose to figure it out."

"Of course you are. Who else if not you? Is there anyone else who knows me better?"

I thought for a bit, then said penitently: "It's no use. I can't figure it out. I give up."

"Ah, no. You don't get to surrender. I'll offer you one more opportunity to guess it. Until seven o'clock tonight. If you don't succeed by then, I'll tell you, but I'll be really disappointed."

"Why until seven?"

"Because that is when the reception we have been invited to starts. What's more, I've promised that we would go."

"What reception?"

"A gala. They'll send a limo for us at six thirty. Nothing less befits a rich person. You will tag along with me."

"Who is holding this gala reception?"

"The buyer of the inventory and books from the Papyrus. We will finally find out who it is."

I wanted to ask something more, but my work phone rang.

"I hear it," said Vera. "And my taxi is also here. I'll call you later."

I quickly hung up one telephone and answered the other.

12

"Inspector Lukić," said my colleague Bumbaković, "there is someone on the line asking for you—a Mr. Gvozden Vidojević. He says that he has something for you."

"Transfer the connection to my office."

I went to the desk and picked up the landline telephone, which rang immediately.

"Inspector Dejan Lukić. How can I help you?"

"Hello, Inspector Lukić," a deep male voice responded. "This is Gvozden Vidojević. It would be a good idea for us to meet." He paused for a moment. "Something . . . appeared . . . at my place. Something that belongs to you."

"What is it?" I asked, even though I could have guessed the answer.

"I don't know that. The object is in an envelope, with the inscription that it is for you. Judging by its shape, I would say that it is a book. Should I open it and take a look?"

"No. Don't touch anything. I'll come pick it up immediately. Where are you?"

"At home, 14 Oak Street, second floor, apartment 3. It's the small street in. . . ."

"I know where it is," I said, interrupting him. "I will see you soon. Thank you for calling."

"You're welcome, Inspector. I'll be waiting for you."

After putting down the receiver, I briefly looked around the office then left, locking up behind me. Once again I didn't have to wait for the elevator, and it was again the right-hand car that was there. Obviously someone had just taken it to the fifth floor. As soon as the elevator started moving, I was tempted to run my bare palms across the three walls, but I didn't because it didn't make any sense. I wouldn't have found anything. There simply could be no way out in those three directions. Twenty-six seconds passed more slowly than they had fifteen minutes earlier.

I sped out of the garage and headed towards the part of town that I had had no reason to visit in eight months. Any other day it would have been only a curious coincidence—work taking me almost to the same place where the "Grand Manuscript" case had played out. However, that was not so today. Not after everything that had transpired since this morning.

By clinging to Occam, I had underestimated events. The warning light should have gone off as soon as the white book appeared, but even after it was in my hands I had carried on with the assumption that what had happened at the City Cemeteries Administration Building was actually the act of one of the many twisted people who had been pestering me since the case of the "Last Book."

I then tried to squeeze the episode from the National Library into the same mold, even though that was an even greater stretch. Indeed, how could it have even occurred to me that two or more connected weirdoes were behind everything? Such people don't get together; they always act on their own, convinced that the entire world is against them. If there was any connection between Mr. Trpimirović, Miss Šuvaković and perhaps Mrs. Leleković and Mrs. Ognjanović, then it must be of another kind. They certainly were not the common variety paranoids or conspiracy theorists; on the contrary, they were participants in a well-devised deception. What they had carried out so far—and what they continued to carry out—was possible only with the logistical support of a serious organization. This especially applied to the performance at the Department of Old and Rare Books, if it were to turn out that the incunabulum was in fact authentic.

A fresh inspiration impelled me to raise my foot abruptly from the gas pedal for the second time today. Luckily traffic was not as dense as it had been earlier, and this time there was no sound of squealing brakes behind me. I knew only one organization capable of putting together something this complex. They had convincingly demonstrated what they were capable of in both special cases: in the "Last Book" and the "Grand Manuscript."

Perhaps the best proof of the exceptionality of the secret society was that it had emerged from both affairs without suffering any consequences, at least as far as I was aware. After the second case I had been more relentless in determining whether they had gotten their just punishment. Above all I owed that much to my colleague, Inspector Vesić. However, despite all my efforts, I did not succeed in digging up any details. I was only vaguely told that everything had been handled and that I should not pursue my inquiries.

If it was in fact the secret society that was pulling the strings of everything that had happened since this morning, then my third encounter with them was unlike the previous two. First of all, they were no longer trying to get their hands on a book or manuscript that they believed was in my possession; on the contrary, they were now leaving identical copies of a strange empty volume at different locations.

Since we still hadn't started to show our hands, and everyone I had met so far had been wrapped up in their own roles, I could not even presume why they were doing everything and why they were once again all over me. The Grand Master had still not appeared to enlighten me as to what they were plotting this time.

In any case, their two past appearances on the scene had coincided with the crossing of our reality and the author's reality. However, now there was no such crossing. And there wouldn't be any, if one were to trust the author. He had firmly promised Vera that he would not meddle any more in our world, because the price was too high; a trail of bodies remained in the wake of his meddling, even when it was well-intentioned. It would have been different if he wrote a different genre, but in detective novels someone always has to die.

I could only hope that the secret society's new plan would not lead to more deaths. Whatever they had devised, for the time being it seemed rather harmless. There were no wrongdoings, other than the fact that they didn't hesitate once more to string along a police inspector. Fortunately, the inspector had finally figured out who was responsible, and he would be able to react appropriately. In any case, they were aware of who had had the last laugh so far in our confrontations. . . .

Since there were no vacant parking spaces in front of number 14, I left my car in the familiar parking lot of number 12. As I stepped out of the car, I looked up at the row of four windows on the upper left-hand corner of the building. The two center windows were tilted open. I wondered who had moved into that small apartment after the conclusion of the "Grand Manuscript" case—the apartment that held strange memories for me.

The adjacent building had four stories and showed the ravages of time. A thick vine partially concealed the decrepit state of the façade. There was no intercom at the entrance. I opened the squeaky door and entered the dim corridor. A acid smell tickled my nostrils. Even if there had been an elevator, I still would have taken the stairs to the second floor.

Apartment number 3 was the closest to the stairwell. I rang the bell. The sharp ring sounded somehow old-fashioned.

An eyeball briefly filled the large eyehole, then a deep male voice asked "Inspector Lukić?"

"Hello again, Mr. Vidojević."

The door was opened by a short older man in a frayed dark red robe, wearing a slightly lighter bow tie and worn-out slippers. He had a small mustache and a large mole on his left cheek. Even though quite gray, his longish hair was still relatively thick.

He gave a brief nod, then stepped aside. I thought that he was letting me in, but an elderly lady in a wheelchair appeared one step behind him. A red plaid blanket covered her legs. She had a wide face, vivid blue eyes and short wavy wheat-blond hair.

"My wife, Sofija," he said, introducing her.

"Pleased to meet you, Mrs. Vidojević," I said with a bow.

She responded with a smile, without saying a word.

"This way, Inspector."

He pointed left, towards a staircase, then stepped out. As he closed the door behind him, I glanced into the apartment entrance for an instant, past Mrs. Vidojević. The walls were covered by shelves full of books.

13

HOLDING ON TO THE handrail, he walked ahead of me, down the stairs.

"Don't think poorly of Sofija for wanting to meet you. She has never seen a police inspector in person before."

"I hope she wasn't disappointed."

"Oh, no, on the contrary, she was thrilled."

I thought of asking him how he knew this when his wife had not said a word, but I restrained my detective's curiosity. Perhaps couples who live together long enough eventually became telepathic. Vera and I have been together a relatively short time, and we already sometimes understood each other without words.

We reached the ground floor. I didn't know where we were headed; the last thing I expected was that we would continue our descent. Mr. Vidojević held on to the handrail once again as we started going down into the basement.

"People are usually surprised when I introduce myself. This is not how they imagine police inspectors."

"If it's any consolation, it's the same with poets. Almost everyone gives me a suspicious look when I tell them what I do. God only knows how they picture poets."

"You are a poet?"

"There—you see. It seems unbelievable even to you."

"No, no," I rushed to clear up the misunderstanding. "I don't find it at all unbelievable. I am only pleasantly surprised. I actually have a degree in literature."

In the meantime we had reached the lower level and stopped in front of a scratched olive-green metal door. Mr. Vidojević turned his head toward me and gave me a suspicious stare.

"And you work for the police?"

I sighed. "If you only knew how many times I've been asked that question. I work where there is work available. There aren't many literary jobs, unfortunately."

"Ah, yes. The literary life certainly isn't idyllic, as many people naively believe."

He took a ring with two keys out of his robe pocket and placed the larger one in the lock. He had to pull the doorknob with his other hand to unlock it, and then lean into the heavy door in order to open it. A strong sour odor struck us from the darkness. He felt around for the switch and turned on the lights.

Extending before us was a short corridor with cellars on both sides. The front and dividing walls were made out of vertical laths. I was under the impression that we were not completely underground, but I couldn't see any windows as we walked down the corridor. We stopped in front of a relatively small cellar, next to last on the left-hand side.

"I don't know whether during your literary studies there was any mention of the downsides of the poetic profession," said Mr. Vidojević, "but you will see one now."

He used the smaller key to unlock the miniature padlock. As he pulled on the door, the bottoms of the laths scraped the cement floor, making a squeaking noise.

What I had already made out through the grated entrance was now clearly visible. Resting against the only brick wall, opposite the door, was a shelf nearly full of identical copies of a thin book with a brown hard cover. I couldn't easily guess the number, but there were certainly several hundred of them.

Mr. Vidojević was the first to enter the cellar, then invited me to join him. "Welcome to the scene of my poetic penance."

I stepped in after him, keeping my sight fixed on the brown wall. He walked up to the shelf, pulled out a copy and handed it to me. Beneath his name, written in ornate script, was the title *Small Poems of Death*, and the lower part of the cover had a picture of a yellow flower. I leafed through the book. The eighty or so pages contained a series of short poems. When I got to the end, he held out his hand. As he returned the volume to its place, an expression of discomfort appeared on this face.

"Please, don't hold it against me. I would gladly give a book to a person with a literary education, but unfortunately that is not possible. All the copies of this collection of poems have to be in this cellar."

"All of them?"

"Yes. A total of 509 copies were printed. I bought most of them from the publisher: four hundred and forty-one. He was very pleased to have the opportunity to sell them to me. It was the first sold out book of poetry that he had ever published. He even offered to print a second edition immediately, if I would also buy it up."

"Really generous of him," I said with a smile.

"It was much more difficult to find the remaining sixty-eight copies that had gone on sale. I've been searching for them for two and a half years, and I've only managed to get forty-four of them. I've been to bookstores, second-hand bookshops, booksellers, and bought every copy that I could find. Next I took out ads, offering significantly more than the book is worth, but it was all in vain. Twenty-four copies still elude me. It is like they've vanished into thin air." He suddenly lit up. "Perhaps you have one? You are a man of books, you surely have a book collection. I'll pay whatever you ask. . . ."

I shook my head, and his face grew dim.

"Unfortunately I don't. If I did, I would gladly just give it to you. I understand literary passions. Although, this is one that is seldom encountered. If it isn't indiscreet of me, why do you want to buy up all the copies of your own book?" I paused for a moment. "Are you not satisfied with it?"

"Oh, on the contrary, I am very satisfied. Moreover, I think that it is my best collection of poetry."

"Then why are you refusing to share it with readers?"

He didn't respond immediately. I could see in his eyes that he was tormented.

"It's all very strange," he finally said, with a bit more vigor. "Sofija is my first reader. She read every poem back while I was writing them, and then the collection in manuscript. She appeared fascinated. But when

I brought her the first copy of the book, her reaction was quite the opposite. She was horrified. She fell into a stupor. She stopped speaking. I didn't understand anything. It took me a long time even to get her to write something at least. She didn't give me any explanation. She only commanded me to buy up all the copies and put them in the cellar. Only when the last one is in here will she speak again. And, as I said, for two and a half years I have been searching for copies of my own book, to restore Sofija's voice. . . ."

We fell silent. It was apparent that Mr. Vidojević expected me to say something in response to this, but nothing appropriate came to mind. In the end I simply repeated his words. "It truly is very strange." I was just about to move on to the reason why I had come, when something struck me. "When you were searching for your book, did you by any chance stop by the Papyrus?"

A smile came over Mr. Vidojević's face. "Ah, the Papyrus. A dear, dear bookstore. I found there about a dozen copies of *Small Poems of Death*. I liked going to Papyrus even without that reason." He sighed. "Very few such bookstores exist, ones that have a soul. It is a pity that it shut down. Did you frequent the Papyrus?"

"Often," I replied with a nod. "I hope that you will acquire the remaining copies of your collection. If I come across one, I'll be sure to let you know immediately."

The old poet smiled again. "Thank you."

"Very well, let's see that envelope that is addressed to me. It's in here, I presume."

"Yes, yes. Behind you."

He pointed downward, next to me. I turned around and spotted the envelope standing against the inside of the front wall, right next to the door. I hadn't noticed it on my way in because I was completely captivated by the books.

"You found it here?"

"That's right. I didn't touch it. I just bent over to read what was written on it."

I looked around the small cellar. There was nothing in it except the shelf. Mr. Vidojević kept it clean.

"Did you have any reason to come down here?"

"Yes. Less than an hour ago I came down to fetch the newspaper and found a copy of *Small Poems of Death* in the mailbox. The book is thin, so it can fit through the slit. However, it wasn't wrapped, which meant that the mailman didn't bring it. Someone had acquired it somewhere for me. It's no secret that I'm searching for them. The person left it in the mailbox because they obviously didn't want me to reward them. There are still good people."

"You can find them here and there," I agreed.

"In all my excitement I rushed straight to the cellar to add the new copy to the rest. I only noticed the envelope on my way out."

I squatted by the open door and gauged the gap between the laths and then the thickness of the envelope.

"There is also no scarcity of bad people," I said as I got up. "Someone had to gain unauthorized entry to your cellar in order to leave this. The envelope could not have passed between the laths."

"No one else has a key."

I removed the key from the miniature padlock and examined it, then the other one, to the metal door.

"They wouldn't need one. This padlock can be opened with a paperclip. The same goes for the lock over there," I pointed down the corridor.

"You don't say! Well, that's dreadful. Someone could break in here and take my books. . . ."

"I don't think there's any danger of that. I keep some books in the basement too. We recently had a break-in; something was taken from every cellar. Mine was the only one that they didn't even open. I can only imagine how scornfully the burglars went around it, having seen what was inside."

"That's a very sad consolation. Still, someone came in here, as you say, even if it was with the opposite motives. Should I still change the lock and padlock? I'm sure there must be something more reliable."

"Of course, but that wouldn't be enough. In order to have any protection from break-ins, you would have to build real walls, instead of these laths. The only solution would be to move the books to the apartment, but unfortunately that is impossible, as far as I understand."

The old poet sighed. "Alas, it is." He paused for a moment. "May I ask you a question, Inspector? Why did someone choose specifically my cellar to leave this for you?"

I shrugged my shoulders. "I hope that the investigation will give us that answer."

I reached for my gloves, but didn't take them out. There was no need for them. Whoever was behind this was too clever to leave any identifying clues behind. I picked up the envelope with my bare hands.

14

I HAD JUST GOTTEN into my car in the parking lot in front of number 12 when Vera called me again.

"I just wanted to let you know that I made it home safely. No one followed or attacked us, and the taxi driver had no clue who and what he was driving. I probably seemed to him like a serious businesswoman returning from a meeting, with a briefcase full of important papers." She giggled. "Actually, that would be quite the right impression."

"I thought you would put the money in the bank first. Why do you need it at home?"

"To impress an indigent police inspector. Otherwise he would never have the opportunity of seeing so much money in one place."

"The indigent police inspector has seen much more than that, on the job."

"Perhaps, but not legally gained."

"If that makes any difference."

"It is horrible hearing something like that come out of the mouth of an officer of the law."

"People change: officers of the law, as well as bookstore keepers. By the way, I just spoke to one of your acquaintances from back in the day, when you were still involved in that honorable business."

"Did you? Who was it?"

"Mr. Gvozden Vidojević."

Vera paused for a moment.

"The poet?"

"Yes."

"Dear Mr. Vidojević. He was a regular customer."

"And patient."

"Patient? Why do you say that?"

"He told me that he bought copies of his own book at the Papyrus."

"So what? The man obviously liked what he had written. There's nothing unusual about a little narcissism. Everyone loves themselves, more or less."

"But you considered others, who also bought the same book time and again, to be patients?"

"In their cases we didn't know their motivations. It could have been something weird."

"In Mr. Vidojević's case it wasn't mere narcissism either."

"What was it?"

"It's a long story. And a sad one. I'll tell you when I get back."

"Where did you speak?"

"At his place, in the basement." I sighed. "Overall, I'm spending most of my day below ground."

"Is something unusual happening?" Vera asked after a brief silence.

"Nothing especially," I responded, with the slightest hesitation. "It seems that today I'm meeting all your patients. As you know, first someone rearranged the records of the burials at the City Cemeteries Administration. Then someone else brought a rare book into the National Library. And now this thing with Mr. Vidojević. I hope that's the end of it. In any case, I don't remember any of your former patients' other peculiarities."

"Oh, there were plenty of them."

"These three are quite enough. If there is another such case, I'll start to believe that the former honest bookstore keeper—and now the bored rich person who has nothing better to do—has cast a spell on me. When will you start doing what you've always dreamed about?"

"Ah, you're curious as to what that is. Just you keep trying to figure it out, Mr. uninsightful police Inspector. You have a little over six hours left. . . ."

I returned the telephone to my jacket pocket, drove out of the parking lot and headed back to the office.

Having turned right onto Oak Street, I continued slowly to the cast iron fence beyond which two arched windows extended from the basement. I stopped the car next to the curb. Everything looked the same as it had eight months earlier, except there was no metal sign in the shape of a teapot hanging above the door. There was no reason to get out. There was no teashop there any more, and even if there had been—my memories of it were not pleasant. I drove on.

Mr. Vidojević and his wife seemed, very convincingly, to be the persons that they claimed to be. However, the same had applied to the other members of the secret society, both the ones I had previously met and those whom I had today suspected to be part of it. Furthermore, Mr. Vidojević was one of the Papyrus regular patrons, and many of them were followers of the Grand Master.

On the other hand, if this today was truly a performance put on by the secret society, its main problem was the complexity of the three acts. It was true that the society was logistically capable of carrying them out, but why would it invest so much effort and money just to deliver three books to me? I could have received them in a far simpler and cheaper way: by regular mail, for example. Unless, of course, the purpose of the performance wasn't to deliver the books but something completely different, something that was yet to be revealed. And if it was so, then new scenarios could be expected. In any case, the performance was still far from over.

I walked towards the elevator in the garage, carrying the third envelope with me. I was just about to press the call button when I wondered which door would open this time. If it was the right-hand one, and it also turned out that the elevator was already there, it would be quite incredible. When I completed the motion, however, something equally incredible happened: both doors opened.

I stood there indecisively, feeling as though I was being tested somehow. It was like I was supposed to decide something far more important and far-reaching than which elevator I would take. Who knows how long I would have stood there had the doors not started to close at the same time. Startled out of my stupor, I jumped into the left car at the last moment.

The ride to the fifth floor felt neither too long nor too short. I smiled at the two colleagues whom I met in the corridor as I walked towards my office, while taking out my key along the way. I slid the key into the lock and turned it, as I had done countless times before, ever since I was given my own office, as a sort of compensation for the promotion that I didn't receive after the "Last Book" case.

However, the key jammed after a quarter-turn.

Brows raised, I stared at the lock in confusion, then looked up and checked the number above the door, even though I was certain that I had not gotten the office wrong. Something like that had never happened to me before, and neither had it now.

Then I realized what it was: I couldn't unlock the door because it wasn't locked in the first place. I pulled out the key, turned the knob, opened the door—and saw probably the last two people I expected to find there.

15

I COULD EASILY HAVE failed to recognize the two young members of the National Security Agency. Stanislav Mirić, the information and communications technology wizard, and the photographer, who often smiled at me, had completely changed their appearances.

He no longer had unkempt hair; it was neatly combed, even slicked back. He wore an elegant suit and tie, instead of the hooded sweatshirt and sweatpants, and there was no conspicuous earring dangling from his right ear. Her black hair was no longer shaven above her ears, a dark suit replaced the torn skin-tight jeans and colorful knit vest, and gone were the rings from her lower lip, right nostril and earlobes. Even now, however, they didn't seem like agents, but rather like yuppies ready for an important meeting.

They sat in the armchairs in front of my desk. The girl had the two envelopes and two white books in her lap. I glanced at the safe where I had left them. It was closed.

"It seems that fashions change often at the National Security Agency," I said as I made my way to the chair on the opposite side of the desk. Along the way I dropped the third, still unopened envelope into the girl's lap. There was no sense in trying to keep it, especially since they had come for it. I got a brief smile in return.

"Not only fashions, Inspector Lukić," Mirić responded. "There are also other, greater changes. For example, Commissioner Milenković is no longer with us."

"Is that so?" I asked in surprise. "Why is that?"

"He was retired after the last case that we cooperated on."

"What was he blamed for? Didn't he do everything that he could under the circumstances?"

"He wasn't blamed for anything. He retired at his own request. It seems that he was just worn out. As you are well aware, this is a very exhausting job, and his age had caught up with him."

"So, that's what happened. We've had similar cases where people retired at their own request, because of exhaustion and age. And who is your Commissioner now, if I may ask?"

"You may ask, but I cannot answer. In any case, the two of us have been assigned this new case because of our experience with the previous one. Regardless of the fact that it didn't end well."

"What new case?"

The two of them looked at each other.

"Inspector Lukić," she said to me, "we don't want to make the same mistake that Commissioner Milenković made. Based on the two previous cases, it is clear to us that we must genuinely cooperate with you in order to get anything done. I solemnly promise that we will not keep anything from you, if you are completely open with us in return. We can all only benefit from true cooperation."

"And this is a good way to start true cooperation?" I pointed to the books and envelopes in her lap. "You break into my office, and my safe, and just take everything from it. Commissioner Milenković did have an unusual understanding of cooperation, but he never did anything like this."

"We removed the books in order to safeguard them. They are not secure in your safe. Someone else could have gotten a hold of them as easily as we did, and we have to assume that they are very important. We also wanted our experts to take a look at them. Still, they will be made available to you whenever you need. Also, if we had dishonorable intentions, we would not be here waiting for you, would we?"

I looked at the girl for several moments without saying a word.

"It isn't easy for me to trust the honorable intentions of someone whose name I don't even know."

A shadow of reluctance passed over her face, as though she had been asked to disrobe in front of a stranger.

"Senka Veselinović," she said finally, blushing slightly.

"I'm glad to make your acquaintance, Agent Veselinović," I responded with a smile. "Very well, now let me repeat my question—what new case?"

"The new case of crossing realities," Mirić said. "Three extremely unusual books have mysteriously appeared. It might be possible to find an explanation for two of them, but not for the third—the one from the National Library Department of Old and Rare Books. Not to mention the incunabulum."

I was again briefly silent.

"How long have you been following me?"

"We've never let you out our sight. For eight months. Both previous cases started with you, so it was natural to assume that the third, if there ever was one, would too. As soon as you got the call from the City Cemeteries Administration about problems involving books, the alarm was raised. And we weren't wrong."

I sighed. "I think you were. This cannot be a new case of crossing realities."

"Why can't it?" the girl asked.

"The fact that the cases start with me is beside the point. The much more important issue is that there need to be dead bodies. The author who is pulling the strings from the other reality writes detective novels, and you simply can't have one without murder victims. Just remember how many there were in *The Last Book* and *The Grand Manuscript*. Nonetheless, this time no one is dead."

"Not yet," Mirić remarked, "but victims could still appear. In *The Grand Manuscript* quite some time passed before the first corpse turned up."

"Perhaps, but until that happens, we cannot dismiss other possibilities, besides crossing realities."

"What other possibilities?"

I glanced from the young man to the girl and back again.

"There is someone else capable of pulling off everything that has happened today. Even the thing at the National Library. You know, of course, who I'm talking about—the Grand Master and his secret society."

I paused, expecting them to say something, but they just gazed at me in silence.

"If we are truly to cooperate, then the time has come for you to show that you are actually prepared to do so. You have to answer one question: how is it that the secret society got away scot-free in the first two cases?"

This time agents Veselinović and Mirić looked at each other a bit longer.

The girl finally cleared her throat and turned towards me.

"Someone is protecting them. Someone very influential. We really don't know who it is. Whenever the Agency tries to take action against them, our efforts are thwarted. Without any explanation. After the "Grand Manuscript" case, Commissioner Milenković wanted to get revenge against the Grand Master, even more than against the author, because he had insolently taken both him and the service for fools, but he wasn't allowed to. That is the main reason why he took retirement."

For a brief moment it was as though no one knew what to say.

"Yet there is something," the young man spoke up, "that the secret society could not pull off, regardless of how powerful it might be."

I shook my head. "What?"

"It couldn't make your colleague Ana Mirković disappear from a moving elevator."

"Perhaps, but that event is not linked to the others."

"You think so?" the girl asked.

"All right, perhaps it is, but don't underestimate the secret society when it comes to elevators. I personally saw how skilled they are. In any case, who knows what happened in that elevator. The new chief inspector has decided to handle that personally. We'll see what her investigation uncovers. A pity there wasn't a camera inside. We would easily have solved the mystery."

A fresh pause ensued.

"There was," Mirić finally said softly.

"Excuse me?" I asked in disbelief.

"We would never have told you if we were not truly cooperating, Inspector Lukić," said Agent Veselinović. "The camera is hidden behind the mirror. I ask that this remain strictly between us."

I nodded. "Of course, of course. And what did it capture?"

The girls put her hand in her bag and pulled out a large tablet.

"Here, take a look."

I rose to take it, then sat back down. The image on the tablet was frozen. It showed Ms. Mirković, who had just gotten on the elevator on the fifth floor. The door behind her was still open. I touched the round icon with an arrow at the bottom of the screen and the image came to life.

The young lady first pressed the lowest button on the left-hand row, then went to the mirror and looked at her face curiously, obviously looking for something that she could touch up. However, there was no time for beautification because everything went dark as soon as the doors behind her came together in the center.

There was no sound. I stared at the monotonous darkness which was interrupted only by the small digits of the clock in the upper right-hand corner. It measured even thousandths of a second. At the moment when the lights went back on in the elevator, the clock stopped at 00:26:118. The car was empty.

I continued to stare at the image on the tablet, which was frozen again, then got up and handed it back to Agent Veselinović.

"What happened?" I asked as I sat down.

"We have no idea," Agent Mirić responded. "It isn't normal darkness. If it were, we would see at least something in it. The camera is infrared. It would show the girl's face radiating heat."

"Such an image" his colleague added, "would be produced if someone were to have covered the mirror with something opaque, but it wouldn't have foiled the camera's microphone. It is very sensitive, it would have picked up even the faintest sound. However, it didn't capture anything; it is as though the girl had stood there motionless, not even breathing."

"The clock in the corner," I said after thinking for a moment, "is it part of the recording or was it added later?"

Agent Veselinović looked at her colleague questioningly.

"It was added later. Why do you ask?" he responded.

"Then there is another explanation. The camera and microphone were switched off for the twenty six seconds of the elevator's descent."

"That simply isn't possible. In order to get to the

camera, one would have first to remove the mirror, and it would have captured that."

"The camera can also be reached from behind, without removing the mirror."

Agent Mirić watched me carefully for several moments, then shook his head. "While the elevator was in motion and in such a short time? Impossible."

"Not then, but beforehand. If the secret society had decided to switch off your cameras when it needed to, it would have taken care of that in time."

"In the middle of the Police Headquarters building?" the girl asked in disbelief.

"Even in the middle of the National Security Agency building. They are by no means to be underestimated. It would be best for you to check whether your hidden cameras have some upgrades that you are not aware of."

The young man sighed. "Even if it were as you say, Inspector Lukić, we still face two very difficult questions. First, how did the secret society pull off the disappearance of the girl from a moving elevator in less than half a minute? All right, perhaps they have installed something that switched off the cameras, but they could not remove someone from an elevator that doesn't have any secret hatches. We are positive about that. Second, why would it undertake something so complex only to make someone so insignificant disappear?"

"Perhaps she isn't insignificant," I responded, just to have an answer.

To my great surprise, Agent Mirić nodded. "I agree, she's important. That is to say, she will be soon. As soon as we find her dead somewhere. Perhaps even in the elevator from which she mysteriously vanished. A corpse will be the last missing piece to complete this—the new detective novel by the author from the other reality."

I opened my mouth to contradict him, but my work cell phone rang.

"Hello?"

That was all I said. Fifteen seconds later I hung up and returned the telephone to my pocket. I then looked first at one young face across from me, then at the other. I stood up without a word, and at that moment their cell phones rang.

"Let's go," I said before someone else could give them the news. "Ms. Mirković has been found."

16

THEY STILL ANSWERED THEIR phones. Like me, they restricted themselves to listening. They skipped even the opening "hello." After about half a minute they both hung up. They stayed seated.

"You go ahead, Inspector Lukić," said Agent Mirić. "We'll be just a moment."

I wrinkled my eyebrows. What seemed so important to them, right now, in my office, that it was more pressing than the appearance of the girl? Still, I didn't ask them because I considered the latter to be more important. Who knows whether they would even tell me, despite the new openness between us. I just shrugged and rushed out of the door.

For some reason I was convinced that at least one elevator would be there, but it took a good three minutes for the left-hand one to arrive. I pressed the lowest button and stood with my back to the mirror. It didn't stop at any of the other floors, so I reached the garage in half a minute. The right-hand car was standing there with the doors open, as though the elevator was blocked or shut down.

I briskly opened the basement door and burst into the corridor. Three of my colleagues curiously watched me run by. This is already the second time today, I thought to myself. I rushed into the lab, again without knocking.

The only person inside was the chief. He was seated on the other side of the large table, as he had been the previous two times.

"Where is she?" I asked, while looking around in confusion.

"At the infirmary. The chief inspector took her," answered Mr. Grubijanić, who was the one who had notified me that Ms. Mirković had returned.

"Is she hurt?"

"No. At least she wasn't complaining of anything. Chief Inspector Uskoković still wanted a doctor to take a look at her." He paused. "Have a seat, Inspector Lukić."

I hesitated for a moment, then pulled out the nearest chair and sat down.

"What happened?"

The head of the lab sighed.

"We have no idea. The girl just turned up about twenty minutes ago. As though she had been absent for only a short while, she went back to her workstation," he pointed towards the part of the table where the instrument with two eyepieces stood, "and pored over her work. She was shocked when I told her what time it was. She was convinced that it was quarter to eleven, not almost one thirty."

I stared at Mr. Grubijanić for several moments.

"Did she say anything about the elevator ride?"

"Only that it was quite normal. She got on at the fifth floor, pressed the button for the basement and arrived here without stopping at any other floor. Nothing special happened."

"Did you take a look at the footage of her coming out of the car? Where did the elevator come from?"

"That is another mystery—from nowhere. It was already on the basement level. Two of our colleagues had taken it down several minutes before. The elevator remained here because no one had called it from above.

Then the doors opened again—and Ms. Mirković stepped out."

"They are still open."

"Yes, the chief inspector ordered that the elevator be shut down."

"Perhaps she should have done it sooner, as soon as the girl disappeared."

"How then would she have come back?"

I was left speechless again for a moment.

"Good question," I replied with a nod.

From behind me came the sound of the door opening. I turned around quickly and found myself facing Ms. Mirković. She stopped for an instant, smiled sheepishly as though she were justifying herself for some reason, shut the door behind her and turned to the left. She looked quite normal, as she had this morning. She sat down, briefly stared in front of her, then looked first at her boss, and then at me.

"How are you?" was all that I could think of.

A smile passed over her face again. "Fine, thanks."

"What did the doctor tell you?"

"That I should spend more time in the sun. Other than that, everything is all right."

I paused a second before speaking again. Without my even intending it, my voice grew softer.

"How was it . . . in the elevator?"

She shrugged. "Like always." It seemed that was all she had to say, then she added: "I smiled once."

"Did you?" I asked curiously.

"I remembered a funny sentence from Saramago's novel about death."

Before I could ask which one, the girl turned to her superior.

"The chief inspector suggested that I go home, but I said that I'd rather stay. I hope you have nothing against that."

"As you wish."

"Can I take a look at your . . . book, Inspector Lukić?"

"There are now three of them. Unfortunately, none of them are in my possession any more."

The girl continued looking at me, expecting me to say something else, but at that moment my work cell phone rang again. I was a little clumsy taking it out. Instead of the caller ID, a number appeared on the screen.

"Hello?"

"Inspector Lukić," said a flustered female voice, "this is Hristina Leleković, Administrator of the City Cemeteries Administration. You must come immediately. Something dreadful has happened."

17

I DIDN'T LEARN WHAT the dreadful thing that had happened was, because she immediately hung up. I returned the telephone to my pocket and rose.

"Please excuse me, something has come up. I'd like to come back later to chat, if you don't mind."

"I don't mind, Inspector. I'll be here."

As I left the laboratory, I thought of how she had already told me that once before. I hoped that this time she would not be foiled in such an extraordinary way.

I didn't turn on the police light, as I would have done in any other emergency. Mrs. Leleković sounded agitated, but it had been the same this morning, and there turned out to have been no reason for haste. It was quite possible that she'd avoided telling me what trouble had befallen the City Cemeteries Administration because then I might not have come at all. In any case, I didn't need the police light to get through the sparse traffic.

The mysterious disappearance of Ms. Mirković from the moving elevator was only a conjuring trick compared to the fact that she had experienced the passing of almost three hours as only half a minute. The secret society might have been able to pull off the former by some form of prestidigitation, but not the latter. Or perhaps it could? I knew very little about hypnosis, so I didn't know whether someone in such a state could be convinced that actually much less time had passed.

I shook my head, as I occasionally do when I ponder a problem. I did this while standing at an intersection, waiting for the light to change. An older lady in the car to my left looked distrustfully at the weird guy talking to himself. Occam would have scolded me for accumulating increasingly complex assumptions like this. It was necessary to look for a significantly simpler one.

The moment I set off from the intersection, the simplest solution occurred to me. There was no need for hypnosis, and the disappearance from the elevator, however it may have occurred, would certainly be significantly simpler to pull off if my young colleague was a accomplice, and not a victim in the secret society's performance. Occam would have liked this. The girl's odd literary taste—funny novels about death—supported this possibility.

The only opponent of this idea was my intuition. As a rational person I had to dismiss it, since nothing supported it. I would have already done so had my intuition not proven to me on several occasions that the solution does not necessarily always have to be arrived at by following Occam.

Preoccupied with the enigma of how the performance in the elevator had been carried out, I had lost track of perhaps a more important question—why had it been set up in the first place? The secret society makes a huge effort to organize the seemingly impossible disappearance of a member of the police staff from an elevator—regardless of whether she took part in the performance or not—only to simply return her. What was the meaning of this? What did they aim to achieve?

And why were they playing hide-and-seek with me? On the previous two occasions when our paths had crossed, they immediately let me know what they wanted—*The Last Book* and *The Grand Manuscript*. Now they were nowhere to be seen, leaving me to speculate about their intentions. And they certainly had something in mind; they were not doing all this just to toy with me. It was high time that they came out of the shadows and revealed their hand.

The area around the City Cemeteries Administration Building was bustling as usual. There were considerably more cars than there were parking spaces. Even though I did so reluctantly, this time I had no choice: I stopped the car where it was explicitly forbidden, took out my police light and placed it on the roof. It would serve a purpose after all.

There was quite a few of people in the corridor, but the guard noticed me immediately. He waved to me from the glass booth, then reached for the telephone. He put down the receiver after a few words and came out.

"The administrator is on her way," he said with a squint. "She'll blame me again. . . ."

"What happened?"

He looked at me as though to ask "Don't you know?" Then his eyes turned for a moment to the stairway leading to the basement.

"The administrator will explain everything to you. I'm not authorized." He paused, then repeated: "It's not my fault."

I wanted to calm him, but at that moment, just like this morning, a piercing "Mr. Rabrenović!" reverberated from behind me. Many heads turned towards the administrator, who was approaching from the left with a crisp step. The guard swiftly retreated to the booth.

"It took you a while to get here again, Inspector."

"Perhaps I would have come faster had I known why I had been summoned this time."

"I told you that something dreadful has happened."

"It would have been more helpful if you had told me what exactly had happened. Then I would have assessed how dreadful it actually was and I would have adjusted the speed of my arrival accordingly."

"You should have relied on my assessment. Anyway, we don't have time for this sparring. Come this way."

18

She walked ahead of me, towards the basement. On reaching it, I saw a man standing in front of the last door on the left.

"You may go now," the administrator told him as we approached. "I'll call you shortly."

She waited for the large older man to move away.

"I told Mr. Rosić to guard the archive until the locksmith comes to replace the lock."

"What happened to the lock?" I couldn't see it; the administrator obscured it by standing in front of the door.

"It's broken. We had to break in."

She stepped back. At first glance everything seemed fine. Then I bent down and noticed cracks in the doorframe.

"Why did you break in?"

She glanced at the corridor behind me, as though making sure that we weren't overheard. Even though there was no one there, she continued in a softer voice.

"To see what was going on with Mr. Trpimirović. I arrived around one o'clock. I knocked, but he didn't open. I thought that he might have gone to the restroom. He was required to notify me if he was going anywhere else. . . ."

"Quite a strict regimen," I said, interrupting her.

"It wouldn't do the police any harm either. In any case, I returned about fifteen minutes later; again he didn't answer my knock. I sent Mr. Rosić to check whether Mr. Trpimirović was in the men's room. I thought that he might have fallen ill, even though he is in excellent health, contrary to your unseemly insinuation that the lack of daylight might be harming him."

She paused, giving me a sullen stare.

"He wasn't in the restroom?"

"No, he wasn't. Why else would we have broken in?"

"It would have been simpler for you to presume that he had in fact gone out. Even the healthiest of people ultimately break under too strict a regimen."

"You don't know Mr. Tripimirović. He would never do that. We assumed something much more likely—that he had fallen ill inside. That would not have been strange. He had a very stressful start to the day. Among other things, he was unjustly accused."

"Well, did you find him in the archive?"

She just stared at me for a moment without saying a word, then shook her head.

"There, you see—in the end he got sick and tired of your regimen."

"Don't be so quick to gloat, Inspector Lukić. There was no one in the archive, but there was something that could not have got there under any circumstances."

It was now I who stared for several moments, overcome by the premonition that I had jumped to a conclusion for the second time, in this same place.

"What?" I finally asked.

"A key in the lock."

I felt something tickle the back of my neck.

"It was locked from the inside, and there was no one in the room?"

"Precisely so. Mr. Trpimirović had disappeared from the archive, which was locked from the inside. Didn't I tell you that something dreadful had happened?"

"You should have called me before you broke in."

"We feared for Mr. Trpimirović. Every moment

could have been precious, and you aren't exactly famous for your swift arrivals."

I sighed and shook my head.

"Who all has been inside?"

"Just Mr. Rosić and myself."

"Did you touch anything?"

"Absolutely nothing."

I took out my plastic gloves and put them on.

I entered the archive and examined the lock first. The signs of the break-in were more visible on the inside; the key protruded halfway. I went over to the desk. Everything looked as it had this morning: the large open book, documents, inkwell, pen, vase. I crossed to the first bookcase. The volumes were now arranged properly.

The administrator stood outside the open door and watched me without saying a word. I looked around the room, then surveyed the bookcases. They were the only other thing to look at. I stopped in the middle of the third wall. The monotonous dark gray panorama was interrupted by a void: a volume was missing. I took out my cell phone and took a close-up picture. Mrs. Leleković leaned in a little to see what had attracted my attention. Two bookcases down I again found an empty space and took another picture.

Having completed a full circuit, I looked at the ceiling and the floor. Then I came out, closed the door behind me and removed the plastic gloves. I didn't return the telephone to my pocket, but retreated to a discreet distance from the administrator and called the crime scene team, giving them instructions in a low voice.

"My colleagues are coming to process the scene," I said upon returning to the door of the archive. "Please make sure that no one goes in, including yourself."

For a moment she seemed ready to protest, but then she nodded. "All right."

"By the way, have you noticed that there are two volumes of burial records missing—3361 and 3521?"

"You don't say?" she answered, shocked, then immediately justified herself. "I most certainly would not have overlooked that, but I was very upset by the disappearance of Mr. Trpimirović. It's so dreadful. . . ."

"It's not exactly dreadful. You have the digital archives. You can make a copy of whatever is missing. If it is necessary at all. Perhaps Mr. Trpimirović has the books."

She squinted at me briefly.

"What do you mean? Where is Mr. Trpimirović? What has happened to him?"

"He's not inside, which means that he had to leave somehow."

"But the door was locked from the inside."

"It's possible to escape even from locked rooms." For a moment I was tempted to add that I had recently encountered such a case, but I restrained myself.

"How?"

"Through a window, for example."

"The windows are covered by bookcases, and there are also bars on them."

"Then there must be another way out."

Her voice grew stern again. "That's preposterous! I should know this building if anyone does. There is no other way out of the archive."

"In that case the only thing we can do is to conclude that Mr. Trpimirović simply vanished into thin air. Does that seem more acceptable to you?"

She opened her mouth but couldn't come up with a response, so closed it again. Her eyes blazed.

"I suggest you remain patient. My people will be here soon. Let them check whether there is another way out. The building was originally a private villa, right? They often have secrets that later owners or tenants have no clue about. Stay here until they arrive, please. I will call you as soon as I get the report from the crime scene team."

Without waiting for her to say anything else, I turned and walked off down the corridor at a brisk pace, then ran up the stairs to the ground floor. I was already at the entrance when I heard a muffled shout behind me.

"Inspector!"

I turned towards the guard, who was approaching from the direction of the booth. Before reaching me he looked right and left at the people who were in the corridor just then.

"Do you have a minute?" he asked. "I'd like to show you something."

I looked him over briefly, then nodded.

"This way."

He motioned towards the stairwell. Thinking that he would go into the basement, I was about to warn him that the administrator was still there, which he certainly would not appreciate, but he headed up the stairs. On reaching the second floor, he glanced in both directions first, just as he had downstairs. There was no one around at that moment.

The floor was identical to the two lower levels in every respect—the same row of doors on both sides, the same thick red-and-yellow carpeting. We headed left and soon reached the end of the corridor. When he turned the doorknob on the last door on the left, I thought that he was taking me into an office, but a new staircase appeared beyond it. It was wooden and seemed rather old. Since this was a two-story building, this was obviously the way up to the attic.

He paused with his foot on the first step and turned towards me.

"This remains in the strictest confidence, Inspector. I would be fired immediately if they learned that I'd brought you here."

"Don't worry."

The stairs creaked under our feet as we climbed up. The low door at the top of the stairs also seemed dilapidated. The attic had obviously not been included in the renovation project for the City Cemeteries Administration.

The guard searched briefly in his right pants pocket before taking out a key. He slid it into the lock, but had difficulty turning it. He muttered something. He finally unlocked the door, and with a fresh creak pulled it towards him and slipped inside.

"Come in quickly and close it behind you," he said from the darkness. "Someone might come along downstairs. I'll turn on the light right away."

I complied. Surrounded by murky obscurity, I remained by the door. I heard Rabrenović moving about at an indeterminate distance in front of me. I was just asking myself why the switch was not in the most logical place, next to the door, when there was a flash of light. Yet it wasn't regular lighting. The powerful beam of a flashlight pierced my eyes painfully, blinding me. I instinctively raised my right hand to protect myself.

Everything was calm for several moments. Then from the other end of the blade of light a deep male voice resounded, one that I had not heard in eight months.

19

"Hello, Inspector Lukić," said the Grand Master. "Once again we meet in the dark."

"Doesn't seem that way to me," I replied, still shielding my eyes with my hand.

"Oh, forgive me." The blade instantly slid back into the sheath of darkness. "Is this better?"

Even though I was again overcome by sightlessness, the blazing image lingered on my retinas for quite a while.

"More acceptable. I was just wondering when you would show up."

"You were expecting us?"

"Could this have transpired without you? The only thing I didn't expect was that we would be brought into contact by a not-overly-conscientious guard. Congratulations, Rabrenović. I would never have suspected you."

A "thank you" could be heard from the deeper darkness.

"The others deserve commendations too. You've always had excellent actors. Are any of them here in the attic too?"

"Who do you mean?"

"You know very well who I mean: the administrator and Mr. Trpimirović, the two ladies from the National Library, Mr. and Mrs. Vidojević. The acting ensemble probably also includes my colleague, Ms. Mirković."

"You're wrong, Inspector. Those aren't at all members of our society."

"There's no need for you to pretend. We know each other well enough. Better just openly tell me what it is that you want from me this time. Why are you organizing extremely elaborate performances just to deliver empty books to me?"

The darkness remained mute for a while.

"You didn't get them from us."

"It could only be you. No one else is capable of pulling off something like that. Especially not the act at the National Library."

"Think about our previous encounters; we never gave anything to you. On the contrary, we were always trying to get something from you."

"That was in the previous two cases. Now it's the other way around, for some reason. Let me hear what you're planning. We're just wasting time playing hide-and-seek in the dark."

There was another brief bout of silence.

"I'd like to propose something," proclaimed the Grand Master. "If you are truly convinced that you received the books from us, simply return them to us. We will disappear instantly. We won't bother you any more. I'm aware that my word doesn't mean much to you, but I'm giving it to you anyhow."

Now it was I who didn't respond immediately.

"Even if I wanted to, I couldn't," I finally said. "I no longer have them."

"The National Security Agency took possession of them, yes, but that's not a great obstacle. They told you that the books were at your disposal whenever you wanted them."

"You're very well informed, as always."

"Poorly informed persons don't go into this line of work."

"By the way, the Agency is burning with desire to know who is protecting you. It certainly must be someone exceptionally powerful. Even I am itching with curiosity as to who it might be. Would you agree to a trade—the books for that information?"

"I would not," the deep voice from the darkness responded without any hesitation. "There are much cheaper ways for us to get a hold of those books. Let the Agency keep trying to figure out who is protecting us. In any case, even if I were to agree, how could you be sure that you'd received the correct information? It cannot be verified."

"Why do you even care about those empty white books? What is it this time?"

Another short pause ensued.

"Your condescending tone is inappropriate, Inspector Lukić. We're on opposite sides, but that doesn't mean that we shouldn't respect each other. We will do anything to finally defeat you, but we greatly respect you as an adversary who has outwitted us on two occasions. It would be honorable if you could at least appreciate our goals, since you can't appreciate our means."

"It isn't only the means that are questionable, but also the fact that the goals concern only a very small number of people. You wanted to get your hands on *The Last Book* so that the members of your secret society alone might be spared the apocalypse. In the case of *The Grand Manuscript* it was even more exclusive: eternal life awaited only one person—the one who read it first. I assume that you were saving that privilege for yourself."

"If that worries you, then I have good news. There is no more discrimination. None. The empty white books, as you mockingly call them, concern all people. Without exception. And not only the living, but also the dead. Actually, primarily the dead. Do you know how many people have lived out their lives and died since mankind appeared in this world?"

Of course, I had no idea, so I gave a safe assessment. "Many."

"Many, yes. Very many. Unimaginably many. Around a hundred billion. All of them are listed in *The Compendium of the Dead*. No one has been left out."

"Then we're not talking about the same thing. There is no one listed in the three volumes that I received, and even the title was omitted."

"All that will appear when you receive the last, fourth volume."

"Ah, so. Another one is expected."

"That's right. It has to appear soon. Without it the first three are worthless. Only with the fourth does it become *The Compendium of the Dead*."

"Even if I got hold of four million more such volumes, it still wouldn't be enough to inscribe even the most basic information for a hundred billion people—nothing but their names and dates of births and deaths. And even that in the smallest possible lettering."

"I agree. However, there are also other types of records, other than alphabetic. We live in a time of quantum marvels, don't we? Four volumes made out of very special paper are sufficient to hold a lot more than the most basic data about a hundred billion people. There is enough space for a detailed biography of each of them."

"All right, let's assume that there is. But why are you interested in *The Compendium of the Dead*? What is the use of this four-volume set with quantum-inscribed information about all the people who ever existed? You must see some benefit, otherwise you wouldn't get involved in all this."

"Your negative opinion of us is clouding your perspective, Inspector Lukić. We don't have any benefit in mind. We only want to prevent the disaster that would inevitably occur if *The Compendium of the Dead* were to fall into the wrong hands."

"What disaster?"

"This certainly is not a mere list of deceased, as it seems to you. It is a miraculous artifact that makes mankind's most ancient dream possible; the realization of the hopes that are the purpose of the existence of all great religions; the rectifying of nature's greatest mistake." He paused for a moment, for dramatic effect. "Whoever has *The Compendium of the Dead* will be able to bring back the dead."

There seemed to be some commotion in the darkness in front of me, but it was also possible that I had imagined it.

"Resurrection?" I said questioningly.

"Resurrection," the Grand Master confirmed.

I sighed. "I still don't understand what kind of disaster is looming."

"How isn't it clear to you? Imagine if *The Compendium of the Dead* fell into the hands of someone who, like you, was overly democratically oriented, and who decided to bring back to life all the deceased. This poor planet is already struggling even with seven billion people on it, and with a hundred and seven it would instantly collapse."

"So, there's no good news. You will be acting out of elitist motives once again."

"That is inevitable. There is not nearly enough space for everyone. A selection must be made. In any case, not everyone actually deserves to be resurrected. However, space would be found for the chosen. For many of the chosen. And that is actually good news, isn't it?"

"And the chosen would be selected by you, I assume?"

"It would be best that it is done by someone who is up to the job. Otherwise it could lead to disaster of another kind."

"Would the chosen also include those whom you deprived of their lives in carrying out your harebrained schemes? It would give you an opportunity to make up for the crimes you had committed in pursuit of your goals."

There was no reply from the darkness. When the deep voice was heard again it had lost its previous friendly tone.

"There would hardly be room for them on our list."

"You can go ahead and tear up your list. It's all nonsense. There is no resurrection, just as there was no end of the world or eternal life."

"How is it then that three parts of *The Compendium of the Dead* have already appeared?"

"Because you planted them. I'm sure you have a reason for doing so. Otherwise, you could have come here this morning before me and taken the first volume. You feel quite at home in this building, don't you?"

"We were a little late, unfortunately. Rabrenović did not deserve your commendation."

"And what do you have against Trpimirović? Why did you get rid of him? He did his job impeccably."

"I have nothing against him. If he were my man, I'd never get rid of him."

"You really are persistent about this."

"Just as you are in not believing me."

"We're going around in circles. Perhaps I would believe you if there were someone else who could have done everything that has occurred since this morning. But there isn't."

"You think so? It seems that your insightfulness really has faded, Inspector Lukić."

At that moment the pounding of a myriad of running feet could be heard, first from the second floor, then from the wooden stairs behind me. The commotion in the darkness before me was definite this time, but it lasted only for an instant. When the door flew open, there was only a squinting police inspector in the attic.

20

A LARGE GROUP BURST in. There was a good deal of confusion, even though no one spoke. Several flashlight beams wandered around, appropriating small patches of visibility from the darkness. One pointed briefly at my face, blinding me again. I covered my eyes with my hands for a second time, and it was just then that someone flipped the light switch behind me. I lowered my hands but my loss of sight lasted a few more seconds.

Upon recovering it, I finally saw the large attic where I had spent the past ten or so minutes in complete darkness. There were no partition walls, only a series of load-bearing columns and horizontal cement beams supporting the roof. The space was almost completely empty. In the rear and to the right was a stack of large cardboard boxes, towards which two of the men headed.

The others gathered around me. I ran my gaze over

their inquisitive faces. There were Senka Veselinović and Stanislav Mirić, as well as four others. I had difficulty recognizing them too because they had all changed their appearance. They were all now clean cut and dressed like yuppies—the complete opposite of the look that I remembered from eight months earlier.

The burly young man no longer had short hair or sports clothes, and the tattoo on his left earlobe was gone. The small young lady with a mole on the tip of her nose had short light hair instead of long and dark, and she had lost a few pounds. The elegant suit made the greatest difference on the long-haired young man who had previously worn faded jeans and the brick-colored sweatshirt, with loosely-laced running shoes. It was also difficult to imagine that the round-faced girl, who looked the best in a business suit, until recently had unruly hair and went around with her bellybutton showing.

"I'm glad that we meet again, young colleagues," I said with a smile. "You've really scrubbed up nicely."

The two girls responded with brief skittish smiles.

"The Grand Master and his band, right?" Agent Mirić said.

"I'm certain about the Grand Master. If the band was present too, they didn't make a sound in the dark. Although there was some commotion, but that could have been the guard, Rabrenović, who brought me here."

"Why did he bring you?" Agent Veselinović asked.

"For a chat. A very useful one. First of all, I learned what is going on this time. After *The Last Book* and *The Grand Manuscript*, they are expecting *The Compendium of the Dead*: a set of four books that contain information about all the people who ever lived. Around a hundred billion of them."

The six agents silently exchanged quick glances.

"You mean the empty white books that you have

been receiving since this morning? There are three of them, not four," Mirić noted.

"For now. The fourth should appear soon. The books will then, allegedly, cease to be empty, although I didn't quite understand how so much data is to be stored in only four volumes. It is some sort of quantum recording."

Agent Mirić turned towards his colleague Veselinović.

"We have the report back from the lab," she said. "The source of the paper that was used to make the white books is unknown. No one produces it. Actually, it isn't even paper but rather some sort of foil. They're currently running tests on it."

"All right, let's say that someone puts all the data on foils," Mirić said. "Why does the secret society want *The Compendium of the Dead*?"

"Because," I responded, "they believe that whoever has the four-volume set will have the power to resurrect the dead."

Mirić watched me for several moments in silence, then rolled his eyes. "No less."

We were joined by the two men who had been inspecting the cardboard boxes. It was only when they came quite close that I realized it wasn't the first time I had encountered them either. I had seen them eight months ago, dressed in jeans and orange t-shirts, first going into 12 Oak Street, and then removing Inspector Vesić's corpse from there.

The taller of them shrugged as he looked at Agent Mirić.

"You will have a hard time figuring out how they disappeared," I said. "Even Commissioner Milenković was unsuccessful. They kept eluding him. I was present on one occasion when more than fifty of them vanished in around twenty seconds from a large chamber beneath a villa. They are very skilled at that."

"Skilled," said Agent Veselinović, "or capable of pulling off the impossible."

"There is no need for the impossible. They have obviously been interested in this building for a while, for some reason, if they had a man here. Probably even more than one. There was time to make a secret escape route in the attic, which isn't in use anyway. You can't expect to find it with a cursory inspection."

"Do you still think that they are behind everything that is happening today?"

"It seems the most likely thing to me."

"Then we have serious difficulties with at least one episode, the one at the Police Headquarters. We didn't give it just a cursory inspection, but a very thorough one. The disappearance and reappearance of Ms. Mirković cannot be explained."

"Did you consider the possibility that she is a member of the secret society? That would provide at least a partial explanation—we would know that she didn't stay in that car for only half a minute, as she claims."

"Even if we were to assume that, the main riddle remains unsolved—how did she first disappear from a moving elevator, and then reappear in it almost three hours later?"

"Patience. The answer to that may yet emerge."

Agent Mirić cleared his throat. "Did you tell the Grand Master that you think that he is pulling the strings?"

"I did. Of course, he denied it, but that doesn't mean anything. He would have denied it whether my assumption was correct or not: in the first case to protect himself, in the second to maintain my misconception. However, when I offered to give him the three copies that he allegedly cares about, he declined."

"Why did you offer him the books?"

"To do you a favor, in the name of our new cooperation. I asked that in return he reveal who is protecting them. This information, however, was more precious to him than *The Compendium of the Dead*, and the power that comes with it."

Agent Veselinović raised her hand to her right ear. Her eyes wandered away from me for a moment. She nodded twice without saying a word.

"We have another inexplicable episode," she said, lowering her hand. "The disappearance of Mr. Tripimirović from the locked Archive. Our experts have just determined that there is no other way out of the room. Perhaps the Grand Master was in fact being sincere when he denied that they were behind everything. Except, of course, if they are actually capable of performing the impossible."

"The archivist could have left the room, and then from the outside turned the key in the lock on the inside."

"The late Inspector Vesić told you that was impossible," Agent Mirić reminded me.

"That was in regard to a significantly more complex type of lock. The one downstairs is quite ordinary. I could probably pull that off."

"That might be the case, but it would be a tricky achievement for someone to whom the dip pen and inkwell are the pinnacle of technology."

"Perhaps someone more skillful helped him, if he too is a member of the secret society. . . ."

"You really are persistent, Inspector Lukić," Agent Veselinović interrupted. "You grasp at increasingly complicated explanations only to avoid the simplest one—that this a new case of crossing realities. It is as though you've completely forsaken Occam."

"Of course I haven't forsaken Occam. The only problem is that I don't think that crossing realities are the simplest explanation. On the contrary. By the way, you used the same words that the Grand Master and I exchanged when parting—'you really are persistent.'"

"There you have it."

"Why do you reject the possibility that realities have crossed again?" Agent Mirić asked. "I agree that it is not the simplest solution, but it is the only one that we have for the impossible. And there is a growing number of emerging impossibilities."

"I reject it because realities cross only when the author is writing a novel that is set in our world. A detective novel. It doesn't really matter that no one has been killed so far, and that such literary works don't exist without murder victims. Perhaps they will appear later, as you've said. What is crucial is that nothing that has happened so far looks like a detective novel. Not only is there no crime, but there isn't even anything that falls within the jurisdiction of the police. Someone is leaving for me, at different locations, empty white books, made of unusual paper. That is weird, I agree, but no laws were broken in the process. The lab technician disappeared in an elevator, then reappeared after a while. The circumstances are mysterious, but the girl is all right. Now the archivist has vanished. There are no signs of a struggle or any reason to suspect that something bad has happened. Why wouldn't he too return unscathed?"

I paused to catch my breath, only then realizing that I was speaking too quickly. Eight young faces were staring fixedly at me.

"If realities have crossed again," I continued, more slowly and softly, "if this truly is a detective novel, whoever is writing it is very unskilled in the art of writing."

Or very, very skilled, I thought to myself.

21

Senka Veselinović was about to say something, and it seemed that Stanislav Mirić also wanted to speak his mind, but they were forestalled by the ringing of my work cell phone. I held up my hand, asking them to wait, and took out my telephone. The chief inspector's name appeared on the screen.

"Inspector Lukić. How may I help you, Chief Inspector Uskoković?"

"Are you at Headquarters?"

"No, but I will be soon."

"Please come and see me as soon as you get here."

"Very well."

I returned the telephone to my pocket, then shrugged.

"I'm afraid we will have to resume our interesting discussion at another time." I smiled. "I have a feeling that it will be very soon."

"It looks like we will be seeing a lot each other today, Inspector Lukić," replied Agent Veselinović, also with a smile.

I left the attic and ran down the creaking wooden steps. As I headed down the second-floor corridor, two or three curious heads peered out of the doors that had been left ajar.

On the ground floor I ran into the crime scene team just as they were arriving. I showed them where to go. "People from the National Security Agency were there until a little while ago. They didn't find anything. Even so, check it again," I added.

My two colleagues, wearing white protective coveralls and carrying large duffel bags, nodded and headed towards the basement. On the staircase they passed the administrator, who was on her way up. Having run into me, she first looked me over in surprise, as though asking what I was still doing there.

"Hasn't the crime scene team already finished?" she asked, nodding downstairs.

"Yes, it has. These are reinforcements. This is not a simple case, as you are well aware. Has the locksmith arrived?"

"Not yet." She gave me a reproachful look. "People are very careless about time. Mr. Rosić is again standing guard at the Archive door." She paused. "The first team didn't find anything?"

"No, they didn't, but I have good news for you. You won't have any more problems with Rabrenović, the guard. He has decided to take early retirement."

Mrs. Leleković glanced towards the guard's booth in confusion. I didn't wait for her to turn towards me and ask for an explanation; I quickly left the building, and after taking two steps down the gravel path I was already at the gate.

There was a surprise awaiting me on the car. Tucked beneath the left windshield wiper was a parking violation ticket. As I removed it I realized that it was actually two tickets. The second was for unauthorized use of an emergency light. The traffic warden obviously hadn't bothered to check whether it was an unmarked police car. I guessed that people often used unauthorized emergency lights around here, and he had simply assumed that this was the case. I shook my head, folded the two pieces of paper and placed them in my pocket. I removed the emergency light, got in the car and placed it in the glove compartment. Just as on the previous occasion, two drivers pounced on the place that I had vacated, without any consideration for the fact that it was illegal to park there.

As I set off down the street, it crossed my mind that since this affair had started this morning, it was only when driving that I had had the opportunity to think things through without any interruption. The rest of the time had passed nearly without let-up.

There was one weak link in what I had told the National Security Agency agents at the end. I had avoided taking a stance on the disappearance of Ms. Mirković, vaguely describing it as mysterious. Had they pressured me into being more specific, I would have had to agree that the episode was the strongest corroboration of their assumption that it was a new case of crossing realities.

What happened in the elevator at the Police Headquarters could only be explained by the interference of a higher power. And the only higher power in our world was the author who acted out of his own universe. His interventions, however, were not arbitrary. He had to take into account the coherence what he was writing. He could not just introduce an episode that made no sense, which is precisely what the event in the elevator seemed to be.

The girl should have disappeared in a more natural way, and then either not appear again or turn up dead somewhere. That would have been not only coherent but also in the spirit of detective novels. However, this way it remained unclear why he had resorted to a mysterious disappearance, only for her to return a while later, as though nothing had happened. It seemed that the episode was an end in itself. It was like something an inexperienced and up-and-coming author would write, only to flaunt his imaginativeness, without any concern for its purpose in the novel as a whole.

Unless, of course, this was a case of what had occurred to me at the end of that long monologue in the attic. What I had left unsaid. I knew for a fact that the author was not inexperienced. He would not have failed to notice such a big slip-up. Perhaps the episode made sense, only I could not see how because it was masterfully concealed, and I still didn't have the time to focus on figuring it out.

Caught up in thought, the drive to the Police Headquarters seemed to me quite short. The doors to both elevators in the garage were closed, which could mean that the right-hand one was back in service. I pressed the call button. A full minute passed before the left-hand car arrived. On the way up, the elevator stopped on the ground floor. Two colleagues and a young woman I didn't recognize got in. They were deep in conversation, but fell silent as soon as they saw me. The men just nodded to me briefly, and then again as they got off on the third floor.

Having reached the fourth floor, I headed left and knocked on the last door on the right. The inscription on the brass plate read "Chief Inspector." Although her official title was "Chief Inspectoress", she didn't like it and had left the plate unchanged.

I could barely hear the invitation to enter over the parrots' loud screeches. I didn't see them, however, when I went in. Chief Inspector Uskoković was in the middle of pulling a heavy cover over the large cage. Once she had lowered it all the way, the squawking stopped.

"They don't usually make so much noise when someone comes in," she said, returning to the massive desk. She kept it very tidy, but it seemed somehow bare without former Chief Inspector Đorđević's two bonsais.

"Have a seat, Inspector Lukić."

She indicated the right armchair in front of the desk. As I sat down, it crossed my mind that this was the first time I had been seated there. Her predecessor had always offered me the left one.

"First of all, I want to confirm to you what you already know: Ms. Mirković is all right. The doctor didn't find any . . . irregularity . . . and she feels fine. Let's hope that it stays that way."

"I saw her shortly after she . . . returned. She seemed all right to me too."

"In order for it to remain so, it would be best not to remind her of what she has been through. I would ask that you avoid talking to her about it. I recommended the same to Mr. Grubijanić. The two of you are the only ones fully informed of . . . the event."

I nodded.

"The investigation will be suspended. Officially—nothing happened. Ms. Mirković has a little amnesia, that's all."

I nodded again.

"Unofficially, as you are well aware, the case has been taken over by the National Security Agency. The building is full of their people." She paused. "It seems to me that they are especially interested in you."

"Yes, we had a long talk in my office."

"About what, if it isn't a secret?"

"About three unusual books that I received during the morning. You saw one in the lab."

She watched me for several moments in silence.

"Your previous . . . special . . . cases also started with books, correct?"

"A book and a manuscript, to be precise."

"A book and a manuscript, yes. Is this the third such case?"

Now it was I who looked at her for a few seconds mutely.

"I don't know," I responded at last, shrugging my shoulders. "The Agency believes that it is, but I'm not sure. It could also be that someone else is behind everything."

"Who could pull off this thing with the elevator?"

"There is a rather powerful secret society. . . ."

"So powerful that it can perform miracles in the Police Headquarters?"

"So powerful that it seems that even the Agency can't do anything about it."

We looked at each other again without words.

"I would very much appreciate it, Inspector Lukić, if you would keep me informed about any further developments in the case. I hope that the Agency has not prohibited that."

"No, it hasn't. At least not yet."

"Very well." The chief inspector stood up. "Call me if you need any help."

"I will. Thank you."

I too got up and headed towards the door. Before reaching it, Chief Inspector Uskoković spoke again.

"I'm glad that you like Saramago."

I turned around and smiled.

As I walked away down the corridor, a muffled screeching resounded behind me. I climbed the stairs rapidly to the fifth floor. I reached for the doorknob, convinced that the two agents had left the office unlocked, but I was mistaken—they had thoughtfully locked up. As I pulled out the bunch of keys, I heard the rustling of the tickets that I had placed in my pocket.

Having entered, I placed the two pieces of paper on the desk. It was something that could be taken care of later. I returned the keys to my pocket, sank into the chair and sighed loudly. Finally, an opportunity to gather my thoughts.

However, it wasn't to be. A moment later my work cell phone rang. Shaking my head, I took it out. The name on the screen was Bumbaković.

"Mrs. Evgenija Ognjanović from the National Library is on the line for you."

"Put her through."

"Inspector Lukić?" The voice of the head of the Department of Old and Rare Books was on the verge of tears.

"What has happened, Mrs. Ognjanović?"

"Please come as quickly as possible."

"What has happened?" I repeated my question.

"I . . . I can't tell you over the telephone. Please, come."

"I'm on my way."

I didn't waste any time locking the office. There was no longer anything anyone was interested in, and a regular lock certainly wasn't a serious obstacle if someone really wanted to get in.

I reached the elevator in three strides and pressed the call button with unnecessary force. About half a minute later the doors of the right-hand car opened. I had already taken a step inside, when a sudden realization stopped me in my tracks.

Stepping back, I turned around and no less hastily returned to my office. It was unclear to me how I hadn't noticed immediately that which had twice been right in front of my nose: first where I had parked illegally in front of the City Cemeteries Administration Building, and then a little while ago when I had placed the parking tickets on the desk.

I grabbed the two crumpled papers from the desk.

22

I DIDN'T HAVE ANY of the envelopes to compare the handwriting, but I didn't need them. I remembered it well. There wasn't much text written in pen on the tickets, just a few words. However, it was enough. The same hand that had addressed the three envelopes to me had also filled out these two forms. At the bottom, in the space indicated for the signature, was an illegible initial.

Of course, it was pointless to call the Department of Transportation and inquire who had been on duty in the vicinity of the City Cemeteries Administration Building. The local traffic warden would know nothing about these papers. Also, there was no reason to take these tickets to my colleagues at the Department of Transportation to have them canceled. They had no record of them at all. Actually, there was nothing I could do about it.

I folded the papers and returned them to the pocket with the keys, then I hustled to the elevator. Fortunately, the right-hand car was still there, and I reached the garage without making any stops. I took out the emergency light and switched it on; I drove out into the street faster than usual, with tires screeching.

Whoever had written those tickets felt such superiority that he had decided to toy with me. It was no longer enough to bamboozle me by sending unusual books and performing disappearing acts. He was convinced that I could not find him, so it pleased him to play a joke on me. What other purpose could this move have?

Then it occurred to me that perhaps he hadn't gone unnoticed. The Agency surely had installed video surveillance at the City Cemeteries Administration Building and in its vicinity during the operation. It was routine procedure. I would call them up and ask that they check the footage. I was already reaching for the telephone when I realized that I didn't have the telephone numbers of Stanislav Mirić or Senka Veselinović, or anyone else from the Agency. My only contact with them was the former Commissioner. I still had Milenković's phone number, but it had undoubtedly been disconnected after he retired.

Perhaps, however, I didn't need the telephone at all. My car was most certainly bugged, despite our cooperation. Just in case. It would probably be enough to ask out loud for them to call me. Or not. I could get them into trouble, which wouldn't do anyone any good. Whatever the case, it was very likely that the footage would reveal nothing, just like the footage from in front of the Café Mocha eight months ago. The superior prankster, who had left the fake tickets, must have been aware that the Agency was recording, and would have made sure to execute everything without being detected.

Few people would be bold enough to amuse themselves so arrogantly. Actually such brazen insolence was typical of only one person's nature—that of the Grand Master. I strained to recall whether I had even seen anything that he had written in his own hand. Anything at all. Unfortunately, nothing came to mind. He must have been convinced that I hadn't, otherwise he would not so openly flaunt his handwriting.

If, however, it was the Grand Master and his secret society who were behind everything, then I was once again confronted with the question of how he could pull off the episode in the elevator at the Police Headquarters. They were very powerful, but they were not wizards. The impossible was not within their power.

I barely controlled myself sufficiently to avoid slowing the car down one more time as something else occurred to me. What if the idea of some force being "behind everything" were wrong? All my thoughts, both the conversations that I had had with the two agents, as well as the one with the Grand Master, had led me to the conclusion that someone from another reality was pulling the strings, controlling everything that was happening.

But that didn't necessarily have to be so. Perhaps there were in fact two separate series of events. What had happened at the Police Headquarters was impossible without crossing realities, fair enough; but nothing else required sorcery, not even the latest event—the disappearance of Mr. Trpimirović from the locked archive. This did in fact seem more like a magic trick, no more complex than the speedy escape of at least two people from a pitch-dark attic.

If the other events were being directed by the Grand Master—and it could be no one else—it was understandable that he wanted me to believe that these too were under the author's influence. The Grand Master had offered to withdraw immediately if I gave him the three books. He wanted to assure me that he had not sent them to me, but it was just a bluff. He knew that I could not give them to him because I did not have the volumes, and if I were to ask the Agency for them, they would certainly oppose my handing them over to him.

The idea of two independent narratives resolved many of the dilemmas, but not the main one: what was the meaning of everything that had transpired since the morning, and which was obviously still not over? How did *The Compendium of the Dead* fit into it?

23

THERE WERE NO FREE spaces in the parking lot behind the National Library, but the guard recognized my car as I was approaching and quickly opened the gate. He waved me to follow him and went towards a separate section on the left. He removed the metal sign reading "Reserved" and signaled me to park there.

"The director just left," he said after I had gotten out of the car. "He won't be coming back."

"Thank you," I said, with a small nod. It was obvious that he could barely contain his curiosity, so I hurried towards the staff entrance, to avoid giving him the opportunity to ask me anything.

The administrator was waiting for me behind the glass doors, just like Miss Šuvaković had that morning. She just said briskly "Follow me" and led me towards the elevator with her head bent. As we passed through the lobby, I turned towards the receptionist and smiled broadly at her. She too looked down, breaking off her obvious stare.

With a wavering hand Mrs. Ognjanović inserted the security key into the slot under the number "–3." As soon as the elevator started moving she began to weep. For several moments I didn't know what to do, then I went up to her and put my arm around her shoulders. She was so short that it felt like consoling a child.

"What has happened, Mrs. Ognjenović?" I asked softly.

She tried to answer, but had barely managed to get a word out when we reached the Department of Old and

Rare Books. She had previously taken a handkerchief from her sleeve and dried her eyes and cheeks.

"Forgive me. This is too much for me." She paused. It looked as though she was about to cry again, but she controlled herself. "She's gone."

I looked around the Department. We were alone.

"Miss Šuvaković?" I asked.

She nodded.

"When did this happen?"

She looked at me for a moment as though she had not understood what I was asking. Then she collected herself.

"Shortly before I called you. I had gone upstairs briefly. A professor who had an appointment at three o'clock had arrived. We canceled all the others who were supposed to work here today. We didn't have his phone number. It was his first time here. Olivera usually greets and sees off all the visitors, but this time I asked to go. For decades I've been spending my workdays deep underground and never had a problem with it. However, after what had happened earlier, I felt confined. I decided to go up to the ground floor and apologize to the professor, just so that I could get out into the open."

"I admire you. I would definitely not be able spend all my time in the underworld."

"I thought so too in the beginning, but you get used to it. You even learn to love the underworld—as you call it. Nonetheless, the professor was waiting for me by the elevator. We spoke briefly, no longer than five or six minutes. He was considerate and expressed understanding for the extraordinary circumstances, even though, of course, I did not tell him what had happened."

"The elevator was open the entire time?"

"No, but it stayed on the ground floor. I would have heard if it had moved. In any case, when I pressed the button, the doors opened straight away."

"You didn't want to stay upstairs any longer? Perhaps go outdoors?"

She shook her head. "No. That was enough. I hurried back so that Olivera would not be alone. It was as though I had sensed something. . . ." She paused briefly. "When I came out, there was no one here. The Department was empty. Olivera had disappeared. I immediately called you. . . ."

Her eyes filled again.

I scanned the large room once more.

"You didn't think that Miss Šuvaković had perhaps gone to the restroom?"

"She couldn't have. The restrooms are one level up, and you can only get there by elevator."

"That's not exactly convenient if a person is in a hurry, and the elevator is occupied."

She gave me a serious look. "We've never had such issues."

"Very well, if your deputy could not have used the elevator, as far as I understand, there is only one other way she could have gotten out—the emergency exit."

The administrator fiercely shook her head. "Out of the question."

I waited for her to say something more, but she just kept on staring at me.

"This time you will have to disclose more about this exit, if you want me to try and determine what has happened to Miss Šuvaković."

She shook her head somewhat less vigorously this time. "I . . . am not authorized. Please, you have to understand. . . ."

"In that case the only thing I can do is conclude that your colleague mysteriously vanished into thin air—and close the case. That wouldn't be unusual—about ten percent of missing persons disappear without a trace. As though they had fallen off the face of the earth."

"Oh, God! You don't know what you are asking of me. Only a handful of us know about it and it has to remain so. If it were to get out. . . ."

"You can be at ease. I'm a police inspector, and I absolutely understand the importance of this secret. I assure you that no one will learn it from me."

Looking away, she started to fold her arms. It was a good half-minute before her inner struggle was over.

"Stay here and face the elevator doors. You must not turn around under any circumstances until I call you. Under any circumstances. Do you understand?"

"I do."

By her barely audible steps I could tell that she had gone to the right of where I was standing. I didn't turn around; I wasn't interested in what she wanted to conceal—how the emergency exit was opened. There was a brief silence, and then a soft mechanical noise reached my ears.

"Inspector Lukić," Mrs. Ognjanović called out to me.

I turned around. She was standing alongside the left-hand wall, in the middle. A part of the bookcase, around two meters high, had moved inward, like an open door with a metal outer surface. As I approached, the administrator stepped into the darkness, from which a moment later came the sound of a switch being flipped.

"Here you are," she said after coming out. The motion of her hand towards the opening seemed to express capitulation.

24

I PAUSED IN FRONT of the entrance, looking at the illuminated interior. The square space was no larger than an elevator shaft. It was almost completely filled by an iron spiral staircase of the same dark gray color as the unplastered concrete walls. A round post extended through the center of it like an axle.

I stuck my head in and looked up. My view was somewhat obstructed, so I couldn't judge how far up the spiral extended, but it had to be high.

"Where does it lead?"

"To the room with the safes on the second floor."

"I'd like to climb up, if you don't mind."

She nodded.

I went in and looked up once again, then stepped up next to the handrail on the left-hand side, because that was where the steps were widest. As soon as I started climbing the automatic counter in my head went on. The ascent was tedious. Every three revolutions there would be a pair of lights on the walls opposite each other. There were no landings or level markers. The ascent ended after a hundred and thirty-seven steps. Breathing with slight difficulty, I reached a small platform with a railing and a low metal ceiling.

A steel door stood in front of me. A key ring with a key hung on a hook next to the doorpost. I looked around, but there was nothing else to see. I started back down, my eyes fixed on my feet. I didn't feel it as much on the way up, but I was getting lightheaded from the constant spinning, so I grabbed the handrail. When I emerged from the shaft I felt a tightness in my calves.

"Please stand near the elevator and turn away again," said the administrator, as soon as I stepped into the large room.

I moved complacently enough, but stopped before reaching the elevator. Something wasn't right, although I couldn't quite put my finger on it. Then a realization broke through to the surface of my consciousness—on the way down my counter had reached a hundred and thirty-six. It took quite significant willpower not to turn around and glance suspiciously at the stairway, but to continue on as I had been instructed.

"Has there ever been reason to use the emergency exit?" I asked with my back to Mrs. Ognjanović.

Once again I heard the mechanical noise as the secret door on the left-hand wall started to close, but I didn't notice the administrator walk over to me. She was already standing by my side when she answered.

"No, there hasn't, but twice a year we have drills. We rehearse leaving that way. I dread it. It hasn't been easy for me to clamber up those stairs for some time now."

I turned around. "Why did you say that it was out of the question that Miss Šuvaković had left that way?"

"First of all, because it's not allowed. There are strict rules on when that exit may be used. Only in the event of a natural disaster or war, and even then there is a complex protocol."

"People don't exactly always stick to what has been strictly prescribed. . . ."

She shook her head. "You don't know Olivera; the future administrator of this department considers the rules to be sacred."

"We still have to assume that she broke them for some reason. As far as I can see, the only way that she could have left is by way of that staircase." I pointed in the direction of the secret door.

"Impossible, Inspector. Had anyone appeared upstairs, in the room with the safes, I would have immediately been notified. There are always two people on duty there. Nonetheless, more importantly, my deputy is not allowed to leave the Department while I am out. At least one of us must be here during office hours. Olivera would never break that rule."

I looked around the large library, then shrugged my shoulders.

"If that is so, then we are confronted with an unsolvable puzzle. Miss Šuvaković's disappearance seems impossible, yet she is gone. Furthermore, this is not the first impossibility that has occurred here today: we still don't know how the two books appeared."

"So it was in fact only a book in the envelope? Nothing more dangerous than that?"

"Just a book," I responded with some hesitation.

"Also an old edition. . . ."

"No, quite new. Nothing that would be of interest to you."

"Why did they send it to you here?"

"I have no idea. Another puzzle. Incidentally, speaking of books, I'd like to leaf through the incunabulum, if you would permit me to. Not with my bare hands, of course." I pulled out plastic gloves from my inner pocket and started putting them on. "It is unlikely that I will ever have another opportunity."

She studied me for several moments without saying anything.

"Face the wall again," she said finally.

I complied for the third time. Now I couldn't determine by her footsteps where she had headed, but judging by the time it took her—I would say that she had almost reached the opposite end of the room. There was a brief silence, then the administrator spoke up in a changed tone.

"Inspector Lukić. . . ."

I turned around and saw her standing to the left of the furthest bookcase. She was looking down. I hurried towards her.

Nearly at the bottom of the bookcase a small drawer was pulled out. Empty.

"It's gone. The incunabulum has disappeared," Mrs. Ognjanović said almost in a whisper.

"Are you sure that you placed it here? Perhaps it's in another bookcase."

She shook her head. "This is the only one that has a secret drawer." She leaned over, touching the inside, as though she didn't believe her eyes, then she pushed it back. When it was in all the way, there was no visible sign that it was there. It obviously no longer mattered that I too knew its location.

"Did Miss Šuvaković know where you had hidden the incunabulum?"

"She was the one who put it there. Why do you ask?"

"I'm just checking," I responded while taking off the gloves.

"You don't mean to say. . . ."

"I mean to say," I interrupted her, "that now in addition to the mysteriously missing person we also have a mysteriously missing precious book, and that is more than enough reason to launch an investigation."

The administrator started speaking very quickly. "That must be avoided at all costs! We've explained to you. The reputation of our Department. . . ."

"I'm sorry, but I have to abide by the regulations. I'm sure you understand. In any case, I will do my best to act as discreetly as possible, as I promised."

"Oh, my god. . . ." she muttered and clutched her head.

"Of course, an investigation would not be necessary if by some miracle both your deputy and the incunabulum were to appear. The Department would be spared the unpleasantness."

I waited a little while for a response, but Mrs. Ognjanović just kept looking at me while holding her head.

"All right, I have to go now. I hope that you will call me soon with good news."

25

STEPPING INTO THE ELEVATOR, I was about to touch the button marked zero, when the call of nature, which I had been feeling for some time, reminded me that the administrator had said that the nearest facility that I required was above the Department of Old and Rare Books. My finger slipped down to the "–3" button.

After the short ride, I proceeded down a well lit corridor, which after about fifteen meters turned sharp right. I didn't know what was located here, but it seemed as lavish as the lower level. The walls were covered in reddish marble panels, and thick carpeting of the same color covered the stone floor. Along both sides, at regular intervals, were padded doors without any nameplates. There was no one in sight, nor were there any sounds.

I finally found the restrooms just before the turn—first the women's then the men's. The inside was even more luxurious than the corridor: marble also covered the ceiling, a huge mirror filled the upper half of the wall above the porcelain sinks; there was even a shower, and the shelf next to it was stacked with towels and various personal hygiene and grooming supplies.

Feeling slightly like an intruder in this place—which was not intended for ordinary visitors to the National Library, including police inspectors—I entered the nearest stall. As soon as I had closed the door the sweet scent of air freshener arose, accompanied by soft music.

The circumstances were quite inappropriate, but the peace around me brought me the focus that I had managed to achieve today only when I was alone in the car. Actually, here it was a bit more favorable to contemplation since I did not also have to focus on driving. There were no distractions.

There were two possible explanations for the seemingly impossible disappearance of Miss Šuvaković.

The first was that she wasn't missing at all, but was still hidden somewhere in the Department of Old and Rare Books. Perhaps there was another secret exit or hiding place behind the bookshelves that I was not aware of; perhaps she had sought refuge in one of the large bookcases, taking the incunabulum with her. The administrator claimed that the small drawer, in which the ancient book had allegedly been placed, was the only secret compartment, but I had no reason to believe her.

The second was that I also didn't have to believe the administrator's claim that her deputy had stayed in the Department while she went to the ground floor to meet with the professor. They could have left together, and Miss Šuvaković could have gotten off at one of the underground levels, carrying the incunabulum. The National Library doubtless had good security camera coverage, but anyone aware of their placement would know how to evade them.

In both cases, the administrator and her deputy would have been in cahoots, with the aim of achieving something. Two options presented themselves here too, depending on whether the two of them were members of the Grand Master's band or not.

If they were members, then the purpose of removing the incunabulum would be to deny me the opportunity to verify whether it truly was a second copy of *The Book of Resurrection*, as I had been told. The question here would be why it had been felt necessary to bring the false incunabulum to the Department, along with the envelope addressed to me, when the same result could have been achieved without it. The answer might be that it was in order to present everything to me as being foggier and more mysterious,.

The pattern from the City Cemeteries Administration had been replicated. In that case the books had first been moved around, mimicking the patient from the Papyrus, only for the archivist, along with two books of burial records, to disappear in the end, even though it was unnecessary. Here someone had brought the book in first, copying a different patient from the Papyrus, only for the deputy to disappear later, along with *The Book of Resurrection*, which didn't need to appear at all in the first place.

Even if this was true, however, I was still no closer

to solving the main puzzle—why was the secret society leaving me the volumes of *The Compendium of the Dead* and why was it denying that it was doing so?

On the other hand, if the two women had no connection to the Grand Master, as he himself claimed, then it must be a real incunabulum, which the two of them were trying to steal, forsaking the high ideals of which they were so proud. We would see whether they would accept my closing offer—that I would stop the investigation if the book was returned.

Though, in this case again, the main puzzle remained unsolved—how did the second copy of *The Book of Resurrection*, along with the second volume of *The Compendium of the Dead*, appear at the Department?

Even though I was still surrounded by puzzles, after careful contemplation I came out of the stall feeling relieved. I walked up to the first sink and washed my hands, pleased that no one had come in, so I didn't have to come up with an explanation as to what I was doing there. I dried my hands in the almost noiseless stream of warm air and walked towards the door.

26

The corridor was still deserted. It crossed my mind at that moment that this might not be an active department, but rather a shelter for the Library staff in the event of an emergency. A little luxury wouldn't hurt if one were forced to stay here for an extended period. I would have expected the deepest level to be chosen for housing people, but the dedicated librarians had the final say, and they didn't hesitate to put the safety of the old and rare books ahead of their own. The two ladies who worked downstairs and their refined visitors had a private restroom at their disposal, which was fitting. Perhaps they would have minded if they'd known that I had used it.

I had already reached the elevator when it occurred to me that something was not right. I turned around and looked down the corridor. Everything seemed the same as when I had come in, but I could not shake the feeling that something was off. I stood there for several moments, than headed back, while looking around, although there wasn't much to see. I was about halfway down the corridor when I finally realized what it was.

Attached to the frame of the door in front of which I had stopped, was an oval brass plate that had not been there earlier. I could trust my memory: I certainly had not overlooked it. Previously there had been nothing interrupting the upper portion of the wooden frame. I looked around and checked the doors that I had already passed, and then the ones in front of me. Of the ten of them eight now had such plates—five on the left and three on the right. The plates on the two remaining right-hand doors were plastic and depicted a woman's and a man's shoe; they were the only ones that had been there when I had passed down the corridor the first time.

I returned to the elevator, then moved slowly from one door to the next, looking at the plates. They all had eight-digit numbers. These didn't mean anything to me. At first glance they were not special nor was there any progression, expect that they started with the same two digits: one and nine. Having reached the end, I took out my cell phone and started taking pictures of them. I could analyze them later.

I had been in the restroom for no more than ten minutes, but that was long enough to install these plates. There were no visible screws, which meant that they were glued on. I could try to remove one or all of them, but I had no reason to do so.

Had it been any other situation, I would not completely dismiss the highly unlikely possibility that during the precise time that I was in the restroom, members of the National Library maintenance staff had installed the plates in this part of the third underground level, with these very unusual inscriptions. However, today such a coincidence was out of the question. Only the members of the secret society could be behind this.

I had no clue what they wanted to achieve. They obviously had access even to restricted areas of the National Library, regardless of whether it was with the help of the administrator and her deputy, or unrelated to them. They were following me, so they had taken advantage of my time in the restroom to leave me this message, the meaning of which eluded me completely.

I pressed the elevator call button. The doors opened immediately, but this didn't mean that the car had been here the entire time since my arrival from the lower level. The Grand Master's people could have called it from somewhere, taken it to this level, finished the job, then retreated, sending back the empty elevator. If this was not the case, then they had arrived in another elevator. There was certainly more than one leading to the shelter.

I had no more reason to stay here, so I entered the car and pressed the zero button. As the doors closed I glanced at the corridor one more time. There were no more changes. When the two halves of the door parted soon after at the ground floor, I faced a welcome committee. In addition to Senka Veselinović and Stanislav Mirić, there were also the girl with the mole on the tip of her nose and the young man who had had a tattooed ear.

27

"You were down there for quite a while, Inspector Lukić," said Mirić. "We were starting to get worried."

"You could have come down to see what was going on."

"We would have done very soon, had you not appeared," said Agent Veselinović.

"Luckily, I wasn't in any trouble, because if I had been, how could I call for help? It's questionable whether there is any cell coverage four levels underground, and even if there is—I don't know your phone numbers."

"We can fix that immediately." Mirić took his telephone out and with his thumb started typing on the small keypad. A moment later there was a ring in my pocket. "There, you now have my number. Although you didn't really need it. We would have been in contact even if you had called someone else."

"Ah, yes. How could I forget that? Eavesdropping in the spirit of true cooperation."

"Would I have told you if it was eavesdropping? We're only keeping an open line with you so that we can come to your aid if need be. Precisely in the spirit of true cooperation."

"By the way," the girl spoke again, "the underground levels of the National Library are equipped with microrelays. Network coverage is as good as it is above ground."

"That won't be of any use to me. I don't think I'll have any more business at the Department of Old and Rare Books."

"How is that?" Mirić asked. "Nothing has been resolved here, quite the contrary. Everything has become more complicated with the disappearance of Miss Šuvaković and the incunabulum."

I thought of asking how he knew all that. Mrs. Ognjanović hadn't told anyone except me. But I had just been given the answer. The microrelays obviously had another purpose, besides ensuring cell phone coverage.

"Her disappearance is the conclusion of the second act in a performance being put on by the secret society. They did the same at the City Cemeteries Administration. The main purpose was to deliver these books to me. The rest is there to create the illusion of mystery."

"The illusion is outstanding. Like the archivist, the deputy seems actually to have magically disappeared. We have the National Library under tight surveillance. She did not leave the building. She is actually in the Department of Old and Rare Books."

"Then search it and you will find her. And the false incunabulum too."

Agent Mirić stared at me for several moments.

"We checked all the places where she could hide. She's not there. And there is no incunabulum, genuine or fake."

It was pointless to ask how they had checked it without being detected, or how they even knew about all the places. He most likely would not have told me, despite the unreserved cooperation between us.

"We're going around in circles," I said. "You are still underestimating the Grand Master, and he feels so superior that he is toying with us." I took out the two pieces of paper from my pocket and handed them to Mirić. "This is what he placed under the windshield wipers of my car while we were at the City Cemeteries Administration. There's no need to check the cameras—you won't see anything."

The other three gathered around Mirić and gazed at the supposed tickets.

"The handwriting is the same as that on the envelopes," said the girl with the mole.

I nodded. "That's right. It seems that even that wasn't enough, so he continued his toying just now. While I was in the restroom on the third underground level, his people placed brass plates with numbers on the surrounding doors. I suspect that they did this to send me on a wild goose chase to make some sense of them. You can try for yourselves if you want—the plates are still down there."

Mirić nodded to the other pair without a word and they headed to the elevator, which was still at the ground floor.

"So, that's what kept you," said Agent Veselinović. "I was just wondering. . . ."

"I don't know what it's like for secret agents, but ordinary police inspectors occasionally have the need to visit the restroom."

"I'd like to take this for the moment, if you have no objections," said Mirić, holding up the two pieces of paper.

"Be my guest. Do you perhaps have a sample of the Grand Master's handwriting somewhere on file?"

"I don't know. I would have to check. However, let's assume that you are right and that he is the person pulling the strings. There's one thing I don't understand. Why would he send you the books that he himself is so interested in?"

I shrugged. "I have no idea. There is surely some reason. And I guess it will have to be revealed when he finally delivers the last, fourth volume to me."

I expected them to respond to this, but no one said a word. We spent about two minutes in silence. Once I glanced at the otherwise curious receptionist. She kept her head down. It looked like she didn't dare raise her eyes in our direction.

The silence was interrupted by the elevator doors opening. The young woman and man came out of the cabin.

"There are no plates above the doors in the corridor," she said, shaking her head.

"So they removed them after I left," I said. "It doesn't matter. I took pictures of them."

I took out my cell phone and flipped through the menus. When the first photo appeared on the screen it took great effort for me to keep a steady face. I was saved from my predicament by a sudden ringing. I removed the picture with a quick swipe and answered the call.

28

"Gvozden Vidojević is calling for you again," Bumbaković said to me. "He says it's urgent. He sounds upset."

"Patch me through."

"Inspector Lukić?" said the old poet in a trembling voice.

"Yes, Mr. Vidojević."

"My Sofija . . . She's gone."

Under different circumstances I would probably have asked a question; the way things were I just responded "I'll be right there." I put the phone back in my pocket, then turned to the agents. "As you've heard"—I pointed to their barely visible earpieces—"we have another disappearance: Mrs. Sofija Vidojević, the disabled wife of the man who received the third volume of *The Compendium of the Dead*."

"A new illusion of mystery?" Mirić said calmly, without irony.

"We'll see," I responded, then hurried towards the glass door.

"Send us the pictures of the plates," Agent Veselinović shouted after me.

Without stopping, I turned and nodded.

I left the National Library and went to the car. There were now more free parking spaces around. I sat behind the wheel and took out my cell phone. I was in a hurry to see Mr. Vidojević, but this took precedence. Before anything else, I had to see the other seven photos taken in the corridor on the third underground level. It would only take a few seconds.

The pictures passed quickly because it was easy to make out what I was interested in. The change was significant: the numbers had been halved. Instead of the eight digits I had seen with my own eyes, the phone camera had captured four-digit numbers. At first glance, I would say that it was the second half that was lost, because the numbers still started with "19."

I paused briefly at the last photo, then entered the instructions for all eight of them to be sent to Agent Mirić's cell phone. I put the phone back in my pocket, started the engine and drove to the parking exit. The guard was standing by the ramp. As I passed by him he grinned from ear to ear and gave me a military-style salute.

Regardless of how skillful the Grand Master was at creating illusions, he could not have been behind this. Perhaps through hypnosis he could make me believe that I was seeing something that was not there, but when had he the opportunity to hypnotize me? There was not a living soul in the corridor or the restroom, and in the attic of the City Cemeteries Administration Building, which was the only place where we had met today, we were in the dark the entire time. I guessed it wasn't feasible to hypnotize someone in the dark.

No, what had happened above the Department of Old and Rare Books was not possible. And the impossible could be pulled off only by someone who influences our reality from another reality. I finally had to accept what I alone had stubbornly dismissed this morning, when everything had started—that realities were crossing again, and that in the other one someone was once again writing a novel that was set in our reality.

I should have realized this right after the first very obvious impossibility—the episode in the elevator at the Police Headquarters—but all this time I had been trying to explain it away. Quite rightly, I had been criticized for my stubbornness. I had been even more persistent in my attempts to convince the Grand Master that it was he who had been organizing the intricate performances in order to deliver the unusual books to me, even though it was simpler to assume that these, too, displayed signs of interference by the author.

Until now I had hesitated to accept that these were once again his actions, primarily because the purpose of them eluded me. It was the same this time. Why would he suddenly decide to make it clear to me that he was pulling the strings?

That was, presumably, the purpose of this game involving the disappearing digits in the photos. Or perhaps not? That is to say—perhaps it wasn't only that. What else could it be? I couldn't know until I had the chance to take a closer look a the numbers. If there was any meaning whatsoever, that was the only place where it could be concealed.

My conscience pricked me for betraying the young people from the National Security Agency. They had been fair to me. I should let them know that the photos I had sent them did not correspond to what I had seen on the plates. Very well, I told myself, I won't keep it from them. I'll just delay telling them for a little while, until I get a chance to look into the matter. Soon, I hope.

29

Once again there were no empty parking spaces in front of 14 Oak Street, so as before, I left the car in the parking lot of the adjacent building. In the upper left corner, the first and fourth windows were now open. An old lady had just made her way up to the glass front door, leading a white poodle on a leash.

In Mr. Vidojević's building I was once again greeted by semi-darkness and the same acid odor. I ran up the stairs and rang the old-fashioned doorbell. An eye instantly appeared in the large peephole, as though the old poet had been standing right next to the door. He still had on his dark red robe, bow tie and worn-out leather slippers.

"Come in, Inspector Lukić."

As he stepped back to let me through, he tried to smile, but it came out as a grimace. He closed the door behind me and led me down the corridor. The shelves, which completely covered the walls, were packed with books. The only illumination came from a weak light bulb which hung from the middle of the high ceiling. The air was dry and dusty, with a prevailing odor of stale paper.

At the end of the corridor we turned left into the study. Here, too, shelves full of books covered all the walls. The few pieces of furniture were pushed towards the center of the room: a desk buried in a disarray of papers, books and magazines, a worn-out dark red plush love seat, a matching armchair, a chair that seemed very flimsy. The blinds were lowered at an angle on both windows, and the soft light was provided by a desk lamp with a green shade, and a floor lamp in the opposite corner with a yellow one.

"Please," said Mr. Vidojević, indicating the armchair.

I settled down in it. For a moment he seemed to have doubts as to where to sit, then he took the other chair, which made a cracking noise.

"What happened?" I asked.

He shrugged and shook his head.

"I don't know . . . I don't understand. . . ."

"Tell me everything that you know."

"Someone rang the bell. Sofija and I were here. I was at the desk, she over there—in her wheelchair." He pointed towards the left-hand window. "She likes to sit there, although she won't let me raise the blinds. . . ." He fell silent for a moment. "I went to see who it was. I looked through the peephole—there was no one. I thought that it might be kids; they sometimes ring the bell and run away. I was on my way back, when I heard the doorbell again. I immediately opened the door. Again—no one. I looked down the stairwell—everything was deserted. I was about to close the door, when I noticed two copies of *Small Poems of Death* on the doormat. You can imagine how delighted I was—three books in one day."

He looked at me as though expecting me to respond. I nodded.

"I have received deliveries like this before," he continued. "People know what I collect. When they come across the book somewhere, they buy it and bring it to me, but they won't give it to me in person. As I've told you—they don't want any reward. In most cases they place the books in the mailbox. On two occasions they left them on the doorstep, like today. Once they rang the bell and quickly went off, the second time they just left it. I brought the books inside to show them to Sofija. She was also very glad. Then I went to the cellar to put them away. When I came back. . . ."

His voice trembled, then he fell silent. Not wanting to rush him, I waited for him to pull himself together.

"When I came back, Sofija was gone. I first thought that she had gone to a different room. In the wheelchair she moves around the apartment with ease. Outside I always push her. But she was nowhere to be found. I looked everywhere, the apartment isn't big. . . ."

"Did you lock the door before going to the basement?"

"No, I didn't. I never do. That would be insulting to Sofija."

"There's something I don't understand. . . ." I paused. "How long has Mrs. Vidojević been in the wheelchair?"

"Since the publication of *Small Poems of Death.* She didn't only stop speaking, but also stopped using her legs."

"So, medically there are no problems with her legs, she just refuses to use them?" I asked.

He looked at me for several moments without speaking.

"What are you trying to say?"

"I'm trying to establish whether she was capable of leaving here on her own, while you were absent."

"Physically she is, but she would never do that. You don't know Sofija. She wouldn't get up and walk even if the apartment was on fire and I was out, and there was no one else to come to her rescue."

"Perhaps there is something that she considers worse than death by fire, something that would make her change her mind."

"What could that be? As you can see, everything is normal here, except that Sofija is gone. And I was in the cellar for no more than five or six minutes."

"It didn't have to be something external. Perhaps it was something within her. Mrs. Vidojević is obviously a woman with a very . . . particular . . . personality."

The old poet shook his head.

"You're on the wrong track, Inspector. Sofija truly is an exceptional woman—would she have been my muse my entire life otherwise? But she did not leave here on her own two feet. If she had, why would she have taken the wheelchair with her? It is also gone."

Of course, I should have noticed that, but somehow I had overlooked it.

"All right, so what do you think happened?"

"Someone took Sofija away in the wheelchair. They brought me the books to lure me out of the apartment. They knew that I would take them to the cellar straight away. They used my absence to get their hands on Sofija." His voice fluttered once again. "I only hope that they didn't hurt her in order to subdue her. Had she resisted while being taken out, I would have heard it from the cellar. I had left the main door open. But everything was quiet. . . ."

"If it is a kidnapping, as you believe, then we must

first try to figure out why she was abducted. I have to ask you—are you wealthy? Perhaps the kidnappers are hoping for a ransom."

"My dear Inspector, you of all people know about literature. Have you ever heard of a wealthy poet? Everything anyone could hope for from me are these books here." He smiled sourly. "And the ones in the cellar. And no one would resort to kidnapping for that."

"Is there anyone who wants to harm you? Are you at odds with anyone? After greed, revenge is the most common reason for abduction."

He shook his head. "I've never clashed with anyone. No one has reason to seek revenge against me."

"What else could it be? Do you have any suspicions?"

He looked at me silently for several moments. When he spoke again his voice was softer.

"Envy."

I thought I hadn't heard him well. "Excuse me?"

"Envy. They envy me because of Sofija."

"Who?" I asked confusedly.

"Other poets. Each and every one of them. No one has such a muse."

Now it was I who was without words for a few moments.

"Did any of them ever say anything to that effect?"

"They didn't have to. I know. Poets are very, very envious."

"All right, perhaps they envy you, but that would hardly give cause for abduction. At least I have not heard of such a case in criminology. And if my memory serves me, there are no instances in the history of literature of muses being abducted out of envy, either."

"So why then would someone kidnap Sofija?" The old man's face seemed to shatter into a dozen pieces. He was on the verge of breaking down in tears.

"We should know that very soon."

"Soon?"

"Yes. Kidnappers usually call after a short while to state their demands. Until then we can't do much. Stay here and wait for their call, then inform me immediately. Don't do anything on your own."

I got up out of the armchair, as did Mr. Vidojević from his chair, which made a cracking noise again.

"Do you think they will . . . harm . . . my Sofija?"

I shook my head. "They won't, don't worry. They wouldn't be able to achieve their aim that way. In any case—who would dare harm a muse?"

I went into the corridor. The old poet followed me. I was already at the front door when he spoke again.

"How is you investigation going, Inspector?"

"Investigation?"

"You know, the envelope with your name on it. Did you find out why it was left in my cellar?"

"I haven't yet, but I'm working on it. It should be cleared up soon too."

30

Just as eight months earlier, I felt a brief weakness as I approached the parking lot in front of 12 Oak Street. The ensuing rumble in my stomach reminded me that I hadn't eaten anything since the morning. Events had followed one after another, without giving me the chance to catch my breath. I looked at my wristwatch—seventeen minutes to five. I hadn't realized it was already so late.

I unlocked the door and settled down in the seat. Usually at the end of the day I stop by the office. There are always some technical tasks that need to be attended to. Today I could skip it and go straight home, but I still headed down to the Police Headquarters. I wouldn't stay long; I had promised Ms. Mirković that I would pop in. I also wanted to take a look at the pictures of the numbered plates from the National Library, and the archives, which I couldn't access remotely, could be useful for that.

If the disappearance of Mrs. Vidojević had been a regular case, there would have been a simple solution: the eccentric lady had simply wanted to go for a walk, and because she was obstinate she didn't just go out, which would have been simplest, but she also quietly carried the wheelchair down to the street, so that her husband wouldn't hear her through the open basement door. She had then ridden in it somewhere, or pushed it empty. This would have been quite typical for a muse who had suddenly decided not to speak or walk until her poor husband collected up all the copies of his poetry collection, which for who knows what reason she had suddenly found displeasing.

This, however, could not be a regular case because the envelope with my name on it, which had been left in the cellar, did not fit anywhere.

If it was part of the performance by the Grand Master, the disappearance of the muse would have been devised primarily to confuse me; I would struggle to find some connection between the delivery of the third volume of *The Compendium of the Dead* and her alleged kidnapping. My search would be impeded by the excellent actor playing the role of Mr. Vidojević. He seemed very convincing as the poet completely spellbound by his capricious wife.

This too, however, was not possible. Again the envelope did not fit anywhere. The Grand Master did not have any reason to leave it for me, since he himself was also trying to get his hands on what was in it. The first volume had gotten away from him, by his own admission, because the guard, Rabrenović, was not wakeful enough. The second one had appeared in a place that was highly inaccessible, even for his secret society. The third one, however, would have been within his reach had the actor in the role of Mr. Vidojević been his man.

The envelopes did not create problems only if they had been sent by the author. The mysterious books in them were intended for me—and they had reached me. Albeit, they did not remain in my possession, but that wasn't important at the moment. This, however, raised a number of other questions: Why was I getting the books? If there were actually supposed to be four of them, as the Grand Master claimed, where was the last one? What was the purpose of the other events that had accompanied the appearance of the books? All three incidents had ended with a mysterious disappearance—first Mr. Trpimirović, the archivist, then Miss Šuvaković, the Deputy Administrator of the Department of Old and Rare Books, and finally Mrs. Vidojević, the poet's wife. How did these people disappear? Where were they now? What were these episodes supposed to achieve?

And finally, the most difficult of all questions: what was the sense of the totality, of everything that had happened since the morning? What kind of a novel was the author writing?

There was no time to dive into these questions because I had just entered the garage at the Police Headquarters. At this hour there were numerous free spaces, so I parked the car quite near the elevator and the entrance to the basement section of the building. Stepping into the corridor I looked at my watch: eight minutes to five. I knocked on the door to the lab and entered.

Inside I came across two female and one male lab technicians. They were getting ready to call it a day. All three of them looked at me curiously.

"Is Ms. Mirković still here?" I asked.

"No, she isn't," answered the younger of the two ladies, a slender dark-haired woman with thick eyebrows. "She just went home. She left a message for you. She said she would see you later."

I looked at her confusedly. "When later?"

The technician shrugged, as though apologizing. "I don't know, Inspector."

31

IT WAS ONLY AFTER exiting the car on the fifth floor that I realized I had not paid attention to which elevator I was getting into in the garage. I rode the left one, but hopefully that no longer mattered. The author was unlikely to play with the elevator anymore. He would only be repeating himself, and that is not a mark of good writing. Regardless of the type of detective novel he had come up with this time, above all he would still have to make sure that the writing was good.

I was already reaching into my pocket to retrieve the office key, when I remembered that in my haste I had not locked the door. I entered, sat down at the desk and turned on the computer. While waiting for the system to boot up, I looked around the room. The rays of the low sun filled it with a soft light. Everything appeared as usual.

I took out my cell phone and transferred the eight photos from the third underground level of the National Library to the hard drive, and then on the big screen I studied the images of the brass plates. I could not determine whether the phone's camera had seen slightly smaller plates than I had, or perhaps their size was the same, while the illusion that they were smaller was because the digits on them were larger. In any case, there was no indication that any of the digits were missing; there was exactly space for four digits on the plates.

I didn't have to look at the images for very long; there were no details that I could examine. The only thing left was to analyze the numbers more carefully. I opened a text editor and copied the eight four-digit numbers in the order in which I had taken the pictures.

The numbers on the list generated this way were jumbled: 1948, 1950, 1993, 1964, 1980, 1977, 1973 and 1961. I tried to work out some pattern, but didn't learn anything except that there were four even and four odd numbers. Next I split them into two unequal groups—the five numbers that were above the doors on the left side (1950, 1964, 1977, 1973 and 1961), and the three from the right side (1948, 1993 and 1980), but no sense appeared there either.

Then I arranged them in ascending order: 1948, 1950, 1961, 1964, 1973, 1977, 1980 and 1993. I stared at the monitor for a while, trying to make out any mathematical coherence. This was not a sequence of primes—that was obvious at first glance—nor any other sequence that I was aware of, although there were not many of those, since my knowledge of mathematics was rudimentary.

Finally, not knowing what else to do, I temporarily removed the "nineteen" that was common to all the numbers, but the sequence still seemed random. As I restored the first two digits, I wondered whether I had perhaps been looking in the wrong direction. I had struggled to make some mathematical sense of the eight numbers, but maybe what linked them was of a completely different nature.

Why would the author give me a mathematical puzzle, after all? Even if I were to find some pattern, what would be the purpose? Had the case been in its infancy, one could imagine that the author was toying with me by feeding me false leads, but events had moved on a long way from their starting point, so there was no time left for such a ploy. Regardless of what he was telling me with these numbers, it certainly was not just to toy with me.

The moment that the last "nineteen" was in place, it was as though a fog had lifted from my mind, one that had previously obscured my view. Focusing on the search for a mathematical pattern, I had not seen what was staring me in the face: the numbers were years.

In my excitement I rose from the armchair, then immediately settled back into it. I had no reason to be too pleased with myself. Even if it were to turn out that I was right about the years, that was only the first step. Next came an entire series of questions and I had no clue what the answers were: What did the eight years refer to? Why was it important to the author to reveal them to me in such a enigmatic way?—and perhaps the most important one: Why had he first put four additional digits and then removed them?

I covered my face with my hands and rubbed my forehead with the tips of my fingers, in an effort to recollect what I had only briefly glimpsed in the corridor on the third underground level, but the fog had still not cleared from there. The only vague impression that appeared was that the eight-digit numbers had the same fifth digit, but I couldn't make out what it was.

I pulled up the police database search and entered the eight years. There were six-and-a-half thousand hits, although not a single one contained all the years. There were none with seven, or even six of the years. I had expected that there would be many documents, since the search was rather ambiguous. There would certainly have been far fewer of them had I been able to provide any other information, but I had absolutely nothing.

Going through the six-and-a-half thousand hits in search of a clue would take hours, so it was out of the question at the moment. In any case, it wasn't necessary for only one person to do this. Undoubtedly an entire team of experts at the National Security Agency was at that very moment busy with this same task. I was sure they would immediately let me know if they dug anything up, in the spirit of true cooperation.

I switched off the computer and the monitor. Before

returning the cell phone to my pocket I briefly illuminated the screen to see the time: five thirteen. It was as though this piece of information also reached my stomach; it started to rumble again. I left hastily, quickly locking up my office, then headed to the elevator. I smiled, thinking of how lucky I was, when the doors to the right-hand car opened without delay.

32

I PRESSED THE BUTTON for the garage. The instant the two halves of the door came together, everything went dark. I sighed. So much for being lucky, or for the author ensuring good writing and not repeating himself. Well, that was his responsibility. Let's see what he had in store for me in this magic elevator. Hopefully he would not do what he did to Ms. Mirković—keep me inside for hours, regardless of the fact that it would seem quite brief to me and I wouldn't die of starvation. No excuse in the world would save me from the trouble I'd be in if I didn't make it to the reception that Vera wanted me to attend with her.

That's when it dawned on me that perhaps I would be spared the fate of the young lab technician. There were differences between what had befallen her and what was happening now. Everything had seemed normal to the girl: the lighting was on in the elevator the entire time; the darkness was there only for the camera that was concealed behind the mirror. Furthermore, she had felt the car move, but this time it was stationary. So, a different performance awaited me.

Just as I was starting to wonder what to do—whether to wait patiently for it to begin or perhaps take out my cell phone and cast some light around me—a familiar voice broke the silence, making me flinch.

"Here we are once again in the dark, Inspector Lukić," said the Grand Master.

It seemed to me that he was standing across from me, next to the elevator door, even though that was not possible. There was no way that he could have suddenly appeared in the cabin. The voice must be coming from a speaker, although I could swear that I was hearing him directly, just like in the attic of the City Cemeteries Administration Building.

Was that perhaps the explanation for his magical disappearance from there? The Grand Master had not actually been in the attic at all, and it was the guard who had briefly held the flashlight pointed at me. That is why everything had transpired in sightlessness.

Once again I thought of turning on the phone screen and solving the mystery, but I gave up on it because there were more pressing matters. He had some reason for insisting on acting this way. He might have retreated if I'd tried to expose him; that could wait. Finding out why he had appeared now was more important than whether he was in the elevator or not.

"Feel free to turn on the light," I responded. "I have no objections."

"All in good time. It's better like this for the time being."

"You don't want me to see something?"

"Not you. There are other curious eyes."

"The camera behind the mirror? I'm blocking it. It's pointed at my back."

"It's not the only one. There are two more."

"Is that so?" I asked, honestly surprised.

"You mustn't allow yourself to be naive. The Agency will never tell you everything, even when it is actually cooperating with you."

"And what about sound? The darkness hasn't muted it. Don't you care that they can hear us?"

"They can't. We've taken care of that, of course."

"I assume you are aware that they are keeping a close eye on me. They know that I got into this elevator, but that it is still on the fifth floor. They will be here any moment to check what's going on."

"They won't. Don't underestimate us, Inspector Lukić. They think that you are still in the office."

"It seems that you have become more powerful than the National Security Agency."

"Now you're overestimating us. No one is more powerful than the Agency. We are just taking advantage of an opportunity. They are convinced that their main opponent is on the other side, so they're not paying much attention to us."

"They finally convinced me too, even though I had claimed for a long time that you were pulling the strings of everything that has happened today."

"I was the first one to tell you that it wasn't the case. You should have trusted me."

"If my memory serves me well, I don't have much reason to trust you. Wouldn't you tell me the same even if you were behind everything, but you wanted to keep it secret?"

"Nevertheless, I am glad that we are no longer your main suspects."

"You might not be the main suspects, but you are far from innocent. You are still making my life difficult. What is the purpose of this new ambush? What do you want from me?"

"You know very well what we want from you."

"*The Compendium of the Dead*? I don't have it. You know that. The three volumes that I received were taken by the National Security Agency. The fourth never appeared. I was just on my way home. I'm done for today. This entire case is not my concern anymore. If the volume that you are hoping for appears somewhere, you will have to discuss it with one of my colleagues on the next shift."

"Ah, if life were only that simple, that your worries stop when you punch out. Of course everything is still your concern. You are up to your neck in this case, whether you like it or not. And the fourth volume is just about to appear. Believe me when I say this, even if you won't believe the rest. I organized this meeting so that I could warn you one more time. Soon, when you find yourself holding *The Compendium of the Dead*, don't try to do anything with it on your own. You will cause immeasurable harm. Hand it over to us immediately—and finally you will be able to walk away from this case. Only then will it actually cease to be your concern."

I sighed. "It seems there's no point in telling you. . . ."

"I was afraid that you would be stubborn about this. All right, what can I do—you leave me no choice. Unfortunately, now I have to threaten you, even though the entire matter could have been settled without that. If you don't cooperate, we will have to relocate someone dear to you to *The Compendium of the Dead*. Someone very dear. Then you will scramble in panic to give us the books since you yourself will not be able to bring back that person from the *Compendium*. . . ."

I felt the blood rush to my face. I swiftly reached for the cell phone in my jacket pocket, but I wasn't fast enough. I had only got it half-way out when the lights went on and illuminated the car, which was empty except for me. The elevator departed for the garage at the same moment.

33

Under any other circumstances I would have used the descent, at least while I was alone, to try to find the National Security Agency's other two cameras. I would hardly be able to achieve anything in less than half a minute, and it was also possible that the Grand Master was not telling the truth, but I would not have been able to resist the temptation. Now, however, that was the least of my concerns. With fumbling thumbs I found Vera's number in my phonebook and called her.

It took great effort to keep a calm voice.

"How are you?" I asked, when she picked up.

"All right," she said, a little cautiously, as though surprised by my question. "And you?"

"I am too," I responded, then added with slight hesitation "More or less."

"You don't usually call me from your work phone."

"It was the one that was in my hand."

She was silent for a bit.

"Will you be home soon?"

"I'm on my way to the garage. I'll be at home shortly."

"Very well. . . ." she said, as though nothing better had come to mind.

Now it was my turn to fall briefly silent.

"You don't have any reason to go out until I get there?"

"No. . . ."

"Very well," I repeated in the same tone. "I'll see you then."

"See you. . . ."

The elevator doors opened onto the garage as I was returning the phone to my pocket. I reached my car in three steps. The moment I started the engine, my phone rang. I took it out again and glanced at the screen. I didn't recognize the number, but I knew who was calling.

"What happened, Inspector Lukić?" Agent Mirić asked.

"Wait a second." I took the phone headset out of the glove compartment, connected it to the telephone, dropped it on the adjacent seat and put the earphones in my ears. I had to drive fast, so I needed both hands; I could not be holding my cell phone in one. "I had a close encounter with the Grand Master," I said as I sped out of the garage.

"How close?"

"It seemed to me that he was with me in the elevator. In the dark."

This was followed by a pause while Mirić gave someone brief instructions. I couldn't understand what he was saying.

"All right, we'll talk about it later. Is Miss Gavrilović in danger?"

"Maybe. . . ."

"We'll be there before you. I'll call you back soon."

"Thank you."

Barely three minutes had passed when he called me again.

"We have the house under surveillance. And we will be there shortly."

"Do you want to meet?"

"You'd better hurry over to Miss Gavrilović. We'll be close by."

"All right." I paused. "How is it that the Grand Master is better than you at dealing with the elevators at the Police Headquarters?"

"I don't know. We are investigating exactly what happened. So, you didn't see him?"

"I didn't. I could swear that he appeared in the elevator as soon as the lights went out, and disappeared a moment before the lights came back on, but as you know, he is a very skilled illusionist. By the way, he told me that you have two more cameras, in addition to the one behind the mirror, in the right-hand car."

"We do," he responded, after a slight hesitation.

"You didn't mention them to me."

"I would have if there had been any reason to. What did the Grand Master want this time?"

"The same as last time—*The Compendium of the Dead*."

"Had he forgotten that we have the books?"

"No, he hadn't, of course. He isn't all that interested in the first three. He seems convinced that he will not have any difficulty getting a hold of them when he needs them. He cares about the fourth one."

"The fourth one is still nowhere to be found." He became silent for a moment. "Right?"

"Right, but he believes that it will turn up any time now. He threatened to kill someone very close to me. That way he would ensure that I handed the book over to him, because I would not be able to bring that person back from the dead using the *Compendium* on my own. And there is no one closer to me than Vera."

I could hear Mirić sigh over the phone.

"We'll move Miss Gavrilović somewhere immediately. She'll be safe, don't worry."

I thought of responding that I was still worried, that this event in the elevator was not the first time the Grand Master had outwitted the Agency, but I refrained. The young lead agent was doing everything he could. Even his significantly more experienced predecessor would not have had any greater success.

"Unfortunately, we will not be able to move her immediately. At seven o'clock we have to be at a reception that is very important to her. Can you provide a security detail for us?"

"Of course. Where is the reception being held?"

"I don't know. A car will be sent to pick us up at six thirty."

"Ask Miss Gavrilović."

"She doesn't know either."

"All right. Who is holding it?"

"She doesn't know that either. . . ."

Several moments passed in silence.

"The reception is very important to her, and she doesn't know anything about it?"

"It's a long story. We don't have time for it now. I'm almost there."

"Has it occurred to you that the Grand Master might

be behind it all? That would be the easiest way for him to achieve his goal."

"It has," I lied. "We'll talk more about this. I'll speak to Vera."

"All right. We've freed a parking spot for you in front of the entrance. Do you see it?"

I was just entering Vera's street. "I see it. Thank you. By the way, have you made any sense of the numbers on the plates at the National Library?"

"Still nothing. We're working on it."

34

After parking the car I removed the earphones from my ears and the miniature jack from the cell phone, then placed the phone in my pocket. Even though my inclination towards neatness was quietly protesting, I did not waste any time returning the headset to the glove compartment. I briskly opened the car door and was already with my left foot on the ground, when a sudden thought stopped me mid-stride. I remained frozen in that position for several moments—neither out nor in.

I had a ghastly impression that there'd been a certain inconsistency in my short conversation with Agent Mirić. Something wasn't right, but I couldn't immediately put my finger on it. Pressured by haste I had almost given up, when it finally dawned on me. I jumped out of the car and ran to the building's entrance.

The first time we had met today, Mirić had told me that they hadn't let me out of their sight for the past eight months, since the "Grand Manuscript" case, and that this morning the alarm had been raised after I'd received the call from the City Cemeteries Administration. This meant among other things that they had been monitoring all the telephones that I use.

I had spoken on my private cell phone to Vera about

the unusual offer that she had received, as well as what had happened later, including the mysterious reception that we were both invited to. Mirić would have been aware of that, but a moment ago it had seemed as though he didn't have a clue. There was no reason for him to pretend. He was aware that I knew that my phones were bugged; we had even mentioned it once.

How was this possible? The only explanation was that someone had foiled the Agency in monitoring my private cell phone. The question was not so much who could do it, but rather why. The Grand Master had demonstrated on several occasions that he was capable of performing incredible communications feats, but why would he resort to something so complex and risky?

Mirić himself had offered the answer. The Grand Master was actually the anonymous wealthy eccentric collector who had massively overpaid for the books and inventory from the Papyrus, and now he was holding the gala reception.

I had lied to Mirić, telling him that I had considered the possibility. It hadn't crossed my mind to connect what was happening today, apparently unrelatedly, with Vera and me. However, I should have put it together. Now, looking back, it didn't require any special insightfulness; actually, it was quite obvious.

Why did the Grand Master need the reception? That wasn't difficult to guess either. He had to have an audience for the miracle he was planning on performing—bringing people back from the dead using *The Compendium of the Dead*. And who better to resurrect than someone who had just died before the eyes of the large audience? Since one could not count on a natural death, however, it was necessary to resort to a violent one.

Someone needed to be murdered. Not just anyone, because the performance would sink into anticlimax—

but someone whose death would touch everyone profoundly. Someone young, beautiful, innocent, who embodied the very fullness of life; an exceptional woman whose subsequent resurrection would be a unique triumph of the Grand Master.

Vera. . . .

I raced up the stairs, skipping two or three at a time.

The seven-story building that Vera lived in had an elevator, of course, but I used it only when I was with her. Even though she knew that I didn't take it when I was alone, she respectfully avoided teasing me about it, even though she otherwise enjoyed taunting me. Her conscience would not let her in this case. After what she had put me through with *The Grand Manuscript*, I was sure she felt at least partially to blame for my fear of elevators.

After returning eight months ago, Vera no longer shrunk from my study. She had seen the original in the other reality, so the copy no longer upset her. We could have lived in my place, we even spent two or three weeks in my apartment, but then she still proposed that we move to hers. She said that she felt more intimate there. Since it was all the same to me, and I also spent a lot less time at home than she did—I agreed.

For a while I didn't know what to do about my apartment. I could have sold it, but it didn't feel right. I was even less inclined to rent it out. In the end I didn't do anything. The apartment sat empty, and we went there from time to time for two or three days, for a change. Even though Vera didn't complain, I knew that she wasn't entirely pleased with this arrangement. She would occasionally tell me, in a teasing way, that I was keeping the apartment because I wasn't sure whether I wanted to stay with her.

On the third floor I realized that I couldn't have used the elevator even if I had wanted to. Two repairmen in dark blue overalls were busy working on it. I had almost run past them, when the one who was crouched down briefly looked up at me. I recognized him as one of the two young men who had carried out Inspector Vesić's body, and whom I had seen this morning, elegantly dressed, in the attic of the City Cemeteries Administration Building.

Panting, I stopped in front of the door to the middle apartment on the fourth floor, and started speedily going through my pants pockets, searching for the key. The door opened before I found it. Vera first looked at me speechlessly for several moments, then moved aside so that I could enter.

We stood across from each other in the hallway for a short while, then I hugged her tightly. We stayed like that for some time. Vera was the first to break the silence.

"Have you eaten anything since this morning?"

I looked at her confusedly, as though she were asking me something utterly bizarre. Finally I shook my head.

"Come." She nodded towards the dining room.

"No, stop. I have to tell you. . . ."

"You can tell me while you're eating."

And so I ate and talked. I condensed nearly nine hours of the long day into twenty-five minutes. I didn't leave anything out. Not even the suspicion about what role she was to play in the Grand Master's performance. It was only after Vera had cleared the table that I realized that I had not noticed what I had been eating.

35

I STAYED SEATED IN the dining room while Vera was in the kitchen. I was suddenly overcome by fatigue. I had not had a break since morning. The work of a police inspector is dynamic and tense, but events this packed together exist only in novels. That is why even the digest could not be any shorter.

Talking between bites exhausted me additionally. Also, after the large meal, it was as though all the blood from my head had rushed to my stomach, and I was overcome by sluggishness, drowsiness. It seemed very tempting just to sit like this, staring in front of me and listening to the muffled noises from the kitchen. I was, however, aware that this idyll could not last. The extraordinary day was most definitely not over. The main excitement was yet to come.

Vera returned carrying two steaming cups of coffee. She placed them on the table and sat down next to me. She still had not said anything about all that she had heard. She had gone to the kitchen not so much to do the dishes and make coffee, as to gather her thoughts. She still appeared contemplative.

"I should have let you know earlier," I said, "but for a long time I wasn't sure what was actually going on. Anyway, cell phones are not reliable. . . ."

"I should have realized it myself. My entire life I've ridiculed people willing to believe even the most incredible nonsense if it suits them, and now that is exactly how I have behaved. I mean really—a 'wealthy eccentric collector'. . . ."

"You can't blame yourself. Anyone would have done the same. Nothing seemed suspicious to me either."

The shadow of a smile passed across her face. I thought that she might make a remark about my insightfulness—that topic never ceased to entertain her—but she immediately turned serious again.

"Perhaps you can learn something more from the Samardžić Law Offices, the broker. They wouldn't tell me anything about the buyer, but I guess they would have to share it with the police."

"If not with the police, then certainly with the National Security Agency. It is unlikely, however, that they know very much. I'm sure that the Grand Master was careful. He had no reason to handle it personally.

One of his people took care of that job—anonymously and discreetly. In any case, all that isn't important any more."

"But could you at least dig up where the reception is being held? It was important to the attorneys that I commit to both of us attending, as though they were personally interested in it. Perhaps they do know something."

"There's no more time. And there's no need. We'll learn about the location of the reception from the chauffeur who comes to pick us up. He will have to know where to take us."

Vera didn't reply. The seriousness on her face seemed to change to concern. I quickly tried to calm her.

"Don't worry. I'm with you now. I won't leave you even for a moment until all this is over. The people from the Agency are also here, all around us. You're completely safe."

She continued to watch me in silence, her expression unchanged.

"The Grand Master can't touch you. First of all, we don't have to go to that reception at all. Also, he won't try anything until he has all the parts of *The Compendium of the Dead*, and the last one has still not shown up. I would know if it had. The first three books were sent to me. There is no reason for the fourth one not to be."

She looked at me for several more seconds, then she said something completely unexpected.

"Why don't you take a bath? It would do you good, and you need to change if we end up going to the reception."

I looked at her questioningly.

"Come on. I'll run you a bath."

I followed her into the bathroom without asking any questions. We didn't have a bathtub, only a shower.

She closed the door after us, then turned on the hot water in the shower. The room started to fill with steam.

"I saw this in a movie once," she said softly, with a bashful smile, as though justifying her action. I had to strain my ears to understand her over the running water. "Is it possible that the Grand Master is listening in on us in the apartment?"

"I don't know. I don't believe so, but it isn't entirely impossible. Why?"

"I have something to tell you that definitely is not for his ears."

She didn't tell me immediately. The mist around us was getting thicker. Vera seemed to fade away into it, even though she was standing only one step from me.

"The fourth volume has appeared," came a whisper from the mist.

"Where? When?" I responded with questions, also softly.

"Here. Less than an hour ago."

"Here?"

"Not in our apartment but in the basement. The small apartment of our neighbor, Mr. Ljuštanović, the retired speleologist, whose wife died about fifteen years ago, and he still visits her grave every day. Remember him?"

"Yes. The old man who raves about life underground. His windows are full of yellow flowers."

"That's right. He was leaving for his afternoon walk, and found an envelope with your name on his doormat. He brought it up immediately."

"Where did you put it?"

"On the shelf with the books from the weirdoes. I was convinced that was what it was. That's why I didn't even call you. It even crossed my mind that the old man had made up that he had found the envelope in front of his door. He needed an excuse to send you something. He does seem like a patient."

"It's good that you didn't call me. The book would already be in the hands of the Grand Master." At the last moment I stopped myself from adding: "And who knows what would have happened to you."

"Should I bring you the envelope together with your change of clothes? I can do it discreetly. They won't notice anything if there are cameras."

I turned towards the shower and turned off the water.

"There aren't any microphones or cameras. If there were, they would have immediately understood what Mr. Ljuštanović had brought and they would have been here instantly. We're safe in the apartment."

I left the bathroom and entered the small room that Vera had given me to use as a study, even though I hadn't asked her. I kept some of my books there. She had added the rest—a desk and everything else that a writer might need. She had never proposed anything to that effect. The things were there in case the need ever arose.

Vera had placed the envelope horizontally on top of the books that filled one section of the shelf. I picked it up and examined it from both sides. It did not differ in any way from the previous three. I opened it, took out the white volume and leafed through it quickly. It was identical to the others. I handed it to Vera, who had come into the room with me.

"This is what everything is revolving around this time. The new dark object of desire of the Grand Master and his band."

Vera scrutinized the book for several minutes. She felt the strange paper, smelled it, at one moment it even looked as though she might lick it, but she just held it close to her lips. Just as I had done that morning, she raised a page to the light coming through the window. She didn't say anything. When she had finished, she didn't know what to do with the volume for a moment, but finally returned it to me. I too had second thoughts before laying it down on the desk.

"Truly an unusual book," she said finally. "What will you do with it?"

I shrugged my shoulders. "I don't know. I should hand it over to the people from the Agency, but the Grand Master has hinted that he could get his hands on the volumes that are in their safe. Perhaps it is best if I leave it here for now." I pointed to the shelf from which I had taken the envelope. "It is in good company there. Also, it is better that no one finds out that it has appeared. As long as that remains the case, the Grand Master will not harm you."

Vera was silent for several moments, then she shook her head.

"Something doesn't add up, Dejan. If my murder and resurrection are supposed to be the highlight of the Grand Master's performance, why would he announce it to you during your conversation in the elevator? He not only gave away his main surprise, but also warned us."

"He had to threaten me with something in order to ensure that I would give him the fourth volume, and he knows that that is where I am most vulnerable."

"He didn't have to. If he had already expected to get a hold of the volumes from the Agency's safe, why didn't he just let you give it to the agents, and then simply take all four?"

I tried to come up with an answer quickly, but to no avail.

"I don't know."

"That's not all. The reception is scheduled for seven o'clock in the evening. How could the Grand Master be certain that he would have all the volumes in time? Look, the fourth one is still not in his hands, and there isn't much time left until seven."

I looked at her for a short while without speaking.

"What are you trying to say?"

"I mean that there is to be no performance by the

Grand Master. He only wants the fourth volume. If he gets it, he has no reason to harm me."

"Are you proposing that we hand it over to him?" I asked in disbelief.

"I propose that you give it to the Agency. Let them deal with the Grand Master."

Now I shook my head.

"I can't take that risk. The safest thing is for the book to remain here. Even if it is true that there is to be no performance by the Grand Master, he could still hurt you in order to get back at me. He said that he sees me as his main adversary. I assume he would not take it lightly if he were to suffer a third defeat, following the Last Book and the Grand Manuscript."

Vera smiled at me.

"There is no risk, Dejan. The Grand Master could not touch me even if he wanted to. I have a powerful protector."

I smiled back.

"I'm not that powerful. . . ."

"I don't mean you, but the author."

I blinked. "The author?"

"Yes. The author would never allow anything to happen to me."

"Really? How do you know?"

"I know. Trust me. I'll explain it on another occasion. There's no time to discuss that now. It's past six o'clock. Go back to the bathroom; I'll bring your clothes. I too have to get ready. Don't forget, this isn't just an ordinary reception."

"Are you sure you want us to go?"

"Pass up something like that?"

"But who is holding the reception, if it isn't the Grand Master?"

"We'll learn soon enough. Hurry up."

36

I HURRIED, BUT NOT so much that I couldn't stop at the dining room table and drink the cup of coffee in several large gulps. It was already lukewarm, but it felt very good. I could almost feel it dispel the last traces of drowsiness.

Before entering the bathroom I left the things that I would not need that evening on the dresser: my private cell phone, key ring and plastic gloves. I also pulled out of my pockets my work phone, badge and wallet, but I took them with me, to put in the other suit. Of course, I would be carrying my gun in a shoulder holster.

In front of the bathroom door I passed by Vera, who had already brought me a change of clothes. She smiled at me devilishly, then ran into the bedroom to get ready. I wasn't exactly happy about her joyfulness. What was about to happen was not to be taken lightly. It now seemed to me that this was exactly how I had acted when I agreed that we should go to the reception. I had caved in to her assertion, but what if both she and I had missed something? What if we were thoughtlessly walking into a trap that the Grand Master had set for us?

I undressed and was already in the shower when my cell phone rang. I got out and took the phone from the shelf beneath the mirror, where I had placed it with the other things.

"Agent Mirić," I said, "I was just about to call you. We have decided to attend the reception. As I have told you, a car is picking us up at six thirty. I still don't know where they are taking us. Question the chauffeur. In any case, we are counting on your security detail."

"Of course. I have some news. We have discovered the meaning of the numbers in the pictures that you took at the National Library."

"What is it?" I asked anxiously, then quickly added

"You can also tell me when we meet in a short while, if you think that it isn't safe now."

"It's safe. We're using a double secure line."

"All right. I'm listening."

"They are the birth years of the eight victims in the two cases of crossing realities; six from the first and two from the second."

The line was mute for several moments.

"Inspector Lukić?"

"I'm here. I was just thinking."

"Do you have any idea why those years were placed above the doors on the third underground level?"

This was the right moment for me to reveal what I had been keeping from them. They didn't deserve that I should act that way. They hadn't betrayed our cooperation even once. On the contrary, it was I who had done so. However, I didn't share his trust in the double secure line. One should never underestimate the Grand Master. For that reason I decided to keep to myself the appearance of the fourth volume of *The Compendium of the Dead*. He would get it as soon as we went downstairs, and I would also tell him about the numbers missing from the pictures.

"I have to think about it. We'll talk soon."

"All right."

I put down the phone and returned to the shower. I set the water temperature, then stood beneath the spray. The hot swarm of needlelike droplets stung the top of my head and my shoulders. The water first washed away only the physical deposits of the difficult day. Then it began to remove the accumulated tension and fatigue, and finally it started to scatter the wisps of fog that had settled around in my mind.

In the clarity that was gradually expanding I tried to revive the memory of what I had only glimpsed in the underground corridor at the National Library, and which had later mysteriously disappeared from the photos. I could now clearly see the first four digits, but those following them were still a blur.

I pressed the tips of my fingers against my temples, squeezed my eyes shut and bowed my head, but nothing helped. The second four digits still appeared as though through a dense condensation on the glass. Obsessed by my frustration, I crouched down. I had somehow to see past that murkiness but I didn't know how.

I was already eager to get up and exit the shower—Vera must have been annoyed by my delay—when it occurred to me that I might know a way of revealing what was hidden. If hot water could not dispel the cloudiness, perhaps cold water could.

Unlike Vera, who loved showering under cold water, I was horrified by the notion. I couldn't hesitate for a moment, otherwise I would surely change my mind. I rose quickly, grabbed the tap and moved it in the opposite direction. It took great will not to bounce to the opposite corner of the shower, out of the range of the icy stream.

I endured about ten seconds in it, although it seemed a lot longer to me. I was frozen stiff. I could barely move my hand to switch off the water. I remained shivering for a while, waiting for the heat that filled the bathroom to engulf me again.

And then it happened. As I was thawing out, the condensation on the glass dissipated and beneath it the outlines of the numbers emerged. Staring at the steam that was retreating to the shower cubicle, I clearly saw in my memory what had been beyond my reach only a moment ago.

The cold water was not the only thing responsible for this apparition. Something Agent Mirić had just said had contributed equally. "Six from the first and two from the second." The digits that had disappeared from the photos formed only two numbers: 2013 appeared six times, and 2014 appeared twice.

The years of the deaths of the eight victims from the cases of crossing realities.

Of course, I should have been pleased with myself, but the feeling of frustration came over me again. I should have recognized this back there, in the corridor. I had already seen one of the eight numbers; albeit it had a dash in the middle, but nonetheless. How many times had I stood in front of Olga's grave and looked at the numbers carved beneath her name on the tombstone: "1980-2013"?

There was a knock on the door. "Are you finished?" Vera asked impatiently.

"I'll be right out," I responded, then got out of the shower and grabbed a towel. I was only half done wiping myself when something occurred to me. I flung the towel over my shoulder and took the cell phone from the shelf. My fingers danced across the small keypad. I sent Mirić the two photos I had taken the last time I was at the City Cemeteries Administration. With them I included the text: *"Call Mrs. Leleković; have her find out from which years are the two books that are missing from the shelf. Urgently."*

As I hastily dressed, my thoughts fervently and unsuccessfully spun around the question why the years of the deaths of the eight victims in the "Last Book" and the "Grand Manuscript" cases would be erased from the photos taken in the National Library. What was the meaning of that move? What was the author trying to tell me?

Mirić's text message arrived as I was tying my necktie.

"2013 and 2014. Your limo is here."

I had received confirmation of what I had suspected, but I still wasn't satisfied. I had to ask the administrator immediately. It could not have been irrelevant which books Trpimirović had taken.

"We'll be down in a few minutes," I answered Mirić.

Vera looked at me grumpily when I came out of the bathroom. "Even I would not have taken that long."

"You only get ready in the bathroom, I also do work there." I looked her over. She was wearing a dark blue tweed suit and a matching lighter blouse. "So, that's what you've chosen."

"You don't like it?"

"On the contrary. It looks very good on you. You wore something similar when we first met, didn't you?"

"You remember? I'm impressed."

"Perhaps I'm not famous for my insightfulness, but I have an excellent memory."

"Speaking of insightfulness. . . ."

"We'll discuss that later," I interrupted. "I've received word that the limo is here. I'll just go get the white book, and we can be on our way."

Vera nodded, then went to the coat rack in the hallway to put on her coat, and I went to the study. I stopped at the door, however, and stared at the desk in confusion. The fourth volume of *The Compendium of the Dead* was not where I had left it.

37

"DID YOU TAKE THE book?" I asked Vera as I turned towards the hallway. I instantly realized that the question was redundant. Had she taken it she would have immediately told me so when I said I was going to fetch it.

"I didn't," she responded. She walked over to me as she put on her coat and looked first at the desk, then at me. "Where is it?"

"Did you hear any noise while I was in the bathroom? Anything at all?"

She shook her head. "Nothing, except the muffled sound of water."

I stepped into the study and checked the windows.

They were all closed. I did the same in the other rooms. Not a single one was open. I finally went to the apartment door and saw for myself that it was locked, with the key in the lock. Vera followed my every step.

"How could it have disappeared?" she asked.

"There are only two possibilities: the Grand Master or the author."

"How could the Grand Master enter a closed apartment without making a sound, take the book and leave, with everything teeming with people from the Agency? He is exceptionally skillful, but he's not a wizard. And how would he even know that the fourth volume was here? You said yourself that there was no surveillance."

I shrugged. "I have no idea. I know only that he should never be dismissed. I have seen that for myself many times."

"Be that as it may, there's nothing we can do about the book's disappearance now, regardless of which of them has it. In any case, we don't even need it. On the contrary, life will be simpler without it. Let someone who cares deal with it. Let's go."

"Perhaps it would better if we didn't go to that reception. . . ."

"Don't be afraid. I told you that the author is watching over us. Nothing will happen to us."

I would have continued to discourage her had she not said "Don't be afraid." This way I had no choice—was I supposed to seem like a coward? I too put on my coat, touched my gun holster under my shoulder, unlocked the door and peered outside.

The supposed elevator repairs had moved to our floor in the meantime. The lights in the corridor were off, and the only illumination came from the open elevator car, where two men in dark-blue overalls were busy. When one got up and started walking towards me, I thought it was the one I had recognized on the third floor, but it turned out to be Mirić. He had earpieces in both ears.

I opened the door, stepped into the corridor, and then signaled Vera to join me. She slipped out, turned around and quickly locked the door.

"Agent Mirić," I presented the false repairman to her.

She nodded. "I know."

I looked at her questioningly.

"He appears in my novel, remember?" she said with a smile.

Mirić also lightly bowed and smiled, and then took a small flashlight out from one of his many pockets and pointed the thin beam towards the stairwell.

He and I went in front, Vera was in the middle, and the rear was taken by the other agent, who had also stepped out of the car in the meantime. Mirić chose the stairs instead of the elevator, obviously on account of what had happened earlier at the Police Headquarters.

Despite the poor visibility, we descended at a fast pace, so I started to speak quickly and softly. I wouldn't get a better opportunity to share the new information with Mirić, without the fear that someone might overhear us. Luckily I didn't have to explain much to him.

"The fourth volume was brought to Vera by the neighbor living in the basement. He found it on his doormat this afternoon. The book is the same as the others. I was going to give it to you, but it disappeared from my desk while we were getting ready. Did you notice anything unusual?"

"Nothing. The first three volumes have also disappeared from our safe. I was notified a little while ago."

"That could not be the Grand Master. Nevertheless, we should be cautious. He's still in the game."

"I agree."

Another figure emerged silently from the darkness on the third floor and joined us at the rear of our column.

"About the numbers on the plates: there are only

four digits recorded on the photos, but I saw eight on each one down there. Now I know what the missing four digits represent—the years of death of the eight victims in the two cases of crossing realities."

"Those two that Administrator Leleković mentioned—2013 and 2014?"

"Exactly."

"Why were they removed?"

"I don't know."

On the second floor the column was joined by another member.

"The limousine and chauffeur were hired; an anonymous client. The chauffeur doesn't know where he is supposed to take you. He will get instructions en route, via GPS. He will not receive them if anyone other than the two of you gets in."

"You've checked the car?"

"We have. Everything seems clean."

"Are you ready to tail it?"

"Absolutely. Reinforcements are here. We won't lose sight of you."

In the darkness of the ground floor there were four more agents waiting for us. They were joined by two of the three from our group, and all went out in front of the door and lined the path to the street. Raising his hand, Mirić stopped me. He himself exited, while holding the fingers of his left hand to his ear and speaking softly. He looked left, right, and up. Then he gave us the signal to move.

I turned around and smiled at Vera, then took her by the hand and led her out. I couldn't see her face very well in the shadows. I positioned myself to shield her with my body as much as possible. The six agents closed ranks, and Mirić went in front of us. He quickly opened the large white rear door of the limo and stepped aside. I pushed Vera inside, then slipped in after her. The door closed instantly.

The limo set off at the same moment. It was only then that I became aware of its size. It must have been at least as long as two regular cars. We sat in the rear white leather seat and were almost two meters from the rear-facing front seat. Above the backrest was a tinted glass partition, so we couldn't see the driver. The windows around us were also tinted. Through them we could only catch glimpses of bright lights as we passed by. No sound from the outside world could be heard.

"What did I tell you?" said Vera, leaning back into the wide soft seat. "A real limo, like in the movies."

"There are several of them in the city. They are mostly rented by the *nouveau riche* to strut around in when they have something to celebrate."

"I'm sure there are also police chiefs among them."

"I wouldn't know, I'm just an ordinary inspector." I paused for a moment. "I see that you are taking everything in a spirit of fun."

"It's always more pleasant that way. Tomorrow it will be especially fun when I once again leave the house I live in—and there isn't half the National Security Agency outside protecting me."

"They may have saved your life. And mine."

"I told you not to be afraid. We are under better protection than anything the Agency can offer."

I leaned over to her ear and whispered: "Let's stick to neutral topics. We don't know who might be listening."

She scowled at me.

"Neutral? All right, here's one. At the moment we are in no hurry, so we can talk about it. Have you figured out what it is that I can finally do? What it is that I have always fantasized about? You have very little time left. The deadline expires at seven, as you are well aware. You have to give me an answer before we leave this limousine."

I sighed. "You know what my day has been like. . . ."

"Will a slightly stressful day thwart your famous insightfulness?"

"Slightly stressful?"

"Don't use the day as an excuse. Even on the most stressful of days you have to know the soul of the woman you are living with."

"Insightfulness is not enough for that. One needs to be clairvoyant. How about you help me a little?"

"The famous Inspector Lukić needs help? He can't solve a simple problem on his own? Well, all right, what can we do? It is an art, of course."

"Is it, now?"

"Why are you surprised?"

"I'm not surprised, I just had no idea."

"You would have had some idea if you paid more attention to what I said, and especially if you paid attention to what I didn't say."

"Now you expect me to be telepathic as well?"

"Why not? That would be useful for your job too. So?"

"You want to continue writing?"

"God forbid. How did you come up with that?"

"Well, you tried to be a writer. . . ."

"That one time was quite enough. In any case, you see the trouble prose creates. Next."

"Music? You want to write music?"

"I would like to, but unfortunately I have no real talent for music."

"What's left? Sculpting? No, you're not . . . muscular enough."

"You've gone through every possibility except the right one. You've really disappointed me."

"Painting?" I asked in amazement.

"Painting, of course."

"How could I have guessed that? You've never given me any hint."

"I didn't have to. All it would take is to connect two details that you know about me."

"Details?"

"Yes. Before I couldn't be a painter because I didn't see colors. Now I see them."

I gazed at Vera, not knowing what to say. The amusing conversation had suddenly become serious. She stared back at me, expecting me to say something.

What got me out of the predicament was the fact that the limo suddenly slowed down, then stopped. The barely noticeable vibration stopped, as the driver turned off the engine. I turned towards the door, expecting, for some reason, that someone would open it. When that did not happen after about fifteen seconds, I carefully opened it a little and peered outside.

We were on a well-lit street. Through the narrow opening I saw the window of a pharmacy. It seemed familiar but I couldn't remember where I had seen it. The passersby turned curiously to see the long white limousine. I waited a little longer, then slowly opened the door all the way and stepped outside, signaling Vera to wait.

What I saw was not supposed to be there. I stared for a while in disbelief at the sight in front of me, as though it had magically emerged from the past, then I hurried to offer Vera my hand so that she might join me. To her this would be an even greater surprise.

38

I CLOSED THE DOOR after Vera. The limo immediately drove off, freeing up at least two parking spaces. When it had moved away down the street, pedestrians no longer had any reason to take notice of the couple that had come out of it, who now remained standing by the curb, gazing at the nearby window.

I looked around, hoping to spot the agents who were tailing us, but there was no sign of them. That didn't concern me. Actually, it would have been unusual if I had noticed them. I thought of getting in touch with Agent Mirić, but he would have already called me if something was wrong.

A cosmetics store was supposed to be in front of us. It had been there several days earlier when I had had passed by, going about my business. There had been no indication that it was closing. On the contrary, inside it had been teeming with customers, as usual. I remembered then what had crossed my mind the first time that I saw the shop: we live in an era when people care much more about quick body beautification than the slow beautification of the soul.

Now, however, everything was different.

The metal and glass, the kitsch glamour, were gone, and the previous antique nobility reigned once again. Instead of the products of the famous cosmetics chain, the shop was full of books, as it has been up until two years earlier. Above the shop window the glittering Fragrance neon sign had given way to discreet and elegant lettering reading Papyrus.

It seemed, however, that there was a price that had to be paid for restoring the bookshop. As far as I could see through the window and the door—there was no one inside.

I didn't rush Vera. For a while she just stared at the Papyrus, without saying a word. The barely perceptible quiver in the corner of her lips gave away how excited she was. She finally turned towards me and looked at me inquisitively. I shrugged, not knowing how to respond to her tacit questions.

Then I led her to the entrance. I paused with my hand on the doorknob before turning it. We were greeted by the sound of ringing bells. After stepping inside, we stayed next to the door, hesitating to go in any deeper, as though we might break the spell of the resurrection of the Papyrus.

Our eyes passed over the multitude of colorful volumes on the shelves, the armchairs lined with worn-out dark-green plush, the blossoming potted plants, the neatly arranged ornaments on the mantelpiece above the small lit fireplace, the cash register counter.

"Perfect," Vera said first, quietly. "Everything is perfect. . . ."

She went up to the shelf to the left of the shop window. She raised her hand and for a moment held it in front of the books, then laid her fingertips on the spines. She walked along the wall, running her fingers across the packed volumes, as though she needed to touch them to be absolutely certain that they were real. Having circled most of the room, she also touched the mantelpiece and the backs of all four armchairs the same way. Finally she approached the counter and pressed something. The cash register drawer opened with a rasping sound. Smiling, she pushed it back, then nodded for me to join her.

I stopped in front of the cash register and looked around once more.

"As far as I can remember, it looks the same, down to the smallest detail."

"Not only looks, but is. This is the old Papyrus, not a reconstruction. The books are the same, the furniture, the things, details, the whole lot. Even the place is the same."

"The place was certainly very expensive. The owners of the Fragrance chain had no reason to sell the shop. Their business was booming. They must have been made an offer that they could not refuse."

"It's easy for the author to make such offers in his novel. Money is not a issue there; he can have as much of it as he wants."

"Lucky him. But why do you think he brought the Papyrus back to life?"

"Who knows? Perhaps for some sentimental reason he had the desire to hold the reception right here. If you have more money than you know what to do with, you are in a position to indulge your whims."

I shook my head. "That would be very *nouveau riche*, and the author is not like that. We both know him; what's more, such whims would put the novel in jeopardy. No, it must be something else, something deeper."

"Deeper?"

"What will happen to the Papyrus after the reception is over?"

Vera shrugged her shoulders. "Fragrance will replace it again. Perhaps the author didn't buy the shop but only rented it short-term."

"If it were so, he would not have gone to the trouble of reviving the old Papyrus in every little detail."

"Then he will keep it closed, until a new reception or some similar occasion. Why not? He can afford to."

"That too would be a *nouveau riche* whim."

Vera hesitated for a brief moment before responding. "As far as I can see, there is only one option remaining—he is planning to reopen the bookstore."

I nodded. "That is the only thing that makes sense. The old Papyrus is not back only temporarily; it's here to stay."

Vera watched me in silence for several moments.

"Yet this is not the old Papyrus in every way. It can never again be that. The bookstore is not only the inventory and the place, but also the people who run it. And they are no more. . . ."

"One of the two women who founded and ran the Papyrus is still here. . . ."

"Didn't I just tell you that I am planning to focus on painting?"

"One thing does not exclude the other. You can both run the bookstore and paint."

"I don't want to run the bookstore; you are well aware of that."

Now it was I who was silent for a moment.

"I'd say that the author is counting on getting you to change your mind. He wouldn't go to all this trouble if he wasn't sure. He is aware that without you there is no bringing back the Papyrus, and he obviously really cares about that."

"How could he get me to change my mind?"

"With a new offer that you won't be able to refuse."

Vera's voice quivered. "If you mean money. . . ."

"Of course I don't mean money," I interrupted her, jumping in to eliminate the misunderstanding.

"Then what?"

"I have no clue. How can I know what is in an author's head? I'm just a piteous uninsightful police inspector."

I pulled my lips into a contrite smile, which in turn made her smile.

"Take off your coat," she said as she started removing her own. "They've really turned up the heat."

I stood briefly, unsure where to put it away. Vera got me out of the predicament.

"Give it to me; I'll put them over there."

She turned around and went towards the back room behind the counter, but it was locked.

"That's odd," she said. "We always kept the back room unlocked; I don't even know where the key is." She came back to the register and placed the two coats on the counter, then looked at her delicate wristwatch. "Seven thirteen. Were only the two of us invited to the reception? Not only are there no other guests, but the host is also missing."

I looked towards the entrance. "Someone is bound to turn up. Let me take advantage of the fact that we are still alone to ask you something. I didn't have a chance in that crowd before we came here. You spent almost a year and a half with the author. Have you ever seen his handwriting?"

Vera thought for a second. "I have. He showed me

his notepad where he had written one of his short novels in pencil. Why?"

"Would you be able to recognize it if you saw it again?"

"I think so. It's rather specific—the letters are small, square, almost printed."

"It's not the handwriting on the envelope that the neighbor Ljuštanović brought you?"

"No, it's not," Vera answered unwaveringly. "That was large, round; it doesn't at all look like the author's. Why?" she repeated her question.

"I'm trying to solve one of the many riddles that I've been given in the new novel. If it isn't the author's handwriting on the four envelopes, then whose is it?"

"Does it really matter? The author knew that I would recognize his handwriting, so he asked someone to write the inscription on the envelopes. It doesn't make any difference who it is."

"There was no reason to involve another person. The text could have been printed."

"Why then was it written by hand?"

I was silent for a few moments, then spoke softly, as though saying something in confidence. "Because that would be an opportunity for the novel's real author to leave his signature."

Vera squinted. "Real author?"

"Yes. We all assume that this is the author's new novel, but it doesn't necessarily have to be so. Perhaps the author is a mentor again, as he was to you in the previous case, while someone else is writing the novel."

"Who?"

I shook my head. "I don't know."

"Even the Agency can't determine whose handwriting it is?"

"They are still trying."

"Could all this be just a trick by the author; using the unidentified handwriting on the envelopes to try to get you to believe that he is a mentor, while in fact he is writing the novel?"

"That's also a possibility, but there are other indications that it is a different author."

"For example?"

"This novel is missing something that the author stuck to in the previous two. For example, my dreams, without which I could not find the answers."

"That is only because everything is happening in the course of one day." Vera smiled. "One cannot expect a police inspector to sleep on the job, even if it helped him solve cases."

"It wasn't necessary for everything to happen in one day. The author chose so himself. Also, the teashop is also gone. It has a pivotal place both in *The Last Book* and *The Grand Manuscript*. In *The Compendium of the Dead* I haven't even smelled tea."

"So, that is the title of the new novel—*The Compendium of the Dead*?"

"I guess. What would be more fitting? However, the most important is the third thing—there are no bodies."

"You don't know that. Three people have disappeared without a trace. It could turn out that they are dead. Then there will be more victims than in my novel."

"I doubt it. We have been given a hint as to what will happen to the missing persons. Among other things, that is the purpose of the episode with the lab technician. We can expect their miraculous return."

"The novel still isn't finished. Someone might be killed at the reception."

"If this turns out to be a reception only for the two of us—that threat is excluded. You are convinced that you enjoy the author's protection, and I think that I can hope for it too. However, even if the Papyrus fills with people, no one will be killed."

"You can't be certain of that."

"I can. The purpose of this work is to achieve exactly what you had aimed for—to show that a detective novel is in fact possible without murder victims. I was mistaken when I claimed that it was impossible."

"If no one will be killed at the reception, then what will happen at it? This is supposed to be novel's finale. What dénouement awaits us? What is there to resolve? The return of three missing persons, even if it is miraculous, is hardly a grand finale."

I nodded. "That's a very good question. Unfortunately I don't have an answer. I have only a certain premonition that the dénouement has been announced in the events of today, but any kind of clearer picture eludes me."

"What do you mean?"

"First of all, ever since it became evident that realities have crossed again, I have not been able shake the feeling that whoever is pulling the strings from the other reality is doing so in such a way as to make my life difficult. He is confronting me with unsolvable riddles, clouding everything around me as soon as it seems to me that I have understood something, and giving me false leads. I am constantly being led astray. It is as though he is angry with me and is taking revenge, although benevolently. At the same time it is as though he is indicating to me something very significant, which he must not reveal prematurely; something that he is keeping for the very end of the book."

"I don't understand you."

"I don't understand very well either. Here's an example. Death appears as a leitmotif in all of today's episodes. In the case of Mr. Trpimirović, the archivist, it is most apparent—actually there is nothing but death around him. Mrs. Ognjanović and Miss Šuvaković were very excited about *The Book of Resurrection*. The old poet, Vidojević is doing penance for the collection *Small Poems of Death*. Finally, our neighbor, Ljuštanović, has been visiting the cemetery every day for the past decade and a half."

"Those are all more or less serious forms of necrophilia, if you ask me."

"Perhaps it's not only that. There are other leitmotifs. All four books appeared in underground spaces: the Archive of the City Cemeteries Administration Building, the National Library Department of Old and Rare Books, the poet's cellar, and in front of our neighbor's basement apartment. Yellow flowers are another commonality of those places. There are some in the police lab as well, which is also underground." I paused a little. "Also, as I mentioned earlier, there is the imitation of the behaviors of patients from the Papyrus: someone first switched books around on the shelves, then placed a valuable volume in the library, and lastly—the copious purchases of copies of the same work."

"So what is the meaning of it all?"

"I don't know. I just have the feeling that it cannot be meaningless. It isn't just random. Finally, the four missing persons are connected to the underground, which weighs heavily on them in different ways. They all want to free themselves from it. The poet's wife is no exception. She lives in an apartment that looks like it doesn't have any windows."

"That's natural. No one feels pleasant underground."

"No, of course not, but there is something more here; this aspiration—like everything else—seems to have a certain symbolic meaning. However, I am missing the key to that symbolism. Perhaps I might find it if I could figure out who the author of the new novel is. It seems to me that everything would become simpler."

Vera watched me expressionlessly for several instants, then smiled.

"Perhaps it isn't that difficult to find out who the author is this time. It wasn't difficult even when the writer was my mentor. All it took was asking the right question."

"What question?"

"Who is absent from our reality? Who isn't here, and is connected to the events?"

At that very moment the bells above the entrance rang sharply.

39

WRAPPED UP IN OUR conversation, we were both startled by the unexpected noise and turned around swiftly. It took me a moment to recognize the man who had entered; I had only ever seen him in a white lab coat. Dr. Dimitrijević, the pathologist, looked distinguished in his three-piece gray suit, with a wide tie of the same shade. We hadn't seen each other since the "Last Book" case.

He came up to us and bowed to Vera. "Good evening, Miss Gavrilović. I am very honored by your invitation to the reopening of the Papyrus." He turned to me, missing her confused look. "Inspector Lukić, it's nice to meet you on a pleasurable occasion at last."

"We are glad that you were able to come, Dr. Dimitrijević," I rushed to preempt Vera, who had already opened her mouth to express her bewilderment.

"How could I miss it? When you are in my line of work, you only get invited to somber events. This is truly a welcome change. I only hope that I won't bring you any bad luck. They say that Thanatos follows me everywhere." He smiled awkwardly, as though apologizing. His propensity for dark humor had obviously not abandoned him.

"Don't worry, Doctor. Thanatos will not dare even look at the Papyrus. We're protected by Eros."

"There's another reason I'm glad to be here. To my great disgrace, I can't remember the last time I stopped by a bookstore. I would like to take the opportunity to have a look at the books, while it still isn't crowded."

"Please do."

Without waiting for Dr. Dimitrijević to move away enough, Vera muttered through clenched lips: "Only the reception was mentioned. There was no suggestion of reopening the Papyrus."

"That's how it is when you deal with lawyers. Legally speaking, they didn't deceive you. This is obviously the reception for the reopening of the Papyrus. You should have gotten the details before agreeing to come."

"And what should I do now? The Doctor is convinced that I'm behind the invitation. Others will surely think the same."

"Let them think it."

"What do you mean—let them think it?" Vera almost shouted. "What will happen when everyone gets here? They will all be looking at me, expecting me to say something. I can't just say: 'Good evening, the Papyrus is reopening.' And what am I supposed to serve the guests? I have absolutely nothing. Even the glasses are locked in the back room. In any case—there wouldn't be enough of them; only three or four, if I remember correctly."

I could barely refrain from laughing at Vera's panic.

"Calm down. The author will take care of everything. I'm sure he didn't organize all this just to embarrass you."

"The author! If he doesn't appear soon—I'm out of here, and then you can all deal with it however you want."

The bells rang again. A short young woman with a snub nose entered, elegantly dressed in lively colors. She gave us a brief smile, then headed towards the bookshelves.

"You don't recognize her?" Vera asked me softly.

I shook my head.

"It's because of the hair. It wasn't medium length

and light brown, as it is now, but rather short and dark. You saw her more than two years ago. She stood over there," she indicated with her head, "next to the veterinary student who died. You spoke to her."

"How can you remember what kind of hair some woman had more than two years ago?"

"You're not the only one with a good memory. In any case, what's difficult about it? She was a regular at the Papyrus."

"You think that she was invited because of that?"

Vera shrugged. "I have no idea."

On the renewed ringing of the bells she looked at me questioningly. Two men paused for a moment near the entrance, as though unsure which direction to go in, and then moved to the nearby corner. The older one nodded to me, the younger one waved. I responded with a slight bow.

"Former Chief Inspector Đorđević," I explained to Vera in a low voice.

"He has a brief role in my novel too, but you don't see him. Only a voice on the telephone. That's not how I imagined him."

"He retired after the 'Grand Manuscript' case. That's Inspector Jovan Petronijević with him. We shared an office during the 'Last Book' case. He passed on news from the Papyrus to the tabloids. That's why he's hesitant to come and say hello to you now."

"He looks like someone who has dealings with the tabloids."

"Excuse me for a moment; he might have similar ideas tonight."

I walked up to them and first cordially welcomed my former superior, then standoffishly greeted my colleague whom I had rarely seen since I had been given my own office. I pulled them aside for a moment.

"It might seem to you that tonight is an open house, but it isn't. People from the Agency are all around."

"No one asked me for an invitation at the entrance. Should I show it to you?"

"I mean someone who might come uninvited, because they've received word that no one is checking invitations."

"Who might that someone be?"

"I think we understand each other."

I patted him on the shoulder, then returned to the counter. I had just joined Vera, when the bells announced a new guest. I turned around and saw a short man with disheveled hair and a bushy mustache. The resemblance to Einstein was even greater than the first time I had seen him, in this same place. Professor Anatasije Nedeljković approached us boldly and in full flow.

"Dear Miss Gavilović! Dear Inspector Lukić! This is wonderful! The Papyrus is opening again! You've made me so happy! How I've missed it! It all comes down to this bookstore. This is where the solutions to all the secrets lie! I'll get right to work!"

He started going through the numerous pockets of his coat and suit, looking for his famous notepad, but since it was nowhere to be found, he shrugged his shoulders mournfully and went to one of the corners to continue his search there.

Vera smiled as she watched him leave, then her face turned grim. "Where is the author?" she almost snarled at me. "There are more and more people."

As if to confirm this, the bells announced the arrival of a party of four: one woman and three men. The petite older woman in a gray coat and beret, as well as the gentleman in the plaid jacket, with an unlit pipe in his mouth, seemed vaguely familiar, but not the other two. The larger one was compensating for a complete absence of hair with a full beard, while the slimmer, shorter one wore a coat reaching almost to the ground.

"That's all I need right now," Vera whispered after giving the new arrivals a broad smile.

"What?" I asked, also softly.

"As though Einstein wasn't enough, the other patients were also invited. It's going to be interesting here tonight."

The lady with the beret sat down in one of the armchairs, took a small book out of her large handbag and started to read. The gentleman with the pipe quickly followed her example. He walked up to the bookshelves, chose a large book full of illustrations and sat down in the second armchair. The other two surveyed the situation in the bookstore, then headed in opposite directions and dived into browsing.

"Remember the old lady?"

"Is she the one who brings a collection of love poems to read here?"

Vera nodded.

"I think that I've seen the gentleman with the pipe too, but I'm not sure."

"You saw him the same time that you saw her—during your second visit to the Papyrus. Whenever he comes in he looks at the same book with illustrations."

"You truly have a better memory than me. Now I'm impressed."

Vera bowed slightly. "I also mentioned the other two to you. The bald one with the beard always buys the same book. We've sold him nearly a hundred and fifty copies. The other one is probably concealing the volume that he has brought for us tonight. The longer the coat, the larger the book that he will leave on the shelf."

The bells this time announced the arrival of a larger group. Even though I saw these seven colleagues almost every day, I stared at them because I had never seen them dressed like this. Formal wear best became the new chief inspector, Vesna Uskoković. It also suited Grubijanić, the head of the laboratory, and Bumbaković, the young officer who worked the switchboard. Inspector Prokopović appeared quite uncomfortable in a suit, even though it looked good on him. Inspectors Kostić and Zarić seemed ill at ease, while the bow tie around the neck of the mustachioed Vranešević looked like a noose.

I stepped towards them, but the chief inspector signaled me to remain at the counter. They didn't stay together but rather scattered around the bookstore. Chief Inspector Uskoković stood with her predecessor, which finally freed him of Petronijević's company.

"My colleagues," I told Vera. "You know most of them from *The Grand Manuscript*. The lady is the new chief inspector, Vesna Uskoković, and that one over there," I nodded, "is Bubmaković, the switchboard operator."

I saw in Vera's eyes that she was preparing to say something about this invasion of police officers, but then her attention was completely consumed by the appearance of another colleague of mine at the entrance. I almost didn't recognize her. Ana Mirković always wore a ordinary white lab coat at work. She now looked very elegant, in a long black dress with an exceptionally low cut neckline and high heels. She smiled at me, then headed over to where her boss was standing.

"Let me guess," said Vera. "The young lab technician, who is interested in your literary recommendations, right?"

"How did you guess?"

"It wasn't difficult. She intentionally hung back at the door. She wouldn't have received the same attention if she had come in with a bunch of police officers as she did when she stepped in by herself. If you could only have seen how you stared at her. And then that smile she gave you. Certainly a sign of appreciation for an exceptional recommendation. Now you are connected by Saramago, and that is a strong bond. . . ."

"God, Vera. . . ." I said, but there was no opportunity to get into a discussion about Saramago being a pimp, because two new guests had just appeared at the door. A younger and an older lady were headed our way. I had never seen either of them before.

"Inspector Lukić, perhaps you will remember me," said the larger one, with the prominent double chin. She was already past fifty. "We spoke on the telephone. Leposava Žutić, from Magnifying Glass Press."

"How could I forget?"

"You weren't patient enough to hear our offer. . . ."

"You are lucky I didn't; it wasn't at all healthy to have anything to do with that manuscript."

She wanted to say something, but I turned to the younger woman. She was about thirty-five years old; her bangs fell over her eyebrows, and she wore an excessive amount of costume jewelry around her neck.

"I hope you haven't forgotten me either. Jelisaveta Šumanović, from *The Evening Courier*."

I started looking around for Petronijević.

"No one helped me get in," the reporter interrupted my search. "I'm here as a guest." She took out an elongated invitation and showed it to me. "However, if you want to give us an exclusive interview about the turbulent day behind you, whose finale we are attending. . . ."

"I can't, unfortunately. I'm here as an admirer of literature, not as a police inspector."

Miss Šumanović also wanted to continue our conversation, but she was thwarted by a fresh ringing of the bell.

"Excuse me," I said to the two ladies, as I walked around them and towards the door, where Mrs. Leleković, Mrs. Ognjanović and Mr. Vidojević stood, looking at the gathering in confusion.

"What is the meaning of this, Inspector Lukić?" asked the administrator of the City Cemeteries Administration. "It is quite inappropriate to invite people in mourning to a party."

"I didn't invite you. I myself am here because I was invited."

"So who invited everyone?"

"We still don't know, but we should find out soon."

"I certainly have no intention of waiting for that. My time is valuable."

"I would still recommend that you be patient. Perhaps you will no longer have reason to be in mourning."

She scowled at me. "What do you mean?"

There was no time to answer her, because the most conspicuous group so far had appeared at the bookstore entrance. The guests who had already arrived had stopped paying much attention to newcomers; it was as though only Vera and I were interested in who was arriving. This time, however, all heads turned to the entrance: led by the Grand Master, a procession of members of the secret society was filing into the Papyrus.

I reacted as quickly as I could under the circumstances. In great strides I rushed towards Vera, making my way around the people who stood between the door and the counter. They were slowing me down, but were also blocking the Grand Master from having a clear shot at his target, if he were to decide to fire immediately. From the corner of my eye I saw Kostić and Zarić quickly approach the counter from the left and right. I put my hand inside my jacket, ready to draw my gun.

We reached the register at the same time and stood in front of Vera like a human shield. As I turned around I faced a multitude of looks from guests who obviously didn't understand what had caused the sudden confusion. There was no threat to Vera or anyone else. The members of the secret society stood calmly in the corner farthest from the counter. The people who had previously been there had moved out of their way, giving them space.

After our two encounters in the dark that day, I finally had the opportunity to see the Grand Master. His tall stature made him stand out not only in the group around him, but also in the entire bookstore. He looked the same as he had the last time we had met, at the teashop eight months ago. His thick salt-and-pepper hair, pulled back in a pony tail, emphasized his high forehead and bony face, and the sparkle of the green jade in his eyes was simply captivating. He smiled at me for a split second when he caught me looking at him.

Six followers had come with him. The sister and brother who ran the teashop, the alleged cleaning lady Mrs. Sokolović, the woman who had impersonated attorney Jovana Timotijević, the girl who had first phoned me, then appeared before me when I was paralyzed, and the guard, Rabrenović.

I removed my hand from my jacket and whispered to Kostić and Zarić to back down, but the guests were still staring at me with discomfort. This would have continued, had the door bell not rung again. Almost everyone turned in that direction.

Finally arriving at the Papyrus were those who were actually supposed to have been here to begin with. A moment earlier, when the Grand Master and his band appeared, my first thought had been to wonder how they could have gotten past all the people from the Agency. I hadn't seen them, but nonetheless I was confident that they were keeping a close eye on the bookstore. Mirić would owe me some answers.

The eight young agents behaved just as the police officers had before them—they didn't stay together but rather scattered around the Papyrus. Mirić came to the counter.

"We are all here," Vera said excitedly from behind me. "There's no one else left."

I turned towards her. "How do you know?"

"Don't you get it? Everyone who appeared in the first two books was invited, with the exception of the dead, of course, and a few extras, such as the Oriental teashop proprietor and his twins. Everyone who has any significance in *The Last Book* and *The Grand Manuscript* is here. The author has brought together all his characters. He is the only one still missing."

I squinted long and hard at Vera, then started to shake my head. She looked back at me with confusion in her eyes.

"Actually, not everyone is here," I said in a low voice.

"Who's still not here? Who's missing?"

At that moment Mirić came up to me, leaned over and whispered in my ear: "We've determined whose handwriting is on the envelopes."

"I too have just deduced the same," I responded.

I didn't have the chance, however, to say anything because suddenly a loud gong sounded behind us.

40

The sound had come from the room behind the counter. In the general commotion I hadn't noticed that someone had unlocked the door and opened it wide. The chatter ceased instantly and everyone looked in that direction. For several moments nothing happened, then three figures, dressed in tight black pants and dark red Mandarin jackets, buttoned up to the top, emerged in quick succession. Each was carrying a large serving tray with a dozen blue-and-white steaming porcelain cups.

It was not unexpected that the older man with slanted eyes who headed the procession should have looked exactly the same as he had the last time I saw him, at the Mandarin Teashop: lean, with thinning hair, rheumatic movements. Two years barely made any difference at his age. A genuine transformation occurs, however, between the ages of twelve and fourteen. Yet by some miracle, it seemed as though the passage of time had had no effect on the teashop proprietor's twins. They also appeared unchanged, so I still couldn't distinguish which was the girl and which the boy.

They spread out in three directions among the guests, offering them tea with a smile and a bow. The trays with the many full cups must have been rather heavy for their small hands, but the children carried them seemingly effortlessly. The father made his way to the counter. As he approached us, he also bowed and gave us a wide smile.

"Miss Gavrilović, Inspector Lukić, meet again. Very pleased."

"We are pleased too," said Vera, as she took a cup. "We have greatly missed your teas."

"I especially missed the one for head work," I said, also taking a cup. "It could have spared me many headaches in the past two years."

"This one more good. Tea for ending."

"Tea for ending?" Vera repeated inquisitively, staring at the yellowish liquid. "What ending?"

"Happy ending. That always best."

Vera had already opened her mouth to continue questioning him but the teashop proprietor beat her to it. "You excuse me. Must take tea other guest. Should drink while hot."

He went around the counter, but then remembered something and came back to Vera. This time his voice was lower, and I could barely hear what he was saying.

"You wrong. I and children not extras. We important role. No happy ending without our tea."

Vera blushed as he continued toward the guests in the center of the bookstore with a renewed smile.

"How did he hear me?" she whispered when he was slightly further away.

"He probably has a tea for hear good. That's how he heard your lament about the refreshments earlier and rushed to help you out. Didn't I tell you that you shouldn't worry about it? The tea for ending certainly is more original than any of the typical things that are served at receptions."

Vera raised the cup to her lips, blew a little into the yellow liquid and sipped carefully. She remained straight-faced as she sampled the tea in her mouth, then she lit up.

"Marvelous. Go ahead and try it. It won't harm you."

It seemed to me that it was still scorching, but I couldn't disgrace myself. I took a modest gulp. The tea was truly magnificent. No single flavor was dominant. I had the impression that a plethora of indistinguishable ingredients were competing for precedence. First one prevailed, then another, toying with the taste buds.

"So?"

"It really is superb. The guests will be amazed. Actually, come to think of it, you and the mandarin could team up. Rent out the back room to him. You never used it for anything important. He can prepare teas there for your customers. Tea for read good, for example, or tea for buy book. Your business would flourish."

"You're joking at such a serious moment. Anyway, that topic is off the agenda; I am not going back to the Papyrus."

Having finished serving the refreshments, the father and children remained standing at three different places in the bookstore. With a smile, they held out the serving trays in front of them, waiting for the guests to place their empty cups on them. Under different circumstances Vera and I would have taken our time drinking this excellent beverage in small sips, but now we just downed it in silence. Mirić offered to take our cups to the nearest tray. I didn't notice what the other agents had done, but he did not have any tea.

"All right, let's hear it," said Vera.

"What?"

"Now that the mandarin and his twins are also here—who else is missing?"

"You don't have to be at all insightful in order to work it out. All it takes is to look around carefully yourself. Who is only person who is absent, and who should definitely be in the bookstore?"

Vera squinted at me, then got on her tiptoes and started scanning the guests. She had barely gotten through a quarter of the circle when the gong sounded again.

A three-person procession stepped out of the back room: a man in front, then a younger woman, and an older one. All had their hands full. He was carrying two large dark gray volumes; the woman behind him held a thick incunabulum, wearing plastic gloves; and the lady in the rear was pushing a wheelchair.

Excited voices came from the direction of the entrance and three figures started to push through the guests towards the newcomers. The old poet Vidojević was the first to make his way to his muse, but then he didn't know how to reach her since the wheelchair obstructed him. Finally, he leaned over and hugged her across it. Mrs. Ognjanović also had difficulties. She wanted to embrace her deputy, but the young woman backed away so that she could first raise the incunabulum above her head, and only then did she permit the hug. Only Mrs. Leleković did not have any difficulties. Even if he had wanted to, with his hands full the archivist could not resist her firm clutch. It was actually much firmer than might have been expected of the administrator, who was renowned for being very strict with her staff.

"The return of the three missing people," I explained to Vera.

"I understood. I just didn't expect the welcome to be so passionate in all three cases."

"Neither did I, although I should have guessed. It seems that necrophiliac passion brings people together as does biophiliac passion."

"Why did he take those two books of burials specifically?"

"To correct the mistakes in them."

Vera looked at me questioningly, but there was no time to explain, because another man had just emerged from the back room. Hardly anyone except me noticed him, because everyone was still preoccupied with the three embracing couples. I too would have failed to notice his appearance, had I not been facing in that direction. He walked straight towards us. Vera realized from my look that something was going on behind her and she quickly turned around.

"You don't have to continue seeking the missing person, Miss Gavrilović," said the elderly man in an overcoat. "We are finally all here."

"Commissioner Milenković! How could I have overlooked your absence? Unbelievable."

"There's quite a crowd at the Papyrus. It isn't easy to make out who all is here, let alone who is not. And Inspector Lukić realized who was missing only just before you did. In any case, had you noticed my absence earlier, it wouldn't have been good for the novel. Only now is it the right moment for me to appear."

"I could have figured out long ago who was behind all of this," I jumped in, "had I not relied on what you said."

"What I said?"

"During the 'Grand Manuscript' case, at one moment I proposed that you try to write detective novels. You resolutely responded that it was not for you, that you are more adept at solving than conceiving detective cases. Remember?"

"I remember. I still believe that."

"But you still started working on a novel?"

"I started working on it not because of my own motivation but at the author's incitement."

"He incited you to do something that you are not good at?"

"That's right. Being unskilled, I would be less suspicious, and he as a mentor made sure that my lack of talent wasn't obvious."

"Why did the author need you at all? Why didn't he write the novel himself?"

"He wanted to have two stories in the novel. One that would be in the foreground, and which someone else would write, and the other, his own, in the background, which would be best protected by the screen of the first story if it was penned by somebody else."

"Why did he choose to offer co-authorship to you? It can't just be because your ineptitude at writing would draw less suspicion. Many others meet that criteria."

"It was also convenient that I had retired. Everyone had lost track of me. The main reason, however, was the same that had previously led the author to help Miss Gavrilović: he had done me wrong in the first two books. He felt guilty. He wanted to make amends."

"He had done you wrong? How is that?"

"You of all people should know. You were his main accomplice. No one had ever strung along a National Security Agency commissioner like the two of you did."

"How could he make amends for that?"

"He offered me the opportunity to string someone along too."

I looked silently at him for several moments.

"Me?"

"To tell you the truth, I would rather have taken the author for a ride than you, but that was a pleasure I couldn't really have hoped for."

"So, that was your main motivation in picking up the quill? Bruised ego? Revenge?"

"Very benevolent revenge. I had to show you a little what it is like when you keep smashing your head against unsolvable riddles everywhere you turn."

"As though I didn't already know. The author took me for a ride as much as he did you."

"Yet you came out as the winner in the end."

"And what about the Grand Master? He certainly strung you along a lot more than I did, and you didn't take any revenge on him. Your young colleagues believe that someone is protecting him. Might that be you?"

"I'm not nearly that powerful. Only the author himself could protect him. He needed such a character. It seems that he is inevitable in this type of novel. However, we will soon be getting rid of him too. Permanently."

"Him too? Who else?"

Commissioner Milenković sighed.

"What you said, that my main motivation was bruised ego and revenge—it hurt me. I thought you knew me better. The collaboration with the author would never had happened had he not made me an offer I simply couldn't refuse."

"What was it?"

"He promised that this would be his last involvement in our reality. I would have agreed to anything for such an outcome. Crossing realities are the worst possible nightmare that the National Security Agency has ever faced."

"That's not your concern any more; you're retired."

"Don't be naive, Inspector Lukić. There's no retirement in this line of work."

"The author made the same promise first to Dejan, then to me," Vera interjected. "And he never kept it. It is also naive to believe the promises of an author."

"He will keep it this time."

"What guarantees do you have?" I asked.

"The finale of this novel."

"Finale? I hope you don't mean the return of these three missing people?" I indicated the group that was still the focus of the guests' attention.

Commissioner Milenković shook his head. "No, of

course not. That's just the conclusion of my story in the novel."

"You really put those three couples through hell in order to get back at me."

"They have no reason to complain. Everyone has been compensated for the anguish that they suffered. Mrs. Leleković and Mr. Trpimirović have finally bonded; they couldn't really achieve that at the City Cemeteries Administration. Mrs. Ognjanović and Miss Šuvaković have acquired an exceptionally rare incunabulum; they will have a little trouble explaining where they got it, but I'm sure they will manage. Finally, Mr. Vidojević's penance has ended; his muse can walk and speak again."

"So, the finale of the author's story?"

"That's right, the story because of which *The Compendium of the Dead* was written in the first place. The finale toward which lead the clues the author has sprinkled for the insightful inspector throughout the novel." He paused for a moment. "Now you can guess what comes next, right?"

I remained staring at Commissioner Milenković for several moments, then nodded.

"I can."

"I can't guess," said Vera.

"I know. You are not yet supposed to be able to guess. I have still to prepare you for the finale. There is great elation ahead for you."

"What elation?" Vera asked after a brief hesitation.

"I believe you are aware that the author is a very orderly person. Before he leaves our world for good, he wants to clean up the disorder that he has created, to restore the order that existed at the beginning of *The Last Book*."

"Not everything can be cleaned up," said Vera in a soft, shaking voice. "Unfortunately there are unfixable disorders. . . ."

Up to that moment I was convinced that I would never see a smile on the commissioner's face.

"Is a pitiful retired agent of the secret police supposed to enlighten you—you who live in the world of books—about the power of literature?"

Vera did not have a chance to respond because there was a commotion among the guests. The teashop proprietor and his twins had collected all the empty cups and were on their way through the crowd towards the back room. They had just stepped in there when the gong sounded for a third time. Everyone looked towards the door, expecting someone to emerge, but no one did. Instead the lights started to fade.

Once the room had grown dim, nothing happened for a brief while. Then the silence that had fallen on the guests started to fill with a murmur similar to a prayer or mantra. It took me several moments to make out that it was coming from the corner where the members of the secret society were standing, and a bit longer to realize why it sounded familiar: slightly over two years ago I had heard it in the underground hall of a villa. . . .

The mantra subsided at the moment when something suddenly started to glow on the wall opposite the entrance. At first it seemed to me that it came from several vertical lamps emitting a white light and placed one next to the other in the middle of the highest row of shelves—but I was wrong. The glow was from the spines of four white books that I hadn't noticed previously, because they were hidden among other volumes with white covers.

The four books that had finally come together—*The Compendium of the Dead.*

The glow rapidly increased in intensity, bathing the bookstore in blazing whiteness. I squinted, and a number of hands were raised to protect eyes. It seemed inevitable that the source of light would shatter, but the opposite happened—it suddenly died away. In the restored semidarkness the afterimage of four spines lingered for a while, creating the illusion that they were still high up on the shelf. However, when my eyes adjusted to the dim light, I saw that there was a gaping void where the books had been.

I gave the members of the secret society an inquisitive look and noticed another disappearance. Among the penitently bowed heads, the tallest one, crowned with salt-and-pepper hair, was missing. There was no time, however, to wonder what had happened to the books and the Grand Master. The lighting on the ceiling started to grow brighter, and a fourth gong sounded from the back room.

All heads turned in that direction once again. For a brief moment nothing moved. Then a short old man in a green overcoat appeared at the door. He looked around the bookstore bewildered, as though awakened from a restless sleep, still not able to figure out where he was. The sheer number of curious gazes directed at him caused additional confusion. Not knowing what else to do, he remained at the door, squinting.

I took Vera by the hand. "Do you recognize him?" I asked in a whisper.

She turned towards me and looked deep into my eyes, then made an unclear motion with her head that could at the same time be both nodding and shaking; both denial and agreement.

"Mr. Predrag Todorović?" she said in a whisper.

"Yes, the retired piano teacher."

"But he is. . . ."

"Dead. Yes, but not anymore."

"How. . . .?"

"Does it matter? Go to him."

This time Vera just fiercely shook her head.

"There's no one else," I said softy. "You are the only person here whom he knows. Should no one greet him upon his return from the dead? Look how baffled he is."

Her gaze stabbed me in the eyes once again. I let go of her hand, then smiled.

"Go on."

She started out with a uncertain step. She stopped in front of the old man, observed him briefly, then began to speak to him. She had her back to me so I couldn't make out the hushed words, but I saw their effect on the professor's face. The convulsion of bewilderment slowly thawed into an expression of confidence, which eliminated the need for unnecessary questions and answers.

He let her put her arm about him and walk him to the other end of the bookstore. The guests considerately cleared a path for them. He only hesitated a little before sitting down in the armchair where he had forever closed his eyes twenty-six months earlier. All it took was a light squeeze of Vera's hand to convince him that that forever had already passed.

Having settled him there, she returned just as a new figure appeared at the door to the back room. Vera smiled at me in passing and continued on to greet retired painter Ljubica Matić. The old woman was in a thin dark coat, with a purple scarf around her neck.

The second encounter was shorter than the first. The painter nodded at everything Vera said, as though she was telling her something ordinary, something that was a given. She only said something once at which they both laughed. They continued the talk in the same manner as they walked over to the last free armchair.

Vera also went to meet the third newcomer, but a young brunette was nearer and swifter. She quickly made her way though the crowd to the young man with the bright-red scarf. They didn't say a word. They held hands and stood there for a minute, gazing at each other. Then they went towards the shelf next to which he had once collapsed. There she first whispered something to him, then he whispered to her and then he touched the large earring in his left ear.

When the fourth person appeared at the back room door I restrained Vera, who had joined me in the meantime.

"But that was our highly revered customer," she protested. "Mrs. Dragana Stojanović, curator of the Museum of Modern Art. . . ."

"Someone else longs to greet her."

I nodded in the direction of the corner that Professor Nedeljković had retreated to. He was already making his way through the guests, waving his notepad in the air. After reaching Mrs. Stojanović, he showered her with a torrent of words, not allowing her to say anything. He kept flipping through his notepad, proudly pointing with his finger to different places in it. Finally he more or less dragged the curator to his corner.

"We should have spared the poor woman the experience," Vera said grimly. "She could live to regret coming back to life."

"The poor woman was herself a patient. There is no greeting more fitting for her. He will convince her to accept her resurrection more easily than you would."

A short stout red-haired woman with a large purse and big glasses emerged from the back room. She wore a colorful poncho over her beige blouse.

"In this case I have to welcome her back to the land of the living. Miss Ljubica Aksentijević might be one of the characters from your novel, but you are a stranger to her. Of all the people gathered here, she knows only me." I paused and turned to Commissioner Milenković. "No, I'm mistaken. She also met with you."

"Only briefly. I think that she has fonder memories of you. Please go ahead."

With a big smile I went up to the literary agent.

"Good evening, Miss Aksentijević."

"Inspector Lukić. . . ." she responded after a little hesitation, as though she hadn't recognized me immediately.

"How are you feeling?"

"Somehow deadened . . . as though. . . ." She left the sentence unfinished, looking at me helplessly.

I took her by the arm and patted her hand.

"Don't worry. Everything will be all right. I'm sure that you're just a little tired."

"Forgive me, could you tell me where we are? I'm very embarrassed, I can't remember. . . ."

"It's not a big deal. It happens to everyone. We are at a reception at a bookstore."

"The presentation of a new book?" Her voice perked up a little.

I hesitated for a moment. "Well, you could say so. . . ."

"A well-known author?"

"Not exactly. . . ."

"Do they have an agent?"

"I don't think so."

"Do you know them?"

"Yes, in a way. . . ."

"Could you introduce me?"

"Gladly, as soon as the program is finished."

"I'll wait. I'm already feeling better."

She smiled, then mingled with the guests.

I had just rejoined Vera, when a short man with graying hair and a thin mustache, wearing an elegant dark suit and bow tie, emerged from the room. Had I known that Inspector Tanasije Vesić would be the next one coming out, I would have stayed by the door. I had not returned there, however, which is why Commissioner Milenković beat me to him.

"I'll get this," he said shortly.

He approached the inspector and without any gestures, not even a handshake, entered into a muffled conversation. Someone uninformed would never have guessed that it was a welcome for a man who had just risen from the dead. The scene looked like the encounter of two friends at a reception, exchanging thoughts about something confidential, but harmless. It didn't last very long. In the end, having nodded in the direction of Vera and me, Vesić headed towards where chief inspectors Đorđević and Uskoković stood. Milenković came back to the counter.

"I invited him to join the Agency," he said softly. "He is all round a valuable man, and especially now, with this posthumous experience."

"What did he say?"

"That he would think about it. He said that this experience has changed his priorities a bit."

When the blond and stout Dr. Sonja Vidić appeared at the door of the back room, wearing heavy makeup despite the circumstances, Dr. Dimitrijević was already ready to step in. He went up to her, and without saying a word placed his fingers against her carotid artery. As though that wasn't enough, he first grabbed her left, then her right hand and checked her pulse.

He then pelted her with medical questions. He fired them one after another in quick succession, not giving her an opportunity to answer. Dr. Vidić finally stopped the torrent by placing her hand over his mouth.

"I'm alive." She uttered the irrefutable diagnosis.

He silently stared at her for several moments, and then it was as though his face shattered: the man professionally numbed by death was brought to tears by life. Dr. Vidić embraced him and started to whisper something to him. They remained like that for some time, only for her to take him aside finally, her arm around his shoulders.

Vera grabbed my upper arm.

"Let's go, Dejan. Stay with me."

We went to the door of the back room, to greet the last, eighth person to return from the dead. I could tell how anxious Vera was by the involuntary twitching of her fingers.

We stopped in front of the door and peered inside. All we could see was a thick darkness. Seconds passed, long and tense, but no one emerged. At one moment Vera turned her head and gave me a confused look. I stroked her hand.

When someone finally appeared, it wasn't only Olga. She was holding by the arm an older man with round wire-framed glasses. They were both smiling.

"Good evening, Vera," said the author with a bow. "Good evening, Dejan."

We both returned the bows.

"Here we are at the end," the author continued. "I had to come to say goodbye. It wouldn't have been nice of me not to appear, would it?"

"I'm glad that you came," Vera responded. "I should thank you for all this." She pointed to the bookstore, then with a smile nodded towards Olga.

"I promised that I wouldn't leave any damage in your world behind me, and above all that there wouldn't be any deaths."

"Won't you suffer damage because of that? Fans of detective novels tend to be bloodthirsty. They might not appreciate your vegetarian thrillers."

"I'm not worried by the bloodthirsty readers. Let them look elsewhere for what suits them. There are plenty of books of that kind."

"And you really won't be coming back?"

"I would just spoil everything with a fourth part, now that everything is brought to a close and settled." He paused for a moment. "Not everything, actually; there is just one more detail that I need to restore to what it was before. Unfortunately that concerns you, Vera."

"I was hoping you would forget that."

"What kind of a thriller writer would I be—even if I do write vegetarian ones—if I were to forget the details?"

"Should I close my eyes?"

"That would be easiest."

Vera looked around her. Before she closed her eyes, a shadow passed across her face.

She opened them a moment later, then looked around the bookstore and smiled. "The good old black-and-white Papyrus. . . ."

"Goodbye, Vera." He kissed her on both cheeks, then turned towards me and put out his hand. "Dejan." He finally nodded to Olga. "Miss Bogdanović."

He waved to the guests, then stepped into the darkness of the back room without waiting to hear their applause.

I stood patiently with Vera and Olga until they finally separated after their long hug.

"I'm very sorry, Vera, that nothing will come of your painting," I said. "I hope that running the Papyrus with Olga once more will be compensation enough."

"Why wouldn't I paint?"

I looked at her with a raised eyebrow. "Well, because you are colorblind again. . . ."

Vera smiled. "Yes, but I remember colors. . . ."

Contributors

About the author

Zoran Živković was born in Belgrade, Serbia, on October 5, 1948. Until his retirement in 2017, he was a full professor at the Faculty of Philology, the University of Belgrade, teaching creative writing.

He is one of the most translated contemporary Serbian writers: by the end of 2021 there were 117 foreign editions of his books of fiction, published in 24 countries, in 20 languages.

Živković has won several literary awards for his fiction. In 1994 his novel *The Fourth Circle* won the Miloš Crnjanski award. In 2003, Živković's mosaic novel *The Library* won a World Fantasy Award for Best Novella. In 2007 his novel *The Bridge* won the Isidora Sekulić award. In 2007 Živković received the Stefan Mitrov Ljubiša award for his life achievement in literature. In 2014 and 2015 Živković received three awards for his contribution to the literature of fantastika: Art-Anima, Stanislav Lem and The Golden Dragon.

Zoran Živković has been recognized with his selection as European Grand Master for 2017 by the European Science Fiction Society at the 39th Eurocon in Dortmund, Germany.

Živković is the author of 23 books of fiction:

The Fourth Circle (1993)
Time Gifts (1997)
The Writer (1998)
The Book (1999)
Impossible Encounters (2000)
Seven Touches of Music (2001)
The Library (2002)
Steps through the Mist (2003)
Hidden Camera (2003)
Compartments (2004)
Four Stories till the End (2004)
Twelve Collections and the Teashop (2005)
The Bridge (2006)
Miss Tamara, The Reader (2006),
Amarcord (2007)
The Last Book (2007)
Escher's Loops (2008)
The Ghostwriter (2009)
The Five Wonders of the Danube (2011)
The Grand Manuscript (2012)
The Compendium of the Dead (2015)
The Image Interpreter (2016)
The White Room (2022)

About the artist

Youchan Ito was born 1968 in Aichi prefecture, Japan. She launched her career as a graphic designer in 1988, becoming a freelancer illustrator in 1991 and founding Togoru Co., Ltd. with her husband in 2000. In 2017 the company was reborn as Togoru Art Works. Handles a wide range of genres including cover art and design for science fiction, mysteries and horror titles, as well as illustrations for children's books.

www.youchan.com

www.ingramcontent.com/pod-product-compliance
Lightning Source LLC
Chambersburg PA
CBHW060538310726
48982CB00009B/1293/J

* 9 7 8 4 9 0 8 7 9 3 0 1 1 *